P9-DJV-046

Praise for the novels of Maisey Yates

"[A] surefire winner not to be missed."
—*Publishers Weekly* on *Slow Burn Cowboy*
(starred review)

"This fast-paced, sensual novel will leave readers believing in the healing power of love."
—*Publishers Weekly* on *Down Home Cowboy*

"Yates' new Gold Valley series begins with a sassy, romantic and sexy story about two characters whose chemistry is off the charts."
—*RT Book Reviews* on *Smooth-Talking Cowboy*
(Top Pick)

"Multidimensional and genuine characters are the highlight of this alluring novel, and sensual love scenes complete it. Yates's fans...will savor this delectable story."
—*Publishers Weekly* on *Unbroken Cowboy*
(starred review)

"Fast-paced and intensely emotional.... This is one of the most heartfelt installments in this series, and Yates's fans will love it."
—*Publishers Weekly* on *Cowboy to the Core*
(starred review)

"Yates's outstanding eighth Gold Valley contemporary... will delight newcomers and fans alike.... This charming and very sensual contemporary is a must for fans of passion."
—*Publishers Weekly* on *Cowboy Christmas Redemption*
(starred review)

For a complete list of books by Maisey Yates, please visit her website, www.maiseyyates.com.

MAISEY YATES

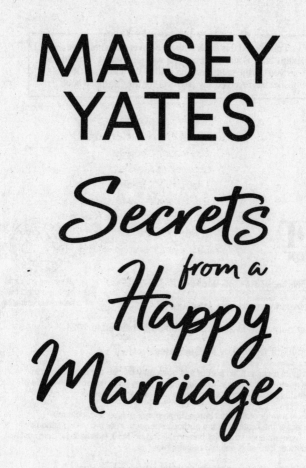

Secrets
from a
Happy
Marriage

HQN

If you purchased this book without a cover you should be aware
that this book is stolen property. It was reported as "unsold and
destroyed" to the publisher, and neither the author nor the
publisher has received any payment for this "stripped book."

ISBN-13: 978-1-335-94818-2

Recycling programs
for this product may
not exist in your area.

Secrets from a Happy Marriage

First published in 2020. This edition published in 2021.

Copyright © 2020 by Maisey Yates

All rights reserved. No part of this book may be used or reproduced in
any manner whatsoever without written permission except in the case of
brief quotations embodied in critical articles and reviews.

This is a work of fiction. Names, characters, places and incidents
are either the product of the author's imagination or are used fictitiously.
Any resemblance to actual persons, living or dead, businesses, companies,
events or locales is entirely coincidental.

This edition published by arrangement with Harlequin Books S.A.

For questions and comments about the quality of this book,
please contact us at CustomerService@Harlequin.com.

HQN
22 Adelaide St. West, 40th Floor
Toronto, Ontario M5H 4E3, Canada
www.Harlequin.com

Printed in Spain

To my mom.
Whenever I showed the slightest bit of interest in something, you made sure I could try it. Not only that, you made sure I got there on time, and always with whatever I needed. From baseball, which I was awful at, to piano, flute, painting, drama and writing classes. I didn't get here on my own. I can drive myself places now, but it's all that driving, and listening, and supporting that you did that made me who I am. Thank you.

Secrets from a Happy Marriage

1

Dear Mr. Hansen,

I am writing to accept your offer of marriage. I will arrive in Newport by train on Saturday, January 6. I have in my possession only one small bag. I have put all of the resources left to me by my late husband into the purchase of this ticket and will not have the funds to acquire a return. I pray we will make a harmonious match.

—FROM A LETTER WRITTEN BY JENNY HANSEN TO OLAF HANSEN, CHIEF LIGHTKEEPER OF THE CAPE HOPE LIGHTHOUSE, DECEMBER 20, 1899, NOW POSTED IN THE PARLOR OF THE CAPTAIN'S HOUSE AT THE LIGHTHOUSE INN, SUNSET BAY, OREGON

RACHEL

Rachel Henderson had known she would be a widow for a number of years now. Knowing that still hadn't prepared her for the day it would happen. For watching the light that made her husband who he was drain away.

This slow unwinding of their lives from each other. Where he would go on, and she would remain.

"I really did want to see her graduation." His voice

was weaker now, even more than it had been a few hours earlier.

He laid back his head on the stark white pillow, his eyes fluttering closed. A few months ago, when he'd started spending more time in bed than out, she'd changed the angle of it. Panting and sweating as she strained to move the king-size piece of furniture on her own. But she'd wanted him to be able to see the ocean without having to move too much.

She'd moved all the pictures into a cluster on that wall, as well—all the photographs he'd taken that they'd had framed, right in his line of sight.

The twenty short years they'd spent as husband and wife, captured in those photos. Frozen. Perfect and happy. At the center of them was a photograph with their hands all together that they'd taken when Emma was a baby.

The three of them.

Her family.

Rachel closed her eyes. "Of course. I'm not going to... pretend we didn't want you to."

There was no easy thing to say. She wouldn't lie and say it was okay.

This old Queen Anne house had stood since 1894, and in those years the one constant had been change. From the age when three lightkeepers had been required to live on-site to keep the kerosene lantern lit and prevent passing ships from being dashed on the rocks.

To when times had changed and innovation had meant only one keeper and a backup were needed.

To the years when bunkers had been built into the landscape during World War II, men ready to defend the country from enemies that might storm the rocky, windswept beaches.

The years when the lighthouse was automated, and the keepers had no longer been needed. When the houses had been used as dormitories and the property an extension for a university.

Then for nearly a decade when the houses and buildings on the property had been empty. Quiet.

Until Rachel's mother had taken over and life had started again in these walls.

Change. New life. Loss of life. Laughter. Fear.

It had all existed here.

And the houses, the lighthouse itself, remained through it all.

Rachel could feel it now. As if the years were layers rather than a timeline. As if it all existed at once, here in this room.

She and Jacob were simply part of it. One row of stitches in a vast quilt.

Rachel found some comfort in that—in this moment where her life felt large and her present pain felt bigger than what she could manage.

That in the fullness of time, she was small. They were small.

But this moment, this time, was all she had. And that moment's relief she felt fell away. Each second on the ticking clock louder, the sound of his rattling breath echoing in her.

Her husband. The only man she'd ever loved.

They'd been hand in hand, all this time. They'd found new ways to stretch a bond, commitment, over the years.

As his needs had changed, her place in his life had changed, and his in hers.

Changed, but not become less important.

She'd been a wife, and a companion, and a caregiver.

More wife than caregiver at first. But that had changed, too. Like a tide, rolling in and out.

His expression, which had been flat for the past few hours, changed. A small smile touched his lips, and he closed his eyes. For a moment she knew a kick of terror. That this might be it. She knew that it was. But just a few more minutes. That was all she wanted.

She had accepted that she would be a widow. But now she was at the stage where she was happy to delay it five more minutes.

Not that anyone asked her about timing.

"Remember when Emma was born?" His voice was thin.

She looked at him; his eyes were still closed. "I remember."

It was like he could read her thoughts, and honestly, she wouldn't be surprised if he could.

"That was one of the happiest days of my life." He opened his eyes. They looked glassy now, distant, like they were seeing something else. "The other one was when I married you."

A tear slid down Rachel's cheek. Because her husband was a good man. And forty was too young to die. Thirty-nine was too young to be widowed.

Being so aware of the history all around, of the ages and generations of time contained in these walls, all the people who had walked across these wooden floors, these years felt all that much shorter.

Far, far too short.

Her eyes skimmed across the orange-and-white bottles of prescription medication that cluttered the top of the nightstand, to the photo of their wedding day. When they'd been eighteen and blissful, totally unprepared for what lay ahead.

Meningitis, which was terrifying on its own. But she'd had no idea—they'd had no idea—of the side effects that were possible.

For that first seizure that would come only a year later. Followed by brain bleeds. Brain surgeries. Endless clotting complications.

Finally, this.

Cancer.

How had this man who had been through so much, who had already had a rare illness with rare side effects—? It didn't make sense.

He looked so different now than he had before. Than he had on their wedding day, or when Emma was born.

For every year she'd aged, she'd watched him age two. The ravages of illness were cruel. It had cost him to keep on living all this time, and he'd done it. Brilliantly.

She knew that people felt sorry for them. For him. For her.

As if loving him had been a burden. As if his love hadn't been sufficient to carry them through this moment.

He had never been a burden.

The love between them had only ever been a gift.

And it was so hard to give up such a beautiful gift.

"I like these pictures," he said. "But you should have hung up the ones I took of you."

Her heart went tight. "The ones you took of me in my underwear? I was not going to hang those on the wall."

His eyes were open again. "But I'd have enjoyed staring at them. I like the ocean but…it's nothing compared to you."

She couldn't speak. Not around the lump in her throat.

She lay down beside him, gripping the edge of the blue-and-white quilt that had been pushed down to the foot of the bed. She pressed her forehead to his shoulder. "Are you flirting with me?"

"Yes." His eyes fluttered closed again and she smiled.

She looked at him, and his familiar profile. And she watched as his breathing became more and more shallow. She didn't want to close her eyes, because she didn't want to miss one more rise-and-fall of his chest.

"I love you," she whispered, the lump in her throat going sharp, painful.

He didn't answer.

She started to get tired, the weight of the moment overwhelming her. She fought closing her eyes for a moment, fought sleep. But then some part of her whispered in her ear.

That falling asleep wasn't a bad thing.

That she should enjoy the chance to go to sleep with her husband of twenty years one last time.

She did.

And when she opened her eyes an hour later, his chest was still.

EMMA

Emma stopped at the mailbox at the end of the private drive that led to the Lighthouse Inn at Cape Hope, her family home and business. Standing there wasn't going to make a letter appear; she knew that.

She'd had a few acceptances already, but not the one. Not the one that she was waiting for. Not the one that she wanted.

The one that she needed.

It was insane, to think that the next four years of her

life, where she lived, what kind of education she would get, was decided by this. And that would decide…everything else. The friends she would have, whom she would meet.

All of it would be decided by this letter.

And she didn't know what she was going to do if she couldn't go to Boston.

So that was fine. She was just standing there waiting for a life-ending piece of mail. Acceptance or rejection into the Boston University marine-biology program.

She jerked open the box and looked inside. There were two letters. She couldn't see to whom either was addressed. She pulled them out and saw that the first one was junk.

And the second…

It was *it*.

Tension unwound inside her, all the bones in her body dissolving. She was afraid she was going to collapse in the driveway.

She couldn't open it out here. She had to go—get inside and light a candle or do a ritual or something.

She took a couple of breaths and gathered herself. The end of the driveway was shrouded by trees, and only a weak sliver of afternoon light managed to break through. But the trees also blocked the wind coming off the sea.

In January, that wind could be bitter, slicing through jackets and gloves to chill you to the bone.

She got back into her car, a late-model Peugeot, which her father had accused of being impractical, as well as an extension of the local landfill, based on the amount of junk—what he *perceived* to be junk—that Emma had inside it.

She had made the case for it being necessary. A mobile extension of her bedroom, not the landfill, thank you very much.

He'd laughed at that and hadn't ever mentioned the state of her car again.

She would miss her dad when she left for school.

And he'd still be here for that. She had to believe it.

She drove too quickly down the drive, and as she rounded the corner, the first thing she could see was the guesthouse, white with a red roof and a picket fence around the outside. The Captain's House. And next to it was Emma's house, the Lightkeeper's House, they now called it. White and red, just like the first, but this one was a duplex, divided in half to accommodate the assistant lightkeepers and their families, back in the late 1800s.

She parked her car and went through the white gate, walking on the path that led around to the front of the house, to the vast porch that the duplexes shared, with one door on either end of the porch.

The sea roared like a monster, booming below, the waves all white foam today as they collided with the large, jagged rocks before frothing into the small cove of coarse, rocky sand, encircled by dark green mountains that helped to shield beachgoers from the worst of the wind.

This view had been there, unchanging, all of her life.

Nearly every morning, she'd woken up, come out to this porch and looked at the ocean.

The idea of leaving it suddenly made her more sad than excited. What if the letter did say yes, and she moved across the country?

For the past two years she'd built up fantasies of a life at that school. She'd built a relationship with the lead researcher at an aquarium there, who assured her she'd have a place to work and get hands-on experience should she be accepted to the school.

Her best friend, Catherine, had applied there, too.

The place, the program...

There wasn't anywhere better.

Oh...what if her letter said no?

She took a breath of the briny, salt-touched air and smiled. She walked over to the wooden door and looked up at the window, the pale sunlight hitting the glass squares and lighting up the colors.

Purple and green and gold.

Then she pushed open the door and stopped.

The sight of her mother standing there immobilized her.

Her mother was waxen. Her dark red hair hung limp down past her shoulders. It was more than the typical marks of exhaustion marring her face. It was like a light had been wrenched from her.

"He's gone," she said.

Emma didn't have to ask what that meant.

Her grip was like iron on the letter, even though her hand trembled. Clinging to it like she was afraid she'd lose her hold on it.

But she knew she already had.

Because whatever had seemed possible outside her front door was impossible now that she was inside.

WENDY

Wendy McDonald finished putting the very last letter into the leather-bound scrapbook and placed it gently on the side table in the lavender sitting room, just next to the table that housed the antique sewing machine.

Those letters and journal entries from Jenny Hansen,

the mail-order bride of Olaf Hansen, the first lightkeeper's wife, had been donated recently by the local museum.

Wendy was on a mission to collect more information from each incarnation of the Cape Hope Lighthouse.

She had recently been promised a batch of letters written by a soldier who'd been stationed here during WWII, offered generously by his family. They were in the process of having copies made so that the family could hang on to the legacy, but the letters would be coming soon and Wendy was pleased at the thought of adding them.

She was having more trouble finding something personal from the time the inn had been a dorm, but she was confident she could find something. A little piece from that unique time.

She took the bottle of furniture polish off the coffee table and began to condition the wood pieces in the room.

This place was her pride and joy. Her salvation.

Thirty-three years ago she'd found herself single, with two daughters and no idea what she'd wanted from life with her ex gone for good.

She had been waiting tables, hoarding the small amount of money she'd gotten from her ex, and trying to stretch it all, worrying every night how it could continue. How she was going to find a way to keep a roof over their heads, to make her girls happy.

She had been frayed down to her soul and the idea of just getting by—after so many years of living a life she hadn't been happy in—had made her want to walk into the sea and let the water wash over her head.

Then she'd heard an ad on the radio that had sounded to Wendy like the voice of God.

The United States Forest Service wanted to turn the Lighthouse at Cape Hope, just outside the town of Sunset Bay, Oregon, into a bed-and-breakfast. And they were running a contest to find an innkeeper.

Someone who could restore the place and find a way to make it attractive to tourists. Someone who could bring in revenue, both for themself and the department.

The time was almost up for the contest.

Wendy wrote a letter with shaking hands and more passion than skill. Then she'd bundled up baby Anna and six-year-old Rachel in their old car, and driven to Sunset Bay all the way from Medford.

She'd slid the letter under the door with a voiceless prayer. And then she'd spent the last ten dollars in her purse buying ice cream while she sat there with a stomach churning from hunger, and nerves.

Somehow, she'd won.

Somehow, they'd seen that a single mother who had two of the most precious incentives a person could ask for would be the one to make this place special.

And she had.

They had.

For six months she'd worked without pay. They'd bought necessities with her settlement, their lodging part and parcel of their role as innkeepers.

And Wendy had prayed harder than she ever had in her life. Because if they could make the place profitable, she could teach her daughters that you could do anything. That you could heal from any wound.

When Rick had walked away from her she'd been devastated. And she'd been afraid that having his children meant she would always live with one foot left in that life. They were pieces of him, after all.

Bit by bit that had changed. As they'd built this property it had bonded her to her girls in a way that went deep. Until they'd been knit together so tightly there was no missing piece between them. Until they were a piece of her, and this place.

As Wendy moved her rag over the banisters, making them gleam, she remembered the work she'd put in back then. How she'd spent days up on a stepladder restaining the cherry trim on every door and window frame—all hand carved in the 1800s by a German artist.

With her restoration budget, she'd combed through antiques shops to find furniture that fit the Queen Anne–style of the home. Vanities with intricately carved legs, four-poster beds and claw-foot tubs.

She'd shown her daughters that they could fashion a life from rubble. That miracles could come in the form of radio ads, as long as you were willing to take the drive, to write the letter and make that miracle happen. That old, rustic wood could shine again, and lace curtains in the window and a coat of fresh paint could make all the difference.

They had lived in various homes on the property over the years. They'd started in the biggest house, the Captain's House—which now boasted six guest rooms—until it was restored and ready for guests.

It was all done now. Beautiful, restored. Like her life.

She had done right.

She had been so desperate to do right.

Both of her daughters had married young, and to very good men.

Rachel'd had it hard. But Jacob was a wonderful husband and father. They were close, at least, living on the other side of the duplex Wendy herself occupied.

Then there was Anna.

Beautiful Anna, with her bright red hair and freckles, who had always been such a bubbly and willful child. And in her she'd seen the potential for the kind of passion that could go wrong.

Wendy knew it too well.

Wendy had never been so thankful as when Anna started dating Thomas Martin. He had been bound for such great things, and it had been apparent even then. He led prayer around the flagpole at school, and gave a bible study at his house that was attended by almost all of the kids in their classes.

It hadn't been a surprise when he'd become an associate pastor at the largest church in town, and then had become the youngest head pastor to ever hold the position at Sunset Church.

Then there was Emma. Her granddaughter. She had grown into such a beautiful young woman, and she had brilliant goals and aspirations. Her focus, her determination, gave Wendy the confidence that Emma would never fall into the kind of trap that Wendy herself had as a young girl.

Falling in love with the wrong man had nearly ruined Wendy's life.

But she hadn't let it. Not in the end.

And she had done everything in her power to instill the right values in her girls, so that they wouldn't have to deal with the heartache she'd had to.

Here, they'd been safe. Here, they'd found refuge.

Just as she finished with her polishing, there was a knock on her door.

ANNA

When Anna walked into her sister's house and saw her, pale, tearstained and silent, the stark reality was undeniable. Jacob was gone.

And Anna didn't have the words.

But her husband, Thomas, did.

Because Thomas always had words for other people.

She was the one that he never had them for.

But it wasn't the best time to worry about that. Maybe she was worrying about it because she was in shock. She'd expected the news of Jacob's passing to come over a late-night phone call.

She didn't know why. She had just imagined that it would.

Instead, it was the middle of the day and she had just taken a pie out of the oven when the phone rang, and it was Thomas telling her that he was coming home from the church office. That surprised her in and of itself because he did not call her when he was working. And he didn't come home early for much of anything.

She knew that her mother had told Thomas because it was easier for her to break it to him than it was for her to tell Anna. But what her mother didn't know was that she and Thomas had spent the entire drive from their quiet row house through town and up the winding drive that led to the Lighthouse Inn in silence.

She couldn't think of a single thing to say to him. And it wasn't just grief, though there was plenty of that.

Jacob was like a brother to them both.

Rachel and Jacob had been married since Anna was thirteen. She could hardly remember life without him.

"Are you all right?" he asked, directing the question to Rachel.

The words turned over in Anna's head, echoed, because, of course, Rachel wasn't all right, but it was also the most obvious question to ask, and for some reason Anna hadn't said it.

"I don't know," Rachel said. "I don't know if I'm ever going to be all right again."

Her sister put her hand on the antique sideboard that sat by the door, as if she was bracing herself on it. And then she took it off as quickly as she placed it there.

Because Rachel was never still for long.

"Can I get you coffee? Tea?" She directed the questions at both Anna and Thomas.

"Yes, thank you," Thomas said at the same time Anna said, "I'm fine."

But Rachel looked relieved at having something to do, and Anna felt that yet again she had profoundly failed at being the one who was more insightful about her own sister.

Her mother was sitting on the couch, pale and resolved. Anna and Rachel's mother was always resolved. She was rarely still, though, and seeing her like that reinforced the wrongness of everything.

Her niece, Emma, was sitting there looking numb. Frozen.

Emma was a kid who'd had to be too serious, too quickly. Self-sufficient, self-reliant. When Emma was younger, Anna had helped with her often, so that Rachel could be there for Jacob when he had surgeries, and Wendy could be there for Rachel.

She'd gotten older, though. And she hadn't needed Anna to watch her anymore.

But suddenly she felt like Emma might need her now.

When Rachel returned with the drinks, she handed one to Thomas. "I guess… Maybe I shouldn't… His body was so broken," Rachel said, "I guess that it's silly to grieve when he needed to be free of it."

"The Bible says that there's a time to mourn, Rachel. You don't have to hold back grief."

Thomas went on, his words building on one another, weaving themselves into a sermon, which was easy for him to do.

He always knew the right thing to say. His voice was calming, comforting.

But not to her. Not anymore.

Anna sank down onto the floral couch, next to her niece.

Emma stretched her lips into a poor imitation of a smile, and Anna tried to return it.

"My mom won't let me go upstairs," she whispered. "She doesn't want me to see him. Um… His—his body." The last word broke. And something broke in Anna, too.

It was almost a relief. To feel broken. To feel pain instead of numbness.

"She's trying to protect you," Anna said.

"My dad's dead. I can't be protected from that."

That word slipped like a shard of glass through Anna's chest and embedded itself in her heart.

There were just some things in the world you couldn't be protected from. No matter how hard you tried. You could do all the right things, say all the right things… And still…

She looked over at Thomas.

And still…

"Thank you," Wendy said, directing her thanks at Thomas. "I don't know what we would do without you."

Those words settled over Anna like concrete. Made her feel like she was weighted down to the spot. But they also triggered something inside her. That pastor's-wife instinct that she knew so well. That was such a practiced role she could put it on like a coat when she wanted to. That was the Anna that they needed. Not the Anna that was broken up, struggling.

She'd hidden that Anna for the past two years, and there was a reason for that.

Purpose turned over inside her and it lit a spark of motion. "I have a pie in the car," she said. "I'll bring it in. Of course, Thomas and I will help arrange the funeral and get the word out at church."

Rachel looked startled that Anna had spoken. "Thank you," she said.

Anna smiled. Serene. Not too big. Not happy. Reassuring. The smile she knew so well. A smile for sad times. One that she'd used so many times before.

"It's what we're here for."

But somehow, the words felt wrong, and so did she.

Because the shape of their family had changed, a great gaping hold left where Jacob had once been.

And Anna had no idea how they were going to go on.

2

This is not the ocean that I know. In California the
water sparkles like a jewel in the sun, and here,
if there is sun, it is swallowed whole by the mist,
the clouds and the relentless gray of the sea.
I fear I have made a mistake.

—FROM THE DIARY OF JENNY HANSEN, JANUARY 15, 1900

RACHEL

Rachel had lost track of how many events they'd hosted
at the Lighthouse Inn. They always used the kitchen as
the staging area, and expanded to the dining room when
the event was to be held outside.

There was a strange sort of sameness in what was happening now. Her mother looking at lists. Her sister putting
last-minute touches on baked goods.

Her daughter, Emma, looking on.

But this wasn't a wedding. It wasn't a bachelorette
party, or a birthday party.

It was a funeral.

Her husband's funeral.

She was staring down at a list of food meant to feed the guests of her husband's funeral.

"Do you think this is enough bread?" She looked across the table, laden with baskets of rolls, at her mother.

"I would think so," Wendy replied.

Rachel had stayed up all night baking, because there was nothing else to do. Make bread. Over and over again. Batch upon batch of rolls, each one feeling imperative.

Keeping busy so much better than trying to sleep.

"Well, we have to be sure," Rachel said. "I don't want anyone to be hungry."

Those words gutted her with their absurdity. She didn't want them to be hungry? They were grieving. A dinner roll wasn't going to help with that.

"I don't think anyone is going to go hungry," Anna said, her voice soft and reassuring. "Anyway, I've baked fifteen pies, and there are some ladies from the church who are going to bring extra food just to be certain."

"Okay," Rachel said, her sister's reassurance throwing her off-balance.

She knew that Anna did this. That she handled all kinds of difficult situations, but Rachel had never needed Anna to care for her.

She was used to being the one doing the caring.

"You've been constantly in our prayers, Rachel."

Rachel gawked at her sister. Anna seemed smooth and serene, which was how she had been for the past fourteen years. Ever since marrying Thomas and settling into her role as pastor's wife. It was like Rachel couldn't touch her anymore.

"Thank you," Rachel said.

And all she could think of was the great yawning distance between them.

She baked fifteen pies.

Yes. She had. But she would have done the same sort of thing for anyone.

"Thanks, Aunt Anna," Emma said.

Her daughter's sincere thank-you made Rachel feel slightly ashamed that she had reacted so angrily.

She took a deep breath. "You know we appreciate it. And I appreciate Thomas doing the service."

"Of course," Anna said, her smile the appropriate amount of sympathetic and warm.

It looked like a mask.

"All right, we have everything," Wendy said, looking down at the checklist. She faced her daughters, her expression serious and determined. "We know how to do this. We know how to plan an amazing event. So let's make this one worthy of Jacob."

Rachel set aside her issues with Anna. She focused on the familiar motions that went into preparing for an event. Her daughter, her mother and her sister just being there made her feel less brittle. Made her feel like she might be able to keep going.

But then, when it was all done, and there was nothing left to prepare, she stood and looked around and realized Jacob was gone. Really gone.

And all that had been familiar a moment before felt dark and uncertain now.

She didn't know how to live in a world without Jacob in it.

ANNA

Anna thought that her face might break. She had been smiling for the past two hours. Standing on this damp grass, her shoes sinking into the muck, the mist clinging to her hair and her grief clinging to her body like another skin.

And over it all, she wore that pastor's-wife coat.

It had been the most important thing she'd put on this morning. Not her black shawl and black pants. Not her black boots.

"They need reassurance," Thomas had said right before they had walked in. And the way that he looked at her—stone-faced enough that she thought he might finally have noticed the distance between them.

She couldn't remember the last time he'd touched her.

Even when they'd walked into the funeral, they had done so side by side, with a healthy amount of space between them.

It felt like a metaphor for their marriage.

For her.

She'd gotten good at separate.

A kick sparked in her heart and she tamped it down, because she was here to be the pastor's wife, not to think about anything else. She was here to support her sister, not to think about her own marriage.

But the loss of her sister's husband had her thinking about marriage. And even more, about Jacob himself.

Jacob was way too young to be gone. She wondered if he'd ever felt like a soul trapped in a body that didn't do the things he wanted, didn't do the things he craved.

Because she did.

She did, and she wasn't even sick. And it felt like an insult to his memory.

"Thank you for coming," she said to two of the guests who were getting ready to leave.

"Thank you," she said to someone else, who looked at her tearfully.

"Are you all right, Anna?"

"We will be," Anna said.

"I'll pray for you."

It kept on like that for the next hour. Greetings and goodbyes, platitudes. She could think about entirely different things, stand there and smile, and say everything she was supposed to.

And her soul was bursting to escape.

She looked over at her mother, who looked like she'd aged years overnight. Which was something that Wendy McDonald would definitely not appreciate if anyone breathed a word of such a thing in her direction. Wendy looked over at Anna, and there was something far too perceptive in her mother's gaze, even through the haze of grief.

Anna always felt like her mother could see it. That no matter how hard she tried to behave, her mother could see that there was something struggling against all of this inside her, and it made her feel transparent.

She had often thought, if she had to choose an era of the lighthouse that had the most relatable history to her, it would be the time it had played host to seventy American soldiers. Because she often felt like up here on the hill, she was keeping her head down and keeping up a brave front, while in reality, she always felt like she was about to be buffeted on all sides.

Dramatic, perhaps.

But, particularly as a teenager, the drama had suited her.

"Thank you so much," she said.

"Can I do something for you, Anna?"

Anna jolted. She realized that she knew the woman that she was talking to more than just in passing. They went to several Bible studies together at church. Laura. Who was always friendly, and always seemed like she might want to spend more time with Anna, but Anna had been spending less time at church things and more time at the Lighthouse Inn.

"No," Anna said. "I don't need anything. Rachel... I'm just concerned about her."

The lie tasted bitter on her tongue. But she lied a lot now. By omission. Without words. With a smile.

She couldn't remember the exact moment she'd stopped feeling guilty.

"Of course," Laura said.

"Thank you for asking."

"If you ever want to go to coffee..."

"Sure," Anna said, not meaning it. "I'd love that. I'll... We'll talk. When everything settles down."

"Okay," Laura said.

She had an overwhelming revelation—Anna realized that things would settle down again. That everything would go back to the way it was, just with a hole where Jacob used to be.

This event, no matter how shocking, difficult and intense, had not changed her life.

She was still the same woman in the same marriage. The same woman, trapped because whatever she felt in her heart, she had restricted herself so tightly she couldn't quite find a way to make the moves that needed to be made.

It was only at the Lighthouse Inn, where she had been a girl, where she had run wild and barefoot through the lawn, that she was able to find that spark in herself still.

She looked toward the Captain's House, and something new sparked inside her. Not habit. Not familiarity.

Determination.

She was not ill. She didn't have an excuse. The only person who was keeping her trapped was herself.

And she thought it might be time to make a move.

3

It is stunning to think that what was home only
months ago is on the verge of becoming the front
lines today.

—FROM A LETTER DATED JANUARY 5, 1943, WRITTEN BY
STAFF SERGEANT RICHARD JOHNSON, WHO, ALONG WITH SEVENTY
OTHER MEN, HAD BEEN STATIONED AT CAPE HOPE LIGHTHOUSE
AFTER THE ATTACK ON FORT STEVENS

EMMA

"Emma." The older woman reached out and squeezed
Emma's shoulder, tears glistening in her blue eyes.

Emma couldn't even remember her name—which was
a common enough occurrence. Everyone knew her because she was Pastor Thomas's niece. But today it felt
overwhelming. The amount of people she didn't know,
offering sympathy and looking at her like they expected
something from her...

She'd done her best to stand between her mom and all
of this.

She was exhausted.

It had been a week since her father's funeral, and her

grandmother was adamant that they all get up and go to church together. She'd been to school, so it wasn't like she hadn't been out of the house.

But kids at school were way less likely to ask about her dad and how she was feeling.

People at church...

They all meant well. They asked because they cared, and Emma knew it.

But sometimes the sense of community was smothering.

It was part of why Emma felt so ready for change.

Her mom wanted her to work at the Lighthouse Inn again this summer, and Emma had been hoping to get a job somewhere else.

There were a lot of things that she wanted to do.

But she didn't see the path to any of them right now.

She sat in the front row with her mother and her grandmother. The stage looked like it always did, with a large wooden cross at the back, lit from behind. She saw a lot of people she knew, some kids from school. But she didn't see her aunt Anna anywhere.

Her aunt had been quiet and distant over the past week, but Emma hadn't thought anything about it because she'd felt quiet and distant. They all had.

They sometimes missed church, but Anna never did. She'd said more than once that going to church was essentially her job. And Emma had never known Anna to... just not go.

The background music faded, and the conversation around them died down. People took their seats as her uncle Thomas came out onto the stage to make announcements.

He was the kind of man who always seemed at ease.

He smiled, no matter what, and not in a way that felt fake. In a way that felt reassuring. Like he was listening, and like it wasn't a burden.

He was tall, with dark hair and a lean build that made it seem like he was always in motion. He usually was in motion. Greeting everyone they passed on the street, helping put dinner on the table, helping with projects that needed to be done at Emma's house.

But today he seemed off. And she couldn't recall her uncle ever seeming off before.

She wondered if he was going to say something about her dad, and her stomach tightened up.

But there was something in the way he took that first labored breath before he began to speak that made her certain it wasn't about her dad.

There was something wrong now. His pallor was chalky, his whole body tense.

He looked like he didn't quite know where to begin.

And Thomas Martin always knew where to begin.

"I know there has been talk," he said slowly. "You've always been there for me, as a family. You've been there as my family suffered a loss this past week, and I am thankful for that, too. But that isn't the only change to take place."

His throat sounded dry, which was a strange thing to notice, except when he swallowed it seemed forced. "I don't take any great joy in announcing this here, but I truly believe, after much thought and much prayer, that this is the best thing to do. The truth is always the answer. And I would ask you to please not take anything that I say and spin bigger stories out of it. I will talk about this once, and only once. I caught my wife in the act of adultery."

The ripple of shock that went through the crowd was audible.

Emma's grandmother grabbed at her chest, as if something had stuck in her heart.

Emma's mother's hands curled into fists, scraping along the textured tan fabric of the pew.

Emma didn't move.

No.

The word, the denial, was explosive inside her brain.

She'd just seen her aunt. She'd been there for them all through this time. She hadn't been… There was no way.

"I've had my faults. No man is perfect. But I have been a faithful husband. And…" He swallowed again, with visible difficulty. "I don't say this to condemn her or exonerate myself. But just to explain what is happening, and why the shape of our church family is changing. I don't have any further details, except to say that we will be getting divorced. I apologize for the role that I played in this failure. There will be a guest speaker today. I will be back with you next week."

He turned and walked backstage then, and voices rose up around them, the sound of the congregation talking, not even bothering to whisper. Why whisper? It wasn't a secret.

Her family didn't talk or whisper. They sat frozen.

It wiped everything out of Emma's mind.

The woman who had done that didn't sound like her aunt, and right now the man speaking from the pulpit didn't seem like her uncle. Because how could he say that? How could he do this to them now? She turned to look at her mother, whose expression was bland, and completely unreadable. Her grandma was waxen.

They exited the sanctuary quickly, rushing out to the

parking lot. Emma felt like they were running from an enemy. Even more terrifying, they were outrunning a wall of questions that none of them would know the answer to. But she knew that she would never be able to look at her uncle the same way again.

Because their family had been fractured before and he had just smashed it to pieces.

That was when she noticed that her grandmother's hands were shaking.

"You don't actually believe that?" Rachel asked.

"I don't know," Wendy said, her eyes filling with tears. "I don't know. Why would he say it if it weren't true?" She twisted the church program in her hands.

"Why would he say anything?" her mom asked, sounding furious. "How could he do that?"

Her grandmother was silent.

But she suddenly quickened her pace, walking to her car and leaving Emma and her mother behind.

"I don't believe it," Rachel said.

She couldn't make her uncle's words match up with what she knew of her aunt, and even if she could…

She knew Anna had a reason.

Her beautiful aunt, whose hair matched her own, and who had always seemed to have a bigger spirit than could be contained in one person.

It didn't…matter to her.

"We need to find Aunt Anna," Emma said.

Her mom rubbed her hand over her forehead. "Do you think she knew he was going to do that?"

Anna wasn't here for a reason; Emma knew that much. And suddenly the ache she felt for her dad was so overwhelming she thought she might break. Her dad, who had always stood tall and firm, even when his body was weak.

She remembered the way that felt. Him holding her.

Remembered being a little girl, sitting up on his shoulders, where she could get a view of the whole world.

She could use a better view now.

"Come on, let's… You should eat. You look pale."

Her mom looked pale, too, but Emma knew better than to point that out.

"I wish Dad were here," Emma whispered.

Her mom nodded, swallowing hard. "Me, too."

4

Perhaps if the walls weren't such a dull color
I would feel more at peace. It's white and gray
everywhere. The clouds, the walls, the sea.
I'm turning gray along with it.

—FROM THE DIARY OF JENNY HANSEN, FEBRUARY 1, 1900

ANNA

Anna closed her eyes. Then opened them again. Tried to catch her breath.

She was lying in bed in the Lightkeeper's Room, a room that was currently unoccupied at the Lighthouse Inn, under the sheets. Staring through the white fabric, the sunlight penetrating the thin veil.

She'd done this when she was a kid.

Tearing through the house, breaking one of her mother's vases.

Hide under the covers.

Collect the ladybugs that ran rampant in the house rather than exterminating them as ordered…and spill the jar in a guest's luggage.

Hide under the covers.

She wished that she was hiding from rampant lady-bugs now.

She *was* hiding from her mother.

From her husband.

From the world.

Service would be over by now. And everyone would know. He'd warned her he was going to do it. That he'd have to announce that their marriage was over and why and Anna had been too sick and ashamed to argue, all the guilt she'd pushed away during that bright, glaring moment of freedom tumbling in on her like a stack of bricks.

She closed her eyes again, and she went back a week. To the night of Jacob's funeral.

She'd been lying under the covers. In this room.

She just hadn't been alone…

Anna waited to feel guilty. Lying there in the dark, with the curtains drawn closed and Michael breathing beside her. Slow and steady, dozing the way men did after they were satisfied.

She couldn't sleep.

But not because of guilt or regret or any of the emotions she had expected to feel, in that small space of time when she'd still been thinking clearly enough to make a decision.

The breath between him leaning in, and their lips touching.

You'll regret it.

I don't care.

But her conscience—or whatever had whispered to her just before the kiss—had been wrong.

When her lips touched his it was like all the pieces of herself had finally come together. That woman, that shell, who had talked to everyone at the funeral with a smile pasted on her face, had shattered into a million pieces.

Her path had been leading up to this for a couple of months now, no matter how she'd pretended it hadn't.

She'd told herself she was only being friendly with a guest. That it was okay her heart leaped whenever she saw his name on the registry for the week.

That when he said she was pretty it was only talking.

But then he'd called her sexy.

Had said rough things to her that shocked her, things that her husband certainly wouldn't have ever said.

He'd pursued her.

Like she mattered. Like she was the center of his life.

The intensity of it was...

It made her heart ache even now.

And there had been some point when she had realized she'd crossed some invisible line and there was no going back, but by that point she'd been so far gone she hadn't even cared.

And standing at Jacob's funeral, so disconnected from herself, then spending the whole drive home with Thomas in silence, she'd known.

Michael was staying at the inn. And she was ready.

She couldn't be sorry.

She felt free. Like she was breaking shackles. Her face burned with heat, her body filled with adrenaline.

She'd never been with another man. She married her husband at eighteen, and they'd both been virgins on their wedding night.

Sex was sacred. And sharing it with someone else was...

It was the biggest betrayal she could have committed.

But no one had ever told her that you could live with

someone and feel alone. That you could share a bed with them and feel cold.

That you could go into marriage shiny and young and full of hope, and fourteen years later feel worn down to nothing.

Until Michael had checked into the Lighthouse Inn.

A traveling medical tech, he made rounds in Sunset Bay often, and he had begun to use her family's property regularly.

He didn't know her. Everyone in town knew her and, more importantly, knew Thomas.

There had been no one to confide in.

And that was how it had started. Because Michael had asked why she was sad, and he had been the only person to notice that she was. That no matter how wide she was smiling it didn't reach her eyes.

But he had seen it. He knew.

No, she didn't feel guilty.

And if he knew... Oh, if Thomas knew, he wouldn't be able to ignore it. Not like when she had quietly told him she was lonely.

Not when she had asked him if he still thought she was beautiful and he'd said yes without even looking at her, asking why she had doubted it.

Not like when she'd said she missed him, and he looked at her like she was insane, because they lived together, and half the time they even worked together at the church, so how could she miss him?

On the nightstand, she saw her phone light up.

Michael stirred in the bed, his eyes opening, but he didn't make a sound.

She didn't answer the phone because she couldn't bear

to speak to anyone. But it was late, and if she was starting to get calls...

She touched his shoulder. "I have to go."

He stirred, and he took her in his arms, pulling her
against the length of his body, kissing her. She melted.
She hadn't been touched like this in so long.

His hands skimmed over her curves. Reverently. Lust-
fully.

Had she ever been touched like this? Had Thomas ever
looked at her with this kind of intensity?

"Do you really have to?"

"Yes," she said. "I... My..."

"Yeah." His lips lifted into a smile. "I get it."

She rolled away from him reluctantly and got out of
bed, dressing slowly.

She put her phone in her purse. Her wedding ring was
still in there. She wasn't going to put it on while she was
still with Michael.

"Regrets?" he asked.

"None."

And that would have stayed true if Michael hadn't followed her.

But he did.

Right out of the bedroom. Right when her eyes connected with her husband's.

Thomas was standing at the bottom of the stairs, his
expression tense, his left hand resting on the banister.

His gold wedding ring shining bright. His eyes met
hers, grave but with no trace of anger at all.

"I've been trying to get a hold of you..."

Her phone buzzing brought her back to the moment.
She unburied herself from the sheets and rolled to the

side, reaching down and fishing her phone out of her purse.

It wasn't Thomas this time.

It was her mother.

RACHEL

"You called me?"

Shock bloomed in Rachel's stomach when her sister walked into the dining room. And it was also shock that registered on Anna's face when she looked around the room and saw that they were all here.

Her sister no longer looked unflappable. No longer the smooth, perfect pastor's wife.

No.

She had felt, strongly in her soul, that her brother-in-law had undone all of that with a few words from the pulpit this morning. But she could see, judging by the bruises blooming underneath her eyes from lack of sleep, and the lines that bracketed her mouth, that perhaps Anna had unraveled it herself.

"We were looking for you," her mother said.

"We were worried," Emma said.

Rachel felt a momentary stab of guilt that her daughter had been the first one to offer concern.

But Rachel still felt like she was lost in a fog of her own grief, and she resented the guilt. She didn't have the room for it.

"Is it true?" Wendy asked.

"Is what true?"

"You must have known he was going to announce it today at church," Wendy said.

"I…"

"You did," Rachel said. She tried to keep the accusation out of her voice. But why hadn't Anna warned them? They had just been sitting there exposed to...

"I guess I didn't really believe that he would," Anna said. "I mean, I wouldn't have thought that he would want to make such a—a spectacle out of it. But I guess that he needs to... He needs to have it done."

"He shouldn't have done that," Emma said, the conviction in her daughter's voice filled with the kind of purity that only the young could feel.

"Were you going to tell me?" Rachel asked. "Ever?"

Anna blinked. "Why would I tell you right now?"

"I don't know. You couldn't wait to blow your life up until I was through all of this? You might as well have confided in me. You could've talked to me."

"Enough," Wendy said. "It's not time to fight. If you need a place to stay, Anna, you know you can always stay in the Shoreman's Cabin. It's available."

"Right," Anna said. "I'm sure the Forest Service won't mind at all if we negatively impact the revenue by giving me a place to stay."

"We built this place," Wendy said. "For us. And I reserve the right to benefit this family with what we've built. You need a place. We have a place."

"Thank you," Anna said quietly.

Rachel couldn't remember the last time she'd seen her sister quite so unraveled. It reminded her of younger Anna. Who used to explode at the drop of a hat and then put herself back together and become a cheerful, sweet child minutes after the storm.

She had been replaced by the smooth creature that had made Rachel's stomach hurt the day of the funeral. But she wasn't entirely sure she was ready for windswept, hurricane Anna yet, either.

She wondered what was wrong with her that she couldn't find any compassion right now. Maybe it was just that the well was dry. Because her husband was dead and Anna had betrayed hers.

Her stomach tightened.

She knew it wasn't that simple. She knew that it couldn't be. Because what Thomas had done rang so hollow and so false that even if he was telling the truth… She knew that it wasn't the whole truth.

But she still couldn't find it in her to be soft. To be forgiving. To let somebody else have a problem when her own life had been destroyed.

And it hadn't been her fault.

It hadn't been her choice.

And when her sister looked at her, Rachel couldn't bring herself to offer any reassurance.

Their mother had given her a place to stay. That would have to be enough for now.

5

The ghost's name is Roo. Ron got out the Ouija
board and asked her. Don't tell Mom. And tell her
the boys are staying in their dormitories, too.
Of course, they would never come over to ours!

—FROM A LETTER WRITTEN BY SUSAN BRIGHT TO HER SISTER, JUNE 1961,
WHEN THE CAPE HOPE LIGHTHOUSE PROPERTY WAS CONVERTED TO
A SATELLITE CAMPUS FOR LOGAN COUNTY COMMUNITY COLLEGE

EMMA

Emma wasn't a liar by nature.

But for the past two weeks it had felt like that was her primary method of communication with her mother.

She bit down on the inside of her cheek and pulled her small car into the parking lot of J's Diner. The shabby yellow building was at the top of a hill that overlooked the main street in Old Town, and she sat for a moment, her interactions with her mom from the past week playing over in her mind…

"How are you?"

"Fine."

"How is school?"

"Good."

"Looking forward to OSU?"

"Yes..."

Not that it was new. Over the years she had honed omission into an art form, and the subtle bending of the truth into a tool she could wield with ease. She'd become skilled at recognizing things that might add weight to her mother's already heavy burden.

She couldn't remove a whole boulder, but she could carry around life's pebbles all on her own without her mom having to worry about them.

Yes, and sneaking out for coffee and a hopeful glance at Luke is definitely in your mother's best interest...

She sighed and killed the engine, then got out of the car and looked around. The town was bustling with people on their way to work, getting coffee from their preferred spots.

The town of Sunset Bay consisted of two main segments—the utilitarian segment of town just across the bridge that led to the highway that ultimately connected them with I-5, and the rest of the state. There you could find big-box stores, dentists' and doctors' offices, autobody repair and larger restaurants.

But if you turned right off the bridge that carried you off the coastal highway, you could get to Old Town, the original main street of Sunset Bay, which ran along the Yachats River, extending nearly to where the river met the sea.

There were tourist traps, with an excess of bright wind socks hung outside, and driftwood animals all in a row. Art galleries, a specialty kitchen shop and little farm-to-table restaurants, coffeehouses and fish-and-chips shacks.

Emma had told her mother that she had an early class,

and it was kind of a crappy thing to lie about where she was going, but she had to get out of the house.

The grief didn't feel like she expected it to.

She'd expected a sense of finality. She'd spent her life dreading her father's death. She'd been so aware of the fact her parents were mortal from the time she was young. Her dad was sick, but if her strong, brilliant dad could be so sick, then anyone could be. There had been a sense of fear in her childhood over every sniffle.

And to an extent she'd thought… She'd thought this would be an end.

She had done her best not to build up hopes of what she might have had with her dad. Had let go of the idea that he might give her away at her wedding someday, or even sit in the front row during her graduation.

Those stages of acceptance that had all hurt. This was just living in the future she'd been expecting all along.

But she hadn't guessed all the little things she'd miss. Like him teasing her about all the sugar she'd put in her coffee. Or him texting her throughout the day to check in.

Sometimes she'd found it annoying. Now she kept scrolling back through every text he'd ever sent, taking screenshots of them so she wouldn't lose them.

It came in waves. An ebb in the pain, where she'd forget, then look at her phone. And remember.

Going toward her parents' room and then stopping because she suddenly remembered he wasn't there.

She just couldn't stand to be home.

The diner was like a strange oasis. A collection of small-town clichés that was comforting in its way. The tile floor was scuffed from work boots, the wallpaper border—with pictures of cars from the 1950s—had seen better decades and no one sat on two of the eight red swivel stools at the counter because the tops were irredeemably lopsided.

But everyone ate at J's, and had ever since Jack Campbell had opened it years ago, and they came still, with his grandson Adam at the helm.

It provided comforting kitchen noises, muffled conversation and familiarity. It also provided an excellent view of the mechanic shop across the street. Which was where Luke would be.

Normally, she would think it was silly to pine after a guy who didn't know she existed. But there was something nice about a relationship that had no expectation on it. A relationship that wasn't a relationship.

These feelings had become a talisman. Something to hold and examine, something else to think of. Away from her house, away from her family. Even from her friends, in a way.

Adam usually asked how she was, but he took her answer at face value and never pressed for information.

She winced. Right. Adam. If he mentioned to her mom that she'd been in today...

She and her mother had been pretty dependent on dinner from here, especially over the past few months.

When things were crazy, Mom always stopped by to pick up burgers or a salad, depending on whether or not she was pretending she wasn't eating her feelings.

Maybe Emma could offer to pick up dinner tonight...

"Good morning," Adam said, his mouth set into a neutral position, the lines on his face giving a suggestion of facial expressions he'd made in the past, but not giving much indication of what he was thinking—or feeling—now.

He'd been in town about three years, which made him brand-new, by the standards of this town. So seldom did things change around here that a fifteen-year-old piece of road construction connecting Sunset Bay with the inland town of Pinecroft was still referred to as "the new overpass."

And Adam was most definitely still "the new diner owner."

If Emma had to guess, he was somewhere around her mom's and dad's ages. But he wasn't married, and as far as she knew he didn't have any kids.

She waited for him to ask about Anna. If he did, she was ready to get in a fight in defense of Anna. If anyone asked.

But he didn't ask about Anna.

She waited for him to ask about the funeral. He didn't.

She wasn't sure that Adam had been there.

Adam might have been one of the few people in town who didn't know her dad in some capacity. Maybe that was another reason she liked the diner. It felt like a different town sometimes.

Maybe that was why this was her mom's preferred dinner spot.

She hadn't really thought of that before.

"Coffee and a doughnut?" she asked.

"No protein?" he asked.

"I didn't ask for a side of judgment."

"The judgment is on the house."

The front door pushed open, and her friend Catherine came in, breathless and red-cheeked. They'd been in pretty constant text contact since the funeral and they'd exchanged a few OMGs about church and Anna, but they hadn't actually talked. Catherine sat down at a table in the corner, the one with the clear view across the street. "Thanks, I..."

"I'll bring it to your table. Hold the judgment."

She nodded and walked away from the counter and over toward the white-and-silver-flecked table where Catherine had taken position, her back to the window, offering Emma the best view.

"This is a great sacrifice," Catherine said.

"I know," Emma replied. "I appreciate it."

"Well, are you ever going to talk to him?"

"No. I'm absolutely never going to talk to him. You made a very good point when you said it's probably for the best he doesn't know who I am."

"You're just going to stare at him?"

"Yes. I am just going to stare at him. I don't need to date anyone right now. I need to get good grades so I can get into the school I want to go to, and then I'll be in college and I'll be busy."

"Boston still?"

Her stomach fell. She'd been avoiding having this talk. "No."

"Em, didn't you get in? I didn't want to ask because of your dad, but when you didn't say anything—"

"I—I got in." She hadn't said those words out loud. "I lied to my mom about it."

"Emma!"

"I got the letter the day he died," she said, her eyes feeling scratchy. "And I was so excited and I wanted to tell him and he was gone. And then I looked at my mom and realized I would be telling her I was leaving and I can't—I can't leave her. And I don't want her to feel responsible for it."

"Emma, that's not like you. I mean, it is like you. Protecting your mom. But not lying. And you want to go to Boston…"

"OSU has a great marine-biology program and it's like three hours away."

Catherine's face fell. "But it's not the same as Boston. By any means. You could go live in one of the most historic cities in the country, and isn't there a specific aquarium there you want to work with?"

"It's not important," she said.

"It's not important that we go to the same school?" Her friend looked wounded and it made Emma want to growl. She didn't have the energy for someone else's wound.

"That's not what I mean." She looked down. "I wanted it, but things changed. Anyway, it's not like I'm abandoning my plans to go to college. I'm just altering course a little bit." Her friend just stared at her. "Don't look at me like that. It makes sense."

"I mean, I guess. I mean, it makes more sense than never talking to the guy you had a thing for *for years*."

"I didn't ask." She was grateful, though, for the conversation shift.

Catherine shrugged. "That's fine. I don't need to be asked."

The coffee and doughnut materialized, as did a mug of coffee for Catherine, even though she hadn't ordered it.

"I don't want coffee," Catherine said.

"Why not?" Adam raised an eyebrow.

"Because diner coffee," Catherine said.

"I can see how somewhere in your teenage head that made sense, but you know I run a diner, so maybe *diner coffee* being used to explain why you think my coffee is terrible isn't the best route to take. Especially when it's being given for free."

"Our judgment is free, too, Adam," Emma pointed out. She nearly earned a smile from him. But only nearly.

"Sorry," Catherine said, and she immediately began emptying sugar packets into the cup.

Satisfied, Adam turned and left them.

And that was when *he* appeared. His truck was loud driving down the quiet main street of town, and when he pulled into the driveway of the mechanic and turned it off, he got out and shut the driver-side door hard enough for her to hear it inside the diner.

Torn jeans and a tight black T-shirt, broad shoulders and the first lips that had ever made her curious about kissing.

All things that were much more fun to think about than her real life.

Fantasy, of any kind, was better than real life right now.

But if that fantasy came with broad shoulders and a compelling mouth, all the better.

"You're embarrassing yourself," Catherine said. "It is so obvious that you're staring at him."

"Who's going to tell? Do you think that Buzz is going to tell?" She indicated the gray-haired man sitting at the bar on one of the red stools.

"No," Catherine said. "But if he looks this way…"

They both stared at Luke as if they were willing him to do just that. But he didn't. He never did.

Instead, he went into the garage, and even then it took Emma's heart rate a full twenty-five seconds to go back to normal.

"Okay," Catherine said. "We have stared long enough. Finish your stuff and let's go."

She chugged down the coffee and picked up the dough-nut, leaving five dollars on the table. Adam gave her a nod as she walked out the door, and she waved.

She waffled between going back inside and asking him

if he would please not tell her mother that she had come in that morning, but that might just guarantee he'd call her mom.

Of course, Adam didn't seem like the type to get involved too deeply in people's lives.

She walked out into the damp, cold morning. The fog hung low over the buildings on Main Street, rolling in off the sea. The air smelled sharp like salt and pine, with an earthy hint of asphalt and dirt thrown in for good measure. The street was mostly empty, with nearly everyone gone off to work or settled in to wherever they might be spending their mornings.

It wasn't high season yet, and the town was populated mostly by locals. Once things picked up, Emma would be busy with the inn. She always helped her family work the inn during the busy season, and they would need her help more this year than usual.

She sighed heavily. She had no idea what it was going to be like at school today. In some ways she could see why her mother had been tempted to call in sick to life.

"Better to just face it," Emma said.

"People probably won't ask," Catherine said.

"Why not?"

"Because it makes them uncomfortable." Catherine smiled and reached for Emma, wrapping her arm around Emma's shoulder. "I'm not uncomfortable, though. I'm here for you. Even if I have to be…here for you while I'm in Boston and you're in Oregon."

ANNA

She was standing frozen in a deserted aisle of the grocery store in front of bags of quinoa with reality bearing down on her like a herd of wild horses.

Thankfully, it was early and the store was mostly empty.

The past two weeks of Anna's life had been like a competition for just how far the phrase *going from bad to worse* could stretch.

Jacob's death.

Her decision to take her emotional affair and make it physical.

Thomas finding out.

She kept replaying that moment over and over in her head. That rush of elation that had turned into dread, her scalp and face hot as her eyes met his.

He hadn't spoken to her for days. It was the silence that had killed her. If he'd yelled, if he'd screamed, if he'd cried, even, she might have felt…

Like it mattered. Like they mattered.

And then she'd had to move back in with her mother.

Even a cabin on the property was a little bit much. Rachel might be able to deal with living in such tight proximity to their mom, but Rachel was…

Well, Rachel was a saint. And that wasn't helping anything, either.

She could still remember, though, when her mom had caught her sneaking in one time, on the cusp of what might have become a misspent youth…

"You have to take your life seriously, Anna. You have to surround yourself with the right people."

"We weren't doing anything! Just hanging out."

"Good people make the difference. Good men do. I was married at eighteen, and I did right, but he didn't. And it's what he did that hurt me for years. You have to be careful whom you associate with, because even if you don't mean to do wrong, the people around you might…"

Thomas had been a good person, in her mom's opinion. And she'd been relieved that Anna was settling down with him. Because, of course, that meant Anna would be spared the ugliness that her mom had experienced in life.

Then she'd gone and made her own ugliness.

Maybe it would be different if Michael had asked her to run away with him.

She waited for some kind of jolt of excitement, a lift in her spirit, but it didn't come.

Honestly, that he'd sort of vanished over the revelation of the affair had killed a good amount of her elation over him in general.

Well, reality had done that.

Fallout.

And she was living in the debris.

She looked down at her hands, wrapped around the cart handle. They were bare. And it was weird how *not weird* that felt after fourteen years of marriage.

She had taken off her wedding ring with ease. But, then, she had taken it off multiple times over the past few months. Every time she'd gone to talk with Michael. Every time she'd kissed him.

And definitely when they'd…

She sucked in a sharp breath and forced herself to move forward. She had a list. She needed to go down the list and get the groceries. She did not need to stand in the dry goods aisle grappling with a minimeltdown. She pushed the cart ahead, and nearly into another cart coming from the left.

And she nearly ran into Laura Keller.

Just great.

Laura had been kind to her at the funeral, but that had been prior to…well, Anna becoming a scarlet woman.

"Anna." Laura sounded surprised, but not unhappy. And that was weird to Anna. But some people were busybodies. Some people would have seen this moment as a full-fat cream indulgence opportunity.

Laura wasn't one of them. In many ways, Laura was one of the most genuinely nice people Anna knew. But Laura was also…good.

She was good in a way that made Anna uncomfortable sometimes.

Her smile seemed too easy. Her laugh too bright. It chafed against the hidden meanness inside her, made her feel emotionally claustrophobic. The weight of pretending she was as shiny, as good, as someone like Laura, had been one of the things that had made her go so brittle over the years.

And she was sure Laura wouldn't—couldn't—like the person she'd been revealed to be.

"How are you?" Laura asked.

She seemed like she might really want to know.

How many times had Anna asked parishioners, "How are you?"

And hoped they'd respond with something light and generic so she didn't have to stay and talk too long?

"Good," she said.

Light and generic it was.

That was a lie, but it was the kind of lie that didn't invite questions.

"I mean, it's been very hard for Rachel," Anna said, just pretending that Sunday hadn't happened.

"Good. But you know, I wasn't actually asking about Rachel."

Anna tightened her grip on the shopping cart and for

some reason became incredibly conscious of the song that was playing over the speakers in the store.

About someone saying it best when they said nothing at all.

It felt painfully ironic on multiple levels.

"I…"

"I didn't like that he did that to you."

Anna blinked. "I…"

"It didn't feel right to me. He's taught, many times himself, that you're supposed to let your critics say what they will and you just go on. Well, he didn't give a chance for anyone to criticize him, did he? He just handed you to all of them."

Anna hadn't expected that at all. Laura had always been such a sweet, sunny presence at the church and she'd assumed her loyalty to Thomas would be absolute.

Apparently not.

Laura looked around, and then she reached out, pulling Anna into a hug. "I'm praying for you."

And, stupidly, Anna wanted to cry. Instead, she forced a smile. "Thank you. Thank you, that's always welcome."

She didn't know what to do, except the quinoa in her shopping cart was looking lonely. And as Laura walked in one direction, Anna walked in the other and took two boxes of cupcakes off the bakery table. They were terrible, store-bakery cupcakes with frosting that would coat her tongue like Crisco, and she didn't even care.

The frosting was bright red and it would stain her mouth, too. Which seemed appropriate. Scarlet cupcakes instead of a scarlet letter.

She stopped in front of a display of local wines, her heart thundering.

And she grabbed one, shoving it in her cart with everything else.

She could never have done this two weeks ago.

She made her way up to the counter and began to put her items on the belt. She recognized the cashier, but she didn't know her. Clearly, judging by the look on the woman's face, she knew Anna.

For all that Sunset Bay was a small town, Sunset Church was large. People drove in from outlying areas to attend, thanks to the popularity of her husband's teachings. He'd garnered a small amount of fame online, which had grown when he'd written a book about peace in troubled times.

It wasn't fame on a grand scale, but in their circles he was well-known. Consequently, so was she.

Now...

Well, now she wasn't the only thing that was well-known.

Be sure your sin will find you out.

That scripture jumped right to the front of her mind and refused to recede. She was sure the words were hanging visibly between herself and the cashier.

Anna pushed her quinoa forward, and the woman looked down meaningfully at Anna's bare hand.

She decided just not talking would be the best route to take in this instance.

The sound of each scanned item seemed comically loud.

When she was finished, she bagged the items.

"Have a nice day," Anna said.

The woman just looked at her. So Anna picked up her things and carried them out to her car.

She paused for a moment and looked across the street,

at the gray line where the steel-colored water met the low-hanging clouds.

There had been a time when she hadn't been able to walk through the store without everyone talking to her. Smiling. Telling her their problems.

Taking note of what she had in her cart.

She could never buy wine. She couldn't walk around looking sad. She could never be short-tempered with anyone.

She could never be honest about the fact that she never felt more alone than she did when she was home with her husband. Her husband, who seemed to have inexhaustible energy for parishioners and none left at all for her.

Anna had wanted an escape. Another life.

She'd gone from pastor's wife to pariah overnight.

She didn't know what it said about her that somehow pariah felt more natural than the other role ever had.

6

I've found friends in the lightkeepers' wives.
Rose and Naomi are kind, and their children
provide a nice distraction. Friends help make the
darkness of this endless winter seem brighter.

—FROM THE DIARY OF JENNY HANSEN, JANUARY 8, 1900

RACHEL

It had been a month and she hadn't changed anything in the room.

The bed still sat at that strange angle, facing the window, and his nightstand was still full of medication.

It smelled antiseptic. She had washed everything. She had washed it a hundred times. She had thrown out the bedding. She had a backup saved for when it was over.

And now she regretted some of that cleaning. Because it all felt too clean. Like she had tried to wipe away his presence, when she had just been trying to wipe away that heaviness left behind by sickness and pain.

She walked over to the nightstand and picked up one of the prescription bottles. Oxycodone. She shook it and turned it over.

Jacob Henderson

His name was printed on it, along with his date of birth.

This was what was left behind of her husband. This was what she was letting sit here. These bottles of pills with his name on them. Evidence of his pain, like some men left behind a stamp collection. Suddenly, it horrified her. She went down to the kitchen and grabbed a plastic bag, and went back up the stairs. And she threw every pill bottle into the trash. Then she looked back at his photos on the wall. That picture of their hands.

Jacob. Rachel. Emma.

Those photographs that were windows into how he saw the world. What he cared about.

The beautiful views of the ocean, gorgeous angles of the house, where the light played across the stained glass.

Rachel paused for a moment, looking at their wedding picture. At the two of them so young and happy, and with no idea of what lay ahead. She was clutching him and a bouquet of yellow flowers. Bright. Happy. New. Those same flowers had been artfully dried and arranged on their dresser for years, but now it felt like a sad metaphor. She related far too deeply. From vibrant and full to sim-ply...preserved.

She opened up the drawer in her dresser and pulled out an envelope. The envelope that contained photos of her. Photos he'd taken before she'd had Emma, and then again maybe ten years ago. Sexy photos that she had joked were only for him, but now that she was nearing forty, she ap-preciated them more than she had before. That there was a record of the way her body had looked when she'd been twenty-one, and didn't have a stretch mark in sight.

And then, even after she'd had Emma, and he'd still

found her beautiful, and had wanted photos of her lying on the bed wearing nothing but her underwear.

She wished that she had pictures like that of him.

He'd been the photographer, and he was always behind the camera. He'd given her this gift. This moment to let her see herself the way he had. How he found her beautiful through the years. A gift he left for her, that she hadn't even appreciated at the time.

"I just miss you," she said. "You used to joke about sending me dirty pictures and you never did. And I really wish you would have."

He had been so handsome when they'd been younger. And she found his body beautiful. Even as sickness had eaten away at him, she found him beautiful, because he was the man she loved. But she had definitely mourned the loss of some of his looks. She just wished that...

She wished that there was more time.

She shoved the photos back into the envelope, back into the drawer. And she took the bag of medication and carried it downstairs and dumped it in the trash.

By the time she was finished she was hungry.

That was significant because for the past two weeks she hadn't felt a single hunger pang. Only the appearance of food in front of her had reminded her to eat at all. And even then, she had struggled to get much down. Everything had sat like lead in her gut and had made her feel like throwing up. But she actually felt hungry today.

She got into her car and decided to brave the drive down the mountain and into town. She hadn't been since church last week.

As overwhelming as the idea of town had been when the only thing to talk about was her loss, the idea of having to make excuses for Anna, explain Anna or hear bad things about Anna along with it was unbearable.

Rachel had too much of her own pain washing through her to give Anna's the attention that it needed. She would get to it.

Maybe after she ate.

Somehow that felt like hope, that desire for food. It felt like waking up.

She turned off the main road and onto a small offshoot that would take her down into Old Town. J's Diner wasn't particularly touristy, like a great many of the places down there, and hadn't been made into something farm-to-table and hipster.

The idea of Adam putting kombucha on the menu was laughable. And that was why it remained popular with the locals.

It was real food.

And as someone who liked fussy food herself, Rachel didn't feel all that guilty thinking that. She made a great many things with a poached egg on top for the bed-and-breakfast. But sometimes all that would do was greasy, fortifying food. And in that case, J's delivered.

And for Rachel it had become something of a refuge to her over these past couple of years. Like a break from life that included French fries, and who didn't need one of those now and again?

The side streets in Old Town were all steep hills, and J's was at the top of one. The parking lot was full, so she pulled her car up against the curb, praying the parking brake did its best work. Then she got out and wrapped her coat more firmly around herself, trying to buffet herself against the wind. The clouds had rolled in, thick and gray this afternoon, and what had started out as a sunny morning up at Cape Hope had turned into a mess of gray soup. But that was part and parcel of living here, and there was something about it that Rachel had always loved.

Because along with weather like this came the urge to curl up with a blanket, a cup of tea and a book. The need to light a scented candle, and simply sit for a while. To pause and reflect.

Of course, she didn't really want to pause and reflect at the moment. But then, maybe that was why, rather than sitting at home with hot soup and a blanket, she'd driven down to J's. She pushed open the worn white door, letting it swing closed hard behind her.

The tables were full, and the bar was mostly full as well, but there were two empty stools—the ones that no one sat on because they needed to be fixed, and for reasons unknown to her, Adam hadn't done it since they broke over a year ago.

She closed her eyes for a moment, letting the sounds of conversation and laughter wash over her.

It was funny how a small town with so few people could contain so many layers.

There were the people who went to lunch after church on Sunday, and the early risers who went to breakfast before. The people who didn't go out on a Sunday at all, least of all to church. There were the people who preferred the trendy cafés, or who never went out unless it was to one of the nice Italian restaurants, which might cost more, but made for an infrequent and welcome treat.

There were those who went to Fog in the morning for their coffee, served in cups that were only one size, the brew containing a tangy aftertaste that Rachel just couldn't acclimate to. And those who went to the Sunset Bay Coffee Company, which had been there for more than twenty years.

J's attracted the older crowd that had lived in town for years. It attracted the loggers, the ranchers, the fishermen.

And it suited her perfectly.

Because it was where she went to be known only by name.

Her life had changed in the weeks since she'd been down to town.

But she also knew that they wouldn't have changed here.

When she saw Adam come out from the kitchen, her whole chest lifted. Like a breath had been drawn for her.

They had an unconventional friendship, that much was true. One that existed with a diner counter between the two of them, but that didn't make it less important than any other friendship.

In fact, over the past few months it had been the most important friendship she had. Because there was a freedom in it.

She'd met him when he'd first come to town—J's had been a go-to for her to get takeout for years—but it wasn't until Jacob had gotten cancer that she'd started to rely on the diner, and Adam.

One night after Jacob had gotten discouraging blood work, she'd been too exhausted to cook, and too tired of herself to stay home. She'd gone to town to get hamburgers for herself and Emma, with Jacob sound asleep and with no appetite to speak of, anyway.

And she'd sat down on one of the red stools, and Adam had come over. Asked her about baseball and what she wanted for dinner, and nothing about Jacob's health. And the profound relief she'd felt to just…talk about something else had been a gift she hadn't known she'd needed.

She'd started getting dinner from J's once a week after that.

And for a few moments she'd sit, let someone make food for her, let someone take care of her. Talk to her. Maybe even make her laugh. And then she was able to go back and be the caretaker she had to be.

She wondered if the real reason she hadn't come here since Jacob died was that she was afraid to see if she'd lost this sanctuary. That Adam would want to look at her gravely and offer platitudes, and she didn't think she could stand platitudes from Adam. Not when he'd never given them before.

"Rachel," he said, a slow smile crossing his face. "It's been a while."

Her shoulders sagged. Her forehead relaxed. Eyebrows lowered.

Just looking at him was comforting. Made her want to settle back into that old routine. Sitting down, waiting for food, talking about nothing. It was funny that she found Adam soothing, because she didn't know that he was innately soothing as a human.

He was sort of hard-edged and crabby, which was at odds with his appearance. Bright blue eyes, dark blond hair and beard, and an athletic build. He looked approachable. But he could be gruff, and it had taken quite a while for her to work up a rapport with him.

"Yeah," she said. "I need a cheeseburger. Really bad."

He lifted an eyebrow. "And a side salad, I assume?"

Some of the weight she'd carried down the mountain with her lifted away. It was always like this. A mini vacation from her life. From herself.

She got to pretend, for just a while, that things were okay, and she couldn't do that with her family.

"You know where you can take your side salad and shove it," she said, feeling the first real smile tug at the corners of her mouth in a good while.

"French fries, then." He started writing before she confirmed it. But he knew the answer.

"Yes."

"And for Emma?" he asked.

"Her usual. Don't let a vegetable touch her cheeseburger."

"You know potatoes are a vegetable," he pointed out, writing down Emma's order, too.

"Just never tell her. She won't eat them."

"I wouldn't dare." He slid her ticket over the back counter and into the kitchen.

"How is your team doing?"

She blinked. "In what sport?"

"The one that's playing right now."

"You know full well that I have no idea what sport is happening right now."

"Basketball."

She squinted. "Isn't there one that has a clover on its uniforms? Because I kind of like that."

"A Celtics fan?"

"Stop it. I refuse to talk to you about sports. I refuse to let you trick me into learning anything about that subject."

"I would never trick you."

She rolled her eyes. "My mother always told me to beware of strange men talking about sports."

He picked up a dishrag from the counter and slung it over his shoulder. "No one forces you to come in here. In fact, you can order ahead."

"I know." She paused for a beat. "There's a reason that I don't."

She could feel the drop in her chest when she said those words, and she didn't know why she'd done it. Because he hadn't said anything at all. In fact, he had treated her exactly the same way he always did. He had smiled, and he had started talking about something stupid. And she had gone and made it real.

His expression flickered, but only slightly, his large hands pressed down against the countertop. Then he shifted one hand, his knuckles brushing against hers. "You don't need to order ahead."

She took a deep breath, her chest feeling tight. "I'm not going to. Not because I have your permission not to, you understand, but because I don't want to."

And she knew that that was all she would get out of him, unless she asked for more. And she was grateful.

"I respect that about you," he said.

"Yeah, well."

He looked past her, at the tables in the dining room, and she wondered if he was going to abandon her and pay attention to other customers. Which was reasonable, she supposed. But he didn't. "I saw Emma this morning."

Rachel frowned. "She told me she had an early class."

"Maybe she did. But she stopped by here first."

Her frown deepened. "Oh. She didn't mention."

"She had a doughnut and coffee," he said. "Though, apparently, my diner coffee is subpar."

"Did she say that to you?"

"No. Her friend said it. Emma's expression implied it."

"Well, she shouldn't come here and be rude to you."

"Rachel, it's fine. I can handle it." He smiled. "I have broad shoulders."

Now that he mentioned it, yes, he did. She turned her attention away from that and quickly.

"I was just thinking," he said. "I have a job opening. And it would mostly be after-school hours. Is Emma looking for work at all?"

"I…" Rachel frowned. "No. I mean, she works at the bed-and-breakfast. And as we gear up for high season we are going to need her."

"Just thought I'd ask."

She felt a momentary stab of guilt. She was lying. But…she felt like the ends justified the lie, or something. Her life was changing; her daughter was going to leave her. Couldn't she have her close for the next few months?

"Besides, I doubt you want a waitress who's disdainful of your coffee."

He shrugged. "To be honest, it wouldn't be that different from what I already have."

A plastic bag appeared in the window of the kitchen.

"That's you."

Adam passed her the bag. "Now, I'm not trying to compete with you or your baked goods, but there might be a piece of pie in there."

She winced. And she didn't mean to, but she'd lost control of her face for a moment. And there was nothing left but honesty. "Your pie is terrible."

"Wait a minute. You said that your daughter couldn't come in here and insult me and my diner coffee, but you're insulting my pie."

"Your *coffee* is fine. Your *pie* is not. I'm serious, Adam, you can't have a fry cook making your pie. You need a baker."

He huffed. "You volunteering?"

"No. I don't do pastry unless I have to. Anna, on the other hand… Now, she could make you a pie."

"I don't have a lot of complaints," he said, grumbling a little bit now.

"You don't have a lot of complaints because half of your customers don't have taste buds anymore because they smoke too many cigarettes."

"Ouch."

"Don't worry, the food is good. If it wasn't I wouldn't eat here."

"Are you at least going to eat the pie?"

"That depends on what's back at my house. I'm going to eat something with sugar. Believe me. And in desperate times… Sure. I'd eat the pie."

"Not that you deserve it," he said.

She stood up from the stool and shrugged. "Life owes me."

"Sure as hell does," he said, nodding.

She shook her head and pushed her way out of the diner, out into the cold.

It had been far too cloudy to have seen the sun for most of the day, but she could tell it had gone down while she was inside because the light around her had deepened from pale gray to blue.

The lightness she'd felt when she'd walked into the diner stayed with her.

She carried it with her, along with the terrible pie, all the way home.

7

1907 May 30: Heavy NW wind with light rain
shower first part of 24 hours. Last part of 24 hours
moderate NW breeze clearing weather. Sea smooth.
1st ass't whitewashing fences. Had a visitor today.

—FROM THE LIGHTHOUSE KEEPER'S LOGS OF
THE CAPE HOPE LIGHTHOUSE

WENDY

The occupancy of the inn was still relatively low. It was late February and they had quite a bit of availability. But they'd had four rooms booked for the Captain's House—three couples, and one man who was by himself, which made for a fairly straightforward breakfast.

They had a young couple who had traveled down from Washington. The woman was a nurse, the man an auto-body technician. And there was a couple, around Wendy's age, who were bird-watchers, and had traveled extensively through the state of Oregon, favoring B and Bs as their place to stay.

The breakfast at the inn was famous. Seven courses, local and seasonal fare. Not only was the inn itself his-

MAISEY YATES   73

toric, and on the list of haunted buildings, but they were
also renowned for their food.

Then there was another couple in their sixties, both
men former sailors who took every chance they could to
be near the sea.

And there was the man who was traveling by himself.
John. He was from California, all the way up from En-
cinitas. He was tall and lean, with thick silver hair, cut
short. He was fairly quiet at breakfast, nodding as she
introduced each course, but not joining in with the chatter all that freely. She noticed that he was always looking
around the room, seeming to study the details, the pictures on the wall, with deep interest.

There were some new photos from WWII that had remained classified until recently, because the locations of
lookout points were considered a military secret.

Wendy introduced the first course—a fruit salad with a
coconut lime sauce—and then went back into the kitchen,
where Anna was working on scones.

"Looks good," Wendy said, looking over at the batch
her daughter had just pulled out of the oven, before making her way to the fridge and taking out the clotted cream,
the jam and the lemon curd.

"Thank you," Anna said, sounding out of breath or annoyed, Wendy wasn't sure.

"You're welcome. Have you—have you started paper-
work for your…? Are you going to go ahead with the divorce?"

"Do you really want to discuss my divorce over lemon
curd?"

For the past month she had been trying to build a bridge
between herself and Anna. Had been trying to find a way
to connect with her.

She'd been…so oblivious to what was happening with her. It was a stunning realization. That she'd lived so near Anna, seen her so often. Seen Thomas so often. Seen them together and even then hadn't noticed a rift between them or her own daughter's unhappiness.

Maybe you didn't want to see it…

"If not over lemon curd, then when?"

"I'll let you know when it's finalized." She sighed. "No. No progress on that front. If you ignore a marriage, will it go away?"

Wendy's laugh came out on a breath. Anna was funny, and always had been. No matter her circumstances. "Not in my experience."

"Shoot. I guess someday I'll have to figure that out, then." Anna went back to work on her food and Wendy let silence reign.

They maneuvered around each other with a certain amount of practice. Anna had learned to bake here when she was just a girl, and she had assisted Wendy from the time she was in fifth grade all the way through high school. A few moments later Anna swept out of the kitchen and collected the dishes, and then grabbed hold of a serving platter with her scones and their fixings, and went back out into the dining room. Wendy could hear her explaining each element, before coming back into the kitchen.

Wendy was already at work on the peach-and-rose lassi that would go out next as a palate cleanser.

And after that was the slightly more time-sensitive puff pastry and eggs.

Wendy whisked the smoothies out and Anna cleared. The conversation of the guests was light and easy, and that was a source of some relief.

You never knew what you were going to get when it came to guests.

This group was laughing together and seemed perfectly at ease.

John, though, was quiet.

Oh, he would nod his head or chuckle at a story, but he didn't offer up any of his own.

Not that there was anything wrong with that. As long as there were no dustups she was happy enough. And no uncomfortable silences.

The awkwardness of a group of people sitting there, the only sound spoons hitting their glasses, was the kind of thing that compelled Wendy to rush things along and start her historical talk a little bit early.

"It's a good group," she said to Anna when they were back in the kitchen.

"Yes," Anna agreed. "It will be interesting to see if that changes tomorrow, since the birdwatchers are going home, and we're getting two new couples."

"You never know." Silence trailed on after those words. There were always moments of normal. And then afterward the tension crept back in.

"I'll do the history talk today," Anna said.

Anna hadn't done a history talk in ages, and Wendy wasn't quite sure why she was offering now.

"You want to?" Wendy asked.

"Yeah. I don't have anything else to do." Anna sighed. "You are helping me, Mom. And I know it's been weird between us, but I'm appreciative I have a place to stay and a job to do. I want to make sure I'm actually doing that job."

"You don't have to do anything to earn a place, Anna," Wendy said.

"I want to."

They both worked together assembling the eggs in the puff pastry, and then when it was time, presented it together, though she let Anna explain that the cheese had come from Rogue Creamery, and the chanterelles had been foraged in the woods behind the lighthouse. To the best of their ability, they used local and Oregon-based products.

It was a part of what made the Lighthouse Inn unique.

It was a piece of history, up there on the rocks, a piece of this state that was her home, and this town that had been her fresh start all those years ago.

The food that she made—the food that she and her daughters made—was a love letter to that. And sharing it with those who came was a great joy to Wendy.

In fact, it made her wonder if it was time to consider providing other meals at different times during the week. She had extra help now. Her flock was back home, even if it wasn't under the best of circumstances.

And Anna wanted more work. God knew they needed to find a way to talk to each other.

Maybe building something here would be the key to fixing what was broken. Again.

The Lighthouse Inn had healed her. It had healed them.

Maybe it would again.

Breakfast finished up with a piece of pound cake, and when everyone was fininshed eating, they walked out of the dining room and into the parlor for the beginning of the history talk. There was a fireplace there that had been made propane for easy starting, and a couch that wasn't exactly authentic to provide large, comfortable seating.

There was also an antique table beneath the window with a Tiffany lamp and books about the area. There were historic photos hung suspended from the crown molding all around the room.

Anna began her talk, moving easily through the historical dates and facts about Cape Hope, and the Cape Hope Lighthouse. The cape had been discovered in the 1700s by an explorer and his crew who'd all had a bad case of scurvy. And here they had found fresh drinking water, huckleberries and the rather inedible camas plants. This place had been *hope*.

And it had remained.

While Anna spoke, Wendy moved quietly to the end of the parlor, looking at the pictures that were set up on the antique piano in the corner.

Pictures of the lightkeepers' families, who had lived here for generations. Pictures of the different iterations of the property. Of times when there had been barracks everywhere and doghouses for military dogs, and when the carriage house had been used as an armory.

Of times when the trees had been burned away by intentional fires set for gardening purposes.

When the trees had grown back, and began to reach toward the sky, like they did now.

"An interesting fact about the barracks," a low, soft voice said behind her. "I didn't know about that."

She turned sharply. It was John.

"Yes," Wendy said. "Of course, after Pearl Harbor, the government was very concerned with the protection of the coastlines, which became all the more intense in Oregon after the shelling of Fort Stevens, and the balloon bombs."

"Of course. My father didn't talk about that, but then, he was deployed overseas."

"Yes, I think it's easy to forget."

"I came here because I needed to see the place," he said. "You see, my father just passed away."

"Oh," Wendy said, feeling a sharp twist of pain in her chest. His loss reminded her of all of theirs. "I'm sorry."

"He was ninety-six. He had a very good life, and I'm sorry, too, but I am glad that he was so healthy for so long. But in any case, he spoke with fondness about this place, and I thought it was time that I come see it. Because nothing makes you realize that time isn't infinite quite like loss."

Wendy's heart twisted. She understood that, and all too well.

"Yes. That is true."

"My great-great-grandfather was Olaf Hansen. The first lightkeeper at Cape Hope. Back in the late 1800s. I believe Jenny Hansen was his wife."

Wendy blinked. "Oh. Of course. Hansen. It's such a common last name…"

She couldn't believe she was looking at Jenny's relative. Jenny was like a friend, in many ways. When Wendy had first come here and had learned to adjust to the gray of the Oregon coast, to her new life, the story of Jenny, the mail-order bride, had connected with her particularly.

She'd spent years compiling letters and tracking down journal entries, so that she now had as complete a story about the woman as possible.

And here was her great-great-grandson.

"I know it. But yes, this was…the first place my family lived in the United States. After Olaf came from Sweden."

"Yes, that's right," Wendy said. "He was a lighthouse keeper there originally, wasn't he?"

A strange smile touched his face. "What an interesting thing, to meet someone who already knows your family history. At least, some of the ancient family history."

Wendy supposed that would be strange. "Your family history is a part of mine," Wendy said. "I've been innkeeper here for... Well it's been thirty-three years."

"About as long as my family was here. So it's in both our blood, I suppose."

"Yes," she agreed.

"Do you have anything here that's part of the Hansen family? Any photographs?"

"Oh, yes," Wendy said. "All of these." She gestured to a line of photographs on the top of the piano. "Olaf and his wife, Jenny."

"I haven't seen this one," he said, leaning forward, his blue eyes glittering. "Incredible."

"Your great-grandfather was born here. In this house," she said, and goose bumps rose on her arms.

"Of course he was," John said, looking around the room as if the space had just taken on new meaning. "What a thing."

Wendy fell back and stayed silent, and she could hear Anna continuing to give her talk in the other room. She was all the way up to how their family had come to be the innkeepers.

"I would love to continue to talk to you about this," John said. "Perhaps over dinner."

Wendy drew back. She hadn't expected that. And she couldn't sort through whether or not he was asking simply because he really did just want to have a discussion with her about his genealogy, or if he was interested in *her*.

Not a lot of single men came to the bed-and-breakfast on their own. Quite a few single women did, typically when they were experiencing a major life change.

It was a good beginning point to someone's emotional journey.

But she didn't often have handsome men in her age group roaming around without a wife attached to them.

So it was entirely possible that he did have a wife.

Though there was no wedding band on his hand.

Not that that meant anything, necessarily.

"I'm busy," she said.

Because being busy didn't require her to sort out what his intent was. Because it just allowed her to avoid it. Avoid him.

"Sorry to hear that," he said.

"If you have any more questions, though, today, my daughter Anna is an expert."

"Oh," he said. "She's your daughter."

"Yes," Wendy said. "And I swear if you say she looks like she could be my sister..."

"No," he said. "I'm far too old to try a line like that. I might have done it twenty years ago, but I know better now. She does look like you, though. She is also lovely."

Her face felt warm. She didn't like that. Not at all. She didn't give men the power to affect her, not anymore. She hadn't given him anything. He'd just taken a response right from her.

"Well, thank you."

"Have a good day," he said.

"Enjoy your stay," she commented.

"That I will."

Wendy practically fled to the kitchen, and it wasn't until the door closed behind her that she realized her heart was beating far faster than it should. Especially since she didn't even know if he wanted to go to dinner for her, or for the house.

It was easier to calm the beating of her heart if she assumed it was for the house.

She didn't have time to worry about that, though.

Because thoughts of beginning a seven-course dinner at the lighthouse were beginning to swirl through her head. And she might not be able to solve Anna's problems, or Rachel's. And it wouldn't fix the strange flush of reaction she'd had to this tall, handsome stranger.

She couldn't fix any of this. But she could give them all something more to do. And sometimes, when there weren't answers, activity would do just as well.

8

If you can focus only on the ocean as you patrol,
you can pretend you are simply walking along the
beach, rather than keeping watch for the enemy.

—FROM A LETTER DATED JULY 4, 1943, WRITTEN BY STAFF SERGEANT
RICHARD JOHNSON DURING HIS TIME STATIONED AT CAPE HOPE

ANNA

It was a Monday night. Things at the inn were quiet, and Anna's mother had asked for all of them to gather in the kitchen tonight.

Anna had been in the kitchen since late afternoon, working on batches of Jenny Hansen's soda bread, pound cake and raspberry bread, with berries that had come from the garden last spring that they'd frozen for use throughout the year. They had gotten a few recipes over the years from earlier inhabitants of the lighthouse.

Anna had modified an oatmeal recipe that had been fed to the soldiers during WWII, which was now called Lookout Porridge, and contained steel-cut oats and dried fruit and nuts. But the favorites of the guests were Jenny Hansen's breads.

She hadn't gone down into town for over two weeks now. It had been…great. She had stayed up here on the cliff top overlooking the sea, and she had…regressed.

Her life felt cleaned. Uncluttered. She'd swept aside everything annoying, like her actual life and the fact that she was going to have to deal with a divorce, look her soon-to-be ex-husband in the face again. That she'd have to go back to town. That Michael hadn't called for weeks.

None of it mattered. She had purpose here. Cleaning guest rooms, cooking, giving history tours and manning the gift shop that was on the property.

And she didn't mind at all.

If things were tense sometimes with her family… she just did her best to ignore it. Her mother's judgment weighed heavy on her. Her sister's silence grated sometimes. But at least silence was…silent.

She could keep her head down and do her work, and not worry about it.

Maybe that was reverting to type, but honestly, she'd take a little bit of type reversion without Thomas and still call it growth.

All things concerning the inn itself were familiar. Easy. Some things were uncertain, but for her, piecrust would always be a steady constant.

That also gave her a momentary kick of cheer.

Piecrust was the undoing of a great many home chefs. And, in Anna's personal opinion, a great many professional pastry chefs who sold their pies in restaurants and bakeries. It was a difficult art to master, one that required cold water and hands that weren't overeager.

Anna had mastered the art a long time ago.

And feeling in her element, feeling like she knew what

she was doing, was such an important thing in her life just at the moment.

"Don't keep us in suspense, Mom," Rachel said when she walked into the crowded kitchen, positioning herself far away from Anna. "What's your idea?"

Emma and Wendy trailed in behind her. Emma was carrying baskets of berries.

Emma looked a bit pale and drawn, but her expression was very Emma—her mouth set in a slight smile, her eyes full of light.

Rachel looked sallow and thin, and the moment she got into the kitchen, she started wiping the counter.

Wendy looked as implacable as ever.

"I'm not trying to keep you in suspense," she said. "But I don't know if it's a good idea or not. But it feels like… It feels like we're starting over. And if we're going to start over, then we might as well shake things up a little bit."

"*You're* advocating for shaking things up?" Anna asked. "I feel like I should check your temperature."

"Not a dramatic shake-up, Anna." Anna couldn't tell if that was a pointed remark. "But… If you girls are going to be here to help, maybe we should try and take on some more meals. The couple of dinners that we've done for outdoor events and weddings and things have gone over hugely well. Perhaps it's time we add them as a weekly event."

"What spurred that?" Rachel asked.

"I need a distraction," Wendy said. "And with Anna here now, and you with…more free time, and Emma helping out. Well, we can do it. So why not? We're in no hurry. We can launch in spring when town is busier, and until then we can plan."

Anna figured it was not the time to joke that she'd had a similar thought before cheating on her husband.

"That…sounds good to me," Anna said cautiously.

Rachel's face was doing something Anna couldn't read. "Funnily enough I was just talking to Adam Campbell about pie," she said.

"Were you?" Wendy asked.

"He gave me a free piece of pie from the diner the other night."

Emma grimaced. "You didn't tell me that."

"I threw it away. We had candy bars in the house. There was no need to try and choke that down."

"Definitely not," Anna said.

They might not be able to talk about much right now, but they could all agree that Adam's pie was a travesty.

"Maybe we need to make pie. Well, not me," Rachel said. "Anna."

She was slightly surprised that her sister was suggesting that, but not mad.

She hadn't realized that she would miss the act of being there for others that came with being a pastor's wife. Yes, it had chafed in the end, but there had been a time when it had been her calling.

Thomas had joined the staff of Sunset Church a couple of years into their marriage, first as a youth pastor, then an associate pastor and finally as head pastor. Her role had evolved along with his and she'd honestly enjoyed it.

For the first ten years she'd been all in.

She'd coordinated most of the women's events, and a lot of the community outreach. She'd spent days meeting with people, listening to their struggles. Praying for them, in earnest.

And as time went on she'd felt like her body was hollow and every word coming out of her mouth was just a practiced response.

One day she'd ended a conversation with "I'll pray for you."

As she'd walked away, she'd realized she probably wouldn't. Not intentionally. But that at some point over time, those words had replaced the prayers.

Once she'd realized it, she'd begun to withdraw.

She'd still shown up to everything. She'd talked and she'd smiled. Her body was there. The rest of her wasn't.

At first she'd been angry with herself.

Then she'd tried to talk to Thomas.

And tried.

And tried.

Can we go out more?

What about a day of rest?

We haven't had sex in a month.

I miss you.

And then she'd tried to seduce him. She'd been embarrassed, which was stupid. He was her husband of fourteen years; she shouldn't be embarrassed about anything, but the distance between them made it feel like seducing a stranger.

Candles. A sexy dress. High heels.

He hadn't even looked at her.

The next day she'd sought solace at the inn, and Michael had checked in for the first time.

He'd asked, "Are all innkeepers as beautiful as you are?"

"Let's get baking," Wendy said, her words jolting Anna from the past into the present moment. "Do you have ideas for what dinners we might make?"

That led to a lively discussion on how to accommodate

different diets—which was something they had to contend with for breakfasts, but dinner was only bound to make it that much harder.

It was exhilarating. Like the world faded away. Like time faded away.

Like she hadn't been married for the past fourteen years. Like Rachel's husband hadn't died.

Like they hadn't been distant for two years and her mom wasn't disappointed in her.

They were family again.

Here in the kitchen.

Like an open window letting fresh air into a stale room. And she could feel how much they all needed it. Could sense that they were all filling their lungs with this reprieve.

"Gluten," Anna said, laughing in spite of herself, "is what makes you stretch. Without it, you break. Gluten holds us together."

"I'm just saying," Emma said, with all the unearned wisdom in her voice that seemed innate to teenagers, "you're going to need a gluten-free option for dessert."

"I've known about this new initiative for five minutes and it's already a chore."

"It'll be fun," Emma said. "Honing your creativity."

"My creativity is a finely pointed blade, child," Anna said. "I don't need to hone it with subpar baked goods."

There was laughter filling the kitchen, and it reminded Anna of simpler times. Happier times. Something she would have said couldn't happen on that terrible day when everything had changed. That this quickly they would get back to talking, to laughing. To being them.

"Can I just supervise?" Rachel asked. "Because all of this sounds like it's above my pay grade."

"I'll supervise you," Anna said. "I'll tell you what you're doing wrong."

"That doesn't sound very fun."

"It will be lots of fun. For me."

Anna rolled out the crust for the pies they were making and placed them in the pie plates. Emma and Rachel mixed together the fillings.

"So does everyone get surprise-pie hour instead of wine-and-cheese hour tomorrow?" Rachel asked.

"I was thinking," Wendy said. "It isn't a bad thing to have surprise pie."

"Unless it's Adam's pie," Emma said.

Rachel was laughing, and wiped a swipe of flour from her cheek, which only added more. "Yes. And can you imagine if you were going to work at the diner you would have to be around his subpar food all the time."

Emma frowned. "Why would I work at the diner?"

Rachel sputtered and shook her head, blowing a strand of red hair out of her eyes. "It's just… He mentioned to me that he was looking for someone. And he asked me if you would be interested. I told him no."

Emma frowned. "You didn't ask *me*."

"You have a job here. And we're… We're adding to the menu."

"But you can't just tell him no. It's up to me."

"Adam asked me if I thought you would be interested. He didn't ask you. And, apparently, he could've asked you that morning when you came in, which you did not tell me you were doing. You told me you had an early class."

Anna recognized that maternal tone. Shock layered with deadly disappointment. She'd heard it often enough when she'd been around Emma's age.

"I didn't realize omitting that I'd stopped at the diner

for a doughnut was a cardinal sin. I didn't think that it was relevant. I *did* have an early class." She also recognized that answer back. And knew Emma didn't realize what danger she was in.

"You just normally tell me things."

"It wasn't something that I needed to tell you. I decided to stop for a doughnut. It's not like I decided to stop for some weed."

"Well, the problem is you might have, and if you're not telling me things—"

"The bridge from doughnuts to drugs is a pretty long one, Mom. I wouldn't get paranoid."

"My *job* is to be paranoid. And I didn't think that taking a job at the diner was the right thing for you. Not right now."

"But that's not your decision."

"Yes," Rachel said, her hands buried in a bowl of blackberries. "It is my decision to make. Right now it is. You still live here. You're not eighteen yet. It's not up to you."

Emma growled and stalked out of the room. A few minutes later Anna heard the front door slam.

Rachel sighed and pulled her hands out of the bowl. "I made a mess of that." Her hands were stained with juice. She stared at them, hopeless, and Anna had the feeling it had nothing to do with the berry juice at all.

She felt for Rachel, she did. But she recognized herself in Emma. Emma wanted something more, something different. Anna had wanted the same in that summer of sneaking out and smoking cigarettes. The one before she'd seen how she'd broken her mother's heart and had decided that Thomas could be the right change.

If Rachel didn't let Emma go, Emma might turn into

Anna. And there was nothing Anna wanted less for her niece.

"It's not that big of a deal if she wants to work somewhere else, is it?"

"That's not the point," Rachel said.

"It's not," Wendy said, backing Rachel up, of course. "When you have children, it's your job to set the boundaries that you want them inside of. It doesn't matter if it makes sense to them. If she wants Emma here, that's her decision."

"I didn't say it wasn't," Anna said. "But you can't force Emma to be here. It's not like that's going to make it a good time to be had by all."

"Sometimes you do have to force teenagers to do things," Wendy said. "They don't know what's best for them all the time. I had to get tough with you sometimes, Anna."

"Excuse me? Are you turning this around and making it about me?"

"You were… I'm just saying you were difficult sometimes, and maybe I did something wrong…" Wendy said.

Anna felt like her mother had reached inside her and hollowed her out completely. "You think you did something wrong. You think there's something wrong *with me*?"

Thomas had thought so, obviously. Why wouldn't her mother?

"Can we please not have a giant fight?" Rachel asked. "My hands are covered in blackberry juice, my daughter is mad at me—"

"And God forbid it not be about you for a second," Anna said, rounding on her sister. "We must remember, after all, that your pain is greatest."

"Anna," Rachel said. "That's not fair." Rachel sounded like all the breath had gone out of her and Anna regretted that. Because the blow had landed a whole lot sharper than she'd meant it to.

"I don't need either of you to act like teenagers," Wendy said. "One is enough."

Well, there was the truth of it. All that tension with her mother that ran beneath the surface of her help. Of their interactions. This was what she thought of her. That she was still a teenager rebelling.

"I didn't ask for commentary on my life. If you don't want me to act like a teenager, then don't treat me like one. If you want me to act like an adult, then you don't get to intermittently school me whenever you feel like it over what you consider to be my poor life choices. I couldn't tell you when my marriage was falling apart because I knew you would just blame me! I don't blame Emma for not wanting to work with all of this…" Then Anna turned and walked out of the kitchen, breathing hard.

It felt good to scream it. To shout what she'd believed deep in her heart. To stop trying to make them feel better when she felt broken.

Well, maybe she would storm out of the house, too. It wasn't every day she identified with her niece, but today she was definitely Team Emma.

If only she could find someone to be Team Anna.

9

You worry too much about rules. When you get older you'll realize that Mom and Dad don't know everything. And no, of course the ghost isn't real.

—FROM A LETTER WRITTEN BY SUSAN BRIGHT
TO HER SISTER, JUNE 25, 1961

EMMA

Emma found that it was difficult to sulk at an empty room. But that was the decision she'd made when she'd stormed out of the Captain's House and gone back to the Lightkeeper's House.

There was no one here to witness her disgust, and that felt injurious.

She had given up Boston. And maybe her mom didn't know that, but it was true, and that choice was bearing down on her, harder and harder every day, and it only got worse when she was in this house.

Staring at this oppressive sameness that was now so unalterably different.

The house was the same.

But her dad was gone.

And those pieces didn't fit, and couldn't.

She couldn't even go into his room. Couldn't go up to the lighthouse, not when it had been a special place, a special walk for the two of them. Pieces of her home, her life, had been ripped away when he'd died, and she couldn't bear being here and being so…aware of it.

Her mom moved through the house with ease. She slept in that bedroom Emma couldn't even go into. She'd cleaned out her dad's medicine and all the signs he'd been here, and sick.

Emma couldn't act like it was over. It felt like it was still happening.

If she'd gotten the diner job she could have at least had some escape. And Luke… Luke was right there and he was the symbol of her escape. Of just a few minutes to look at something beautiful and wonderful and not connected to any of…this.

Her dad had *died* here. And they were just still…living here.

She didn't know how.

A lot of people had died in this house. She knew that.

And in the Captain's House, too. It was even rumored that they had a ghost living on the first floor. As a result they were part of the Haunted Buildings Registry. Though Emma had never seen one, and she supposed that if anyone should have seen them, it was the people who lived there.

But it felt different, more personal, and it just… She just wanted something different. She had taken that escape from herself.

Sometimes she wanted to be just like all of her friends and shout about the unfairness of life when her mom wouldn't buy her a new cell phone. And sometimes she wanted to shout at God. Because her dad was the best, and he was gone. Because her aunt Anna had been publicly humiliated by someone they all should have been able to trust.

Because she and her mom should at least be able to get along easily since they were all each other had left.

The front door opened, and Emma turned, prepared to sulk at her mother.

But it was her aunt Anna.

"I got yelled at, too," Anna said.

"Did you do any yelling back?"

"Plenty of it." She took a breath. "I figured you had the right idea storming off. But I don't want to go anywhere. So I thought I would storm over here."

"You could've gone back to your cottage."

Anna nodded. "Yeah. I figured I would find you. See if you were okay."

"No," Emma said. "I'm not okay."

"Neither am I," Anna said.

Silence fell between them, but it wasn't uncomfortable. She felt understood, somehow. Their pain wasn't the same at all, but still. She felt like Anna might be the one person who really understood *her*.

She remembered taking her aunt's hand when she'd been little and they'd been waiting in a doctor's office for hours for her dad. Her mom had asked Anna to take her somewhere. They'd gotten ice cream and gone to the beach and Emma had smiled for the first time in two days.

Anna knew her. Emma knew Anna.

"Can I tell you something?" Emma asked.

Anna's expression was cautious, but her words were compassionate. "You can tell me whatever you need to."

Emma hesitated, unsure if she should bring this up.

"I… I don't actually care what happened with you and Uncle Thomas. But I think what he did was messed-up."

Anna blinked. "You do?"

"We were all there. We were all there, and my dad just died, and he didn't even warn us. He didn't warn my mother. He didn't warn Grandma. How could he do that? And he… I can tell that he just expects us to disown you. He just expects us to take what he said as the truth and side with him. I've never felt so…betrayed as I did right then. And whatever you did or didn't do, it won't make me feel as betrayed as that."

To Emma's horror, her aunt's eyes filled with tears. She blinked, and then sat on the overstuffed floral couch that rested just beneath the living-room window, that looked out over the ocean. "That's really sweet of you. I did sleep with someone," Anna said. "Just… If that changes your opinion."

Emma took a moment to turn that over. "It doesn't really."

"Em, have you ever even kissed a guy?"

Emma's face went hot. "No."

Anna huffed out a laugh. "That could be why you aren't as horrified as other people are." She swallowed. "It's a really intimate thing to do."

Normally, this sort of conversation with an adult would make her skin itch, but she felt a strange bloom of pride that her aunt was talking to her like she was an equal. An adult who understood.

It stood out in total opposition to her mom *turning down a job* on her behalf.

Anna looked down. "I didn't do it without thinking about it a lot. And I didn't do it just because… I didn't do it just to feel pleasure. And I feel like it's easy to believe that I did. I feel like everyone is so happy to have me believe that I got…seduced and I'm weak. I mean, I did get seduced. But… Not the way they think. He made me feel special. I really wanted to feel special. Because one day I woke up and realized I didn't know whose life I was living. And once I had that thought, I couldn't let it go. You can't live your life for other people, Emma."

Emma's pride was replaced by a deep discomfort.

Her grandma had lived her life for her mom and aunt. She'd been a single mom, working hard to give them a life. And her mom had taken care of her, taken care of her dad.

Emma didn't want to be a weak link in that chain.

Emma couldn't believe that you could just…set aside all that and live for yourself.

"My mom's lived her life for other people all this time," she said, bald and simple. She could tell those words hurt Anna. She wasn't trying to accuse her of anything; she was just…saying.

She kept so much back to protect her mom; she had to. From having to do makeup work for shaky grades over the years when her dad's health had been compromised, her crush on Luke, any problems with friends… She hadn't ever wanted her to worry. But she could see now that it amounted to a wall. Not stones that Emma carried; rocks that she had built up into a barrier between them.

Anna was offering honesty, and even if Emma couldn't quite believe some of it, she wanted to answer honestly. Wanted to take this moment, this space, to say something that was true.

"Yeah, I guess so. But I don't even mean that you have to be selfish. Because I don't believe in being selfish, either. I know that there's a whole congregation full of people who would laugh at me saying that. But I just mean…

If you bend too much, you're going to make weak spots in who you are. And eventually those weak spots will give. And you will break. Like gluten-free dough. No stretch, all break. Because you can't do it forever. And if you wait until you break, it's going to be a pretty spectacular break that hurts a lot more people than it had to. So if I were you, I would avoid being me. I would maybe hold firm on the job I wanted. So you know… You don't break your marriage vows later."

Emma's eyes felt scratchy. "I guess that makes sense. But I don't want to hurt anyone, least of all Mom."

"I know. But you know what would hurt her worse? If you ended up resenting her. If you ended up angry at her because you didn't know how to be the person that she wanted you to be. If you didn't find a way to lovingly show her that you have to do what's right for you. Because eventually, you lose the ability to do that lovingly. Speaking from the other side."

"Right. Well. Thank you."

"Thank *you*," Anna said. "For…loving me enough to be on my team." She breathed out, long and slow, like she was considering the next few words carefully. "You didn't believe him, though, did you?"

Emma thought about it. "I didn't care."

"So you didn't believe him. Because I feel like if you had…you might have cared a little bit that I cheated on your uncle."

"I know you," Emma said. "And whatever I believed, I knew you didn't do something to be cruel. Or just to be selfish. I'm seventeen, and I know enough to know that. I don't know why everybody else can't figure it out."

"You know, not to cast aspersions on your youth or anything, but part of it is because you never had a husband.

Look at your mom, Em. She stuck by your dad through everything. All of his illness and all of that… I couldn't even stick by my husband, who is perfectly fine, and is good to everyone, and—"

"No one's going to think of it that way."

"Honey, everyone thinks of it that way. People can't help but compare. And on the comparison front, I come out badly. That's just the truth."

"You're not the same person. And Uncle Thomas isn't the same person as my dad. Which I think might be an even more important piece of that."

Anna smiled sadly. "Yeah. Maybe. Go get that diner job if you want it, though. Okay?"

"I promise," Emma said. Anna stood and pulled Emma in for a hug. "If your mom gets mad at you, just blame me. Everyone already thinks I'm a bad person, anyway."

"I don't," Emma said, resolute.

"You have no idea how much that means to me."

Then Anna walked out the front door, and Emma could hear her heavy footsteps on the porch.

And her words replayed, over and over again. She could already see that they were true.

Emma trudged upstairs, her hands running along the familiar banister. She stopped, right across from her parents' room.

She didn't want to go in. Because he still wasn't there.

She paused for a moment and wondered. What he would tell her if she went in to talk to him. If she asked him what she should do.

He would take her hands and walk her up to the lighthouse, when he'd been able, and they would watch the beam of light go out over the sea…

"The world is so vast, Em. And you want to study the

ocean. It goes even deeper. So not only do you want to wander all the land up here, you have to go beneath the waves, too."

"I want to study it all at least." She gripped the railing and closed her eyes, letting the mist coming in off the water spray her face.

"There is more than you'll ever know or see in a lifetime."

"Is that supposed to be comforting?"

"It is to me. There are mysteries in the world we'll never untangle. Depths we'll never explore. So we don't have to regret that we can't do it all, see it all. In life the greatest gift isn't knowing the most, or seeing the most— it's loving the most. Being loved the most. Trusting that when you do go out to explore all that's out there, love will be here. Waiting..."

Except her dad was gone. And she wasn't even brave enough to go up to the lighthouse right now.

She turned away from the empty bedroom and slunk into her own. She climbed onto her twin bed, the mattress punching down beneath her feet. The lavender bedspread wrinkled as she stretched up to look at the carving on the beam overhead. It had been painted over a couple of times with white, but she could still make it out.

Lazy Susan slept here. 1961.

Emma often thought about the college students who'd lived here, and wished she knew more about them. It was strange to think they'd been here on an adventure, when to her it was as worn and familiar as an old pair of sweats.

She flopped down onto her bed and grabbed hold of a pillow, clutching it to her chest.

If she wasn't careful, she was going to break later. She'd spent a lot of time trying very hard not to cause her parents trouble. She didn't want to give her dad any grief, not when he felt so ill all the time. She didn't want to give her mom any grief, not while her mother was caring for him.

But somewhere in there, she had forgotten that she needed to minimize her own grief, too. The diner wasn't Boston, but it was something.

And she was going to get it.

She liked to think that whoever Lazy Susan was, she would approve.

10

He tends the light all night; he sleeps all day.
He's a stranger to me. I have been married once
and thought it would be simple to marry again.
Nothing about him is simple.

—FROM THE DIARY OF JENNY HANSEN, JANUARY 20, 1900

RACHEL

Rachel still felt guilty about the fight with Emma the next day.

She hadn't seen her that night; her door had already been firmly shut, and Emma tucked up in bed, the universal signal for "I am a teenager and I'm not speaking to you."

And she felt marginally guilty about how things had gone with Anna. She had not intended to be part of any ganging up on her sister.

The terrible thing was, in her anger last night she'd suddenly identified that hot, reckless thing in her chest. The one that sat there sometimes when she looked at Anna and Thomas over dinner, when Jacob was too ill to come downstairs.

Anna's life had seemed so easy. So perfect. Her husband was healthy, he was successful and there was something about that vitality that made Rachel feel…jealous. She felt petty even acknowledging it now, especially now.

Maybe you should ask about what happened.

No. Not yet. She did need to talk to Anna. But right now healing the rift with Emma was what mattered.

Emma didn't come home after school, which was strange, and she also didn't return Rachel's text, which had her feeling panicked for a whole five minutes until her phone rang.

She recognized the number as J's—unsurprising, given she'd called it enough times to place orders. She answered.

"Mom?"

"Why aren't you using your phone?" Rachel asked.

"Because I'm at work," Emma said, a note of defiance and steel in her voice that sounded a whole lot like Rachel's younger sister.

"You're…at work."

"Yes. I stopped by before school today to talk to Adam about taking the job. He hired me. And I'm being trained."

"I… I told you that that wasn't happening."

"Yeah, I know. And I decided that it was important enough to me that I needed to make it happen. And I would've come home and talked to you first, but Adam wanted me here now."

"He did."

"Yes."

"What made you decide to do this? We could've talked about it."

"No, I didn't think we could talk about it." Her daughter never, ever talked to her like this and the words felt like a stark slap down the line. "I tried to talk about it.

You were weird. You basically acted like I was doing meth when I told you that I went to get a doughnut. So we'll talk about it later."

"Emma…"

"Talk to Aunt Anna."

Emma hung up the phone, and Rachel suddenly had an out-of-body experience, where she saw herself storming into J's Diner and turning over a table in the middle of her daughter's work shift.

Her daughter, who was seventeen and not seven.

So maybe she needed to get a handle on her reactions. But, honestly, at this point in life she didn't have a whole lot of perspective on what emotions were even supposed to be.

She bit back a scowl. And she stormed straight down to the Shoreman's Cabin, with murder on her mind.

Anna's car was there, so she knew her sister was around. She might be up at the Captain's House, but Rachel would find her.

Luckily, Anna was home. She jerked open the door, looking comically like Emma in that moment. Sullen and defiant.

"Yes?" she asked.

"Did you tell my daughter to go ahead and take the job without talking to me?"

Anna lifted a shoulder. "She did talk to you. You freaked out."

"Funny. She said the same thing."

"Because it's true."

"Adam didn't ask her. He asked *me*. If he'd come to her directly—"

"You would've handled it exactly the same. Because you didn't want her to take the job. You want to have her close to you, and I understand that, Rachel, I do. But if you try to control her too much you're either going to lose her now, or she's going to have a complete freak-out in twenty years."

"What makes you say that?"

Anna huffed and pressed her hand to her chest. "The voice of freak-out experience."

Rachel stared down her sister, her heart thundering. She felt like she was standing in the doorway of a room she wasn't ready to enter.

One that might challenge what she thought about Anna. About herself and her own feelings toward her sister, and she wasn't ready.

She didn't want to be challenged.

"I'm not ready to have this conversation," Rachel said.

"I know you're not. I figure that was why you hadn't asked me about it. But we're kind of in it, anyway."

"Did you do it?" Rachel braced herself for whatever the answer might be.

"Yes."

"I don't know why you think you're qualified to give my daughter advice."

"Really? That's all you can ask me?"

"My husband is dead!" she yelled. "He's dead. I would give anything..."

What, to have him back?

No, she couldn't have him back. That stopped her cold.

In the endless suffering that he'd been in, in his weakened state, where he was just so tired. Living life as a caretaker, and not as a lover. No, she didn't want him back as he was. She wanted him whole. Because if he could have been healthy for their whole marriage... And Anna had that.

She'd had it. Easy. She had thrown it away, and for what?

"I would never have done that," Rachel said. "You threw it all away for sex? I haven't had sex in *years*, Anna, just so you know. And I would never... I would *never*."

Anna's face was drained of color, the dark circles under her eyes pronounced. "There's a big difference between *can't* have sex and *won't* have sex, Rachel. A big difference. And how it makes you feel... It's just different."

Her sister was getting at something, at a deeper issue, and Rachel wasn't dense enough to miss that. But she was angry enough to choose to. Because Anna had taken this moment, the hardest time in her life, and made it about her.

She'd advised her daughter to take a job somewhere else. She couldn't have waited to end her marriage, even a few more months.

Her pain. Her own pain was so big she couldn't see around it, and right now she didn't want to. She'd taken care of other people all this time and worried about them, and right now, looking at her younger sister, she chose to just let all that poison flow right out of her.

"Our marriage vows were the same," Rachel said. "The same as everyone's. And it doesn't matter if you have more sickness than health, it's still the same promise. It doesn't matter if things are hard, it's still the same. That much I know."

She turned and stormed away, the rage that was driving her now something she couldn't control. She didn't want to control it. She had been... She had been the best that she could be for everyone.

For years.

She hadn't been able to fall apart when Jacob had died, because what was the point? There was too much to handle. She worked until she was exhausted. Fell into bed and slept dry-eyed and then woke up and did it again the next day. It would have hurt everyone if she lost it. Emma, her mother… What was the point of it all?

She felt close to falling apart now.

And maybe this was why she and Anna had struggled to find closeness as adults. They were united by a love of the Lighthouse Inn, their mother. Shared memories from their childhood. But Rachel had always taken care of Anna. Anna was five years younger and she'd helped with her sister from the beginning, been a proud big sister who'd adored her sister's chubby cheeks and fuzzy red hair.

When she'd been a teenager she and her friends had stayed at her and Jacob's house sometimes, to feel more independent, even though they were just on the other side of the wall from their mother.

And somewhere in there Anna had grown up. Separated herself. Found her own life. But Rachel had always been the caretaker. The one who'd watched over her. Anna had always been rowdy, wild and in need of caring for. Until she'd started dating Thomas, whom Rachel had imagined was the kind of steadying influence she'd needed.

But it hadn't brought them closer together.

They were different. Too different to get along. Too different to deal with each other.

She was just so angry right now. It was better than being wounded.

Giving in to it, right in Anna's face, had felt amazing in the moment. To unleash it all instead of shoving it down had been a high and she wanted to ride it as long as she could.

She stormed back to the Lightkeeper's House and grabbed her car keys, then drove furiously toward town. When she pulled up to J's, she took a deep breath before getting out of the car, and she asked herself if she was really going to do this.

If she was going to be that vision of angry Rachel that she'd had of herself about a half hour ago, storming in and causing her daughter a massive amount of embarrassment.

She wasn't going to cause her daughter embarrassment. But she was going to talk to her.

She got out of the car and slammed the door shut, crossing the street. And then she stopped.

She could see Emma there through the window, talking to customers. Laughing. She had a pad in one hand, and she was writing down orders.

Her red hair was up, and she was wearing a gray T-shirt, white apron and a pair of jeans. She looked...impossibly like an adult. Like the college student she was soon going to be. And very much not like a little girl whose life Rachel could control.

It wasn't even about control.

It was just about having to let go of way too many things and not wanting this to be another one of them.

She let her arms fall slack at her sides, and her purse dropped to the sidewalk.

She saw herself way too clearly just then. A ticking time bomb pretending she had it all together while yelling aimlessly at her sister, just looking for a target for the anger and pain that lived in her and finding her convenient.

She was pushing away her sister. She was smothering her daughter because she was terrified of what her

life might look like if she had only herself to be responsible for.

She was ruining everything.

Not Anna. Not Emma.

And all that righteous rage drained away and left her
feeling exactly as she was. Sad. Tired.

Alone.

The door to the diner opened, and Adam popped his
head out. "Did you want to come in?"

"No," she said, deep in the throes of thwarted anger.
What a terrible feeling that was. Worse than being turned
on with no relief. Worse even than looking forward to
leftovers all day and finding out someone else had eaten
them first.

She closed her eyes and breathed in, then out.

"Maybe I'll come out, then." He slipped out the door
and stood in front of her. It was weird to not have a counter between them. She wasn't sure she'd realized how tall
he was. She was usually sitting, and he was usually standing, and the counter space was between them.

He dwarfed her. She barely came up to the bottom of
his chin. It was weird that it surprised her.

She'd talked to Adam multiple times a week for the
past couple of years, but she didn't know much about him.

He was the grandson of Jack, the original owner. But
she didn't know what had brought him to Sunset Bay. She
didn't know why he'd chosen to take over the diner. She
hadn't asked. Because he did her the great mercy of not
asking her about her life, and on some level maybe she
felt like not asking him about his made it all safe.

"Why did you hire my daughter without talking to me?"

He lifted an eyebrow. "Was I supposed to talk to you?"

"You asked me if she was interested and I said no."

"And then she came by this morning and told me that she was. You didn't tell me not to hire her, Rachel. You told me that she wasn't interested."

"Did you think that might be the same thing?"

"No," he said. "I didn't. Because as far as I know you're a pretty levelheaded woman."

"You don't know me."

"I guess not."

She made an exasperated sound. "I am her mother, and I just need to know what's going on with her. And... I was counting on her to work at the bed-and-breakfast."

"Were you?"

She took a breath and looked up and down the street. It was deserted, and it was dark, the streetlights casting an overly yellow glow onto the sidewalks. She hadn't confided in her family. She hadn't told them anything about what she was feeling because it didn't feel fair to burden them. But Adam... She could tell Adam.

Things were always easier with him.

"No," she said. "I wasn't. Not in a practical way. Just an emotional one. She's going to college in the fall. And... I am not handling that well."

"You're doing okay," he said.

"I'm here, ready to yell at you for committing the great evil of giving her a job."

"You didn't actually yell at me, though," he pointed out. "And you didn't storm inside and yell at her."

"I wanted to."

He shoved his hands into his pockets. "But you didn't."

"You're a pain. Has anyone ever told you that?"

"More times than I can count."

She cleared her throat and looked behind him, into

the diner window again. At Emma. "Will you take really good care of her?"

"She's waiting tables in Sunset Bay, not taking work as a human pincushion in Vegas."

"Can I come visit?"

"I was under the impression that you would be spending as much time in my restaurant as you ever have."

"Okay. She can work for you."

"I didn't ask for or need your permission."

Rachel sputtered. "You… You did, though."

"I mean, you wanted me to need it. *She* needed your permission, but I didn't need your permission."

"I'm pretty sure you did, to hire my minor child."

"I don't have a form for you to sign. This isn't a field trip."

"Didn't you care about my feelings at all?"

"Of course," he said. "But caring about them and thinking they're reasonable are two different things. And I figure, even if you needed a minute to sort your feelings out, you weren't going to keep her from working here, not in the end."

"You're enraging."

"Do you want a cheeseburger?"

She sighed. "Yes, I want a cheeseburger." She picked her purse up off the sidewalk and followed Adam back into the diner. Emma looked up from the table she was waiting on and froze. Rachel waved her fingers, a small white flag. She sat down at the counter. "Do you want it to go?" Adam asked, putting himself back behind the counter, and happily restoring the order of things.

"I might eat here," she said.

"Only if you promise not to harass my waitstaff. Or ground them."

"I promise," she said.

A few minutes later he put the cheeseburger in front of her. The intense…normalcy of the moment felt wrong when she'd left things with Anna like she had.

"What's wrong?"

She looked up and met his eyes. "I thought you had a policy against asking me that."

"Did I…ever say that I had a policy about anything?"

"No. But you've never asked me that. And it's the only thing most other people have asked me for about two years."

The corners of his mouth turned down. "Sure. You also never stormed up to the front of my restaurant before, stood frozen outside like you'd been hit across the face with a marlin and then stared at my cheeseburger like it had stolen your best friend from you." He winced. "That was a bad choice of words, and I'm sorry. It's not my place to dig into what's going on."

"It's not about him…" She said the words softly.

It was the first time either of them had ever come close to talking about her husband.

He nodded. "Okay, then."

"I yelled at my sister earlier. Because she's the one who told Emma to come get the job. And I said some things to her that I… That I shouldn't have said."

He considered that for a moment, and she could tell he wasn't especially thrilled that he'd gotten himself into the position of being the advice giver. "We all say things we don't mean when we're angry."

Rachel let that comment settle over her for a minute. "No, I meant them. I shouldn't have said them. Not the way that I did. Because… I feel things. Some complicated things. But I'm also not interested in cutting her out of my

life. So I guess I need to figure out a better way of dealing with my feelings."

"Yeah, I think they call that *life*. The thing where you
spend a lot of time working out better ways to handle
your feelings."

"Have you managed that yet?"

He nodded. "Yep. I do it pretty well. By not having
feelings."

He said it light and funny, but the words hit her in a
way that made her feel unaccountably sad. Adam seemed
easygoing, but when she really thought about it...

It didn't make a whole lot of sense that he had moved
here to run the diner. She imagined he made an all-right
living with it, but it wouldn't be anything extravagant.
Not really anything worth uprooting a life over. She supposed that he could be married, though she never heard
anyone say that he was, and he didn't wear a ring. Even
more possible, he had a girlfriend, because it wasn't like
they talked about those sorts of things.

But if he was what he appeared to be, he was single,
alone. And he was...an attractive man. Probably forty, in
excellent shape...

All those things didn't add up. Not without something
dark and hollow and sad behind them.

But she wouldn't ask. They didn't ask each other those
kinds of questions.

"Okay, but what if *I* have feelings?"

"You'll probably have to talk to her."

"I was afraid of that."

"It's up to you. You could also just not worry about it
right now. Maybe it'll fix itself."

"Nothing fixes itself," Rachel said. "Though, in my

experience, not a whole lot seems to get fixed with my effort, either."

"I don't know. I think you fixed this pretty well."

They both looked back at Emma, who was happily seeing to the next table.

Happy.

She looked happy here. Less burdened and pale.

And she'd tried to keep her from this to make herself feel better.

She'd fought with Anna, who'd made life choices without her—her permission. Her guidance.

She wondered then if the thing that scared her most was what her life looked like when she wasn't needed.

And she was afraid she was perilously close to finding out.

11

Today the chaplain came with a timely reminder:
we are troubled on every side, yet not distressed;
we are perplexed, but not in despair.

—FROM A LETTER WRITTEN BY STAFF SERGEANT RICHARD JOHNSON,
AUGUST 25, 1943

ANNA

Anna hadn't spoken to Rachel in the two days since their fight. But she knew that she wasn't going to be able to avoid her for much longer.

For one thing, they worked on the same property. For another, they were supposed to bake croissants from scratch for a large party that was coming up just for breakfast in the morning. And that meant not only would they be seeing each other, but they would also be interacting in that tiny kitchen. Trying to work together to make something happen.

It was too bad she was going to have to try to pretend her sister didn't think the worst of her the entire time.

Rachel's response hadn't surprised her, even if it had hurt her. Emma's reaction had been surprising, but welcome. Anna was afraid to have a conversation with her mother that went too deep, because she knew that in her mother's eyes she was the worst kind of woman that could ever exist. While Rachel was currently exemplifying what it meant to be the best.

And Anna felt petty unto her soul to even think of it that way. It was like being trapped in the middle of a storm-tossed sea and worrying about your hair being wet. The waves might pull you under, but God forbid you be a little bit damp.

She wondered if Rachel would even show up and help her bake. She couldn't actually imagine her sister backing out on an obligation, but in truth, baking wasn't Rachel's special skill and she wouldn't be looking forward to seeing Anna any more than Anna would be looking forward to seeing her.

She wondered, though, if she didn't really have anything to blame but the distance between herself and her sister for the blowup that had happened. They had pulled away from each other over the years. Nothing dramatic.

But it was like the pain in their lives was a loose thread, and the more time pulled at it, the more the fabric between them unraveled and they began to separate.

She walked into the kitchen and just stood there, and then she began to assemble ingredients. It was fifteen minutes past their agreed time to meet, and she had dry ingredients, bowls and lots and lots of butter set out on the counter, and she had just come to the conclusion that Rachel probably wasn't going to come, when her sister walked through the door.

"Oh," Anna said. "You came."

"Of course I did. I said that I would."

And Rachel did like to martyr herself to a cause, even if that cause was pastries.

Anna bit back the uncharitable comment.

"Emma is really happy working at J's."

Rachel said that while she was taking an apron off the peg, and she was very carefully not looking at Anna.

"Oh?"

"Yes," she said, tying the apron around her slender waist and taking a scrunchie off her wrist and putting her long red hair up in a bun on the top of her head with practiced ease. "I'm sorry that I got angry about it. She's happy. And I think... I don't know why I didn't see it. I think she needs a break from being here. From the grief. I mean... He died here. We had the funeral here."

It hit Anna then how strange it was to see her sister like this. Not knowing what to do. Not being certain. Anna had always found Rachel's certainty about the world intimidating. Rachel just did things. What needed to be done. Always.

There was only five years between them, but sometimes Anna felt impossibly young standing next to Rachel.

Even more so now.

Rachel had buried a husband. Rachel had a daughter who was getting ready to go to college.

Rachel, for her part, looked far younger than she was, the blessed side effect of living where the sun rarely shone. That, and a combination of what Anna assumed were blessed genetics. At least, they definitely were from Wendy. They wouldn't know about their father. Neither of them knew him.

Rachel had told her once that she had some vague memories of him, but he'd left for good before Anna was born, and she didn't have any of her own. She'd never been particularly sad about that. He'd hurt her mother terribly. He'd abandoned his daughters.

He was a cheater.

A cheater…like *her*.

But she'd had reasons for what she'd done.

Maybe he did, too.

"I'm glad that she's happy," Anna said quickly. "And that… It makes sense. I know what it's like…" She blinked hard, debating whether or not she should say the next thing. "I know what it's like to need a break from your life. And that really is all I said to her. That if she really wanted something that she needed to come forward with it now. Because if you don't you're just going to end up hurting people later."

"I… Thank you for saying that to her. I don't know how to do this part."

"Your daughter growing up?"

"No. People not needing me."

The silence settled between them for a moment. "What do you mean?"

"I've always had someone to take care of. You. Emma. Jacob. You grew up." She pulled a face. "Jacob died. Emma is getting ready to live life on her own. I don't know what that means for me."

She stared at Rachel, unsure of what to say. She'd never imagined her sister feeling insecure. Not ever. "You don't…have to take care of us," Anna said.

"I know," Rachel said. "I mean, I'm realizing it."

"I meant you don't have to take care of us for us to… need you." Things might be difficult with her sister, but she was her sister.

"Thank you," Rachel said, her voice thick. She drew in a shaking breath. "Let's start laminating, though, okay?"

They both started with their own large batch and began endlessly folding chunks of butter into the dough so that it would bake just right and make the delicate, flaky layers they would need for good croissants.

They worked in silence, which was preferable to fighting.

"I'm sorry," Rachel said.

They both kept folding. Layer after layer.

"For?"

"For what I said. For the… The way that I said it. I don't understand, Anna, and I don't even know… I haven't had the capacity to even try for the past few weeks. And it definitely wasn't something I should have gone off at you about when we haven't even had a discussion with any kind of civility yet."

"Oh."

"I can't say I didn't mean it. I did." She blinked.

"You're just sorry you said it that way?" She turned the dough and folded it again.

Another layer.

"I don't know that it was right that I said it at all," Rachel said softly.

"Oh." Anna's heart was thundering as she continued to work the dough.

There wasn't anything to say after that, Anna supposed.

"I wanted to hurt you because I was hurt. It's that simple. And I guess I'm that small."

"You didn't have to be mean to me."

"I know," Rachel said. "Do you ever just feel mean?"

"Oh. All the time. But I haven't been allowed to show it."

"Why?"

She snorted. "Really? Look at who I was married to.

I was the pastor's wife. I had to be happy and perfect all the time."

"I never needed you to be."

The words took the air out of her. "Well, I don't know. Mom did. Because you were so good and easy and I was… me. And when I found Thomas I know Mom was sure the issue of *me* was solved."

"You really think Mom thought of you as an issue?"

"She was afraid. I know she was. Afraid I'd end up… I mean, I guess like I am."

"I didn't know that."

"Because we don't talk. I was thirteen when you got married. You had Emma. Jacob got sick. I had my own friends, and then I threw myself into my life and…we just never talked."

Anna just wasn't happy to let things lie. Not anymore. She'd destroyed her marriage with her actions. There was no more decisive act than the one she'd committed, so why she shouldn't face her sister and their distance she didn't know.

They'd both just gone with it. For years.

Anna was done just going with it. It had been the way she'd dealt with life for far too long, and it had been dry. Arid. It was no life at all.

Rachel herself had lived more vividly. Somehow, she'd responded to the way their mother had raised them and found happiness, even though she'd found trials, too.

Rich. Layered. Life.

Anna had been hiding instead. She'd found a stark, literal way to behave. To make herself perfect. And she'd learned just how little that meant in the end.

She wanted more. Better.

"It doesn't have to be like this," Anna said. "I mean, it

makes sense that when we were younger and we were in such different places in our lives we didn't connect. But now...we have this great place we all love between us. We're close to each other in proximity. We had big family dinners all the time. There was always a feeling of being a close family. Jacob and Thomas, and Mom and Emma and then there's you and me. And all those connections but ours is just...polite. Why?"

Rachel's cheeks were red. "I don't know. If you don't know, why should I know?"

"I—I don't know, but you're older, so you should know."

"Oh, thanks. I—I really don't think about it. I didn't even realize it until I was...alone like this. Until Jacob wasn't there. And then it seemed so obvious how things between you and me aren't like they should be." She paused for a moment. "I guess there were some things about your marriage that I resented. And the worse off Jacob was, the more..."

She sucked in a sharp breath and her head lowered, a tear spilling down her cheek. And Anna dreaded what her sister might say next, but she knew she had to listen. Because she'd asked the question. Because when you set off a bomb you can't hide from the destruction and wasn't she learning that?

She had asked the question.

So maybe she should bridge the gap, too.

She reached out and pulled her sister in for a hug.

"I loved him so much, Anna," Rachel said on a choked breath. "I love him so much. Still. And I wanted more and better for him than what he got. And sometimes... I wanted easier for me. And that isn't fair. It's not fair, because he wasn't a burden. He was my great joy. He was the love of my life. But sometimes I just... I got tired, and

I got sad. I wanted things to be like they were. I wanted us to be able to have what we did. Because I loved that. We found something that worked. We found happiness. It wasn't like it was a long slog of sadness. It wasn't. But it was hard sometimes, watching you two. Watching you get to be a wife the way you were. I let it make us distant. And knowing it wasn't perfect now doesn't change how I saw it then."

Anna didn't know what to say to that, because she would never have guessed that being around her was hard for Rachel for those reasons, not for a moment. Not when Anna could see plainly that Jacob had more affection for Rachel in his every breath than Thomas had for her, particularly in the end.

And she had to think of her own *whys*. Which she'd been avoiding for a long, long time now.

She'd hidden her own issues with Rachel, with her life, behind the careful, perfect pastor's-wife facade she'd built around herself. She'd used it to keep her own feelings a mystery from even herself. But it was all crumbling now.

She could see clearly now that Jacob and Rachel had been together in a way that had worked a sore spot into her own heart over the years.

Because after those family dinners, she'd imagined them together. How they talked, laughed, behaved, kissed, after everyone had gone home.

Thomas just closed the door on her and went back to his important work.

"I pulled away from you," Anna admitted finally. "Because watching the way that he looked at you made my heart break. Not because I felt sorry for you, and I know that maybe I should have. It made my heart break because

I'm selfish, and I could see that he… He loved you. He loved you so much, Rachel."

"Thomas loves you."

"No," she said definitely. "And if he did, he doesn't now."

Rachel paused for a moment, then met her sister's gaze. "I was afraid to ask this before. I was being selfish. But I want to understand now. Why did you do it?" There wasn't any condemnation in the question. And Anna knew if she wanted Rachel to understand her, she had to give her a chance to understand.

But how could she do that when she hardly understood herself?

What had seemed clear while she was in it felt muddled in the rubble.

Anna blinked, and she rolled the dough again, created another layer. "Do you remember what it was like in school when a boy would smile at you and it made you feel warm all over? And it could make your whole day. Your whole day could center around that smile. I remember feeling that way about Thomas. He was so…important. And he cared so much about everyone. He cared so much about being a good person. I admired that. And I wanted it. Because you know… Mom always made it sound like marriage was the most important thing. The absolute most important thing for us to do was marry a good man. So that we didn't end up in the same situation as her. And also, to not have sex before we got married so we wouldn't get pregnant."

Rachel laughed. "I failed at that." She rolled and folded another layer.

"You did?"

A sly smile curved her sister's lips. "I slept with Jacob

before we got married. I couldn't help myself, in spite of Mom's pregnancy fearmongering."

"Well, I didn't sleep with Thomas. I waited. We both did. It was important to him. And it was important to me for the same reason. But that's the thing. I loved that about him. I loved that he could wait. I loved that he had restraint. And that he wanted to do the right thing. I knew that if I could just marry him that my life would be perfect. That it would be everything that I was supposed to be. Rachel, I knew that it was the right thing. But somewhere along the way he quit smiling at me. And then he quit looking at me. And I realized that I lived with a stranger."

"Did he hurt you?"

"Yes. Not with his fists. And, no, he didn't sleep with another woman, but he… I thought I lost the ability to even feel the kind of joy that I used to feel when he looked at me. I tried to talk to him, but you can't talk to someone who isn't going to talk back. You can't fix what someone else doesn't think is broken. And I… I felt that thing again. When I met Michael."

"Michael," Rachel said. The word had a strange weight to it. Anna looked over at her sister and saw that the tips of her ears were red.

It reminded her that even though they were talking now, it didn't mean everything was fine. It didn't mean it was a smooth path.

"Yes. He made me feel beautiful, Rachel. And everything he did felt so good. And he hasn't called me since Thomas walked in on us."

"Thomas walked in on you?" Rachel's movements stilled again.

It was Anna's turn for her ears to turn red. "Not like

that. But we were…just coming out of the bedroom. Thomas was looking for me…

"It was awful. But I can't go back, and on some level that's a relief. If I had taken it to the edge, or if it had happened in a different way, then I would have… It wouldn't have gone this far. He would have wanted to fix it and I don't know what I would have done. But now… There's no choice, is there?"

"You said that you didn't… That he didn't…"

"Oh, are you talking about the sex?"

"Explain that to me," Rachel said.

Anna shook her head. "I mean, I can. But there's nothing really to explain. It became more and more infrequent, until…basically nothing. Not anymore. And I wanted to fix it, and he told me that I cared too much about the things of this world." She huffed a breath and tried to do something about the shards of glass in her chest. "What does that say about me, Rachel? I would go to bible studies, and the women would all be giggling, and talking about their husbands wanting sex even though they were tired, and acting like it was the worst thing in the world that they wanted that from them. I knew that whatever Thomas was doing wasn't some Christian, pious purity thing. I knew my sex drive wasn't a sin. I knew it because I was surrounded by women in the church who had happy, healthy marriages with lots of sex. And I… Look, he never wanted it all that much. What I thought was restraint prior to marriage turned out to be…disinterest. But it became nothing. *Nothing.* Everybody is always going on and on about how much men want sex, and how much they *need* it. And if he doesn't, then what's wrong with me?"

She'd never told anyone else this. And the words felt

like a rope thrown out to Rachel. And Anna could only hope she'd grab on, that she'd let it connect them.

"I… I don't know what to say."

Roll. Fold. Roll. Fold.

"I understand that me standing here and complaining to you about a lack of sex is… Maybe it's not fair. Because I get that you had to make a marriage work without it."

"It's different," Rachel said, and the vehemence in her voice told Anna she'd grabbed onto that rope. "It had nothing to do with the lack of care, or lack of interest in me. And I know that. It was medically difficult. And then… not happening. And, yeah, on a physical level I miss that. But I missed it from *him*. Because I missed the closeness that we had. The love that we have between us. It's because we had intimacy that I miss it, and I don't just miss it in a general sense."

"Well, I wanted it. And when Michael showed up, and he started flirting with me… For the first time I thought maybe I *wasn't* the problem."

"Why didn't you talk to any of your friends about this?"

"How?" She turned to face Rachel fully. "How do you talk to any of your friends from church about how their pastor won't…? That I feel like he doesn't love me. That I'm so lonely, and my entire heart feels like a dry desert. Michael showed up and it was like water refreshing me, reviving me. For the first time in so long."

She turned away again, staring intently at the pastry dough. "I wanted to keep it to myself. I didn't want to talk to anyone about it, because I knew that what I was doing was wrong. I knew if I talked to one of my friends, or to you, you'd ask me why I had to do it *this* way. Why I didn't get counseling or leave him before I slept with someone else. I just wanted it so much. I decided not to care. I decided to go ahead and keep it to myself. I talked to everyone at church less and less. I talked to you less and less. Because I didn't want anything to come up that might make me stop. That might turn me away from the path that I was on, because I knew it would end with me having sex with him. And I wanted to. I *really* wanted to."

A tear slid down her cheek. "I'm so angry at Michael for abandoning me. And that's what you get, isn't it? I am the cautionary tale. I'm the scarlet woman from our child-hood. I destroyed a marriage, even if it was mine. And I was punished for it. I'll never be able to go down into town again. I'll never be able to look anyone in the face. I lost my husband and I lost my lover, too. So there you go."

They went on working for a while after that in silence. The only sounds in the kitchen the buzz of the fridge and the rolling pins.

"It's funny," Rachel said slowly. "I had kind of the same thought that you did. That I would marry a good man who would never leave me, and everything would be fine. And he did leave. He didn't choose it, but he's gone all the same."

Rachel cleared her throat and continued. "Marrying a good man certainly didn't insulate me from pain. I'm so thankful for the life that I had with him. And it was stu-pid of me to get bound up in being jealous of you. But I thought…a good marriage was a good marriage. The same as any. I said the other day that our vows were the same, but the men weren't. It isn't the same."

Rachel shook her head definitively, and she reached out, putting her hand on Anna's arm. "The way things were with Jacob and me… It wasn't a sacrifice in the way people think it was. He showed me that men could be good. And he showed me that a good father could make such a difference. Emma had the best father, Anna. I'm so thankful for that. For him. He made me believe in love in a way that I didn't before. I didn't want to fall in love head over heels, because I didn't want to get hurt. Mom might have made you afraid of passion causing you pain. She made me afraid of love. But I couldn't resist him. Not at all. I was head over heels the minute that he asked me out in math class. And not just because he was more interesting in comparison to the subject." She took her hand away from Anna's arm and wiped her forearm over her cheek, dashing away a tear. "He made me something better. He took a girl who was scared of emotion, and he made me embrace it, all the way to the end. And I am hurt. I'm heartbroken. I don't know what to do with this new shape my life has taken. I can't regret the time we had together. I can't even look at it as a sad ending. Not when it was such a happy life."

Anna's heart felt crushed. A martyr. She'd thought of Rachel as a martyr. And she'd forgotten about love. Because if she'd had her marriage, and had to end up caring for Thomas…she would have resented him. Resented being stuck. "Jacob was a good man."

"Thomas isn't," Rachel said. "What he did to you at the church… It was wrong. What he did to you during your marriage was wrong."

Something in Anna rejected that, too. "I don't know what Thomas is. I think Thomas isn't a good husband. But I don't think he's a bad man. That's another thing, Rachel, and I haven't had the words for it until now. I was afraid to talk to anyone about it because I know that Thomas has changed people's lives for the better. And…a person doesn't have to be perfect to be useful. To be used. And he has been. His books have…changed people. He's brought people out of the depths of despair. He's taught them how to hope. He's made them feel closer to God. He's made them feel joy. And what was I going to do? Talk about his failures? Invalidate what he's done?"

"I don't know," Rachel said. "But...making yourself the bad guy can't be the solution, either."

"I don't know what I am."

She'd thought her sister was a martyr. Maybe *she'd* been the martyr the whole time.

She felt like the kitchen had been turned over on its head, but the dough, the rolling pins and everything else were right in the same position.

"Well," Rachel said finally, "there's nothing stopping you from being whoever you want."

That felt like a revelation, and it washed over her like a wave. Maybe she had been the martyr. But that didn't matter now. Because now wasn't the end.

"Isn't that the whole point of a new beginning?" Rachel asked. "Starting again?"

"I'm afraid," Anna said.

Because now she felt like she was staring at the horizon line of the ocean, at the angry waves, knowing she was going to have to cross them. Knowing she was staring at vast, endless possibilities that she would have to work through, and it was going to be hard.

"Me, too," Rachel said. She seemed to consider something for a long moment. "We don't have to be alone in this, though. We're both here at the same time."

Anna looked down at her hands, down at the dough. "We are."

"We're sisters," Rachel said, the words coming slowly, as if she was testing them out. "And we're both still here, alive and...if not well, then just alive. We didn't miss a chance at having a relationship, a friendship. We don't have to be alone."

"Okay," Anna said. "Okay."

"You chose to start again. I didn't. But in the end, it doesn't matter, because what we have to do is the same. So now we have to…find that life."

She stared down at the puff pastry. They'd rolled and folded and created layer after layer after they'd talked.

They'd found new layers with each other.

"Mom never wanted us to be heartbroken. Not like she was." Anna didn't know how she would begin to repair the relationship with her mother.

"Of course she didn't. She didn't want us to be hurt. Life happens. We can't be protected from it forever."

"And you would be so relaxed about that when it came to Emma?"

"No. I'm not relaxed about anything when it comes to Emma."

Anna smiled slyly. "Well, you let her have her job."

"Yes. I did. One point to me," Rachel said.

"Yes. And no more, not if you're going to keep handling the dough like that."

"You're so critical."

"And you're going to make sure it doesn't laminate properly."

"Well, you can put the failed croissants in a basket and label them Rachel's Follies."

Suddenly, Anna wished it were that simple. That she could bundle up the misshapen aspects of her life and put them in a labeled basket.

Anna's Follies.

But she was living them instead.

Rachel was right. It was the chance to start over. And she really wouldn't go back. Not even if she could.

So starting over was what they were going to have to do.

She was just glad that she didn't have to do it alone.

And maybe just like dough, and just like her relationship with her sister, it wasn't about sailing toward new, infinite horizons.

Maybe it was just about making things better. Layer by layer.

12

Sometimes the right thing isn't the fun thing.
But the fun thing hurts later on. Still, if he's
cute enough the fun thing is worth it.

—FROM THE DIARY OF SUSAN BRIGHT, AUGUST 1961,
DURING HER TIME AT THE CAPE HOPE LIGHTHOUSE

WENDY

It was much more common for a guest to stay at the inn
for two or three days than it was for them to linger for two
weeks. John Hansen was lingering. And he made Wendy
feel like she was on the verge of a hot flash, which she
hadn't had for more than ten years.

It was strange, being exposed to a man who made her
feel quite this off-kilter.

When it came to swearing off men, Wendy was a champion. She had been hurt so badly by Anna and Rachel's
father that it had been the simplest thing in the world to
simply shut down that part of herself and focus on raising her girls and running her business.

She was attracted to John, though.

Wednesday morning he had been the only guest, and Wendy had been the only one preparing the food.

She felt a little bit guilty that she had time to think. Time away from the tension between everyone. Emma and Rachel, Anna and Rachel, Anna and herself.

Sometimes there were moments where they were the family they'd started as. Where they could bake and chatter and laugh. And then the reality of where they were at now would creep in and shatter the solidarity.

They did all of their bread baking at the beginning of the week, often prepared the crab cakes for a whole month and then put them in the freezer. And that meant that on days like today, Wendy didn't need any backup in the kitchen.

But it also meant that she was alone with her problematic guest.

Who was as polite as a man could be, and hadn't made any untoward advances or anything like that.

No. All of the untoward everything was inside of her.

"Another cup of coffee?" she asked.

He was taking breakfast at the small, round table in the lavender parlor. The small table with the lace tablecloth and floral china set on top of it seemed almost ridiculously fussy in front of this no-nonsense man.

He had a directness to his manner that suggested he was not a man who much cared for lace.

But he also hadn't complained.

She suspected it would go against his sense of chivalry to do so. He had that air about him, as well. A man who cared deeply about manners and the right way of doing things.

Rare, in other words.

He was a very nice break from real time. A piece of

this place she loved brought into the present. A chance to feel something other than grief or sadness, worry over the present state of the family.

"Yes, please," he said. "Would it be all right if you set down for a spell?"

"Well, I was planning on giving you a history talk once you were finished with breakfast."

"Does that mean you can't sit now?"

The thing was, she could. She had one last course to bring out for him, a slice of cake with cherries baked into it, and there was no reason that she couldn't sit.

Except that… It would be crossing the line between innkeeper and guest. Not that she was inherently opposed to that. If he had been a pleasant woman whom she enjoyed speaking with, she would have done so without thought. Or a pleasant couple.

Truly, if he had been a man that she didn't feel attracted to, she would have done it.

But she did feel attracted to him. And that was the problem.

"Have a cup of coffee," he said.

It was a pleasant-enough-sounding invitation, except it wasn't actually an invitation so much as a command, and she should be annoyed by it.

But she was hard-pressed to be annoyed by him.

"All right," she said. "Let me go get your final course."

She returned with cake. Two pieces of it, because if she was going to sit, then she was going to eat.

She couldn't pretend that she was doing it for any reason other than that she wanted to. Couldn't pretend that she was trying to be polite because he was a guest and he had asked her to sit.

If she'd been a younger woman with slightly less self-awareness, then perhaps she could have.

But she was too old for games like that. Even in her own head.

She was sitting with him because he was handsome. Because she wanted to be near him.

Because even though she was never going to allow anything to happen between the two of them, it was nice to have someone look at her like he might want something to happen.

She'd spent years avoiding situations like this, but she didn't feel vulnerable anymore. Didn't feel like she would lose her sense of self over a man.

What was the harm in a flirtation?

"I'm sure you must find it strange that I am lingering around here by myself," he said.

"I don't ponder the strangeness of guests overly much. If I did, I wouldn't get anything done."

He chuckled. "I bet you have some stories."

"Working in hospitality for this long… Yes. A lot of stories."

"And they are?"

"Honestly, it's difficult to think of only one. But what I will tell you is that no matter where people come from, no matter what they do for a living, how much money they have, what corner of the world they're from… People are strange. That is consistent." She lifted her coffee cup to her lips. "And half of all guests leave a pair of underwear under the bed."

That earned her a laugh. "Really?"

"Yes. I'm not sure why. Or how they don't think to look. Because I assume that if they lose that many pairs of underwear at my inn, then they lose them everywhere. And you would think they would start checking."

"Well, I will be sure to check for my underwear beneath my bed before I go."

Her face got hot and she took a bite of cake, resenting that he'd somehow managed to make her blush. She didn't even know she could blush anymore.

"Good plan."

"I told you that Olaf Hansen was an ancestor of mine," he said.

"Yes. You did mention."

"Well, this is all news to me. You see, my father had a falling-out with his father. And as a result, all my family history was basically lost. There is no one for me to ask. And I'm discovering that there's this whole rich history to my family I didn't know about. That when we came to this country, Oregon was where we landed. I'm fascinated by it. And maybe I'm trying to feel closer to those people that came before me because I'm getting older. Because my father dying kind of drew a line beneath my own mortality."

"I can understand that," Wendy said softly. "It's a difficult thing, those family grudges. I was estranged from my own mother, and she died without us ever fixing it. I just tried to make our own history here. Because… My family history is filled with spite and judgment."

"For all I know my father's was the same. But I'm curious to know the history of my family." He paused for a moment. "Sorry about your mother."

"It was a choice I made," she said. "A choice not to live beneath her judgment. We make the choices we have to. But it doesn't mean they don't have unintended consequences. Like you not knowing where you came from.

And, of course, those things become more important... Now."

"I find that I tend to wonder a lot more about where we came from. You know, I know where I'm going. We're all going there. But... I don't know, something about that makes me want to feel more anchored to the past."

"I have some letters," Wendy said. "Some letters and diary entries from Jenny Hansen. Did you know she was a mail-order bride?"

"Can't say as I did."

"We keep all the walls here pastel in her honor. The lavender parlor has been lavender for over one hundred years. We've freshened the paint up, but the color is the same. Jenny hated the gray Oregon weather, having come up from California to marry Olaf. She convinced the Coast Guard to allow her to paint it. And you know how hard it is to convince the government to do anything. She was something, was Jenny."

"Well, that stubbornness certainly runs in my family," he said.

"I have pictures." She stood up and went to the small antique table that housed an old sewing machine and the stereoscope, with specially made photos of the lighthouse. She picked up the photo album, and took a seat next to John. "This, here," she said, opening it up, "is a photo of Olaf and Jenny on their wedding day."

She looked up at John, and was struck by the resemblance between him and his ancestor. Oh, they weren't carbon copies, but there was something there that she could see. Similar lines and angles, and the way that he held himself.

In the photo, the man was wearing a dark jacket and

hat, reminiscent of a naval uniform, and holding the hand of a woman in a white dress.

"'Keeper Olaf Hansen,'" John said, reading, "'and his bride Jenny. Nineteen hundred.'"

"That's her. She was unhappy for a while. A long while. But from what I can gather of her diary...that changed."

"What do you suppose changed?"

"I—I think they fell in love."

"Well, that would be a nice story."

"I can get you some pages from the diary if you'd like. A lot of it is down at the museum, but some of it we have here. You can go over them while you're here. It's your family. You have a right to the history."

"I'd like that," he said, looking at her, his blue eyes intent.

She suddenly wished it was that easy.

Just falling in love.

Sadly, in her life it never had been. Or for Anna and Rachel. And as simple as she made it sound when she spoke of Jenny, she knew that it hadn't been for Jenny, either. It had been change and sacrifice and compromise.

All things that Wendy hadn't had to do in a very long time.

Things she didn't want to do.

No. She didn't want that.

But it made her ache a little bit when she looked at him.

"Well," Wendy said, standing, "I had better get to doing the dishes."

"I can help, if you like."

"No," she said quickly. "It's a...certified kitchen. You need a food-handlers card." He didn't really need one to help her with dishes, but she didn't want him back there. She needed a break from him. And she certainly didn't need him acting gentlemanly and confusing her feelings even further.

"Suit yourself. I'll be checking out tomorrow. I'm hoping that I can come back soon."

"Well, we always like return guests."

"Well, I hope that you look forward to me returning, too," he said.

"I'll set the diary pages on the table for you. You can go over them this afternoon."

"Appreciate that."

He looked at her for a long moment, and Wendy felt a blush rising in her cheeks again.

And then she turned and ran like she was fleeing temptation.

But she tried to pretend it was just that she had dishes to do.

EMMA

"Can you run this across the street?"

Emma looked at her boss. Then looked around. "Me?"

The first month at her new job had gone by quickly. It was a relief, especially after the weirdness that she experienced every day at school. People were so strange with her. So careful.

She was thankful for Catherine, who was real, and normal, and who had been with her the whole way through the journey of her father's illness, and seemed to be able to handle his death a lot better.

What a stupid thing.

That complete strangers couldn't cope with her father's death. Because that was what it seemed like.

That they were uncomfortable with her because someone she loved had died. That they expected *her* to be un-comfortable all the time.

It clung to her like a film and made her feel separate from everyone around her. At first that had been fine, but now she just felt…outside. And she didn't like it.

She had messed up a test, and a teacher had been nice to her. Sympathetic. Had said that it was *understandable*.

But that wasn't true, and it wasn't fair. If people didn't know her, they wouldn't be okay with her failing at a test or at something basic, just because of her circumstances.

She didn't want to be held to some kind of weird low standard just because something in her life was sad.

There was no sanctuary, no escape.

Except for at the diner.

She liked the sound of food cooking, loved the smells. The chatter of the people. The customers ran the gamut, from friendly to absolutely terrible, and she even enjoyed that.

There was something about dealing with a grumpy old man who didn't bother to smile, not even at her, that made her feel…*human*.

It made her feel like a normal person.

And then, of course, there was Luke.

Luke came in and got dinner at the diner almost every evening.

He would walk across the street from the mechanic shop, in a pair of battered, dirty jeans, and a faded T-shirt, even though it was cold out, and lean over the counter, getting an order to go.

And she would watch him.

Sometimes he would catch her watching him, and then she looked away quickly. Eventually, she started trying to smile, because she realized the looking away quickly was not only suspicious, but it was also weird.

And so it went on like that, for the whole month.

And now Adam wanted her to take Luke his lunch order.

Adam's face was too neutral, which meant he was probably well aware of how she felt about Luke. "Yeah, Luke wasn't able to get away for lunch, so he said he needed some food, and he was going to come pick it up, but I think he got caught on the job, so I thought it might be nice to run it over to him."

That was nice. And it also meant that she was going to have to be face-to-face with the object of her very distant crush.

He'd been an escape. A distant, easy fixation. And this was about to bring him into reality.

"Okay," she said, taking the bag and whipping out the door, letting it close hard behind her.

She moved quickly and decisively across the street, looking both ways as she did. Because if she stopped and even took one breath, she was going to get all weird.

It was crazy, how handsome she thought he was. With his dark hair that was always sticking up at odd angles, like he'd run his fingers through it. His dark brown eyes, and his square jaw. When she looked at him, sometimes her heart pounded so hard against her breastbone it made her feel dizzy.

She understood the term *lovesick* now. Because she definitely felt a little bit sick when he was near.

She'd never felt this way about any of the guys at school. They were all too narrow and awkward, and she was awkward enough for all involved and didn't need anyone else contributing to it, thanks.

But Luke…

Luke wasn't awkward at all.

She wished that she could be like Catherine, who didn't seem to get all that bothered about boys, even when she liked one. If they didn't like her, she just sort of shrugged and moved on.

Emma did not feel like she was in a shrug-and-move-on place.

She walked into the front office of the mechanic shop and saw that it was empty. She moved cautiously toward the side door that led to the actual garage and peered inside. She could see legs sticking out from under a car, legs that she was sure were Luke's and didn't belong to the owner of the garage, Dusty, who was round in the middle and had stick-thin legs that pointed outward, in opposite directions from each other.

She cracked the door open slowly. "I—I brought food."

The legs moved, and then his whole body emerged as he pushed forward on the roller board he was lying on and maneuvered himself out from under the car. He had streaks of oil or some other car-related something on his face.

And she had never seen anyone more handsome.

"You didn't have to do that," he said.

"I did. My boss…asked me to. Not that I wouldn't have done it just because. But in this instance… I work for him. And he told me to. So. I did have to."

That was too many words.

"Well," he said. "Thank you."

"Busy today?"

"Dusty is laid up at home with a broken leg. So it's going to be a hell of a couple weeks."

"Oh." She frowned. "Does no one else work here?" She

was a little embarrassed that she had to ask that, but her awareness of this place boiled down to Luke.

"No," he said."

She handed the bag to him, and he took it. "That's... too bad."

"No kidding. But gotta keep overhead down."

He opened up the bag and set it down on a workbench, then sat down on a stool. There was a cheeseburger and he took it out, biting into it.

She grimaced.

."What?"

"You didn't even wash you hands," she said.

He huffed a laugh and took another bite. "What's your name?"

"Me? Emma."

He swallowed. "Luke," he said.

As if she didn't know. But she wasn't going to say that she knew.

"I know."

What was wrong with her?

A smile quirked the corners of his mouth. "I would offer you a French fry. But I didn't wash my hands."

"That's okay. I kind of have...limitless French-fry access."

He shook his head. "What a life."

"Are you going to come for dinner tonight, too?" she asked.

"Probably," he said. "I'm never going to get all this done if I don't put in some late hours."

"You always eat dinner at J's."

"Mostly."

"No one's waiting for you to come home for dinner?"

"Nope," he said, stuffing another fry into his mouth.

She wanted to ask more questions. Why he lived by himself. Why he didn't have a girlfriend. *If* he didn't have a girlfriend. Where his family was. Why he was here all the time, and why, if there was no one here to wait for him for dinner, did he live in Sunset Bay at all, when he could have gone anywhere else.

Cars broke everywhere, after all.

But she didn't have an excuse for staying and chatting with him, and she had to get back to work.

"Maybe I'll see you later," she said. "I have to go."

"I've been working late all week," he said. "Do you work Friday night?"

She was supposed to go home Friday night and help with dinner at the inn. Their inaugural dinner, which was fully booked.

"Yeah," she said. "I'll be here."

"Maybe you can bring my food over after your shift ends? If that's not too much to ask. And bring something for yourself?"

She froze. Was he...asking her out in a very strange way? Or was he just asking her to be a food-delivery person who lingered?

She didn't have any idea. So the only thing to do was ask, since she'd already revealed that she knew him and scolded him for not washing his hands. It wasn't like she was knocking it out of the park here.

"You...want to have dinner with me?" she asked.

"Yeah. It gets kind of old eating alone."

"Yeah," she said. "I'd like that. But only if you wash your hands."

A slow smile crossed his face. "I think I can handle that."

When she turned to head back to the diner, she could

barely breathe, and her hands were shaking. She had no idea how she was going to make it through the rest of her shift. Or the whole day tomorrow.

And she needed to come up with some excuse to tell her mom, or anyone in her family for that matter. Luke was hers. Her crush on him was hers. And whatever might happen next was hers, too.

She needed something. Something separate and safe from all the tangled, snarled things in her real life and her family.

As soon as she got back inside, she sneaked into the back and grabbed her jacket, pulling her phone out of the pocket. And she fired off a quick text to Catherine.

More secrets. More little lies.

But if her mom thought she was having dinner with Catherine, it would only be easier for her.

Luke hadn't looked at her like she was sad. He didn't treat her like an alien. He wanted to have dinner.

She wasn't going to worry about anything else. Not when something was finally going right.

13

Surprise inspection. We were warned by the keepers in Yachats they were coming. Rose and Naomi helped me push the laundry into the parlor closet. We locked it and when they went to check the closet, we claimed we'd lost the key some weeks earlier. When the Coast Guard left, we laughed so hard our sides hurt.

—FROM THE DIARY OF JENNY HANSEN, FEBRUARY 20, 1900

RACHEL

"I bet you're so glad to be back," Rachel said, stripping the linens off the bed. She looked around carefully to make sure there were no hidden undergarments anywhere.

"Sure," Anna said cheerfully. "I missed vacuuming up beetles."

It was a cleaning day, and a bread-baking day, and Rachel and Anna were busily straightening guest rooms.

Rachel had been a widow for a little more than two months. Cleaning felt like a gift next to that reality, as did planning dinners at the lighthouse.

Even ladybugs felt like a decent distraction.

Anna was standing up on a chair, her vacuum pointed at the light fixture as she did her best to deal with the influx of ladybugs.

Rachel remembered being a kid and thinking it was mean to dispatch the ladybugs in such a way, but over the years they'd become the bane of the inn, and while in small numbers they could be somewhat charming, when they got to this point, it wasn't charming at all.

Any animal in large quantities was unsettling.

A collection of ladybugs all over a guest room wasn't the best look.

"Well, I missed having you here. This reminds me of when we used to clean the rooms to try and make an extra couple of dollars when we were kids. We were severely underpaid."

"That's the point of using family," Anna said.

"I suppose so."

Over the past two months she and Anna had begun strengthening their relationship. Their honest conversation that had happened over pastry making weeks ago had set the tone, and things had been easier between them since.

They were sisters. Friction still existed, along with moments of perfect ease. But the balance of good and tough had started to shift.

"I wish that Emma were here," Rachel said. "I mean, she would still be in school now, even if she was working here. But... I want to spend this time with her. Things are going to change after she graduates. And I'm not ready for any of it."

"That's what happens, though," Anna said. "They grow up. And, hey, at least she's not obsessed over some boy like the two of us were."

"I can't even think about that. Her birthday is coming

up. By the time I was her age I was already with Jacob. *Having sex* with Jacob."

"Yeah, better not think about that."

That comment brought Rachel right back to what it had been like to be seventeen. Desperately in love, giddy with the prospect of being naked. Having his hands on her.

That was a bygone era. The kind of thing that only came with youth and innocence in a new relationship. It had faded a long time ago for the two of them. But then... Then they hadn't been able to have physical intimacy at all. Not in that way. And she'd been fine with it.

There was no point in... There was no point in missing it now.

She had been focused when she'd been with Jacob. Focused on everything they did have. And it was only now that he was gone she was starting to think about all the things they hadn't had. It didn't feel fair. It felt disloyal.

"What?" Anna asked, stepping down from the chair, the ladybugs thoroughly vanquished.

"Just thinking about Emma."

"Are you?" It was clear from the look on her sister's face that she didn't quite believe her.

Rachel hesitated. "No. I'm thinking about me. But it's stupid. There's no point to it. Not to any of it."

"What? What's going on?"

"I just..." She blew out a breath, trying to ease the knot of tension that had built in her chest. "I keep thinking about what you said to me. About the way that Michael made you feel. I haven't thought about my body in a long time. I haven't thought about being beautiful. I've been comfortable. I've been with a man who loved me, and he always... He always made me feel beautiful. And it's hard to explain the way that our relationship changed, because I feel like I'm saying it was lacking something, but it wasn't. It was all that it could've been. And I never dwelled on what we didn't have. But now I'm starting to feel like I... Like I miss it. Because I could have it. I mean, that's the thing. When I was with Jacob, I had Jacob. Now that I don't have him—"

"It makes sense," Anna said. "You miss what you don't have. All that you don't have. Because you don't have anything to fill the void."

"Exactly. And Emma would be a great distraction. I don't like thinking about me. I don't like thinking about my feelings. It was easier in so many ways to just throw myself into being a caregiver. Then it wasn't about me."

"And how bad you felt."

"I guess," Rachel said. She laughed. "God knows it's not because I'm actually selfless."

"I don't know," Anna said. "You're about the most self-less person I know."

Rachel shook her head. "That's the thing. I'm not. I'm just a person." She saw a ladybug crawling on the wall, and she moved her hand, letting the little thing crawl up on her finger. She opened up the window, the old thing sticking as she shoved it upward. The view of the ocean was below, and the mountains that curved around the inlet—stunning. She let the little bug out onto the roof. "This one gets to live."

"But if it comes back, I'm just going to vacuum it up."

"Do what you have to in pursuit of debugging," Rachel said. "Anyway. It's not as simple as me being a good person, you're right. There was a blessing in being busy, and having something to do. There's a reason that I never hired someone to come care for him at home. Better to stay busy. To focus on everything that was right there,

Emma and Jacob, and it kept me fulfilled. Even though my heart was breaking, I was fulfilled. My life was full. Now I'm sitting around thinking about me. And I want to feel pretty."

The admission caused a whole avalanche of terror to rain down inside her. "Anna," she said. "I don't know what to do. I don't want to go out and find a man to have sex with. A new man. The very idea horrifies me."

"It's not really that horrifying," Anna said. The corners of her mouth kicked up into a smile. "Rachel, you're—you're a woman and you're beautiful and don't you want to be able to feel that?"

"I mean, I can feel it on my own," she said dryly. "I've had to a great many times over the years."

Anna cackled. "Well, you and me both. But don't you think it would be nice for you to…be with someone who could take care of some things? At least…climax things?"

"I love Jacob. I loved being married to him. But the idea of being in a relationship again makes me want to crawl into that bed and sleep forever. Ladybugs be damned."

"You don't have to be in a relationship with someone to have sex with them," Anna said.

"Speaking from your vast experience?"

"Well, no. Okay, I didn't go into my… I thought I was in love with him," she said. "I thought he was going to take me away from Thomas and marry me. And I would have gone. I still wanted to get married. Even though I hated my marriage. That's still… In my head that's the inevitable end."

Rachel sagged, feeling defeated. By everything. If the one champion of casual sex in the whole room couldn't even claim an experience of it, there was no hope. "I can't imagine that. Getting married again. I don't want that."

"I don't think I do, either. But I don't know how to imagine... I want to be loved," Anna said. "I want to be loved in the way that I think I can be."

"I was loved," Rachel said, her voice hushed.

But she ignored the yawning cavern in her chest. Wouldn't it be nice to be loved again? Wouldn't it be nice to have it be different?

A man who could take care of her.

Her heart kicked violently against her breastbone. Guilt assaulted her. She couldn't think like that. She couldn't. It wasn't fair.

"You really want to never be loved again?"

"It's not that I don't want to be loved, it's that..." She swallowed. "I mean Mom has never dated anyone, has she?"

"Uh, yeah...no. I mean how many times did we watch her friends from town throw eligible single men at her while she destroyed them with a single look? Unless she has a layered secret life we know nothing about."

They exchanged a glance, and Rachel knew that both of them were thinking there was no way Wendy McDonald lived her life with secrets. She was too...her.

"I doubt Mom has dated," Anna said. "But she's also been bitter about Dad and everything for years. She's... held on to that. And I don't want to hold on to my past. I needed to get out of my marriage. I don't want to keep pieces of it with me."

Rachel felt... She didn't know. "I never let myself think about my life past him. I knew it would happen. I knew for a long time. I watched him die for years, Anna."

"I didn't let myself think about a different life for a long time. I didn't even tell myself I was unhappy. I hid it. So that I wouldn't...well, so that I wouldn't do what I did. And once I really looked at my life I knew I couldn't go on the same way I had been."

"Well, I know I can't. But doesn't loving someone mean… Doesn't it mean not moving on fully?"

"I have no idea," Anna said.

"That's not helpful at all."

Anna moved over to the window and moved the lace curtain, and revealed a clump of bugs. She wrinkled her nose. "Well, until then we can vacuum ladybugs. Endlessly."

"That seems like a poor substitute for sex."

"It's less complicated," Anna said.

Rachel looked around at her surroundings—her haven for all these years, her first job and her continued passion.

Yes. It was simple. Here in this bedroom, cleaning with her sister, things seemed manageable.

Maybe she should just be happy with manageable.

Heaven knew that there was less guilt involved.

WENDY

It had been over a month since John Hansen had left the inn, much to her relief. He unnerved her. Not because he was off-putting in any way.

That was the problem.

He wasn't off-putting at all. He was the best-looking man she'd seen in she didn't know how long, and he was also plainly interested in her.

And not just in *her*, but in the house. In its history.

Basically, in absolutely everything she cared about.

And that made him feel…dangerous.

She was fifty-seven years old. She should not be thinking about a man like that. Dangerous. Handsome.

And she shouldn't be…nervous around one.

She was way too jaded for that. She knew exactly how this sort of thing ended up.

She'd been happy enough in her life as it was for years. She'd wished, of course, that Jacob had been in better health. But she'd been surrounded by her family, her girls. Now it was all changing. Emma was going off to school. Anna and Rachel seemed to be finding a bond with each other, but Anna was still so distant from Wendy.

She tried to put it out of her mind as she knocked on the door with her elbow, her hands full of a cheese platter that she had made for the night's cribbage game.

She and a few of the other female business owners got together once a month to talk about business, town politics and everything else under the sun. Mostly it was an excuse to eat and laugh, and this was the first time she'd gone since Jacob's death three months earlier.

The group fluctuated and rotated, depending on the season, who was in town and who wasn't, who was busy and who wasn't.

As soon as Cynthia let her in, the woman who owned one of the jewelry stores in Old Town, Wendy could see that there were a few more than just their core group there tonight.

One of the younger women, Jo, who ran Fog coffee along with her husband, Nick, was there. She was in her early thirties, and had a nose ring and the sides of her head shaved, while the top was left long and black and glossy. She was the same age as Anna—Wendy assumed—but she didn't engender maternal feelings in Wendy. She was bright and sharp, and utterly unintimidated by anyone or anything.

In Wendy's past experiences, younger women were sometimes cowed by a group of older ones. But not Jo, who was always happy to lead a discussion on what it took to make nondairy yogurt at home, or how to brew your own kombucha. Which was something almost no one who came to these gatherings was ever going to do.

But they all smiled and nodded along, anyway.

Lisbeth, the owner of the yarn shop, was there. She was always popular, as she tended to bring overstock to share around the table.

Wendy didn't often knit anymore, but it was something she had once enjoyed doing, and she'd taught her girls how as well, so she was always happy to take extra yarn and hoard it, even if she didn't have anything pressing to make with it.

She set down the platter on the table. "Hi, everyone," she said.

She received a round of cheerful greetings from the group.

Wendy made a beeline for the wine, which was already open and sitting out on Cynthia's sideboard.

Cynthia's house was like an architectural representation of her as a woman. Bold, eclectic and deliberately unfussy. Her business, her home, her wild black hair and the locally made jewelry she wore all seemed to flow together. She was one of the most truly *her* people Wendy had ever known.

She could be bold, and outspoken, but with Cynthia it was always genuine and never from a place of manipulation.

She'd developed a good friendship with Cynthia over the years. Though, like with everyone in town, she talked mainly about her life as if it had started the moment she'd come here. But it had been more than thirty years now. It was the only life that really mattered.

When Wendy saw Lillian Chase, who owned the little children's-clothing store, Peapod, she felt a kick of concern.

Lillian was very involved in Sunset Church, and where Cynthia was open-arms and authenticity, Lillian was narrow, polished reserve. Wendy had a feeling genuine conversation sometimes hit her perfectly coiffed hair and bounded right off. Because of all the hair spray, or maybe the real reason was that her heart was smooth and polished, too. With no space for love or compassion to slip in and take hold.

But then, the owner of Sunset Bay Coffee Company, Natalie, was involved in the church as well, and she gave Wendy the brightest smile imaginable upon entry.

So it wasn't really fair to assume that it would be difficult with people from the church.

But, then, that wasn't the real issue. It was Lillian's involvement in the church, plus Lillian being who she was. It made Wendy feel on guard.

Lillian seemed to find new heights in the falling down of others, as if she saw an opportunity to step on the back of someone who stumbled and raised herself up higher.

Natalie wasn't like that at all.

"Is there any business gossip?" Wendy asked.

"Pico's is closing," Cynthia said, tapping brightly painted nails against her wineglass. "It's a shame."

She didn't actually think Cynthia thought it was a shame, as the store had crossover competition with Cynthia. They weren't a jewelry shop, but an eclectic mix of different local goods.

They'd only been there for a couple of years.

It was Wendy's experience that most people didn't

know how to get through those first years in a town like Sunset Bay.

They didn't understand that you were going to have to lose a lot of money before you could find a groove. Before you could figure out how to cover the lean months, and live for Christmas, and summer, and those times that brought an influx of people to town.

There was just a limit to the amount of local people who were going to stop in on a regular basis and buy clothing at a boutique store, when they could go down the road from the cute little walkable tourist community and buy things cheaper in a big box store.

They settled in and began the game, conversation continuing lightly between moves.

"So," Lillian said, her blue eyes sharp and cold, like fractured ice. "How are you, Wendy?"

The words didn't sound light, or casual. And the fact of the matter was, she hadn't asked them when Wendy had come in, so it was clear that this was a buildup to something.

The thing about small towns was that everybody wasn't inherently nice. They were territorial, and the connections ran deep, like roots of old-growth trees into the soil. Or blackberry vines. You might see the plant on one side of the street, but the roots could extend all the way across, originating from another place entirely.

She had learned to navigate sticky situations over the years as a result of these realities.

And she could sense when words had more weight to them than they should.

"Well enough," Wendy said. "The loss of Jacob has been hard. He was a good man. We all miss him. Rachel is doing as well as can be expected. And Emma has a job in town—I'm sure you've seen her."

"I wasn't even thinking of that," Lillian said. "Of course, that's been difficult. But after what Anna did… Honestly, Wendy, I think the way that you've been showing your face about town is brave. Poor Thomas."

Lillian shook her head and clucked her tongue. The divide of reactions across the long table was sharp and stark, and would have been funny if it wasn't Wendy at the other end of Lillian's verbal sword.

The reactions were either total disapproval, interest, or a strange, squishy sympathy that Wendy didn't like any more than she liked the interest.

"Anna's life is her own business, and she's my daughter whatever happened," Wendy said, hoping that would put the matter to rest.

"I mean, we all know what happened to you, Wendy," Lillian continued. "Your husband had an affair, that's why you had to come here in the first place and start over. I can't imagine that it's been easy to watch Anna follow in his footsteps, after all the good work that you've done in this community, after the reputation that you've built. And after the way that you were hurt by behavior like that. It's almost a crime against you."

A chasm opened up inside of Wendy's chest. No. This was not supposed to be what her fresh start had brought her girls.

Greater judgment? No, that had never been the idea behind coming here. It had never been the idea behind sharing the story of how she'd made it here.

It had been to prevent them from being judged. It had never been to bring extra judgment.

As a single mom, she had known that she had to get in

there and build up sympathy for her circumstances early, otherwise they would think that her daughters were from an immoral background, and the judgment that would've been heaped on them for Wendy's actions would have been…terrible.

So it had been important that everyone had known the story of her husband leaving her for another woman.

But it had never been for sympathy for Wendy. It had always been for freedom from baggage for her girls.

And here it was, an unexpected bag, being hurled through the air, aimed directly at Anna.

"I don't see what my past has anything to do with what Anna's done now. And I don't see how her behavior is any of your business. Are you friends with Thomas?"

Wendy had avoided this very thing ever since she'd moved here. Judgment. She'd done her best to keep her head down and be a hard worker. She'd turned away from confrontation whenever she could.

But that had been for her.

This was her daughter.

And when it came to defending Anna, Wendy wouldn't shy away.

"He's my pastor," the other woman said. "His pain matters to me."

"But you don't know him," Wendy said. "And it hit me when he announced what my daughter had done in church— without warning me, without warning Rachel or Emma, when he exposed all of us to censure like that, not to mention the way that it immediately cast Anna as the villain in the story—that I didn't know who he was. Because I would've told you that he would've never done that."

"What else was he supposed to do?" Lillian asked. "He didn't want there to be rumors."

"What is this, if not gossip?" Wendy asked. "You know one side of the story. Don't allow yourself to confuse someone being a pastor with being perfect. He was my son-in-law for fourteen years, and I can tell you that at the end of the day he's just a man like any other. Unless Anna has a chance to stand up in church and share her side of it…you won't know the whole truth, will you? Unless you're able to blend the two perspectives into one, then you really don't know what happened. Who can know the truth of a marriage from the outside of it?"

"You're taking this very personally," Lillian said. "I just wanted to express concern for you. Because I feel that you did work very hard to build up a reputation in the community that was beyond reproach… And now—"

"A reputation doesn't matter very much if you don't have your family. And I'm certainly not going to distance myself from my daughters because people can't stop from wagging their tongues down in town. I work with tourists, anyway, thank God. And I would rather see them. At least if this is what I get from the locals."

That seemed to wake up Cynthia. "That's enough, Lillian. I'm not here for this kind of talk in my house, or anywhere."

Wendy stood, shaking with rage, because it was too little, too late, as far as she was concerned. She went over to the sideboard, collecting her cheese platter. "This is coming back with me."

And before anyone could speak again, she swept out of the house and out onto the cold street.

Which felt warmer than that house, particularly after that. And she knew that it was likely shock that had prevented anyone but Cynthia from speaking up in her or Anna's defense, but it didn't much matter.

She had been left on her own to defend.

That, she supposed, was common enough.

And something she was used to.

She had forgotten. Somewhere along the way, she had forgotten.

That everything she was now had been to protect Rachel and Anna.

The way she had reacted to what Anna had done, even just on the inside... She had forgotten who she was. And she had let her fear over Anna being in pain transform into anger, into disappointment.

But nothing that she had, nothing that she was, mattered at all if she lost her relationship with Anna. If she let her own knee-jerk judgment affect the way she treated her daughter.

Because how, then, was she any better than Lillian? She wasn't. Her job wasn't to find out the facts and then decide how she felt after that. Her job was to stand by her daughter.

She was going to do just that.

She might eat this entire cheese tray by herself first, but she was going to do it.

She only hoped that she didn't have too much damage control to do.

That she didn't have too much damage to repair.

14

Inspection today. I negotiated with the Coast Guard
to allow me to paint the walls approved colors.
Mint and lavender. If I can't have sun outside,
I will make it in here.

—FROM THE DIARY OF JENNY HANSEN, MARCH 5, 1900

RACHEL

Rachel pulled into the parking lot of the plumbing store
and put her head on the steering wheel. It was rainy and
cold, as April—even late April—on the Oregon Coast
could decide to be at any given moment, and she didn't
want to be shopping for plumbing parts.

But you didn't always get what you wanted in life.

She was just sick of being the poster child for that particular truth.

She got out of the car and scurried quickly into the
store, dodging raindrops as she went.

They were having their first dinner at the inn tonight,
and people from town had made reservations, as well as
some current guests.

And, of course, they were having a plumbing issue.

Thank God it was a contained, standard sink-plumbing issue, and not an explosive, toilet-plumbing issue. Rachel was intimately acquainted with both.

Rachel, Wendy and Anna had not run an inn by themselves for this many years without learning how to fix things. From basic electrical to plumbing, they were all pretty accomplished in household repairs.

Repairs, epic stain removal—a hazard of working in the hospitality industry—and deep cleaning.

The house was old, and they'd fixed things when the occasion arose more times than Rachel could count.

Jacob had joked often throughout their marriage that his wife was handier than he was.

And it was true. She was.

Jacob had a flair for the artistic, a brilliant eye for photography, and his work had hung all over the different buildings on the property for years.

But he couldn't fix anything.

Rachel had to go buy a U joint, and it would be easy enough to repair the pipe under the sink, but it still necessitated a trip into town.

Willy's Electric and Plumbing was the primary source for projects, and Rachel liked them, because she knew them all, and they didn't try to explain to her how a project needed to be done.

Sometimes, when she went into the chain hardware store that was a little bit larger, and had more product on hand, a random, spotty-faced male employee would try to instruct her on how a job should be done. And she would have to stand there and grit her teeth and not say—to the pencil-slim boy who probably still lived with his parents—that she knew more than him.

She never had to explain that to Mark or Jerry or Willy himself.

The store itself was almost entirely the color of oatmeal, from the floor to the ceiling, with a cartoon mechanic painted on the wall the only real character in the place. The shelves were mainly utilitarian boxes, black drawers and open bins, with small signs indicating what you were looking at. Plumbing or electric. Sinks, toilets. Commercial and residential.

Rachel knew exactly what she was after.

She slipped into one of the aisles and found the U joint in a bin of parts, picked it up and headed toward the counter.

It was Mark Bronson who was working today. A pleasant-looking man with graying brown hair and a beard. He was husky and tall, with a ready smile and dark eyes. He was maybe five or six years older than Rachel, if she had to guess.

"Hi, Rachel," he said, his manner a little bit overly bright. "Haven't seen you in a while."

She braced herself for sympathy.

"Hi," she said. "And, yeah, I haven't had anything break in a while. So I'm not all that sorry I haven't been in a while."

He laughed. A little too loudly. "For sure. This it for you?"

"Yes," she said.

"Plumbing problem?"

She chuckled. "Yes."

"Look, I…"

Rachel's amusement died as she braced herself for a litany of apologies.

"I understand that it's a little bit quick. But the thing is, if I don't say anything now, someone else will get there before me. And you don't need to feel any pressure to say yes. But I just wanted to let you know… I'd like to go on a date with you sometime, if you are interested. When you're interested. If you ever are."

Rachel was completely stunned. Of all the things that she had expected… Well, she hadn't expected that.

"A date," she repeated.

"No pressure," he said. "And it doesn't have to be now. Or soon. But I wanted to give you my phone number. And you can call me. If you're ever ready."

Dating.

A *date.*

She was a little bit thrown by the fact that he wasn't here to offer sympathy, but actually had seen a woman, and not an object of pity. That he had seen *her*, and not a widow.

"I—I don't know," she said.

"Like I said. Don't feel you need to answer now. Or ever. But… I like you, Rachel. You're an interesting woman. I've always thought so. But, you know. Anyway, I have a feeling a lot of men feel the same way that I do. And it's only a matter of time… Probably a more appropriate amount of time before they ask you. But maybe when that happens, or maybe when you think…it might be nice to have dinner with someone, and just have a conversation, you'll think of me."

"Thank you," she said. "I… Sure. I'll take your phone number."

He wrote his personal number down on the back of a business card, and put it in the bag with the U joint.

"I could help with whatever plumbing problem you're having," he said.

"No," she said, a little too quickly. "I... I'm good at that. I've got that covered."

"All right. It was good to see you, anyway."

"Good to see you, too," she said.

She walked out of the store clutching the paper bag to her chest, her heart beating wildly against it.

A date.

That kept playing in her head over and over again as she got into her car and started it.

You were supposed to wait to go on a date for at least a year, she was sure of that.

Of course, she didn't know where she'd heard that.

Three and a half months wasn't a year. She wasn't really ready to...date someone. But it didn't horrify her. No, horror wasn't what she felt.

It was something of a revelation to have a man look at her and see a woman.

She'd been with Jacob since they were teenagers. Since before she'd had a child. Since before she had lines in her forehead that didn't go away even when her expression was relaxed. Since before she had a stomach that wasn't flat, and back when she'd had boobs that held themselves up even when she didn't have a bra on.

And she'd imagined that as beautiful as Jacob found her, he found her beautiful because he knew the *whole* her. That they had that history together that stretched back.

She'd seen all the Jacobs she'd known when she'd looked at him. The young, vibrant boy, the athletic teenager, the handsome man, the sick man. They'd all been there, all part of the person she loved.

So she'd believed him when he'd called her beautiful. But when he'd called her beautiful he'd seen all the Rachels she'd ever been.

Having a man who didn't look at her and see years of history, having a man who had no real emotional attachment to her at all look at her and think it would be good to go out with her... It did something to her that she didn't expect. And she liked it in a way that she didn't expect.

It had woken up something inside of her. Invigorated something.

But she could not go out with him now. The interest was sure nice, though.

She hadn't realized she had wanted it. Not when the thought of intimacy with another man scared her so much. But a dinner date...

She pondered that, on the drive to the house, through the tunnel that cut through the side of the mountain, and carried her over the bridge, to the winding private drive that led to the Lighthouse Inn. And all the way through her mundane plumbing project.

She made sure to push aside the thoughts, shook them away when she went into the kitchen.

It wasn't that it was a state secret that she'd been asked out, but she wanted to hold it close to herself for a while. She wasn't going to do anything with it, anyway.

But her grief belonged to everyone. And this was just hers. Like her conversations with Adam in J's. It was nice to have something that just belonged to her.

She breezed into the kitchen and greeted her mother and sister, then paused when she noticed that Emma wasn't there.

"Where's Emma?"

As if her daughter had sensed her concern floating over the airwaves, her phone buzzed. She took it out of her pocket and looked at the message she'd received.

Can I have dinner with Catherine?

She sent the return quickly. We have our dinner tonight.

I know. But Catherine's mom is making lasagna, and she invited me. And I haven't been over there since…

Okay, Rachel texted back, because she certainly didn't have the energy to argue with Emma about that. Emma deserved a break.

A chance to be happy.

Rachel did, too. A chance to move forward. Take a new step.

Maybe with Mark, maybe not.

But she held on to his number.

15

Things feel calmer now, and though we are
watchful, high above the water like this, with the
great blue waves below and the mountains behind
us, it is easy to simply take joy in the splendor.

—FROM A LETTER WRITTEN BY STAFF SERGEANT RICHARD JOHNSON,
OCTOBER 15, 1943

ANNA

Preparing dinner had gone off without a hitch, and even though Anna missed the ally she'd found in her niece, things were all right with Rachel and her mother.

Things with Rachel had actually been smoother than they'd been for years. Their talk while they were making croissants had shifted something between them. When Rachel said it was up to them how close they were going to be, she hadn't been lying.

She also hadn't been promising a miracle.

It was slow going sometimes, learning to confide in and trust someone you hadn't for so long. But over pastry dough, ladybugs and dusting, they were slowly starting to build a bridge between them.

Anna hadn't confided in or trusted anyone all that much in a long time.

Michael had been a notable exception. She had *trusted* him.

With deep, dark secrets, with her body, with her soul.

A horrifying reality now that he had quit speaking to her so completely.

Ghosting. That's what Emma said it was. Him completely vanishing.

Slowly, but surely, she was beginning to feel heartbroken by the loss of him.

Like part of her heart that had been numb was beginning to thaw out.

She didn't know how she would talk to Rachel about that. It had been one thing to announce her affair and talk about the issues in her marriage.

It was another to admit how much she felt for him. That she missed him, even while she was angry at him.

But she let the smell of dinner rolls wash away her angst. The cleansing scent of yeast, white flour and butter combined with the satisfaction of a perfect bake helped to dull some of the pain.

"Wonderful," Wendy said. "I'll take these out now."

Her mother swept the bread out of the room with a wide smile on her face, and Anna's insides glowed.

Here, now, everything was moving smoothly. Yes, there were a lot of issues left unresolved. But she was happy to slide into the ease she felt when they cooked together.

"Everything looks great," Rachel said, testing the temperature of the roast. "I think it's going to be a big hit. And bring more business in."

"We're good at that," Anna said. "We're good at making people feel like they're home."

And maybe they didn't have it all perfect between them, but these were the things that helped. A home-cooked meal, sitting around a table with friends. Or, in the case of Anna, Rachel and Wendy, cooking together.

Because it took her back to a simpler time, because it meant home to her, even if she couldn't quite grasp the feeling of it now.

She took her potatoes au gratin out of the oven, followed by honey-glazed carrots. Then, as her mother swept back in, she handed her the bowl of tossed green salad. Her mother came back into the kitchen and they all quietly began to eat some of the misshapen rolls that had not gone out to the dinner table. They all liked them with copious amounts of butter. And as they stood there, all three leaning against the island at the center of the crowded kitchen, their eyes caught while they were chewing, and they smiled.

It made her feel hope for the first time. Like there might, in fact, be a path back to something. Something better than what she had now.

"I'll take out the next one," she said.

She grabbed two of the sides, and Rachel followed behind her with the meat. Her steps faltered as soon as she went out into the dining room and saw Laura and two other women that she knew from afternoon bible studies at the church. Her mom wouldn't have known to give her a heads-up, because she probably didn't know any of them.

Sunset Church was large enough that it was impossible to know everyone unless you were part of smaller groups they were in, and since Anna had been a part of most of the small groups, she was more familiar with more of them than her mother would be.

Laura smiled, and the woman next to her—whom Anna

was reasonably certain was named Hannah—shot her a chilling glare. Laura, for her part, kept her expression resolutely friendly, and not focused on Hannah at all.

Anna set down the dishes on the table, and the explanation for them faltered on her tongue, so Rachel took over, brilliantly explaining each element of food before the two of them began to head back toward the kitchen.

But Anna paused, taking a sharp turn toward the sitting room, then made her way over to the front door and tugged it open, letting the cool ocean air wash over her.

It was like every time she thought she had a minute to start over, she was reminded that she couldn't. Not here.

But what would happen if she left here.

She might be able to start over, but she wouldn't have...

Rachel and her mother. Emma.

This house.

It would be like splitting herself in two again, and she had already done that. She didn't want to do it again. She didn't want to believe that she could only have a new life if she left pieces of herself behind.

The door cracked open, and she turned, expecting to see her sister. Instead, it was Hannah.

"I didn't know you worked here," Hannah said, the crystalline words brittle, sharp and deadly. "I would've thought that your mother would've had the good sense to distance herself from you."

Anna felt like she had died and was floating up outside of her body, because she couldn't actually believe this was happening. It was like watching it happen to another person. Like one of her fevered arguments with herself had manifested and was playing out in front of her, with Hannah acting as her self-loathing essence while her actual self scrabbled to make justifications for everything she was. Everything she'd done.

"She's my mother," Anna said.

"And Pastor Thomas is her son-in-law."

"He won't be. Not after we get divorced. That's kind of the law part. Legally, it can be dissolved."

"Well, no one can blame him. Not after what you did. And I don't think it's fair that you're still here in town. It's not fair to him. He didn't do anything."

Anna was stunned by the truth of that. And Hannah would never know just how true what she'd said was. He hadn't done anything. He just hadn't done a damn thing.

He hadn't done anything to fix their marriage. Hadn't done anything to make her feel like he cared. Hadn't done any of the things that a good husband was supposed to do.

He hadn't kissed her. He hadn't held her. He hadn't loved her.

Not by the end.

And it was amazing how people thought that made you innocent.

Doing nothing.

She was *guilty*, because she had done *something*.

Because she'd had an affair. And everyone knew about that. Didn't know that for years she had been the one to do *something*. To talk about their problems, to try to fix them. To try to seduce him. To cook dinner, try to be pretty, try to be supportive.

She had done something.

Something. Something.

While he had done nothing.

"I don't want to have this conversation with you," Anna said.

"Because you're convicted," she said, her words laced with venom. "You know that what you did was wrong."

"If I want to talk about my marriage, it isn't going to be with you. I haven't even had this in-depth of a conversation about it with Thomas. He went and announced it to the entire church without ever speaking to me about it. He's said more to a room of a thousand people about our divorce than he has ever said to me. And you tell me whether or not you think that's right?"

Her lip curled in disdain. "Why should he talk to the woman who let another man touch her like that." Her cheeks went red, her whole body nearly shaking with indignation. "I would *never* do something like that."

And the hardness, the intensity of her tone, told Anna another story altogether.

"Good for you," Anna said. "I hope that doesn't come back to bite you someday. I hope that your marriage never ends up in a place where you question everything you know, and everything you are. Where being somebody completely different, being someone that you would have thought was appalling a few years ago, doesn't become preferable to being the person that you are."

The door opened again, and Laura came out. Anna braced herself. She was outnumbered now.

"What are you doing, Hannah?"

"You *smiled* at her," Hannah said. "But I'm not going to ignore what she is. I'm not going to forget what's right and wrong. And I'm not going to fail to call things like they are."

"Hannah…"

"No. You can have your lazy version of love. Letting people feel comfortable with what they are, but I don't believe in making people comfortable. It's not wrong to call out immorality."

"Don't you see yourself?" The ferocity in Laura's voice surprised Anna, and even more so when she realized that it was directed at Hannah. "Throwing stones like you're without sin. If Jesus couldn't condone casting a stone at a woman caught in adultery I don't know why you think you can. I don't know why it's your job to punish someone. It should be your job to forgive. And *you* should be embarrassed. Not Anna. She's just up here having a life, having a job. You… You went out of your way to be nasty. To be unkind. And it so easy to hide behind platitudes like you do. If you don't care about someone it's easy to call them out, isn't it? Because you wrote her off, so you don't care what she thinks about you. You're embarrassed now, because I'm calling you out. Because you care what *I* think. Where's all that conviction now, Hannah? Where is it?"

Laura was right, and Hannah was looking completely shamefaced. Laura's eyes filled with angry tears. "You run around acting like you're doing the Lord's work. But as far as I can see the only God you have is yourself and your own opinions. You use false morality like a weapon to make yourself feel above it all because if you didn't run around attacking other people you'd have to look at yourself." Laura turned to Anna. "I'm sorry," she said. "I didn't know this was a hit. No one told me. I wouldn't have allowed her to come up here if I would've known…"

"It's okay," Anna said. Laura had no idea how okay it was. Considering that she had been so gloriously defended by someone she wasn't related to.

Hannah sucked up her face like she was drinking lemon juice through a straw and turned, walking through the door at the same time Rachel appeared.

"Come on," she said. "Let's go for a walk. Fresh air."

She didn't know why her sister was holding on to her so tightly, or marching her quite so insistently down the porch stairs. Until she started to shake. And cry.

And she realized that Rachel had seen that the break-down was coming before Anna had. She pushed open the gate on the white picket fence, and the two of them walked down the paved path that zigzagged down the hill and toward the beach. The clouds were low, the mist rolling in, and the sun had faded into nothing, never visible today as it had been hidden behind a thick blanket of gray.

The ocean churned angrily, all froth and rage, swelling up to the shore.

She related to the ocean today.

She hadn't thought anything could shock her like this, not now. After the shock of her own behavior, after the shock of Thomas calling her out in a public venue, she'd thought she'd reached the limit.

But not here.

This place, this house, was her refuge. It always had been. And it had been especially in this last month. And Hannah had come up here and taken that from her.

She had taken this place where she was beginning to rebuild herself, bit by bit, and she had reminded her that wherever she went in Sunset Bay...someone would know. And someone would have an opinion.

And in some cases, would be absolutely and completely bound to making her feel bad.

And maybe for every five of them there would be a Laura.

But she would definitely be rarer than those who came to point and laugh at her failure.

Because it wasn't as gratifying to try to lift someone up as it was to kick them while they were down.

"I don't know what I would've done," Anna said suddenly.

Rachel zipped up her coat, stuffing her hands in her pockets, and continued walking beside her. "If what? If Laura hadn't of come out there? No worries. I was going to punch her in the face."

"No. Not that." Anna kept on walking, the mist stinging her face. But she didn't mind. It gave her some relief from the stinging in her chest.

"What if it wasn't me?" Anna asked. "What if it had been one of the worship pastor's wives? What if it was some other woman at the church? It has been. Over the years it has been. I might not have been Hannah, but I was never Laura for them, either. It was easy for me to just turn away and pretend it didn't happen. For me… partly because I was afraid that if I would have let myself speak to someone who had gotten out of their marriage I would have started thinking about my own. And I put that off for as many years as I could. Trust me on that." She cleared her throat. "I feel alone. And it so easy for me to be upset, but I wouldn't have been a better person. I just wouldn't have been."

"You don't know that," Rachel said.

"No," Anna said. "I do. I do. And the bottom line is whatever motivates someone like Hannah, it's not actually just to make me feel bad. She needs to hold that position that she does because…if she doesn't maybe her life will break apart."

"Or maybe," Rachel said, grabbing hold of Anna's arm as the path ended, turning into sand, "she's a bitch."

Anna laughed. "I mean, maybe that, too. But… I don't

know. This is the problem. I spent a whole lot of time without any perspective at all, and now... I'm so desperate for people to try and see deeply into what I did that I'm trying to see more in what everyone is and does."

"Yeah, being empathetic isn't necessarily a bad thing."

"I don't have the energy for it," Anna said. "I just want to be angry. I can't even have that."

"Maybe that's that personal growth I'm always hearing about? I've been told that I am experiencing an enormous amount of that."

"No way," Anna said.

"Not since Jacob died. But when he was sick. I'm extra strong, Anna. That's what I hear. God gave him to me because I'm extra strong."

"That's..."

"Not fair? Makes him sound like a burden? Makes it sound like God did something to us? Yeah." Rachel laughed, the husky sound barely rising up over the waves. "People say stupid things even when they mean well. But I don't think Hannah meant well. And that was beyond stupid. It was cruel. And you didn't deserve that." Rachel's voice broke. "I'm sorry for what I said to you. Because it was about my feelings. Not yours."

"I imagine that you're even more out of empathy than I am." The constant barrage of idiocy Rachel must have received over the years... Anna couldn't imagine how tired she was.

Well-meaning might not cut deep like *mean*, but it wore you down like a rock being slammed by the waves.

"Maybe," Rachel said. "But I shouldn't have been out of empathy for you."

"I can't get away from this feeling," Anna said. "That what I did was the ugliest thing someone could do. Because somehow I put it all out of my head when I was in it. When it was me, it seemed like there were a thousand different ways to justify it. When it was just me and Micahel, I could pretend the rest of the world—the church, Thomas, you and mom—didn't exist, not in our world. And then…now it's like I see everything real. Not two sections of my life, but one life. It all crashed together and the wreckage is so bad. And I realized that I'm exactly like our dad."

"Not exactly," Rachel said.

A laugh burst out of Anna, in spite of herself. "Just a little bit?"

"No. It's… Dad toyed with Mom for years. Got her pregnant with me, left, came back and got her pregnant with you, and then left again. He—he messed around for years. And he left her devastated and with two children. And I don't think your husband is devastated. And therein lies the problem. The problem with all of this. I kept comparing you and your marriage to me and Jacob. But Jacob loved me. And I loved him. And losing him has left a hole in what I used to be because we were one person. Our souls were one. Losing him is changing the shape of me. Is it like that with Thomas? I don't think it is. I watched him up there in front of the whole church like I was having an out-of-body experience. I watched him talk about you leaving him, and I didn't feel like he was a man overwhelmed by grief. I felt like he was a man doing damage control. I know what it's like to lose your other half. Damage control is the furthest thing from your mind."

They let silence lapse between them, the waves battering the shore.

"I can't go back and change it," Anna said. "And I don't think I would. But that doesn't make it easy."

"You know, all that stupid stuff that people say to me, all that yelling that Hannah did to you… It's all people just trying to explain life in easy, neat ways. Because we don't want to believe that it's messy and painful and sometimes good men die for no reason."

Rachel took her hands out of her pockets and pushed her windblown hair out of her face before she continued. "They want to believe I'm stronger, and special, to be able to handle such a tragedy, because they want to believe that they aren't. And because of that they'll be spared. They're not going to watch their husband waste away in front of them."

She toed at the pile of black, tan and gray rocks piled in a line in the sand. Dropped there by the sea, looking ordered and perfect in their randomness. Like a painting, when they were really just deposited there by water without care at all.

"They want to believe," Rachel said, "like Hannah clearly does, that no man would ever appear and treat them better than their husband, seduce them away. They want to believe that there's a weakness in you that isn't in them, because it's how they sleep at night. The same way they want to believe that there's a strength in me that God won't find in them. So maybe he won't test their faith."

Anna looked up at the hill, at the lighthouse. It was automated now, not dependent on three lightkeepers to stay up all night and keep it burning. It was just there. Eight beams of light turning in a slow circle.

Guiding those out at sea right on back home.

"So," Anna said slowly, "between us, we're Job and Judas. And people are desperate to believe they could never be either one."

"Exactly. Not righteous enough to be tested, not weak enough to betray."

"If only it were that simple."

"The thing is, any of us could be either one, depending on the circumstances. We're all so much weaker and so much stronger than we think."

Anna hoped so. Because her weakness had been tested already and she needed some of that strength Rachel seemed to believe existed in everyone to be found somewhere inside her. "I'm going to need a lot more strength than I've got right now to get through this."

She wondered if Rachel would ask if she was going to leave. She almost hoped she would. So they could discuss it. So Anna could sort through that thought and decide what she wanted.

The problem was, she wasn't sure she wanted to go.

And if her sister did suggest it…

But she didn't.

"I got asked on a date," Rachel said.

Anna looked at her, shocked by that. "A date?"

"Yes." She paused. "And I understand. Why Michael making you feel pretty stopped the world for you. I've never thought of Mark that way at all. I—I still don't. And even then his attention felt good because I haven't had anything like that in ages. And knowing a random guy could think I was pretty, well…"

Anna nodded, her heart clenching tight. "Thank you," she whispered.

"It's like you said. You were afraid to look too deeply at what you missed, at what you didn't have because it would make you discontent. I didn't have a choice but to decide my life was fine. Jacob wasn't doing anything to me. Him being sick wasn't about me, it was about him. Of course, it was hard. Of course, I missed what we couldn't have any-more. Of course, I wished... Of course, I wished we could just...have a miracle. Or an alternate reality. Something where he wasn't sick. But I could never ever let myself wish for a different life for me. It wouldn't have been fair."

Anna touched her sister's arm. "It's okay if you wanted one sometimes, though. It doesn't mean you didn't love him."

Tears slipped down Rachel's cheeks and she didn't have a chance to brush them away before the wind carried them off for her.

"Are you going to...? Are you going to go?" Anna asked.

"I can't go," she said.

"Why not?"

"He hasn't been...gone long enough, surely."

"What's long enough?"

"I don't know," Rachel said. "I feel like there can't be a long enough. For twenty years of marriage? Twenty *great* years?"

"Do you want to go?"

"I don't... I mean... It wasn't like him asking me was exciting because of who it was. But it was nice to have someone notice me. Actually me."

Anna made an understanding sound in the back of her throat. "I mean, maybe I'm not the person you should ask, though. About the appropriate time to start dating a new man. Since I don't exactly have a grasp on that."

The laugh that Rachel let out went over the waves this time, a short, sharp burst, followed by a string of laughter. She put her hand on her stomach, doubling over.

And then Anna couldn't help but laugh, too. Until the

tears were falling down her face, because it was either laugh or cry.

And out here, under the low-hanging sky, the mist all around them, the light from that lighthouse still cut through. And maybe that's what this was. Maybe it was what they needed.

There was no one here to see that they were laughing, anyway. At the sharp, painful, absurd things. There was nothing to do but laugh, because it was either that or cry forever. And right now, Anna was doing both.

Without judgment.

With her sister.

"How did we end up here?" Rachel asked when their laughter had died down.

"I don't know. It definitely wasn't my plan when I was a little girl. My MASH game said that I was going to have one husband and live in a shoe in Italy. Not one husband, one lover and end up in my childhood home in Oregon."

"Yeah, I was supposed to have a Lamborghini," Rachel said. "That didn't pan out, either."

Silence fell again and Anna thought about her sister's date. Yeah, maybe it seemed soon, but a date wasn't marriage. And she knew that Rachel had been a caregiving wife in the end, and that her role had been different than what it originally was. Maybe she needed a little romance. Not love, but romance.

"You should go out with him if you want to. There's not a time. I mean, maybe you shouldn't go getting married again yet…"

"I don't want to get married. I don't even want to fall in love. I don't want to have feelings. I'd like to scoop them out of my chest with a spoon. But… I don't know, going on a dinner date with someone who thinks I'm pretty doesn't sound terrible. Maybe in another month."

"Maybe. That makes sense. You told me... You told me that was part of your marriage that you didn't have anymore. It makes sense you would be ready for that first."

"Sex? Oh, I am not there yet." She paused. "Well, maybe I'm a little bit getting there."

"Do you want to hear a secret?" Anna asked.

"In the spirit of sharing, I suppose so."

"Michael was the best sex I've ever had. And sometimes, when I regret that everything fell apart around me... I just think of that. Because I didn't know it could be that good. Fourteen years with the same man, and I didn't know it could be that good."

"And that is something else Thomas has to answer for. Because I've had some good sex, Anna."

"Well, I hadn't. Not like that." Her mouth twitched. "I guess... I guess that's not supposed to be very important. I mean..."

"But it is," Rachel said. "And I say that as someone who couldn't have it in their marriage for quite a while. We did have it. Real intimacy. And we took pleasure in each other. And I loved being with him. It mattered because it was something only we shared, and something only we wanted to share with each other. It's so much harder when you don't have that. If you never did. We spent so many years taking it for granted, and then clinging to it while it lasted. And then like seasons of life, we let it go, and we did it together. We held the memory. Because it wasn't my life and his. It was *ours*."

Anna couldn't grasp the concept. Not in a tangible way. "We were just never like that. I think we wanted to be. I think in the beginning...even he wanted to be. The thing is, it just didn't ever come together. I don't know if it was getting married young and growing in different directions or…what."

"You don't *have* to know," she said. "The marriage isn't your burden anymore. Sure, you have all this divorce stuff. But…the marriage is gone. You could sift through the wreckage, but it won't put it back together now. You don't have to know what caused it."

She blinked, feeling like she had just been staring at a web of knots and tangles that she'd been trying to sort out for so long she was strained with the effort of it. And suddenly, she realized she could put it down.

That was the gift, she supposed. If you decided to throw something away and start over…you didn't have anything left to untangle.

The only knots left to go through were inside of herself.

Because their lives were separate, and she could begin again from there.

Those knots, though—those she couldn't leave alone. Because they came with her.

"Thank you," Anna said.

"For what?"

"For trying to understand me, even though it's hard."

"It's really not all that hard," she said. "The further I get into examining everything in my life, the more I feel like we're a lot more alike than I realized."

"Well, it means everything to me."

"To me, too," Rachel said.

They turned and walked back up the path, heading toward the Captain's House. Their mom would be wondering where they'd gotten to, and that made Anna smile slightly.

That was the gift of being home.

There were definitely downsides to it as well, but the

gift was that sense that any moment she could step backward in time. Find a simpler version of herself and maybe start from there, instead of contending with this complicated adult version of herself that she had never aspired to be.

Wendy didn't ask where they'd been, but as they worked on dessert, Anna turned to her mother.

"What happens if you don't end up with the perfect life you dreamed of?"

Wendy blinked. "You either change your life, or find a new version of perfect."

"Is that what you did?"

Her mom faltered. "Yes. I found a new version of perfect. And I never looked back. This place, you girls and all the years since became my dream. At first it seemed impossible. When I came here with nothing—nothing but a dream for what this place might become. But gradually... I fell in love with this house, I fell in love with being your mother, and then what I'd lost didn't seemed to matter so much."

Michael was gone. Thomas was gone, and her love for him had faded a long time ago. There was no one left for Anna to love but her family and herself. And no life for her to love but the one she would go and make.

So she supposed she would have to start making something.

16

It's really a terrible thing to fall in love.
You can forget who you are, thinking
so much about another person.

—FROM THE DIARY OF SUSAN BRIGHT, AUGUST 1961

EMMA

Emma had spent her shift in a state of discomfort, because she had chosen her outfit based on what she wanted to wear to have dinner with Luke that night, and not based on practicality.

She had on flat shoes because she wasn't that much of a martyr to beauty, but she was wearing a pair of tight high-waisted jeans and a crop top, which made maneuvering around for the job difficult. And her waist was beginning to feel constricted beyond the point of reason.

They had spoken a little. A few stolen conversations with him during lunch delivery.

They'd kept it light, not getting into details about their lives, but mostly talking about the people in the town, TV shows and other ridiculous things.

She liked him so much more than she'd imagined she even could.

When the to-go order came in at closing time, Luke had placed it for two. She didn't even have to make her own order. Which made it feel much more like a date than the initial request had been.

He had paid over the phone, and she beat a hasty retreat as soon as the clock rolled over and her shift was finished, the bag of food in hand as she scurried across the street to the garage.

He was standing there by the bench and stools that he had eaten at yesterday, but his hands were clean, and the surface itself was entirely clear, with a cloth set over the workbench itself.

"Wow." It wasn't a fancy restaurant, but somehow it felt better. More significant, because he had prepared it all himself.

"Well, I know you're always a little concerned about the cleanliness."

"Yeah," she said. "I… Yeah." She held up the food and wandered over to the bench, and he brushed off the stool quickly before she sat down.

"I hope you got extra French fries," she said as she watched him get the food out of the bag.

He lifted an eyebrow. "Extra?"

"Don't look so surprised. French fries are serious business."

"True," he said. "Fortunately, I did anticipate that."

He pulled out a container that did indeed contain only fries. And she dug into them happily.

There was a soda machine in the corner, and he walked over with a couple of dollars. "What do you want tonight?"

"Orange?"

He smiled and shook his head, putting in the dollar and then pushing the button for orange soda. And he got a Coke for himself.

He brought them back over to where she sat and extended the soda to her, which she took, tapping the can thoughtfully.

"Orange soda," he said. Suddenly, concern she hadn't seen before marred his brow. "How old are you?"

Heat touched her cheeks. Well she hadn't exactly been looking forward to this part of the getting-to-know-you. "I'm almost eighteen."

The crease between his eyebrows deepened. "How almost?"

She laughed. "Three weeks. I'm graduating this year."

He nodded slowly. "That's not so bad."

"Why? How old are you?"

"Old enough to drink," he said.

"By how much?"

"Well… That depends. Do you mean from a legal standpoint or when I actually started drinking?"

"You're the one who introduced it is an age marker."

He shrugged. "I turned twenty-one last month."

"Okay," she said. "I guess that's not so bad."

"Graduating, huh? What's the plan after that?" He got out his hamburger and started to eat, and she followed suit.

"I'm going to OSU," she said, looking down at her food. "I guess."

"What you mean 'you guess'? That wasn't your first pick?"

"I'm studying marine biology. And it's a great school for that. It is. But… I wanted to go to Boston. They have a great marine-biology program there, and a partnership with an aquarium that I was really interested in."

It never got much easier to think about that, even now that it had been a couple of months. But then, none of it was easier. It was harder in new ways. People had stopped giving her sad looks at school, and she'd been grateful for that. But now it felt like everyone expected her to be normal.

"You didn't get accepted?"

"I did," she said. "But I—I can't leave my mom."

There wasn't any indication by his facial expression that he had any idea why she felt she couldn't leave her mom.

"My dad died," she said. "Almost four months ago. The day I got the acceptance letter, actually. And she didn't want me to leave, anyway. If I left her now—"

"I'm sorry," he said. "That's bullshit. You got accepted into your top school, and you're not gonna go?"

She wished they had stuck to talking about TV. Not ages and the future and things like that.

"My dad's dead," she reiterated.

Because as far as she was concerned, it was the answer to any question he might have.

"Yeah, and forgive me for sounding kind of callous, but that's not likely to change anytime soon."

His words probably should have offended her, but they didn't. Instead, they made a strange kind of sense. "No. But there will be more time in between what happened then—"

"And in that time your mom will never learn to not need you. Sometimes you have to take opportunities when you get them."

"Yeah, and when have you had to do that?"

"I'm still here. My dad's dead, too. He drank himself to death. So no one was exactly making a saint out of him and acting sorry he was gone. And it's been a long time. But my mom met some other guy, and she went off and had a couple more kids."

She tried to imagine her mom with someone else and… couldn't. "That must have been hard."

"Yeah…" He lifted a shoulder. "I was seventeen. That kind of sucked. But I didn't want to go, because Dusty promised me this place. He doesn't have a son, and no one else to leave this place to, but he's willing to leave it to me."

Her age. He had been her age when his mother had left him. "I can't imagine that. Being left on your own…"

"There wasn't going to be anything for me where she went. I'm smart enough to know that people like me don't get those chances too often. I've been here working with Dusty for the last four years. That's my version of college, anyway. The best school I got accepted at."

"You're brave," she said. "To stay on your own like that."

"I don't know. I did what made sense. So what about you? You were smart and you got the grades to get into the school. And you just don't get to?"

"I lied to my mom. I told her that I didn't get in."

"Wow," he said. "Because you know she would have told you to go if you did get accepted."

"Or she would have asked me not to," Emma said. "I don't know. I just needed to deal with it on my own. And I meant to tell her the truth…but I just didn't."

"Hey. I don't know what it's like to have people care where I am. Maybe I'm off base. But you should go. You should go because you deserve to have what you want. If I could have gone to school to be a mechanic, I could've gotten all kinds of certifications and gotten a lot further.

As it is, I'm self-taught on a whole lot of things that Dusty doesn't know, and when I take over the place, I'll be able to take on different business. But working toward certifications is going to be slow. If I would've had the chance to go to school… I would have."

"I'm going to school. Just three hours away instead of a country away."

"But it's not what you want. Don't you think that you're worth it?"

She frowned. "What do you mean?"

"You're concerned about your mom's feelings, and that's nice. But don't you think that your feelings matter?"

"Yeah," she said. "Of course they do."

"I don't think you're giving them enough weight," he said. "Just my opinion, as a guy who had to ask how old you were a few minutes ago."

She laughed. They finished eating and moved on to lighter subjects, and by the time she had finished her hamburger, she was 100 percent convinced that he was the most wonderful guy she'd ever known.

He was like a light that illuminated the center of the room. Pushed the darkness into the corners. It was still there. But it wasn't everything.

"I can show you around," he said.

And then she couldn't regret that step toward real conversation, because this really did feel…like a step. They'd eaten together before, but they hadn't delved into each others lives.

This felt like him sharing his life.

"Sure," she said. "I can honestly say I have never been shown around the garage before."

"Well, you're in for a treat."

He said the words somewhat dryly, but she could see

that he was proud of the place. She got the sense that he did a good portion of the running of the business, and that the transition between himself and Dusty had been happening slowly over the last few years.

"How did you meet Dusty?" she asked, looking intently at all the tool racks and shelves full of auto parts. She might not be able to identify anything, but it took on some meaning, knowing how much it meant to him.

That he was working here because this business would belong to him someday. And that mattered to him. Was worth working through meals, and all the sweat and grease and even blood—he had some stories—that went into the job.

"I was looking for work. I had a pretty good sense of how to work on old cars, because I'd been helping my mom get hers running one way or another constantly over the last few years. So he agreed to take me on and train me. I was sixteen. Not going to school."

"You quit school?"

"Yeah," he said. "Not the best move in hindsight, but at the time… I didn't have any use for school. Not when I could be out making money. And… I knew where I was going to end up. Somewhere working with my hands, but definitely not somewhere that required college. So there just didn't seem to be a point."

"Oh," she said. "I guess that makes sense."

"Except you don't agree." He looked combative, and she realized…

He expected her to judge him. To judge this. She was going to college and she talked about it like such a sure thing, while it was clear that to him the only sure future had been one he'd build with his hands. Learning a trade, like he'd done, had been the smartest thing he could do.

And he was used to being judged for it.

She shook her head. "No, I'm realizing that I'm lucky. Because it was definitely something my mom and dad wanted for me, and they made sure that I knew I had that privilege available. I just always assumed that I could go. And you—"

"No one in my family has ever gone to college," he said. "We're just not those people."

"But you're smart," she said. "You have to be to fix engines. To teach yourself?"

"I'm lucky, too," he said. "Because Dusty has taught me a lot about business. I would never have been in this position without him. But you can see why I'm here. There's not a ton of open opportunity in Sunset Bay, but there's this opportunity for me."

"Yeah."

"You know what—I think I have some sheet cake left over in the fridge for my birthday."

"It's probably really old."

"Yeah, it's a little old, but Dusty also brought it in late."

"Okay. You have to take the first bite, though."

They ended up sitting in his truck with the heater on, a plaid blanket over her knees while they ate cake and listened to the radio, since it was the only thing he had in his pickup, not a hook up for a cell phone or anything.

"Do you know what's weird about your dad dying?" she asked.

"What?"

"Everybody treats you like you're an alien. So as bad as you feel about the whole thing, you just end up feeling worse, because you can't even talk to your friends anymore."

"Yeah," he said. "When my dad died, it was kind of a

relief that he wasn't around anymore. But I was sad, too. And…"

"No one understood that, did they?"

He shook his head. "No."

"How old were you when he died?"

"Eight. I took all of his baseball cards out to the back-yard and set them on fire. And then I cried because I wished I had them." He didn't say anything for a while. "I've never told anyone that."

She blinked. Hard. "My dad was a great guy. He was an amazing dad. I'm not sure he felt like it. He was sad sometimes that he couldn't go to everything always. That he couldn't just…get up and have energy when I wanted him to. It didn't matter to me, though. He was the best. Whether he was walking up to the lighthouse with me or just…talking to me. Teasing me about how sweet my cof-fee was, or how messy my car was. He knew me."

She took a deep breath. "He wouldn't want me to go to OSU because he died. He would want me to follow my dream."

"Well, I think you have your answer."

She nodded slowly. "I guess so."

He leaned across the cab, and she suddenly couldn't breathe. "You have a little bit of frosting on your cheek," he said, reaching up and brushing his thumb over her skin. And then he brought it to his mouth.

And then licked it.

"No sense wasting good frosting," he said.

Her heart was thundering so loud in her head that she could hardly breathe.

It occurred to her for the first time that she was *alone* with a boy. Absolutely alone. And they could kiss…or whatever… And she wanted to. At least the kissing. So she stared at him, because she hoped that he would get the message if she did.

He smiled, and he leaned in. It wasn't a long kiss. And it felt…

Strange.

His mouth was warm, and firm, and it made her feel like someone had wrapped her in a blanket and set her by a fireplace, safe and cocooned, but also close to something dangerous and destructive, that if it escaped its confinement would destroy her completely. When he pulled away she felt giddy. Dizzy.

"I want to see you again," he said, his mouth still right next to hers.

"Okay," she said.

"Good."

"Yeah," she responded, leaning back against the seat. She wished that he would kiss her again, but also, she wasn't sure she could survive it.

"It's pretty late," he said. "And it sounds to me like your mom worries about you. So… I don't want to cause worry. And if we want to go out again, then I suspect it's a good time for you to head home."

"It's late?" She reached into her pocket, grabbed her phone and cursed when she saw the eight or nine messages and two missed calls. That meant her mom had probably called Catherine, who had probably ignored her, because she knew that her mom would want to talk to her.

Great. Now they were both in trouble.

"Yeah. I do need to go."

"You look worried? Is everything okay?"

She wished a hole would open up in the truck and just swallow her up. "My mom doesn't know that I'm with you."

He frowned. "Oh?"

"I told her I was having dinner with my friend Catherine."

"Okay." He rested his elbows on the steering wheel and stared straight ahead. "Don't take this the wrong way, but I'm not used to dating girls who still live at home."

She wrinkled her nose. "You really thought I was older, didn't you?"

"Yeah. I should have asked up front."

"Well, I'm *almost* older. I'll be older…well, right now. But older in the way you mean soon enough."

He sighed heavily, then looked over at her, his face shadowed. "I didn't run away when you told me. I'm not running now."

She bit her lip. "Good."

"I don't meet a lot of people who understand losing someone," he said. "And I didn't expect to find that with you. Honestly, I just thought you were pretty. But if you were just pretty I probably would have sent you away when I found out you were seventeen. But it's more than that."

A liquid, giddy feeling shimmered in her stomach, in spite of her anxiety. "I'm glad. Well, to be pretty and to be more than that. I… You know what I mean."

"Handle your mom however you want. But…you know my opinion." He laughed. "You know, the opinion of this guy you didn't know until today. So if you want to ignore me, that's fair enough."

She wanted to tell him that she did know him. Because she'd been watching him for months. But then she would sound crazy, and he *really* wouldn't want to see her again. She was going to try to minimize the fact she was in high school, not maximize it by revealing that she was a girl with a crush. Who had never been kissed before until a few minutes ago.

"I'll keep that in mind."

She got out of the truck and slammed the door behind her, waving as she went back across the street to where she parked her car. "Wait a second."

She turned around and saw him just a few paces behind her. "It's not chivalrous for me to let you go without making sure you get to your car okay."

"Oh," she said.

"If you didn't have your own car here, I would have driven you home and walked to the door."

"Oh," she said again, heat igniting her cheeks.

"And can I get your phone number?"

"Yes," she said, accepting his phone when he gave it to her, and calling herself. Then she handed it back to him. "Now we have each other's."

"Good," he said. "I'll see you."

He didn't try to kiss her again.

She couldn't decide if that made him a gentleman, or if it made her disappointed.

Or if it was both and that was okay.

She considered that while she drove home, her lips burning. Her phone rang, and she answered it, putting it on speakerphone.

"Where are you? Your mom has called me twice, and I feel mean ignoring her."

"I'm sorry," she said to Catherine. *"He kissed me."*

"Wow," Catherine said. "I figured you'd make a guy wait way more dates to get a kiss. Or at least…take you out and not to his garage."

"He kissed me."

"I mean, he seems like the kind of guy who would have

kissed you on the first date. You're the one who doesn't seem like that kind of girl."

She guessed maybe she did think that she was the kind of girl who would wait until the fifth or sixth date to kiss a guy, but this didn't feel just like a date.

It felt like…a shift.

Like he had come into her life and things had rearranged themselves. Like the conversations they'd had tonight had created new ideas inside of her and she wasn't going to be able to go back and not have them there anymore.

The way that he had talked about her caring for herself.

And he thought she should go to Boston.

Maybe it wasn't the best thing for a guy that you liked to tell you to move across the country, but…he believed in her. That felt like it mattered.

"I *really* like him."

"Good," Catherine said, her ire clearly decreasing. "I'm glad you like him."

"Thank you. I'll figure out how to fix it. I'll just say that we lost track of time."

"Okay. And then stop lying."

"You lie to your parents all the time."

"Yes. But *you* don't."

Catherine hung up right as Emma pulled into the private drive and she sighed, trying to figure out exactly what she was going to say to her mom. She parked in front of the Lightkeeper's House and stared for a moment, and then she killed the engine and trudged inside.

"Where have you been?" Her mom was right there, looking pale and afraid. And mad.

"I'm sorry. Catherine and I lost track of time."

"Catherine didn't answer her phone, you didn't answer your phone."

"I know. I'm sorry. By the time I realized how late it was and that I'd missed calls from you it was too late for me to fix it."

"What were you doing?"

"Hanging out," Emma said.

"You normally have your phone welded to your hand, Emma."

"I didn't tonight."

"Why not?"

"Mom," Emma said, "I'm not even going to live at home in a couple of months. You can't police everything I do all the time."

Emma didn't know where her anger came from. Because she was the one who had lied. And she was the one who hadn't kept track of the time. And her mom was afraid, and Emma could understand why. Except for some reason all of it just made her mad, and she didn't want to deal with it.

She didn't want to deal with her mom's feelings. She didn't want to have to live to make her happy.

She didn't want to have to calculate her every move to spare her mom worry. Because she had been doing it for too long.

Tonight had felt amazing.

And she had felt free.

She had had something that belonged to her, only to her. And she hadn't gotten the lecture on safe sex and waiting until after college to get serious about someone. She had just…gotten to see where it went. And she'd liked that.

"Emma Jane," Rachel said. "I pay for your life—your minimum-wage diner job doesn't. And who do you think will be financing your collegiate independence? Not you. So, yes, I do get to know where you are, and who you're with, and what you're doing."

"Not if I don't tell you." Emma turned and stomped toward the stairs, but her mother's hand coming down hard on the countertop stopped her.

"Listen to me," Rachel said. "I have lost enough. I'm not going to lose you, too. Not to some fit of teenage rebellion."

"And I'm not yours," Emma, turning, shouted back. "I'm my own. I lost Dad, too. That *hurt* me. That was my loss, too. And I'm not your possession to sit around making you feel better. I'm my own person. With my own… pain. And I don't have to sit in this house every night so that you still have something to take care of, because you don't know how to go out and have a life of your own."

She went up the stairs, shaking, feeling sick to her stomach that she'd said those things to her mother. But part of her had meant them. Maybe even most of her.

She sat down at her computer, her heart thundering in her ears. And then she saw the pink folder that was sitting on top of her desk, with her acceptance letters inside. She opened it, and she found the one from Boston.

She hadn't confirmed with OSU. She hadn't confirmed anywhere.

Boston.

She was going to Boston.

She wasn't going to let anything stop her.

17

My new husband commands light that
guides ships on the sea, and yet we cannot
seem to find each other.

—FROM THE DIARY OF JENNY HANSEN, APRIL 8, 1900

RACHEL

Rachel was surprised when she didn't cry. She was…
angry. Absolutely enraged at her seventeen-year-old.
Which seemed…silly.

Suddenly she remembered when Emma was two years
old, and had torn up a beautiful, precious book that had
been given to her by Jacob's mother, one that had been
hers when she was a girl. She remembered yelling, help-
lessly. At a tiny child who didn't understand what she
had done wrong and couldn't fix her transgression even
if she had.

And she remembered sitting in the absurdity of that.
The absolute uselessness of her own anger, and the potential destructiveness of it.

Then, she had taken the pieces of the torn book and
gone to her room, closing the door behind her and pray-

ing quietly that God or Emma would forgive her for losing her temper.

She felt that silly now.

Getting angry at this almost adult whom she still felt responsible for. Who had wounded her in the perfect and most precise spot.

Had managed to hone her words into a needle and stab them directly into every one of Rachel's worst fears.

That she didn't know how to live. That she didn't know who she was apart from being Jacob's wife and Emma's mother.

"Well," Rachel said to the empty room, "that's because it's all I've been."

There. How was that for anger? Useless, stupid anger. Her whole life had been them, and now somehow she was supposed to just let go? She had poured herself into them, into their needs, and she did it because she loved them, but to have it turned around on her and...

Fine.

She would do something else. She would be something else.

She picked up her phone, ignoring that it was eleven o'clock at night, and called the number that Mark had given her. "Hello?"

"I hope I didn't wake you," Rachel said.

"Rachel?"

"Yeah," Rachel said.

"No. You didn't wake me." He was a nice man, which she should care about.

"Good. I... I'd love to go out. I would totally love to go out with you." The words tasted weird. "As friends," she added in a rush. "If you're interested in that. Friends."

"Uh...yes."

"Maybe in a couple of weeks? When things calm down on the weekends here at the inn. We are doing this new dinner thing, and until we get it down, I don't think I should be gone. But after that."

"Sure," he said. "Whatever works."

"That would work. So…let's say May 15."

Two days after Emma's birthday.

And after the surprise party that she was going to throw the ungrateful little brat.

Maybe she shouldn't throw Emma a surprise party. Maybe she should make herself a cake in honor of the day that she had destroyed her body only to have it never snap back to its original state ever again, and then had taken abuse for her love in the eighteen years since.

Maybe she should commemorate *that*.

"Yeah. Works for me. I'd clear my schedule if it didn't."

"Okay. Looking forward to it." She hung up, possibly faster than he was ready for her to hang up.

And then she dropped her phone onto the sofa and covered her mouth with her hand.

She was going on a date with a man who wasn't Jacob. As a friend, but even so. Her daughter hated her. She was leaving. To go to college. And she was right.

She was very nearly an adult, and she wasn't going to live here, where Rachel could keep track of her, and all of this was probably some last gasp at control. And hanging on because life had already forced her to let go of the single other most important relationship in her life.

A sob did escape then.

She didn't want to go on a date. She didn't want to be with someone else.

But maybe she needed to do this. Go on some dates. Get out of her house. Figure out who she was without Jacob.

Without Emma.

But she probably *did* need friends. But she'd let some of her long-standing friendships go fallow as she'd dealt with her life.

At least she had Anna. This new, tenuous relationship with her sister that was building up slowly and surely as the weeks wore on.

But right now she just felt alien. Disconnected. Like she was forcing herself to eat broccoli so she could maybe someday have the hope of dessert.

Dessert—in this instance—was a life that didn't feel so sharp. So painful. Where she had easy friendships, and maybe enjoyed going out on dates.

Where she found men that she liked to kiss, and maybe even sleep with.

She didn't think she'd ever get married again.

That thought actually made her...excited.

She didn't have to be a wife if she didn't want to be. She could let go of the responsibility.

Vows that bound you to a man through everything. That wrapped your life in theirs so tight it was one.

She loved Jacob. She didn't think of him as work, not as more work than any marriage was.

But marriage was work.

And she didn't have to enter into that kind of relationship ever again.

But she hadn't *chosen* the loss of her marriage. And she wouldn't have.

But it had happened. So she had to find a new way to live, and figure out what she wanted that new state of living to look like.

Rachel felt numb, and she didn't have anyone to talk

to. Even if she could talk to Emma right now, this would not be the subject she would want to broach.

Her friendships had fallen by the wayside.

Anna.

Of course, she could talk to Anna. Her little sister wasn't little anymore, and she likely would understand more about this whole situation and the reasons behind why Rachel had said yes than even Rachel would.

She grabbed a shawl off the peg by the door and wrapped herself in it, charging down toward the Shore-man's Cabin, which was at the bottom of the winding path that led right to the beach. The little building was nestled in a cove, surrounded by rocks that kept it safe from the waves.

It had been built sometime in the 1930s, and had largely been inhabited by lone fishermen over the years.

And right now, it was inhabited by her sister.

Rachel knocked firmly, and when the door opened, Anna greeted her with round eyes. "What are you doing down here?"

"I said yes to going on a date with Mark. From the plumbing store."

"You'd better come in."

Rachel accepted the offer happily, though was slightly worried that the instant access she'd been granted spoke volumes about the fact that what she had done was a little bit crazy. And worthy of a sisterly intervention.

"I just heated up some water. You want some tea?"

"As long as there's whiskey in it."

Anna laughed. "That's disgusting. Let's try it."

"Do you really have whiskey?"

"I do," Anna said. "Which is a little bit wild, all things considered."

"I guess pastors' wives are not supposed to have bottles of whiskey?"

"Having a glass of wine at dinner with you and Mom was considered edgy by my husband."

"Really?"

"He never would have said anything at the house. But... yeah, he was always a little bit irritated when I would have one. Anyway. We're not here to talk about me. Tell me about your date." She gestured to a small table with two chairs in the kitchen. One was red, one yellow. Anna opened up a cupboard, took out to teacups that were mismatched and poured hot water into them.

"I just... I don't know. I don't have feelings for him. Not like that. I don't know if I'll ever have feelings for anyone like that again. I know that I want to. But I have to...do something. And it's not moving on."

Anna moved around, a ginger blur of motion, strands of hair escaping from her bun as she readied the tea bags and put a generous amount of whiskey into each cup. Then she set one in front of Rachel, and put one in front of the empty chair, before taking her seat.

"It's just about moving. I guess. If that makes sense. Because... I need to find a way to feel something again. I need a new place to have dinner. And a new face to have it across from. Not so I can forget, not to replace anyone. But just... I'm here. I wake up in the morning. I work at the end. And I love it. I love being here. I love you and Mom."

"Sometimes there aren't words," Anna said slowly. "Sometimes it's just your heart groaning. And it takes a good long while for groans to become actual words. For you to be able to understand them. And sometimes you shove them away for a long time, Rachel. Because it's terrifying to try and understand them, because then you'll feel compelled to act on them. But sometimes when there's a deep sadness in your heart, your heart cries out for something. It's not right or wrong—it just is. Your heart needs something. Give it what it's asking for."

"I don't want to fall in love. And I don't think I could fall in love with him. Which, honestly, is why it's such an ideal date."

"Maybe you just want to feel like a woman again. Beautiful. There's nothing wrong with that. It kills you inside, losing sight of that."

"Jacob made me feel beautiful."

"I know. I loved Jacob," Anna said. "I love him. He's the closest thing I've ever had to a brother. And I know—I believe—that he's always going to matter to you. And I don't see this as you letting go of him. Set grief to the side for a moment. Timelines. What other people might think. What do you need?"

"I guess I just want to see what life looks like now. And this feels like…a way to do that. A new view. Like I said. I—I can go out on dates now. There's a new reality that I'm living in, and if I don't do something to explore that, I'm going to end up… Sometimes I walk by our bedroom and I think he's still there. And the more I sink into isolation here, the more that's true."

"It's okay, Rachel. All of it is okay. There are about a hundred guidebooks for things like this, but the people who wrote them still never went through what you did. Because they didn't have your marriage. Your husband. And they don't have your life or your heart. We know what's right. We have a generic set of rules for how were supposed to handle everything… But when you're in the weeds, looking for solutions to your problems, sometimes things that never made sense before look a whole lot different."

Rachel tried to smile, her heart twisting. "You sound like the older sister now."

"Well, that's the thing. I'm not a kid anymore. We've both… Lived some life. We can learn from each other. We can be there for each other. You don't have to just take care of me, Rachel." She slid her hand across the space and covered Rachel's with her own. "Let me take care of you, too."

Rachel looked down into her teacup and took a sip, the whiskey burning a trail down her throat. She coughed, and then started to laugh. "I like the way you take care of me," she wheezed, pounding on her chest.

Anna took a sip, too, and blinked. "That's strong."

"I'm so tired," Rachel said. "And I don't want to go to sleep."

"Bunk with me tonight," Anna said, raising her dainty teacup. "We'll get hammered and watch HGTV."

That was a new view. A new thing.

And as she settled onto the couch with her sister, pulling a wool blanket over her knees, clutching her spiked tea, she thought that for now this was a pretty great view, after all.

18

Patrol does give a man time to think. It reminds
him of what's important. I think often of you.

—FROM A LETTER WRITTEN BY STAFF SERGEANT RICHARD JOHNSON,
JULY 25, 1944

ANNA

She had done a lot of thinking about her life over pie.

Either making it, or eating it, Anna felt that pie was an
extremely good source of clarity. This had always been
true. Whether her problems had been with friends in high
school, or concerns over a child in the church who was
sick and in the hospital.

It was true now, while she went over her own problems.

She had been baking continually at the Lighthouse Inn
over the last week, turning over the altercation with Hannah in her mind, and the conversation she'd had with Rachel after.

A few nights after she'd had her drunken slumber party
with Rachel, when they had been working on croissants
one evening, her sister had asked her why she didn't con-

sider expanding her baking, and reminded her that she'd told Adam to consider using her to bake pies.

Rachel's confidence in her sparked something, and made her feel...well, made her feel like she'd found some of her own confidence, too.

Which was why she found herself on her way to J's, ready to go in and speak to him. And feeling as nervous as if she was going on a job interview, which she'd never done in her life.

It was funny, because she had been avoiding town. Resolutely. But the worst had already happened. Someone had actually come and yelled at her. Gotten in her face. And they had come up to her sanctuary and done that, so the real question now was...what was there to be afraid of?

She could certainly run in to Thomas, which she didn't want, but the thing about Thomas was he hardly went anywhere other than church. It was there, or he was in his office. Sometimes, he did meet with people and have a coffee, engage in some public counseling at the coffeehouse. But he didn't go to J's.

She parked in an empty spot across the street, the nose of her car pointing downhill. She put on the parking brake and got out, standing for a moment as she looked at the yellow, slightly run-down building.

She turned and looked at the mechanic shop she'd parked in front of, glancing through the window and locking eyes with a young man behind the counter. She hoped he wasn't annoyed that she'd parked there. But if he was, he could just join the whole club of people that were annoyed with her.

She didn't care.

A bubble of laughter welled up in her chest.

She didn't care.

She'd had whiskey in a teacup.

She had done the absolute worst thing. She knew, beyond a shadow of a doubt, that people did think the worst of her. Her family loved her, anyway. Her mother might not have accepted her actions, but she hadn't disowned her, either. Emma and Rachel loved her. Defended her. Accepted her.

Who cared what anyone else thought? And they would think. A whole lot of things. Awful things. And she just didn't care.

She might as well park her car where she pleased.

He couldn't hate her any more than Hannah did. Hannah, she suspected, hated her more than Thomas did. In fact, she suspected a host of people did. But that was how this sort of thing went. It was so easy to inhabit someone else's life and trauma. So easy to form pure, undiluted opinions when you didn't know all the facts.

Facts often clouded emotion.

And people didn't like that.

Anna herself hadn't liked it.

It was difficult to judge after having the epiphany that she didn't know how she would have behaved if she'd been on the other side of a situation like this.

But she wasn't. She was her. Standing in solidarity with herself. It was all she could do. She took one last look inside the mechanic shop. The guy wasn't looking at her, so he must not be that bothered.

And she found that whatever she told herself about freedom, she did care slightly. Because she could hardly cast off years of emotional training and just not care at all what people thought.

But she could tell herself she didn't care. And that at

least offered moments of that feeling, whether it stuck around or not.

She crossed the empty street quickly, and walked into the diner. It was mostly empty. Too late for breakfast, too early for lunch.

There was one older couple sitting in the corner by the window, but otherwise there was no one.

Adam wasn't at the counter, but she assumed he was in the kitchen. She'd never been here when he wasn't present. In fact, she was pretty sure he lived upstairs. Not that they'd ever discussed his living arrangements.

She walked up to the counter, and no sooner had her palms pressed down on the mottled silver-and-white surface than the kitchen door opened, and Adam came out, a dishcloth slung over his shoulder.

He crossed his arms over his broad chest, the muscles in his forearms shifting, and not for the first time she thought he was a little incongruous in an old, dilapidated diner.

"Anna," he said. But he wasn't looking right at her. His blue eyes were scanning behind her, and for a moment she wondered if he was looking for Emma, since Emma was his employee.

But…no.

No. It wouldn't be Emma.

He was looking for Rachel. She didn't know why she knew that, only that she did.

"Hi," she said. "My sister mentioned that you have terrible pie."

"Okay," he said. "As opening lines go, that's a strange one."

"It's on-topic."

"Is it?" he asked.

"Yes. I would like to offer to make pie for you."

"Me personally?" He pressed his hand against his chest.

"No. Although, we can start with that, if you want. I want to make pie for the diner. You don't have a pastry chef. And I make a lot of pie, anyway. I do it for the lighthouse. It could be beneficial. For both of us. I can leave a card down here. If people like the food, maybe they'll consider coming to the bed-and-breakfast."

"I don't know what to tell you, and I hate to disappoint you. But I don't exactly get a lot of tourists in here. This is kind of a regular hangout."

"But what if people hear you have amazing pie? Then it might become a tourist hangout."

"See," he said, "that mostly scares me."

"You're a big guy. I don't actually think anything scares you that much."

She didn't know Adam well, but she could see the ripple of charged emotion that went through his body before he tipped up his lips into an overly casual smile. "I've never liked spiders."

"Well, my pies are not spiders. And tourists aren't spiders, either. I just… I don't have much to do right now. And I will literally make you pie at cost. Just…give it a chance. Give it a try. Nobody else is going to take my pie, Adam. And, honestly, if I were you I might hide who's making it first."

"Why?"

She rolled her eyes. "Please. No one's going to want any of your whore pie."

"Is that a kind of pie…?" He grimaced. "Because, I have to admit, it doesn't sound that appealing."

"No. You know… I'm not exactly well loved around here right now."

He let out a gruff sigh. "Look. I try to pretend that I

don't hear any of the gossip around here. Mostly because I don't ever want to be asked to engage in it. Also, I don't care what anyone says."

"Why not?"

"Because people are jerks. And…it's none of my business."

"Yeah. But…still."

"I don't care." He slung the dishcloth from one shoulder to the other. "And, yes, I will carry your pie. I'll put your name on it. I don't especially mind what anyone says."

"Well, people *might* say things. You do need to be aware of that."

"The people here? They all go to the community church, and they don't like the big fancy one, anyway. They think your husband is too shiny. That he's selling a bill of goods. They think anyone who can fill that many church seats can't be a shade too far above a scam-artist televangelist."

For some reason, that made Anna bristle. "Well, I don't think that's true. He's sincere in what he says, in what he believes. He's not scamming anyone, believe me."

"That is probably a bit more generous than you need to be. But again. I don't actually care. About gossip. I *do* care about pie. And you're right. Mine is terrible. Luis makes a good hamburger but he makes a pretty damned awful crust. So…yeah. Let's do it. I can get a pastry case and stick the whole ones out here, make a big deal out of it."

"Don't do that. I don't want charity pie."

"It's mutual charity. Isn't it?" He rubbed his chin. "Actually, we're exchanging money, so it's just mutual business."

"You're all right, do you know that?"

He smiled. "You only say that because you don't talk to me very often."

"So…when. When should I bring the pie?"

"Whenever. Whenever you have one done."

"I can bring them tomorrow."

"Great." He turned and started to walk into the kitchen. Then he paused. "How's Rachel?"

"She's…" She looked at his back for a moment. And while she paused, he turned to face her again and that fleeting thought she'd had earlier felt confirmed as she noticed the way the lines around his mouth deepened when he said her sister's name.

She cleared her throat. "I didn't think you did gossip."

"I don't." He crossed his arms again, rocking back on his heels.

"You could ask *her* how she is. I'm sure she would appreciate it."

"I actually don't think she would. I think she likes it when I don't ask."

"Well, it seems maybe not the best to ask me, then."

"Just because she doesn't want me to ask doesn't mean I don't want to know." He paused for a moment.

"I didn't realize you knew her quite so well," Anna said. She didn't mean to dig, but now she was a little curious.

"She's a customer. A regular. We talk sometimes." Anna knew that wasn't the whole truth. But as someone who'd sat comfortably in lies for a number of years, she didn't want to go forcing anyone out into the open until they were good and ready.

"I'm worried about her," he said finally.

"Me, too. But she… You know, I was going to say she's strong. It's true. But she's just human, too. And maybe she kind of doesn't want you to ask her how she is, but

I still think you should. I think she would like knowing that you care, Adam."

She looked around the diner's empty space. "Actually. On that subject of you caring about my family. Do you think that we can have Emma's birthday party here? Don't say anything to her. Rachel has been planning on making it a surprise, but she was going to have it up at the lighthouse. It's just... I think that place is complicated for Emma right now. She and Rachel had a big fight, and she said something about it being kind of depressing there. Considering that's where her dad died. But she likes it here. Her job here makes her happy."

He nodded slowly. "Sure. I'll shut the place down for her. Just tell me when."

"Her birthday is May 13. It's a Wednesday night, so—"

"Consider it done."

"Thank you. For everything. And I mean it. Ask Rachel how she is."

"I will," he said.

Anna turned and walked away, and she felt...more accomplished than she had in longer than she could remember.

She stepped out of the diner and onto the street, and when she turned, she found herself walking right in the path of a man she recognized. It took her a second to place him.

Xavier Ramos.

She'd gone to high school with him and had seen him at church off and on over the years. He wasn't totally regular, but he'd been around, and they'd chatted pleasantly whenever they'd seen each other.

For a moment, she forgot. And she smiled at him.

Then there was a beat. A terrified beat, where she wondered how he would respond. Would he smile back? Or would he be another Hannah. Ready to judge her and tear chunks off her.

He smiled.

"Anna," he said. "Long time no see."

"Oh. Uh. Yeah. It has been."

His eyes dropped to her left hand and then back to her face. "How are things?"

"Good," she said. "Really good, actually."

Maybe *really good* was an exaggeration. But he'd looked at her hand. He'd looked for a ring. And she'd wanted to just make it clear she was more than okay with that vacant space on her finger. Whatever he'd heard or hadn't heard.

"Oh, and you?" she asked.

He laughed and his smile lit up his face. It was a very handsome face. "Good. I fish, you know, so sometimes I'm here, sometimes I'm in Alaska. I've been back for a few weeks."

So back long enough to have heard rumors about her, that was for sure. But he didn't have any weird energy about him.

"Will you be here for a while?"

He nodded. "I plan on it. I just bought a house and I'm fixing it up. I'm hoping to be more local now."

"Oh, right. Do you have a…fiancée or girlfriend or…"

He grinned. "No."

And she tried to ignore the slight fluttering in her stomach.

"Same," she said. "Except…you know. Men. Not… women. Not that… You get what I mean."

"Yeah," he said. "I have an appointment with a contractor, but hopefully I'll see you around?"

"Yeah," she said. "I'm around."

When he left, she felt slightly breathless. Giddy.

She had done something for Rachel. She had done something for Emma.

And she had done something for herself.

She had built three things today.

And for someone who had felt like nothing but a destroyer for quite some time, that felt amazing.

But that, she supposed, was the great truth of life.

A hammer could demolish, and a hammer could build. It all depended on what you did with it.

She was capable of *both*.

She had been the one to destroy her life. And she was the only one who could build herself a new one.

19

Ron is so funny, you'd like him. Dad wouldn't.
He's got a motorcycle.

—FROM A LETTER WRITTEN BY SUSAN BRIGHT TO HER SISTER,
AUGUST 1961

EMMA

Emma felt strange leaving things unresolved with her mother. She also couldn't claim she was just a benevolent liar now.

At this point, she was simply a liar.

She saw Luke almost every night. And she always made up excuses. Picking up an extra shift, doing homework with Catherine. And her mom hadn't pushed. Likely because she was waiting for Emma to say she was sorry, or was afraid they would have another big blowup.

Emma was exploiting that. She knew she was. But as long as her mom didn't know what was happening, Emma could luxuriate in it.

She was going to Boston. She had accepted.

Luke was her boyfriend.

She could talk to him about anything. About everything. When they weren't talking…there was a lot of kissing.

She had no practical experience with guys. No kissing, and she'd certainly never wanted to have sex with one before.

And she knew it was fast. Really fast.

But she wanted to. With him.

It felt big, but it was the distraction she needed from today. Her birthday.

Today hurt.

Her dad should be here, and he wasn't. It felt wrong.

There was something about being with Luke that helped. At first it had been that crush, that secret that she had that she could hold close when the world felt hard. Now it was the beauty of something new. The healing of it.

Like renewing her heart. Layering something bright and brand-new over the old hurt. It didn't make the pain go away.

It was like a multifaceted gem. If she held it a certain way, the light caught the right edge and it glowed. Making it all she could see. Ignoring the dark spots, for just a little bit.

Luke felt so special, so important.

And she didn't care if some people would think it was too fast, or that she was too young. She didn't. She was going to see him sometime tonight. But there was going to be a family dinner first, and now Emma was helping her aunt Anna take pies to J's. She didn't mind that—it put her in proximity to Luke. Although, it would be difficult to figure out what to do with her face if she saw him, and she was with Anna.

Not that she really needed to keep it a secret from Anna.

But she didn't want to talk to anyone about it. She couldn't quite articulate why, not even to herself.

She grabbed the pies out of the back of her aunt's car and turned, looking toward the garage. She could see him through the window, and he lifted his head and his eyes met hers.

She felt color mounting in her face, and she knew that Anna could see. He knew that she was keeping him a secret, even though he didn't love it. She had explained at length that had nothing to do with being embarrassed of him—she wasn't. She was insanely proud of him.

She just didn't want... She didn't want to *share* him. She didn't want to share these happy spots in her life with anyone. Because the minute that she let the rest of her life in... Well, everything else was sad and complicated. And this wasn't.

"Are you looking at that boy?" Anna asked as she grabbed the second box out of the car.

"Maybe," Emma said, turning away.

"He's cute."

"Yes," Emma said.

Denying that Luke was cute would be more suspicious than just agreeing. She worked across the street, after all. And going to J's was how she'd seen him in the first place. So it stood to reason that she could acknowledge his attractiveness.

"I can't believe you're eighteen," Anna said.

"Why? Because I grew up so fast?"

Her aunt's face did something funny. "No. Because you're still a kid. I know you might not realize it. I know I didn't when I was eighteen. I was getting married. Ugh. Thank God you're not doing that."

Given Emma's recent thoughts about her feelings for

Luke that felt pointed, even though her aunt didn't intend for it to be.

Emma truly didn't feel young. She felt tired.

But when she was with Luke it all felt so much brighter.

"I'm proud of you, Em," Anna said, pulling her in for a one-armed side hug.

Then Anna turned and walked toward J's and Emma trailed behind her.

Guilt twisted Emma's stomach. She had never put a toe out of line, not in all her life, and now she was doing it. But she was doing it in a deceptive, quiet way. And she wondered if that was actually what her entire life was made of.

Pretending to be something she wasn't. Pretending to be someone she wasn't.

Pretending to be good, when she actually wanted to rebel.

She hadn't lied or been overly sneaky, because she had felt like it was wrong. But she also wasn't being honest about what she was. And maybe that was what had led her down the path to being such a liar now. Because it had seemed more acceptable than telling everyone what she wanted. Because that was truly terrifying.

Because it would seem random to them. This sudden desire to date an older mechanic, who had dropped out of high school. The need to spread her wings and separate herself from her family, to move across the country. It would be surprising to them because they didn't know that she was resisting her desires all this time. That she was suppressing them.

It would surprise them because she had never talked to her mom about boys, because it had seemed like such a strange and thorny subject.

She had watched her mom love her dad in a deep, intense way. But she'd also seen how sharp and painful love could be. One time she'd told her mom that she had a crush on a boy, and her mom had looked at her with wild terror in her eyes and said, "You're too young."

She had been fifteen. Now she wondered if her mom had imagined that first crush would mean Emma would want to be married at eighteen just like she had.

She was still brooding when Anna pushed open the door, and Emma walked inside, her arms full of pie, only to stop cold.

The room was full of people she knew. And in that moment that it took her to identify them all, they shouted, "Surprise!"

She blinked. "Oh."

"It's a surprise party," Anna said.

"Right," Emma responded.

She looked around and saw her mom, who was hanging back, reserved, and her grandma. And there was Adam, her boss, behind the counter, as if to announce that he was here, but not really here.

"Happy birthday," Catherine said, standing up from her table and pulling Emma in for a hug as she shoved a gift box with a balloon on the top into her hand.

The cake was beautiful, sitting in the middle of the table, and she assumed that her aunt had made it. She turned to her. "Thank you."

Slowly, very slowly, happiness put cracks into her shock. Into the dark cloud that hung over her head, and had for so long.

"Don't thank me until you try it. But I think you're going to love it." She pulled her in for a hug, too.

Her mom stood, then cautiously crossed the room, holding out her arms. And Emma leaned in.

She wasn't going to be mean. Not at her birthday party.

And she loved her mom. She didn't think for a moment that somehow that had changed just because they'd had a fight.

There was no point in acting that way.

"Thank you, everyone," she said, feeling deeply uncomfortable that she had to make anything remotely resembling a speech. "Just…thank you."

And Adam started bringing out cheeseburgers. So many cheeseburgers. And all of the French fries she could possibly want.

"Thank you," she said, again.

Her boss was a hard man to know. He was easy with jokes, but she didn't know anything about him. And he didn't demonstrate sincere feelings in an open way. But he was kind. One of the kindest people she'd ever known. The way that he supported her aunt with her pies, the way that he had always talked to her mom.

And the way that he'd given her a job, and trained her with patience, but also hadn't treated her like she was damaged.

He had helped to make this place a haven for her, and she appreciated it.

Her presents came, and it was amazing to get such thoughtful, wonderful gifts from her friends.

Each and every one made her feel like less and less of an unknowable alien. And like maybe she was the only one who'd actually seen herself that way.

A journal and frog earrings from Catherine, along with a set of her favorite pens. A succulent in an owl pot from Prathika. A giant, fuzzy blanket that Noemi, Abigail and Chantelle had gone in on together.

All things she loved. All things she would use.

It made the path back to real life seem not quite so long.

Throughout the entire event, her grandmother was unusually quiet. Emma kept looking over at Wendy, who would offer her a smile, but little else.

Emma realized that she was contributing to the way they saw her. She had hidden who she was.

They had no real idea how much Boston had meant to her, or that she had decided to go, anyway. That she was dating Luke.

And that was her fault.

She'd hidden it. And not to protect them, like she'd believed. To protect herself. She hadn't wanted to argue. Hadn't wanted to make the special, secret things in her heart public because there was something about the idea of sharing them that made her afraid she was exposing them to danger.

She didn't trust life, that was for sure.

It had taken away her father.

But that didn't mean…she couldn't keep going on out of fear.

And when she looked at her aunt Anna, she knew well how that ended. With an explosion.

Maybe she could make it all happen without an explosion. If she did it in time.

"Em…" Her mom turned to her once she'd finished with her friends' gifts. "Your dad has something for you."

Emma's heart stuttered. Her mom's eyes were shining as she reached to the edge of the table and pushed forward a wrapped box. "I don't know what it is," she said, her voice thin. "He didn't tell me. But he bought it two years ago. Because he told me he was afraid he wouldn't be here. And he wanted you to have this on your birthday.

Because he's with you, even if he can't be here physically. That was important to him, that you knew that."

Emma didn't know if she could breathe around the lump in her throat. And the room had gone quiet.

With shaking hands, she undid the ribbon. She didn't want to tear the wrapping. She peeled the edges of the tape slowly, then unfolded the plain pink paper, leaving all of it intact and revealing a small, white box.

She opened it and inside was a bracelet, rose gold, with two charms.

A lighthouse, and a round pendant with an inscription.

The Light will always lead you home.

Something clicked inside her. Like a key in a lock.

Her dad had always known she would go.

And he'd known the house, her family, would be there waiting for her, guiding her back, like a ship out at sea.

Her mom was silently wiping away tears and guilt bound up Emma. She was so…unsettled and angry about everything, and her mom was hurting, and she didn't know what to do about any of it.

Except…

She reached across the table and hugged her mom. Tears slipped down her cheeks and whatever was happening around them faded.

Whatever was going to happen in the future didn't matter.

Right now…

Right now she was home.

She released her mom and put the bracelet on her wrist, staring at it intermittently.

He wasn't here, and he should be. He'd given her this instead.

She felt the loss of him more and less all at the same time.

Her dad... He'd had to plan for a future he knew he wouldn't see. And he'd done it. It was the bravest thing Emma could even think of. The kindest.

It made her feel like she wasn't all that brave. Not by comparison. She'd struggled to accept his death. He'd had no choice. He'd accepted it. Planned for it.

And he'd still laughed with her. Smiled with her.

It made her want to be braver now. To smile and cry. To live.

She wiped away her tears and it took a while to recover, as she finished her milkshake and cake.

The party went on, and eventually she...laughed. Without thinking, without pausing first. She felt happy.

It felt normal.

Her dad not being there was strange, like there was a hole at the center of the diner. Friends filled the gaps. In the room, in her heart. For now. For this.

They ate French fries and cake until they were full, and laughed at one of the boys sucking in helium and trying to talk after.

"Idiot!" one of the girls shouted. "Use your phone for that! That's dangerous."

That only egged on more of them. But Emma appreciated it because the more ridiculous it got, the better it was.

When the evening wound down she walked outside with her friends and laughed with them halfway down the block to their cars.

She felt him watching her before she saw him.

"Hey," she said as she hugged Catherine, "thank you. I'll see you. I have to…" She gestured toward the garage.

"Ah," Catherine said. "Boyfriend."

"Who?" Prathika had overheard and leaned in, her dark eyes wide.

"Her boyfriend. The mechanic."

"Ah, no way! He is *hot*," Prathika said, with genuine enthusiasm.

Emma hadn't fully appreciated what she was missing by not telling her friends about Luke. The genuine envy was something she liked a lot better than pity.

"Yeah," Emma said, blushing a little. "I'm just going to run in for a second."

"Her mom doesn't know about him," Catherine said.

"Well, he's twenty-one. I figured I'd wait on that."

"Yeah, my mom would kill me," Prathika said.

"Mine would just worry so hard she might open up a hole in the ground. I'm just…"

"Bye!" Prathika and Catherine said together, and Emma scurried off toward the garage.

Luke was there, just like she knew he'd be.

"Did you bring me cake?" he asked.

"Oh…no. Sorry. That was dumb, I can go get you some cake…"

"I'm kidding, Em. I don't need cake." He pulled her in for a kiss and she sighed, leaning into it.

"I wish you could have been there," she said.

"Well, if your mom knew about me I could have been."

Guilt gnawed at her. Both guilt over lying to her mom, and guilt over what hiding Luke meant for him. "I know."

"I'm not going to lecture you on your birthday. But I do have something for you."

Her heart skipped. She'd really, really hoped he would

get her something and she had spent a lot of time wondering what it might be. When he handed her the small wrapped box her heart skipped.

For a moment she was worried it would be a bracelet. Like it would somehow be…something she had to put aside because her dad had just given her the bracelet and she couldn't put her boyfriend's bracelet over her dad's bracelet.

She turned it over, then started to untie the ribbon. Then the delicate tissue paper. She took the lid off the white box, and revealed a small, delicate necklace with a pearl on the end.

The chain was rose gold.

It matched the bracelet.

Emotion swelled up in her chest and she didn't know what to say or do. It just felt right somehow.

"It's not a lot," he said, "I know. But I know you love the ocean. A pearl seemed right. Maybe someday there will be more than one."

She pushed herself up on her toes and kissed him again, hard. "It's perfect," she said.

So was he.

And it was weird but in the moment she felt caught. Between him and the pearl. Him and her dreams of going away. Of that life she'd created in her head. New experiences and everything else.

He was a new experience she hadn't realized she'd wanted. And leaving here would mean leaving him.

"Let me," he said, taking the necklace out of the box and clasping it quickly around her neck.

She touched it, then looked up at him. "I…"

"Your mom won't notice. You got lots of gifts."

Pain twinged slightly in her chest. He was clearly

slightly irritated about being a secret. And she felt…well, she felt bad about it, too.

About all the secrets.

The bracelet was heavier on her wrist then.

How could she see the light if she was keeping everything in the dark? Her dad had trusted her. To know who she was and what she wanted.

She had to fix this with him. But she had to fix some things with her family first.

"I wasn't going to say anything about my mom. I was just going to say thank you. Again. I love it."

"Good," he said, shoving his hands into his pockets and taking a step backward.

"I have to go." She looked out the window of the garage and saw her mom, aunt and grandma walking out of the diner, holding gifts and balloons. "Everyone is leaving."

"I'll see you tomorrow?"

"Yeah. And I'll text tonight."

He reached out and touched her hand, and Emma smiled. Then she went to the door and ducked outside, running across the street toward her family.

Her mother, grandmother and aunt were loading everything into the back of her mom's car. Emma watched them for a moment, then touched her necklace. Immediately, her mother's eagle eye went right there.

"Where did you get that?" she asked. "It's pretty."

Emma hesitated for a moment, and then decided she wasn't going to hide it. "My… Luke gave it to me."

"Who's Luke?" her mom asked.

"He's my… Over there," Emma said, waving her hand. "He's my boyfriend."

Rachel blinked. "You have a boyfriend?"

"Cute Mechanic is your boyfriend?" Anna asked. "Why didn't you tell me?"

"I—I didn't tell anyone!" Emma said. "And I'm sorry. I should have told you. I should have told all of you. I just... Mom, I've been trying so hard not to do anything to upset you."

Her mom looked like a harsh breeze off the sea could have blown her over.

"Emma," she began, "you don't have to protect me. My job is to protect you."

Her grandmother had a slight reaction to that statement that Emma couldn't read. And her aunt Anna folded her arms over her chest and shrank away.

"No. I wanted to protect you. Because you did so much for Dad, and you've done so much for me. And... I never wanted to add to your burdens."

"You've never been a burden to me. You've been the brightest, most wonderful spot of my life in all of this."

"But I know that you don't want me to leave. And I know that's why you were upset about me taking the job here. I was afraid that if you knew I had a boyfriend you would get worried. And you would ask me questions about..."

"Right," her mom said, looking a little bit pale now.

"I just wanted something for myself. Something that wasn't going to add to...everything else. Something separate."

"I understand," Rachel said. "Emma... I don't want you to feel like you have to keep secrets from me."

"Well, I'm eighteen now. I'm grown up. It's time I started acting like it. The bracelet that dad gave me... It said the light will always lead me home. It will. This is my home. But I need to..." Emma blinked furiously, tears filling her eyes. "I lied to you about Boston. I did get accepted."

The ripple of shock that went through her family was visceral, tangible.

"I know," Emma said. "I shouldn't have lied. But then... I accepted. I accepted the offer to go. I did it without telling you. And... I was waiting... I messed it up. I know I did. But I'm not going to lie anymore. I thought that lying would protect you. But it was just keeping us from being close. It was making me miserable."

Emma couldn't read her mom's expression. She looked large-eyed and shocked. "I want to talk more about this. Maybe we should head home—"

"It takes a lot of guts for you to come down here, Anna."

The four of them turned and saw a woman Emma vaguely recognized from church. Hannah somebody.

"I wasn't aware that it took bravery for me to walk around in my own town," Anna said.

"Hannah," Wendy said, her voice measured, but Emma recognized it as dangerous. "I suggest that you move on."

"I more than suggest it," Emma's mother said. "You have nothing to say to anyone in my family. Least of all my sister. I can only assume that if you're so obsessed with her life your own must be boring and pathetic. Perhaps you should get back to it."

"I'm definitely not going to take any lectures from you, Rachel Henderson," Hannah said. "Everyone knows that you are exactly the same as your sister. Everyone knows that you were down here talking to the diner owner when you should have been taking care of your husband. For all the world to see. Anyone could walk by on the sidewalk and see you sitting on a bar stool giggling like an idiot.

And that's just what you let us see. God knows what the two of you were doing in private."

"How dare you," Rachel said, her voice choked with rage. "I loved my husband."

"Get away from me and get away from my family," Anna said. "How can you say that about my sister in front of her daughter. On her birthday. You're just angry because Laura pointed out what a hypocrite you are. It's tough to feel superior when you've already been knocked down to the ground. I don't know what your issue is—"

"Honestly," Hannah said, "I don't think anyone would ever patronize your family inn if it weren't for Wendy." Hannah turned to Wendy then. "You should be embarrassed. You shouldn't defend them. Anna especially has embarrassed you and undone all of the good reputation you spent years building."

"My good reputation?" Emma's grandmother asked. "My good reputation." She repeated the words as though they tasted bitter. "Is that why you're so angry? Because of my reputation?" Her voice was hushed, but it was deadly, and they all hung on her every word. "Well, let me tell you, my reputation is a lie."

That hung heavily between them, settled in the silence like a fog and wrapped itself all around Emma.

A lie.

Wendy took a step toward Hannah. "And if you're going to come down here and imply that something is wrong with either of my daughters, then you should know something is wrong with me. I had an affair with a married man, Hannah. Would you like to call me a whore? Go right ahead."

Her grandmother stood there, her chin tilted upward, her expression one of fire.

Anna, Rachel and Emma were struck completely silent, just like Hannah was. The waves in the distance, cars moving by on the nearby highway, all seemed deafening.

"Then it runs in the family," Hannah said finally. "And now I don't feel bad for any of you." She turned and walked away, leaving them standing there. It felt like a bomb had gone off—Emma's ears were ringing, and the silence around them deafening.

"Let's go home," Wendy said. "There are some things that I need to tell you."

20

*There are secrets one must keep. Secrets for
one's country. I do wonder, though, if secrets
of the heart ever do anything but hurt.*

—FROM A LETTER WRITTEN BY STAFF SERGEANT RICHARD JOHNSON,
OCTOBER 11, 1944

WENDY

All the way back home, Wendy turned certain revelations over in her mind.

The way that she had judged Anna.

Because she had cast that other woman, that woman who would break marriage vows, as the worst kind of harlot in the years since she had moved to Sunset Bay.

Herself.

She realized that she had done that to herself.

If you told a story enough times for a long enough time, it became easy to believe. But she'd realized how flimsy it was. How…pointless when that woman had gone after her girls on a public street.

Over the years, she had reframed everything in her mind, because it had been the easiest thing to do. But if she unburied everything, the depth of her hatred for her own self was staggering.

And when she had to speak the words, it had all come flooding together.

She had fractured the truth, swept it underneath the rug.

But now that rug had been pulled back, and she was painstakingly putting those pieces back together, trying to put the picture back into place so that she could explain.

Not just to them. But to herself.

And those pieces were sharp. Jagged. And she knew she wouldn't be able to sift through them all without cutting herself.

Without bleeding.

Three cars pulled onto the private drive, and then up to the Lightkeeper's House.

Wendy got out first, inhaling the ocean air, trying to allow the familiar sounds of the waves hitting the rocks, rumbling through her, to soothe her. But she was beyond the point of soothing. She wrapped her lilac shawl more firmly around her body, as if it might hold her together. She walked up the steps of the front porch slowly, and then unlocked the door and pushed it open.

She flicked on the lights, but somehow, the familiar house didn't feel familiar right now.

The whole world felt alien.

Because when she had written that letter, asking to be the innkeeper of this beautiful place, when she had scrubbed and polished, restored and renewed the building, she had scrubbed away pieces of herself.

As she had given a new facade to this place, she had done the same for herself. For her own life.

But just like the house itself, no matter how new the

fixings were, no matter how the wood shone with care from all that polish, no matter the new wallpaper, the new paint, the new appliances in the kitchen, the history remained the same.

Underneath all that beauty, it was still an old house.

It wasn't made new.

And neither was she.

She had covered and covered for as long as she could. But the wear beneath had come out now. And she should have known that was inevitable. It was just like this house. Something always broke. Because no matter what new things they put over the top of the old, the fundamental structure was from 1894. And so there would always be burst pipes and strange noises.

You couldn't change who you were.

You couldn't erase your past.

You could only cover it.

"Mom," Rachel said. "Let's go sit down."

Rachel was taking charge, taking care. Of course. Anna looked tight-lipped and angry, and Wendy was afraid that would only get worse.

Emma looked worried.

The four of them went to the dining table and took their usual places in the chairs.

There were two empty chairs, and that felt like it sat large and heavy in the space.

Jacob's seat was empty because he was gone. Thomas's seat was empty. The shape of them had changed.

And it was about to change again.

She was afraid. Afraid this would mean more empty chairs around her table. Her fictional reputation was hurting Anna. It was hurting Rachel. And Wendy couldn't justify it. Not anymore.

"I'm so sorry," Wendy said. "I blame myself for all of this. I tried to tell you how to live good lives. I tried to guide you into happy marriages. But I don't know anything about them. I told you that mine was ended by another woman, but that wasn't true. The truth is, I was never married. I was the other woman."

Silence settled hard in the house, the only sounds the ticking of the clock and the groaning of the floorboards, as if the house itself was protesting all of this.

"Explain." It was Anna who said that, her face pale and drawn, her voice thin.

"I was never going to tell you this," Wendy said. "It never seemed like there was any point. I made up this story to protect you. You have to believe that. And then over the years I sort of forgot that it wasn't true. Because I told it so many times. Because you would ask me about your father and I would tell you who he was, and I had changed the way it all went. And I repeated it more times than I ever lived the reality of what happened, and it began to seem more real. And I was grateful for that. Because then I could be angry. Because then I could feel justified. Because then I could enjoy the life that I built here with you, because it's easier to be a victim than it is to be the one who—"

"Just tell us what happened," Anna said.

"Anna," Rachel cautioned. "Give mom a moment, she's upset."

"*I'm* upset," Anna said.

"Should I leave?" Emma asked.

"No," Wendy said. "You should hear this, too."

And that was the hardest thing. To let her granddaughter stay. To let her granddaughter be part of this thing that was going to fracture their family, their lives, even more than they already were.

"I was never married to your father," Wendy said. "I started working for him when I was eighteen years old. I never had a great relationship with my mother, and I was eager to leave home and make a life for myself. So I did. I got an office job, and I felt independent and confident. And I liked my boss. A lot. And he liked me. He was… about twelve years older than I was. And it took some time, but we began a relationship."

"Meaning you started sleeping with him," Anna said, pointed and hard. Bitter.

She'd had a hand in creating that hardness. That bitterness. Her own fear had kept her from reaching out to her daughter when she should have.

She had caused all the harm she'd hoped to prevent. Like dammed-up water finding its way around the barrier. Causing damage to places unseen and unguarded.

Eroding that foundation that was made only of sand.

"Yes," Wendy responded, feeling shame lance her chest. "He was married. And I knew that. But he kept telling me that he loved me, and that she didn't love him. He told me all about how his marriage was failing, and I found a way to twist and justify it in my head. Because he loved me better, but he was trapped. And he had to figure out a way to not be in that trap. He had to protect his legacy, his work. His money."

She took in a shuddering breath. "I got pregnant. And he promised that he would leave her. Then he told me it wasn't possible for a variety of reasons. After I had Rachel, he made me leave my job. But he kept paying for my life. He paid for us to have a little apartment and he would come and visit us."

Rachel looked pale, stunned. "I remember that," she said. "I remember him. But not much. He never lived there, did he?"

"No. He never did. And then, he quit seeing us for a while. He said there were reasons… And he couldn't leave his wife just yet, and he had to go away for a while. But I think what happened was she was getting suspicious. And he couldn't chance that. He kept paying for the apartment. But I went out and got another job, part-time, so I could keep taking care of you and only have you in day care for some of the time. And then he came back. He came back, and I was weak. And I loved him. And I forgave everything. His absence, that he hadn't left his wife yet. Everything. That was when I got pregnant with Anna. I found a picture of his family in his wallet after that. His whole family. He had children."

"We have half siblings?" Anna asked. "We have half siblings, and you didn't tell us."

"You had to have assumed that was a possibility all this time. And you never asked." She shouldn't have said that. She shouldn't have been defensive. But that much at least was true.

And it did seem to quiet Anna for the moment. She wasn't sure she had the right to quiet Anna, or to try and mitigate her youngest daughter's judgment.

Because it was Anna she had hurt the most. And she knew it. Not just with the judgment that her lie had contributed to as far as the town was concerned. But the way she had been unable to reach out to her. Because it had touched too close to all these things, and she had still been running from them inside of herself.

She had been running for more than thirty years.

"I would love to tell you that I was the one who cut

things off. And maybe in some ways I was. But I had to disappear to do it. When he found out I was pregnant with Anna, he left. I have no doubt he would've been back when he wanted…what he wanted from me. But I left. I heard about this place. About the contest. And I ran. I found a place here. And an opportunity to start over. I knew that nobody… Nobody would want to be friends with a woman who'd slept with another woman's husband. No one would want to know the other woman. And they wouldn't want to be friends with her children. And I—I wanted better for you. Better for me. Better for this place, and our future. I thought that I'd done it. But the day that Jacob died, all that we built here started unraveling. Suddenly I could see… No matter how hard I tried to spare you from pain, I couldn't. And I didn't. I caused you a different kind of pain by lying. And I'm sorry."

Wendy looked at her daughters, and her granddaughter. Rachel was clearly torn between comforting Anna and comforting Wendy. Emma looked subdued. But Anna… The anger in Anna's eyes burned.

21

I have had far too much time to think up here.
It's become unbearable. If you sit alone with your
thoughts for too long, you question everything.
The whole way the world is put together.

—FROM A LETTER WRITTEN BY STAFF SERGEANT RICHARD JOHNSON,
NOVEMBER 1944

ANNA

Everything that Anna had believed about life had been instilled in her by her mother.

And so much of the shame that she had felt over the crumbling tower that was her marriage over the past several years had come from the way that her mother had instilled such value in the institution.

Right. Because you married a pastor and became a pastor's wife and none of the pressure from town, and church, and yourself, played a role in your inability to walk away like a normal person.

Well, that might be. But her mother was part of that.

And her mother had been…just as weak as she was.

Granted, they hadn't been *her* marriage vows, but someone else's. But it had gone on for *years*.

She was the other woman that she had purported to hate so much.

Anna couldn't wrap her mind around it.

"I don't understand," she said, the words falling from her mouth before she even had a chance to think to speak. "I have to understand how you could talk about a wife and marriage vows as something sainted. Sacred. How you could paint the kind of woman who would come in and sleep with another woman's husband as being evil. When it was you. It was *you*. You were with someone else's husband at night. You were... You were the villain. You were the woman you asked us to hate, that you asked me to hate. And I've been hating myself and...living miserably because of it."

"I believed everything that I said to you. I believed that a woman who would do what I did was weak." Her mother's voice broke, but Anna didn't feel any pity. Anna didn't feel anything. "I believed that a woman who would do what I did was morally compromised. I believe that about myself, Anna. And over the years it became easier and easier to push it to the back of my mind. To pretend. Because the woman that I was and all the things that I believe about her... She couldn't have raised you girls. She was too flawed. She... I..."

Her throat worked and she closed her eyes. Then she seemed to gather herself and spoke again. "It's me. I can't let myself off the hook. Not anymore. I can't distance myself from what I did. I want to. I fell in love and it made me do things that I never believed I was capable of. When I went back home... I was pregnant with you. My mother already thought that I was a sinner beyond redemption, Anna. And when she found out that I'd let him back into bed with me… When she found out I was pregnant again… The things she called me. Well, they were things I had already called myself, believe me. She said it would be better if you didn't know. Or if I gave you—both of you—up for adoption. Because that kind of shame would follow you. She said my mother loved me enough to give me up. She said I should be brave enough to do that for you and for Rachel because I was unfit."

"Mom," Rachel said. "She didn't say that to you. She couldn't have."

"Of course she could have. Why do you think you've never seen her?"

"I knew she wasn't supportive," Rachel said.

"Well, she wasn't wrong. About the way people would see me. What would have happened if we would have come here and people had known that I'd had an affair with a married man that spanned years? That I had two children with him? Do you think they would have been kind to me? They would've locked their doors and never let me anywhere near them. They would've been afraid that I would steal their husbands. They would never have let you play with their kids. It would have followed you. It would have followed Emma. We would have been outcasts up here on the hill instead of being part of the community."

"So it was up to me to make us outcasts, then?"

"No," her mom said. "Of course I don't mean that."

"But it's the outcome. I'm the one that ruined things. And you're all just good. Good people, who have to deal with me."

"Was telling Hannah not enough? Do you want me to get a billboard and put it up in the middle of town, Anna?

Because I will. I'll expose myself—my reputation doesn't mean anything to me in light of what this has done to you."

"Why? Why bother?" Anna said. "You can just go ahead and keep defending me on the street when people come up to shout at me because they're so angry about what I did to my husband. And you all are, too," Anna said, looking around the room.

"I'm not," Emma said. "I never was."

Some of the anger drained from Anna. "No, Emma. I'm sorry. I don't mean you."

"I didn't understand at first," Rachel said. "I understand now. I'm sorry that I wasn't able to be supportive of you at first. I am."

Suddenly Anna felt gross and mean. And she remembered Rachel saying something similar to her only a few weeks ago.

Don't you ever just feel mean?

She felt mean now. Mean and unforgiving, and she just didn't want to see her mom's point of view. She was hurt. Wounded. Destroyed by this lie and how it had shaped her life.

"We lived to make you happy," Anna said. "Because of what you did for us. Because you made us feel like... Like your life was harder because you had us." That wasn't exactly true, but it was something that Anna had always been somewhat aware of. That her mother had it harder because she was single. And that she was single because of the two of them. "Everything that I thought about being married, it's because of you. Because of the sanctity that you bestowed on it. And you didn't even believe in it. You used to tell me that the secret to a happy marriage was love, but how would you know? You've never even been married. And I stayed married so much longer than

I would have because of you. You didn't keep me from becoming that other woman, Mom. You turned me into her, because I didn't know how else to escape. And I'm not sure that I can ever forgive you for that."

Anna turned and fled the room, went out the front door and down the steps, into the darkness.

She looked up at the lighthouse, cutting great swaths of brightness through the endless night.

She felt lost. Alone.

She thought of the soldiers that had been stationed up here, not knowing if there was an enemy out there in the darkness.

She knew where the enemy was.

The enemy was inside her.

She started to cry then. Real, deep sobs, that came from the depths of her soul. And she didn't know what was actually devastating her. That she felt her mother was at fault for her marriage? Because she knew that wasn't the whole story.

That her mother wasn't a saint?

Or that *she* wasn't. And that she had no one to blame but herself.

Not Michael, not Thomas.

Things had gone the way they did because of choices she made.

She let out another wrenching sob as a fat raindrop plunged from the sky and splattered onto her face. All around her, the clouds let down, the rain like ice over her skin, rolling down her back, under her clothes.

So cold at first, but then she stood there, and closed her eyes as the storm raged around her, as the waves began to froth and groan, crashing against the rocks like they were trying to destroy the very foundations of the outcropping the lighthouse sat on.

The very foundations of her life.

And she waited.

Waited for things to crumble around her.

Waited for the rain to make her feel clean.

But she didn't. No amount of rain, no amount of self-righteous anger at her mother… Nothing seemed to work.

And she wondered if this was just life now. Caught somewhere between happiness and guilt. A remorseless sort of guilt that she didn't know if she could ever explain, let alone sort through inside of her own heart.

It wasn't even all about the affair, but how she'd gotten there. How she'd let her life get away from her, and allowed herself to be a passenger in her own existence, rather than the driver.

She supposed all of that, those things that didn't make sense, went right along with wearing her mother's shawl to keep out the chill, even while she was so angry with her.

Her life was splintered. Her feelings were fractured.

And she wondered if they could ever be whole again.

22

We fought. He kissed me. I lost my mind.
I am not myself here. I am not myself with him.

—FROM THE DIARY OF JENNY HANSEN, APRIL 20, 1900

RACHEL

Rachel had no idea if Adam would still be down at J's. But she also didn't know where else to go. She drove too fast down the winding road. The rain, combined with the streetlights, made little dots of gold on the windshield. Maybe he wouldn't be there. She could have called to check. But either way the drive would…help clear her head, maybe.

Emma had told Rachel she wanted to go to Catherine's house and it was probably lazy parenting to let her. Wasn't she supposed to sit with her and have a heart-to-heart? But it was her birthday and it had ended explosively. If she wanted to go hang out with a friend…who was Rachel to stop her? She hoped that Emma didn't think what Hannah had said about Adam was true.

And here she was, on her way to see him.

And you going to see Adam has nothing to do with how weird Hannah made you feel?

Well, maybe it did. She needed to see him to be sure that…it was the same still.

When she pulled up in front of the diner, she could see that there was still a light on. She parked by the curb and walked up to the door. It was locked. But she could see Adam, standing there behind the counter. She knocked, and he looked up, his blue eyes clashing with hers. His beard was a little longer than normal, and it made him look just a little bit dangerous.

Which was weird. More than weird.

Because Adam was her safe space. He wasn't dangerous at all. But she couldn't quite shake that thought, even as he came over to unlock the door.

"Is everything all right?"

She didn't have an answer to that. "Can I come in?"

He looked her up and down. "Of course."

He backed away from the door, and she slipped inside, the smell of his aftershave catching her for a moment. Then she just walked over to her regular stool.

"I hope you're not after food, because I just got everything cleaned up."

"No."

"You want some of Anna's pie?"

Of course, he offered food, even when he'd just said she couldn't have it. "I didn't come for food. I don't really ever come for food. I just need to talk."

He nodded slowly. "Did you want me to turn the lights on?"

She looked around. It was pleasantly dim, the only light coming from back behind the counter. She felt like it offered her just a little bit of privacy. Almost like a confessional.

"Off is fine," she said.

"Whatever you want."

"What do you know about Emma's boyfriend?" Of all the new information she had to process tonight, this was the safest place to start.

"Um, I don't know her boyfriend."

"The boy who works at the mechanic place over there," she said, gesturing broadly toward the windows.

"Right. Well… I don't know that I consider him a boy."

"What? How old is he?"

"I'm not sure," he said. "But…older. Not like… I mean, he's still a kid to me."

She narrowed her eyes. "Is he a good kid? Should I be worried?"

"Probably," he said. "Just because as a parent it's your job to be, right?"

She laughed, hollowly. "Right. Sure." She sighed. "She… She's going away to Boston. And she has a boyfriend. And I didn't know any of it. Because I thought I was there. And I thought that I was part of her life. But I'm not." She felt like there was no ground under her feet.

She didn't know her daughter. She didn't know her mother.

"That's normal. You do know that, right?" he asked.

"Is it normal to not have any idea where your daughter has decided to go to college?"

"Well, maybe not *that*. But it's pretty normal for your teenager to not tell you every detail about her life."

"She had a plan to go across the country. Before Jacob died. She and her friend Catherine both want to do the marine-biology program at that school, and she spent a lot of time talking to this woman who runs an aquarium that has a connection with the college, and she was sure she was going to get a position there. But she told me she didn't get accepted to the school. And I... I was glad. Because I wanted her here. With me. But she wanted to go. And I didn't realize that."

"You still don't want her to go," Adam said.

Those words cut through her chest.

"Of course I don't. I didn't particularly want her to go before I was living by myself. And that's...awful. It's so selfish. I hate that I even have that...feeling inside of me. I want to be the kind of mom who just wants the best for her kids and doesn't take her own happiness into consideration at all."

"I think they call parents like that liars."

She huffed a laugh. "No. Surely there are truly selfless mothers in the world." That comment just brought her back to her own mother, but she didn't want to get into that with Adam.

"Maybe Emma won't like it," he said. "Maybe she'll get over there and she'll want to leave."

"That would be terrible. She would be across the country from me and upset..."

"But at least it would be her decision. Or maybe she'll love it. And she'll come back and visit at the holidays, and it will be hard for years. But God knows you've been through worse."

Silence stretched between them. She hadn't come for advice, but for that neutral listening ear he'd provided all this time. But she had broken their unspoken rule, and she had mentioned Jacob. She had talked about the problems in her real life.

And she hadn't realized it until it was too late.

She splayed her hands over the counter and looked down at them. Her wedding ring was still on her left hand. She should probably take it off before she went out with Mark. Which was such a weird, stupid thought to have right now.

"Yes. I *have* been through worse. You're right. I don't exactly want to go through more."

Adam leaned forward slightly, and his hands went with him, sliding over the countertop, and she watched them. The tips of his fingers were so close to hers.

It wouldn't take much. A slight shift, and their hands would touch.

"How are you?" His voice was low, and it skimmed over her skin in a way that made her feel edgy and uncomfortable.

She should move, because being close to him was making her uncomfortable, too.

But she didn't.

"Ugh. Don't ask me that," she looked up at his face. "I'm here asking you advice at nine p.m. How do you *think* I am?"

"In general," he said.

"We don't talk about that stuff."

He shrugged. "We do now, I guess."

"I don't know. I don't know what to call how I am. Sad, and tired of being sad, because I feel like half of my life has been sadness for years. And it's all kind of bittersweet, because the end that I knew was coming, came, and I don't know what to do with myself. Except… I have a date."

Adam's hands moved back a fraction. "Really?"

"Yes."

"With who?" Another fraction away.

"That is not your business." Her own hands slid back slightly.

"Why not? Do I know him?"

"Probably. Mark."

"Mark from the plumbing store?" They moved an inch.

"Yes. I went in to buy a pipe and he asked me on a date."

"Really?" His hands slid back with that repeated question.

"Yes. You asked me that already." She curled her hands into fists, still resting on the counter. "I mean, we're going out as friends. It's just…practice for being a human in the world. It's not *a thing.*"

"Well, I guess that's the thing," he said. "You go out, you find yourself a guy. You go on dates. That's what you do while your daughter's at college. Because…you can. Isn't that kind of the point of empty nests?"

"I don't want one," she insisted. "Not really."

"Life doesn't tend to ask what you want. It's not a diner. Things aren't made to order."

"Neither is your food."

Their eyes caught. And then he quit moving away.

He leaned in just slightly, and she caught that scent again. His aftershave. His skin. Her stomach fluttered, just a little bit. And she was absolutely and totally taken aback by the sensation.

By her need to stay where she was, right in his orbit.

She had always felt drawn to him. From the moment they'd met. But it was different right now.

She swallowed and leaned back. For some reason, that motion triggered a response in him, and he straightened, taking two large steps backward.

"Am I a bad mother?" she asked.

"I'm not going to comment on anyone else's parenting."

She frowned. "Anyone else's?"

"Never mind. Just…love her, Rachel. Like you do already. You're going to make mistakes. But…don't drive her away."

"I—I don't want to. But I worry about her."

"She's eighteen. You have to trust that the parenting you already did will keep her from doing too many things you don't want her to do. And then you have to remember all the things that you did that your mom wouldn't have wanted you to do."

She laughed. Hollow and bitter. "Except I barely did anything my mom wouldn't have wanted me to do. My reasons were…silly. Because apparently my mom was a bigger rebel than Anna and I combined. Well, Anna up until a couple of months ago."

"Was that the source of the tension from earlier?"

"Yeah. Oh…my dad, Adam. I just… I just thought that I would have to survive going through this huge milestone of my daughter being a legal adult without my husband. I didn't think I'd also have to deal with family secrets, my daughter's secrets and…" She met his gaze and the words died on her lips. "I'll tell you. About my mom sometime."

"Well, if you ever need to talk. You know where to find me."

She did know where to find him. She always had.

Hannah's words echoed in her head and lodged a wedge of discomfort in her chest.

"Yeah," she said, "apparently you never leave."

"It's true. I don't actually have a life. I exist right here in this spot for whenever you show up."

He was joking, but there was something in his blue

eyes that didn't feel like a joke, and she had to turn away from him.

"Good night, Adam," she said, sliding off the stool.

"Good night, Rachel." His voice was low and husky, strange. "Have a good date."

She turned, and it took a lot longer than it should have for her to find some words. "I will."

"You deserve good things to happen to you," Adam said, his voice soft now. "I mean it."

"Thank you." She hoped more than anything that what he said was true. That maybe she deserved good things. And if he thought so…maybe they would happen.

She had no other reason to hope.

23

Well, I did it. My parents would be furious if they
knew. But it can be my secret. Just mine and his.

—FROM THE DIARY OF SUSAN BRIGHT, AUGUST 1961

RACHEL

The next day, Rachel cleaned until her knuckles bled.
Anna was hiding in the Shoreman's Cabin and her mom
was like a zombie.

Rachel couldn't stand the tension.

When Emma finally got back from Catherine's, Rachel
felt like she needed to talk to her. Not only about Boston,
and about this mysterious boyfriend of hers, but also about
the accusations that Hannah had thrown around out on the
street. It was weird, to acknowledge that there needed to be
a shift in her relationship with her daughter. Because when
Emma had looked at her and said that she just wanted to
protect her mother, Rachel had felt shame. Intense shame.

She was supposed to protect Emma. Emma wasn't
supposed to protect her. And, more importantly, Emma
shouldn't ever feel like she had to. But she did. And she

realized that her daughter was carrying a lot more weight on her slender shoulders than Rachel had ever imagined.

It was the same with Anna. The same with her mother, even, and it was hard to acknowledge that because she was still so mad at her mother, but it was true.

She didn't have a solution for the way things were between them. And she wasn't even sure if…being conscious of it now, she could have fixed it before it got here.

She had been lost in her own hurt. In the day-to-day doing, and caring for Jacob. Anna had been lost in trying to maintain the appearance that her marriage was okay. Her mother had been lost in this fiction she had created about herself. And Emma… Emma had been hiding herself.

Rachel sighed heavily and made her way upstairs to her daughter's room. She knocked tentatively.

"Come in," said a muffled voice.

Rachel walked in and saw that Emma was stretched across her twin bed sideways, her legs hanging off the other side. She had a book in front of her, and her phone next to that.

"Can we talk?"

"Yeah," Emma said. "Are you mad at me?"

"No. I'm mad at myself."

"Are you mad at Grandma?"

"A little bit."

"Yeah," Emma said. "I can see why you would be."

"Aunt Anna is furious with her," Rachel said. "She's so mad she's barely talking to me."

"I can't blame her," Emma said.

"Me, neither."

Rachel hesitated for a moment. "About what Hannah said," Rachel said. "About me. And about Adam…"

Emma wrinkled her nose. "I didn't take that seriously,"

she said. "That woman is clearly insane. Like…what's her deal?"

"I don't know," Rachel said. She thought it best to hold back that she thought Hannah might be a frigid bitch. That was the kind of thing reserved for her sister, not her daughter.

"Adam is my friend," Rachel said, something about the words sitting wrong on her tongue. "And I swear to you, nothing… I was faithful to your father. I loved him. I love him still. Nothing will ever… It will never change that. Luke is your first boyfriend, right?"

"Yes," Emma said, frowning.

"You'll never forget them," Rachel said. "Never. Whatever happens after this. You never forget the first time you fall in love."

Emma's cheeks went pink. "I didn't say I was in love with him."

"Are you?"

"We've only been…hanging out for a couple of months."

"It doesn't matter. It's just… Those relationships that build who you are… You never move on from those. Your dad shaped me into the woman I am, just like I shaped him. He gave me you. He gave me twenty wonderful years. I will never not love him."

"That's—" Emma blinked "—good."

"You know, people would never ask you to move on," Rachel said. "They never expect you to get over losing a father because they don't expect you to replace him. People start asking widows and widowers to move on, though. And I'm not sure that's the right way to look at it. I'll love him forever, just like you will."

"Yeah," Emma said.

Rachel nodded slowly. "I just wanted to make sure you

knew that. That you knew I wasn't sneaking off and… I wasn't."

And yet, something about what Hannah had said had tripped a guilt wire in her heart, and she couldn't quite let it go. Because she might not have ever touched Adam, or fantasized about him or anything like that, but she had been down at that diner escaping.

Insulating herself. Building a little space that belonged only to her.

It was one reason she couldn't be mad about Emma and her boyfriend. Because she understood. She understood just not wanting to talk about everything all the time. Not when it played over and over in your mind, and the feelings echoed around your heart all day, every day.

To have a space that was separate from these big, epic changes that were happening in your life was… Sometimes it was the only thing that kept you going. The only thing that kept you breathing.

"You can tell me things," Rachel said. "I mean it."

"I think I've told you everything."

"I want you to go to the school that you want to go to," Rachel said.

"Thank you," she said.

"I got asked on a date," she said, not sure what had spurred that except that she was asking for honesty, so she supposed she better give it.

"Really?"

"Yeah. I don't… I don't know how I feel about it. Like I said, I don't want to move on. I don't want to replace Dad with anyone else… But…sometimes I think it would be nice to go to dinner."

"Just dinner?"

"Just dinner," she said.

"I don't see why you can't do that."

"Really?"

"Mom, I don't want to stop doing things because—because Dad died. I don't know why you shouldn't have a life. It's not like you're going to marry him."

Rachel forced a laugh. "No! No. I'm not going to do that. I'm not... I don't have feelings for him or anything." She blinked back tears. "This wasn't my dream. But, Emma, you always were. You always will be. And you realizing your dreams matters to me."

"Your happiness matters to me, Mom."

Happiness.

They could both have that. They both deserved it.

Rachel was determined.

She sank onto the bed and pulled Emma into her arms. Emma pulled her into a hug, and the two of them tipped sideways onto the mattress. Emma laughed, and her smile looked so much like Jacob's it took her breath away.

Rachel couldn't help but smile back.

Jacob was in her heart. In her daughter's smile. In the young woman she was becoming. Strength and certainty—a gift he'd given her with his steady, loving parenting that had continued after his death. That most perfect gift.

He was in the very walls of the house. The sound of the ocean against the rocks. Because this life they'd built, and the sounds, sights and smells of it, was forever linked to him. To twenty years of love, laughter, struggle, pain, loss and joy.

Nothing could replace him.

And dinner date or not, no one ever would.

24

I'm in trouble. If Mom and Dad find out they will never speak to me again. And he's gone. I don't even have an address for him. I don't feel eighteen right now. I feel all of eight years old, and I'm terrified.

—FROM A LETTER WRITTEN BY SUSAN BRIGHT TO HER SISTER, SEPTEMBER 1961

WENDY

Wendy had seen John Hansen's name appear on the books a few days earlier, but she'd been so lost in her own personal haze that she hadn't been able to process it.

Anna still wasn't speaking to her.

Rachel was frosty. Only Emma seemed to have taken it all in stride.

But when John appeared in the entryway of the inn on the day of check-in, she couldn't ignore him. And she didn't feel like she was in a daze at all.

"Hello," she said, grabbing hold of her necklace chain, and then immediately releasing it.

She was acting like an insecure girl.

"Good to see you again," he said, nodding once. His

voice was pleasantly deep, and his manner would have been reassuring if she didn't find him so…unnerving. He had the slow, steady demeanor of a rancher, and she wondered if she had the right read on him. And then she wondered why she cared.

He was the only guest in the house. Which was strange.

"It's…the wine-and-cheese hour," she said. "Of course, you're the only one. And you had the historical tour already."

"I'll take a beer," he said. "Is there a beer-and-pretzel hour if you're the only guest?"

"Sure," she said.

"And is there a chance that the innkeeper can join me? Since I'm the only guest?"

She didn't see why not, and part of her just wanted to sink into the moment. To quit…guarding herself quite so closely. Because of what it'd gotten her? Sure, she had managed to keep her walls up all these years, and she had maintained a facade for the town.

She had never engaged in liaisons with guests, or anyone else for that matter. She had… She had shut down that part of herself a long time ago.

And just for a moment, she wanted to let it go.

She wanted to feel beautiful again.

She felt like a failure right now. As if everything she'd worked for had come to nothing. Because Anna was so hurt, and her hurt was linked so tightly to Wendy's lie. And Wendy had to wonder—for all Rachel would never say it because her love for Jacob would prevent it—if Rachel was hurt in many ways because of Wendy, too.

If she had also married too young. And jumped into a life far too serious. If she should have let them be free. Given them wings instead of clipped them.

For all she hadn't meant to, it seemed that she had.

Her birds were still in the nest. And didn't that mean she hadn't given them the strength to fly away?

She was ruined inside. And that made her want to embrace this even more.

She wanted to enjoy that a man was looking at her. In all honesty, she had thought that moment had passed. That she had let it go sometime back in her twenties, with lines and gravity and everything else stealing the chance of it ever happening again.

But he seemed to think she was beautiful.

And she thought he was pretty beautiful himself.

There was no one left to protect, and the ones who had counted on her hadn't been protected by her, anyway. And she knew exactly how the world worked. No smooth-talking cowboy type was going to change that.

She wasn't an eighteen-year-old working in an office, not anymore. She was a grown woman, a businesswoman, a mother. Someone who had built a life for herself. She didn't need to be protected or supported. And it was that lack of need that made her feel so confident and easy right now. Like there was no reason to hold him at bay.

"Yes. The innkeeper would love to join you for a beer."

"And since I'm the only guest, I feel like I should do the work of acquiring it. Why don't you have a seat?"

"Well, I'll take you up on that."

He went toward the kitchen, and she could hear him moving around. She went into the sitting room, and sat in one of the antique chairs that was positioned in front of the window. The lace curtains were pulled back, and the weather stormed outside of them, the ocean a ferocious gray.

He returned with two beers, and a bowl that contained pretzels.

"I have a confession to make," he said. "I brought the pretzels."

"Well, that was forward-thinking of you."

"I'm not much for wine and cheese."

"I am," Wendy said. "But this is nice, too."

"If you want to have wine and cheese, don't let me stop you. There is no problem with us each enjoying something different."

"This is different for me," she said, taking the bottle from his hand and raising it slightly. "A nice departure."

"Well, then. Far be it for me to stop you."

He sat down in the chair across from her. There was ample space between them, and it shouldn't have felt charged at all. But it did. They were alone together in the house, and that didn't make Wendy feel scared or insecure. No.

It was exciting.

What a way to run from your problems.

But she wasn't in the mood to be chastised. Not even by herself. Perhaps most especially not by herself.

"What brings you back here?"

He shook his head. "I can't seem to stay away. Loss makes you think a lot about your life."

"Yes," Wendy said. "That is true. My—my son-in-law passed. A couple of months ago. It's been… It's been a difficult time."

"I'm sorry to hear that. My father was an old man. It still makes you think, but it's at least the order of things. It's terrible when someone that young passes."

"It is. I agree."

"My wife died far too young," he said. "It was... It was hell."

"I'm sorry," Wendy said sincerely.

"It was a long time ago now. You don't get over it, but it fades. Or maybe it doesn't. Maybe it's just that everything around you is fresher. More real. Requires more energy. She's with me still. She always will be. My first love, the mother of my children. That doesn't fade."

"No, of course not."

"I couldn't go on a journey when she passed. I had children to finish raising. I did that. They're all in their forties now, with children of their own. Living all over the country. Which I suppose is evidence that I did something right." He paused for a long moment. "I'm a rancher by trade. I don't have much of anything to do with the sea. It fascinates me that my ancestors did."

So she'd been right. He was a rancher. "I'm sorry to hear about that. Your wife. The family fallout..."

"I don't even know what it was about. I've been collecting bits and pieces of information ever since my father died. It's a hell of a thing, to realize that you left some things too late. Everyone that I could have asked is gone. And my only real connection is...this place. So I know it might seem a little bit crazy that I'm here, but it... It's my only connection to the past."

She nodded slowly. "Funny you should mention family secrets."

"You have some of your own?"

"Doesn't everyone?"

"Apparently."

"I've learned from your great-great-grandmother," Wendy said slowly. "I'm sorry you didn't know about her until recently because she was an amazing woman. I talk to her sometimes up here. Think about her an awful lot. She left everything she knew behind and she made a life here. I always thought I was like her. But Jenny was braver than I am. Jenny came here and shared herself fearlessly. And it's how she found love. I kept my secrets. I kept people out. I let my daughters think a certain thing about their past. About my past. And..." She looked at him. "You were a good man, weren't you? A good husband."

"I like to think I was."

"Were you faithful to your wife?"

He nodded once. "Yes, ma'am."

Well, she would see just what he thought of her—really thought of her—in a moment. Like Anna said, maybe it was time for her to cope with what people would think of someone like her. Because while she had enough self-hatred to go around, she hadn't had to deal with the hatred of others.

"I had an affair with a married man. For years. I've never been married. I loved someone that I couldn't have, and I… You know, I don't know if his wife ever knew about me. I don't know if I hope that she found out, and found someone better, or if I hope that I never got the chance to hurt her."

"Love makes fools out of all of us in time. And there are ample ways to be hurt by it," he said.

"You don't sound shocked to find that out about me."

He shook his head. "Life is long, and it's a hell of a strange trip. Besides, I'm not the same person I was even ten years ago. Much less thirty."

"I suppose that's true. Though, I wonder who I would have been if I would have been up front about what I'd done. With my girls. With everyone. I can't help but wonder. I punish myself all this time. Tried to make myself into something… Something else. Have you been with anyone since your wife?"

His charcoal-gray eyebrows shot upward. "There's a question. But, yes. I have been. It's been a long time, like I said."

"Ever come close to getting married again?"

He shook his head. "No. When my kids were young, there was no chance of that, and then… I don't know. I got kind of accustomed to my own company. Can do whatever I want, go wherever I please. But you've been single a long time, you ought to understand that."

She nodded. "I do. I understand that well."

"And you know, now I'm free to go to a lighthouse bed-and-breakfast on a whim, whenever I feel like it, because I have people to help manage the ranch in my absence, and I don't have anyone to question where I go."

"That doesn't sound so bad."

"It hasn't been. But sometimes it's lonely."

"Sometimes it is," Wendy agreed.

"How about you? I figure the question is fair to ask back."

"No one," she said. "Because I made myself into a lady of virtue, and I figured that I'd better live up to that."

"Well, that," he said slowly, "is a hell of a lot of pressure to put on a man."

"Or an honor," Wendy said. "Though, who said I was going to bestow it?"

"Just wishful thinking, I suppose. Though, I have to tell you, I don't think being with a man you find attractive is a black mark on your virtue. You seem like a pretty damned virtuous woman to me, Wendy, but then, I'm not sure that I'm an arbiter of virtue."

"I don't know that I'm virtuous," she said. "But I'm also not sure I care anymore."

She did feel like a teenager. Giddy and waiting for her first kiss, because she might as well be.

And when he did lean in and kiss her, she melted, grabbing hold of him and clinging.

She *liked* him.

The whole feel of him. His mouth, his broad shoulders…everything.

"I might not be a young man," he said. "But I know what I'm doing."

And Wendy believed him.

And for the rest of the night she was determined to focus on nothing more than all the things that John Hansen knew how to do with a woman's body.

25

The man infuriates me. And he obsesses me.
It wasn't like this with Matthew. I have a sickness.

—FROM THE DIARY OF JENNY HANSEN, MAY 21, 1900

RACHEL

It had been a very long time since she had gone out to a nice dinner. And it was a *very* nice dinner. It was a newer restaurant, one that tended toward fresh, farm-to-table type foods. And something she wouldn't have necessarily pegged Mark for liking.

"My sister told me this place was great," he said after the server set the single-page menus down in front of them.

She looked around the small dining room and saw people she didn't know well, but vaguely recognized, and she felt oddly exposed. Like she wanted to get up and announce she was just out with a friend so they wouldn't judge her for being here so soon after Jacob's death.

She wondered if Anna felt like that all the time. Like

people were looking and knew her business everywhere she went.

They didn't know. They didn't know Anna's, and they didn't know hers.

They knew bits and pieces of their lives, but not the whole story, and from there they made up their narratives.

It suddenly seemed deeply unfair.

She shrugged off the feeling and turned her attention to Mark. She couldn't help what people thought.

They made small talk at dinner, and Rachel was pleasantly surprised at how easy it was. They might as well have been chatting in the hardware store. Yes, she learned some things about him that they wouldn't have talked about there—including that he had been divorced for eight years now, and that he and his ex-wife were on decent enough terms, with visitation that had been worked out so that things were as easy for the kids as possible.

"It wasn't easy to get to that point," he said, taking a sip of his wine. "But…once we did it was fine. She's remarried, and he's a nice enough guy. And, hey, if you can't be happy together you should do your best to be happy apart. It's better for the kids. To see us both happy."

"I suppose that's true," Rachel said.

"It's not how I wanted things to end up, of course. I meant to stay married, but there's no use hanging on to the past. We're almost friends now."

Rachel couldn't imagine that. Except… With a guy like Mark, she could see how it would be possible. He was affable, and he was friendly. He seemed willing to roll with anything. He let her choose the wine, and he seemed happy to drink it.

He ordered the steak and potatoes, because it was what

he recognized, but didn't make any disparaging remarks about anything else on the menu.

He was nice.

In a *genuine* way, not in that cloying way that made you suspect the kindness was more an oily film that clung to the top of entitlement.

Plus, he didn't strike strange sparks off of her. He didn't make her uncomfortable. He didn't make her tense. When dinner was finished, he walked her to her car, and dropped an easy kiss on her cheek.

And she was…fine with it.

But she didn't want to kiss him again, and she didn't want to kiss him on the mouth. It was so easy that it was disconcerting. And when he asked if they could go out again, she said *yes* just as easily, because she would be happy to share a nice meal with him on any given day. It was so much easier than she had anticipated. Shockingly so.

She had expected for it to feel conflicting and it hadn't. Because it was just so perfectly and easily platonic.

So maybe she didn't need romance. And maybe she didn't need sex.

It was a relief. That's what it was.

She intended to drive home. But somehow, she found herself driving toward J's.

It was late, and the restaurant was probably closed. But Adam had been there the other night. Maybe he would be there tonight.

When she pulled up to the front of the diner, she could see that he was. He was bent over a table, wiping it clean, his expression tense. And she wondered what made him tense when the diner was closed.

For all that she talked to Adam on a regular basis, she

didn't know a lot about him. That was by design, it occurred to her. Because they had been a careful, safe space for each other for a good while now.

Was she that for him? She felt so certain of it, all of a sudden. And with that suddenness came curiosity.

Yes, she was curious. About him.

The realization made her skin feel too tight. Made her dress feel too tight. Which made her feel self-conscious about her outfit.

She hadn't felt awkward at all earlier tonight. She had chosen the dress intentionally as something she hopefully looked nice in. And she had felt… It had been nice to feel pretty.

But she hadn't felt *exposed*. Somehow, imagining Adam looking at her in this dress made her feel just that.

She walked up to the door and was about to knock when he saw her.

His expression went from tense to wary. Then she wasn't sure why she was inspiring wariness in him.

But, apparently, she was.

He straightened and made his way to the door slowly, then unlocked it and opened it.

Whatever the tension had been in his face, he brought it out with him. She could *feel* it.

"Is the doctor in?" she asked.

The joke came out weak, and so did her voice.

"I thought you were on a date," he said, frowning.

"I was."

He backed away, holding the door open, allowing her to enter. She slipped in past him, and he moved away from her. He stood in the center of the diner, his large frame making the space seem small.

She'd never thought of J's as small. But Adam was usually contained behind the counter, not just standing there out in the middle of the dining room.

"Aren't you going to get behind the counter?" she asked.

"Do you need me to be behind the counter?"

"You just *usually* are."

"Well, I'm not right now."

"That's fine." It didn't feel fine. It felt weird.

"So how was your date?" he asked.

"It was good," she said, holding her hands behind her back. She could feel Adam looking at her, up and down. And even though she had a coat on over the dress, she still felt self-conscious. "We had a perfectly pleasant conversation."

"You and Mark."

"Yes."

He shrugged his shoulders. "About plumbing?"

"*No*. About our lives." In fact she officially knew more about Mark's life than Adam's.

"Okay. Interesting. And it was good?"

"Yes. Pleasant, even. We covered a range of topics, but nothing controversial. He didn't ask me about sports. So right there, he exceeds a great many men conversationally."

"Right. Because you don't like sports."

"I do not."

"So what are you doing here, then?" he asked. "You could be out still making conversation."

"Well, dinner was over. I was going to go home…"

"But not with him." The words had bite. And they weren't a question.

"No," she said, as if it was the most ridiculous thing in

the world. As if she had thought about it, at least in a detached way. "It's a little bit soon for that, don't you think?"

"I don't know. You were out on a date. I don't presume to know everything about you."

"Well, I told you it was a just-friends thing." She looked at her hands. "And, anyway, it's too soon. For that."

"But you might go out with him again, and maybe it won't feel too soon?"

She looked away from her hands and back at him. "I don't know. I don't have to know. That's kind of a cool thing about this…life that I didn't exactly choose to be in the middle of. I don't have to know. I don't have to make a choice about it. Not now. Maybe ever. You know, the time might never be right for me."

"Right. Of course."

"How about you?" She crossed her arms, the sleeves on her coat bunching up. "Have you had a date lately?"

He huffed out a laugh. "No. When would I have had a date?"

"Just wondering. We don't usually talk about dating stuff."

"Yeah. You were married until a few months ago."

The words slid under her skin like a barb. And she wondered if he'd meant them to.

Something felt a lot like danger in the air around her. And Hannah's sneering face swam into her consciousness. She ignored it.

"Yes. But I'm not now."

"No," he said, a muscle jumping in his jaw. "You're not."

Silence fell between them. The only sound the humming of the heater and the various refrigerators in the back. The music was off, which was a strange thing to notice, but it was something else that made the diner feel unfamiliar.

Adam wasn't behind the counter. And it was far too quiet.

"Maybe we *should* talk about sports," she said. "I feel like that's maybe what the date was missing."

"It was missing something?"

"Yes. Something. Because I didn't want to go home. I wanted to come here. Because it felt like…" She blew out a hard breath. "I don't know, like the night wasn't done. Ask me about a stupid sports thing."

"What if I'm not in the mood to talk about sports?"

"Well, then, what good are you, Adam? You are my go-to for sports conversations that I don't want to be in."

"Right now you seem to want to be in the conversation, so that defeats the purpose of me harassing you with it."

"How's your sports team?" she asked.

He let out a slow breath and walked out of the center of the dining room, around to the back of the counter. She didn't know why, but she felt like she had just lost ground. She didn't even know what ground she was thinking of.

"Which one?" He was in his preferred position now, his usual position. Him on one side and her on the other, but everything still felt wrong.

"I don't know." She flung out her arms. "The ones playing right now."

"I haven't been watching sports. I haven't been able to concentrate."

"Oh."

He sighed heavily. "What's going on, Rachel?"

"I don't know," she said honestly. "I don't know. I—I had a nice time on my date. I was nervous to go out, and… You know, I realize that I didn't care who it was with. Going to dinner with him felt like going to dinner with an old friend, and it was nice. But… I didn't want to kiss him. And maybe that's the thing. Maybe I'll never want to kiss anyone. That's a relief, actually, because I was afraid I'd have to do this whole thing. And I guess I don't have to."

Silence ticked by, seconds that she counted. And suddenly, she felt very aware of her mouth. Suddenly, she became very aware of that he was looking at her mouth.

She looked away. "Maybe that's the thing. I wanted to rush this, to see if I was going to be the kind of person who needed it, or if I would be happy alone forever. It was the suspense I couldn't take. And now I know. It was nothing. And I was fine with it."

"There you go," he said. "I guess you had the answers all along."

He was dismissing her. And she felt flat and strange. And very silly. She wished she could go back and decide not to come here. Or even just go back and say about half the words she'd said tonight, because she'd just said too many things, and not enough of them had made sense.

"Yeah. I guess so." She didn't have answers. Not even one. She felt hollowed out and awful and like she wanted to cry.

But it was clear that he wanted her to go, and she wasn't going to stay if he was ready to leave. If he wanted her gone.

"Good night, Adam," she said. "I… I'll see you. I'll see you…soon."

"The door locked behind you when you came in, I'm going to have to let you out."

"Oh," she said.

She lingered where she stood for a moment while Adam

came out from behind the counter and pressed a code that she assumed disarmed something. Then he pushed his key into the lock and turned it, releasing the door. And he stood and wedged it open, his arm pressed across the door and his body positioned right at the entryway, like an imposing sentry.

She took a breath, and consciously realized she was holding it to avoid breathing in his aftershave again. Because it made her stomach feel funny.

She started to move past him, and suddenly, he caught her arm, holding her there between his body and the door. His blue eyes were intense, and she felt it then. All the way through. The danger. And she wondered how she had ever thought that he was anything quite as bland as safe.

"Just a second," he said, his voice rough.

And he leaned in and captured her mouth with his.

Heat flooded her entire body, heat and desire and intense, undeniable need.

It was like being caught up in a wave, being pushed under the surface so far she couldn't tell which end was up. Couldn't seem to find her way to air. And she wasn't sure she wanted to. Because as it went on, she started to wonder if *he* was air.

He pulled away from her and she whimpered. She wanted to cry because it was over. Because she had to think again, and she didn't want to.

"I just wanted to be the first one," he said, his voice rough. "Because you're going to be ready, someday. And somebody already got in and asked you out before I did, and it doesn't matter if it was nothing with him—it won't be nothing with everyone. You won't be alone forever."

Sometimes truths came together slow and easy. Like

looking through a soft-focus lens slowly being narrowed in, bringing detail into focus and making all things clear.

This was a soft focus. It was not a gentle truth. This truth fell from the sky fully formed and hit her on the head.

Sharp. Hard.

Adam.

She wanted him.

Wanted.

Not a dinner date. Not a nice conversation.

But to kiss him. Touch him. Taste him.

And it wasn't fresh, or new. There was a reason she sought him out when she needed someone to talk to. A reason she wanted to be near him.

It was a great and terrible realization. It had been an easy thing to go on a date with Mark because she didn't want him. Because he wasn't dangerous. Not like this.

This was the great and terrible truth that had vibrated beneath the surface of her skin all night. She wanted to date because she didn't know what else to call it. She didn't want to date because she wasn't ready for a relationship, and she didn't want to insert another man into her life.

She wanted something much more direct. Something raw and naked.

Something that was about her. Not about anyone else.

It wouldn't heal anything or anyone.

It wouldn't bring Jacob back or make her relationship with Emma better.

It wouldn't repair the relationship with her mother.

Wouldn't help Anna with her present plight.

It wasn't about being a caregiver, or a fixer. A mother, a sister or a wife.

It was about being a woman. A woman who wanted a man.

And…she was going to do it. Before she could lose her nerve, before she could think more about it.

She wrapped her arms around his neck, and she kissed him deeply. She had only ever kissed one man in her life, and it was the strangest thing in all the world to have a different mouth beneath hers.

To learn a different flavor, a different texture. The way that he held her was *different*. So was the way her body fit against his.

And he was… He was hard, and he was strong, his arms like a steel band around her, his chest a wall, his heart thundering beneath.

She wasn't hiding from his scent now—she was letting it envelop her, letting it overtake her senses completely.

She had forgotten what it was like to be kissed like this, and then again, she had never been kissed quite like this, because she had never been kissed by him.

"Maybe we shouldn't stand in the doorway?" he whispered against her mouth.

"Right," she said. "Upstairs?"

He paused for a moment, his blue eyes hot and sharp with need.

"Are we clear on what you're asking for?" He took a step back. "Because I don't want to go upstairs and have a talk."

"Neither do I," she said.

He pulled her inside, pulled the door shut behind her and turned all the locks again. Then he quickly turned off the lights in the diner.

"I figure we don't need to advertise it to half the town."

"Thank you," she said.

She was trembling. She felt like a virgin.

Well, she practically was.

It had been so long since she'd had a first time.

Since she'd been afraid of what it would mean to be naked in front of a man. It had become casual to be naked in front of Jacob.

There was an ease that they had with each other, and with each other's bodies. And even when they'd been unable to have a sexual relationship, that ease had remained. She didn't worry about stretch marks, she didn't worry about cellulite on her butt and her thighs.

She knew that he wasn't comparing her to other women, because he hadn't been with any other women.

She knew that he remembered when her breasts had been fuller, and when they been a little bit perkier, but she also knew that he loved them the way that they were. He remembered when her stomach was tighter, but he loved to run his hands over it when it was just a little bit softer all the same.

She didn't know anything about how many women Adam had been with. What he was used to. What he liked.

She didn't know what he would think of her body, and she kind of wasn't sure what she thought about her body. Because she hadn't thought about it all that much.

Her body had been faithful to her all these years. She wasn't ill, or in pain, and so she didn't much mind the stretch marks and cellulite, in light of everything else.

She minded it all a little bit right now.

"Come here," he said, grabbing her hand and leading her behind the counter.

"Well, we're on the same side of the counter," she said.

"It would be a little bit difficult if the counter was between us," he said.

That was true. Maybe that was why they'd kept it between them quite so resolutely.

He took her into the kitchen, and she looked around, a little bit disoriented seeing the diner from a whole different perspective. But they moved quickly, to a door in the back, which opened to reveal a narrow, dark staircase.

"I promise the staircase is worse than the apartment."

"It would have to be," she said, laughing nervously.

She ignored the staircase, anyway, and she enjoyed the way that it felt to have him hold her hand. His hands were big, and they were calloused.

Warm.

She liked the feel of it.

She remembered when their fingertips had been so close to touching, only a couple of days ago, and she wondered... If they had brushed then, would they have ended up here even faster. She had a feeling they would have. That if they would have touched, this electricity would have been there.

Maybe it had been all along.

Waiting.

Waiting for the moment when they could touch.

That thought settled strange in the pit of her stomach.

He was right. The apartment was better than the staircase. It was homey, and cozy, with battered wood flooring, a small kitchen area, a seating area and a bed.

A *large* bed.

The blanket on top was a blue-and-white quilt, something that had to be either an heirloom or a thrift-store find because she couldn't imagine Adam choosing something like that with great thought.

He closed the door behind them and went over to a heating-and-cooling unit on the wall, then pressed the button a few times. "It'll get warm in here pretty quick," he said.

"You do understand women," she said, shivering slightly, though it wasn't from the cold.

"Yeah, I remember some things."

He closed the distance between them, and he cupped her chin, holding her steady as he leaned in to kiss her again. He took it slow this time, achingly so.

And with each pass of his mouth over hers, the kisses went deeper. Until she was utterly and completely lost in them.

In him.

And it was like freedom. Because for a moment she just felt good. Aroused in a way she hadn't been in longer than she could remember. The excitement of his hands roaming over her body, even with her coat and dress on, was so intense she could hardly stand it.

It was bright, and it was new, and during this long, gray season, it was a gift.

He pushed her coat from her shoulders, and let it drop to the ground. He moved his hands down her back, to her bottom, pulling her up against him.

He touched her cheeks when she came into contact with the evidence of his arousal.

He wanted her.

And maybe he hadn't seen the stretch marks, and maybe he hadn't borne witness to the cellulite, but he wanted her as she was now, and that was truly something.

He took a step away from her, and he grabbed hold of the back of his shirt collar, pulling it forward over his head in that way that men did that was both mystifying and glorious all at once.

His body was…well, it was shocking.

If she had been hoping for him to maybe meet her at her insecurities, she knew that she was out of luck.

Because he was stunning.

A man, mature and in his prime, with muscles that were much more well-defined than she'd imagined beneath his typical uniform of a black T-shirt and jeans. She wasn't sure if it excited her or terrified her to know that they were so unevenly matched on this score.

He wasn't *normal*.

Mark's body would have been way less intimidating than all of this—this perfection that nobody would have expected out of a diner owner in his forties. There should have at least been rumors going around about his abs, and yet, there were none. At least none that she had heard.

"What?" he asked.

She had probably been standing there staring like an idiot.

"I feel like you should probably warn people that you're this hot."

Half of his mouth rose upward, and a laugh that sounded somewhat helpless escaped his lips. "I'm sorry, what?"

"It's really not fair. I had no idea."

"You had no idea I was…hot?"

"I knew you were *handsome*. *Very handsome*. And in decent shape. But, I feel like you should warn a woman that you're quite so…you know—" she waved her hand "—*this*, before she commits to coming upstairs and getting naked with you."

"Why is that? Is there something repellent about me being hot?"

"No. But if you're expecting…that," she said, pointing

to his stomach, "to be under here—" she pointed to her own "—then you are sadly mistaken."

"Rachel Henderson," he said, his voice a growl. "I have had inappropriate thoughts about all the things that might be under your clothes for a lot longer than I care to admit. Based on the amount of time I've spent looking at your body, I'd say that I have a pretty fair idea of what I'm going to find there. And when I do, I'm not going to be disappointed—I am going to say a damned prayer of thanks. And then I'm going to touch you, everywhere. And I'm going to taste you, everywhere."

The erotic thrill those words elicited sent a shiver through her entire body. She wasn't inexperienced, not by any stretch. She had been married for years, and they'd had a fulfilling, uninhibited sex life during most of that time.

But that was him. Jacob. And this was Adam. And it was like two completely different things.

Jacob, she had known. Jacob she had *loved*.

Their intimacy had grown and increased and changed over the years.

They had learned sexuality with each other, and they had honed it to something perfect between them.

He knew just how to touch her, and she knew just how to touch him. Desire created and satisfied between just the two of them. She knew all the things he liked.

She had known how to speed him up when he was taking too long, and she had also known just which way to move to help herself get where she needed to go if she was having difficulty.

They had a routine. A dance. Something that had been raised to high art after all that time together.

This was an unknown, and she felt both inhibited and

secure in the moment. And utterly, completely captivated by the promise in his words and his eyes. No matter how afraid she was, she couldn't stop now. Didn't want to. And while all her experience might be reduced to essentially nothing as she stood before this man, there was something to be said for age.

Because at the base of it all she didn't fear rejection. She didn't fear disappointing him. She was more afraid of her own disappointment. Of putting herself through this monumental event, and having this brilliant body at her disposal, and it not living up to what it promised.

She reached behind her back, ready to undo the zipper on her dress, but he stopped her.

"Let me," he said. "You're a gift I've been waiting to unwrap for a long time."

He approached her, grabbed hold of the zipper tab and pulled it down slowly, achingly so. And what she hadn't told Anna or her daughter was that she had gone to even more care choosing her underwear for the evening.

It was black lace, and her bra matched her panties, because *just in case.*

She had also shaved and waxed herself within an inch of her life, so that everything was neat and orderly and smooth. And she wondered who she'd had in mind when she'd done that. Wondered what she'd been thinking in her subconscious.

Especially when she'd driven over here.

He let out a curse, short and sharp, as her dress pooled at her feet.

"You're perfect," he said, pulling her body up against his again. His skin was hot, his body hard, and his chest hair beneath her palms was...just right.

"Beautiful," he whispered as he kissed her mouth. As

he stripped the rest of the clothes from her body, and the rest of the clothes from his. As he laid her down on the bed, those rough hands skimming over her body. Unfamiliar hands, unfamiliar movements. But they brought out a response in her, all the same. So intense, almost too intense. She was so afraid she was going to cry. And almost more afraid that she was going to come with him barely having touched her.

She had missed this.

This intimacy.

Skin on skin, a kiss that could take you to a deep, heavy place, transport you somewhere new. Desire that knotted up your stomach and made you feel like you couldn't breathe.

It had been so long since she'd felt this.

So long since she'd allowed herself to feel it, and she hadn't even let herself acknowledge how much she missed it.

She'd just pushed it away, brushed it to the back of a cupboard to be dealt with later, because there were too many big things in her life that needed doing. Needed mending and caring and loving.

And this hadn't mattered. She hadn't let it.

She'd forgotten it, and she'd done it on purpose.

Now that cupboard had been pushed on its end and this had spilled out before she was ready and maybe it was all the better for it.

Because for her, sex had always been linked with love, with intimacy. And they didn't have that. But they had chemistry.

And it was *real*.

Terrifying.

Wonderful.

She'd never known this before. The heat that could exist between two people built with nothing more than their desire.

Everywhere he put his hands, it was like fire. Desire that she hadn't realized still existed in her. And everywhere she put her hands on him...

Learning the landscape of a new male body was intense, so bright and sharp and brilliant. She wanted to memorize the moment, him, every dip and ripple in his muscles, the texture of his skin.

She wanted to live in the moment, this moment, for as long as she possibly could. Because everything felt so good.

And she wasn't sad.

She kissed his face, his chest, his abs, and he turned her over onto her back, strong hands pinning her to the mattress as he made good on his promise, and kissed her everywhere.

As he wedged apart her legs with his broad shoulders and pleasured her with his mouth until she shattered.

Until she was nothing more than a scattering of bright, brilliant pieces that she didn't even want put back together.

And when he surged inside of her, his face filled her vision. And his body was so deep in hers that she didn't know where she ended and began anymore.

Somehow it was sacred. A prayer in the dark stillness of the bedroom, even though it shouldn't have been. A vow made with their bodies. That he'd give her pleasure if nothing else. That his strong arms would hold her together even while she was afraid she was going to fly apart.

She was so acutely aware that it was him. It hit her then that she hadn't been afraid, not for one moment, that she wouldn't be. That she would wish it was Jacob, or have difficulty not fantasizing about him.

No, this had been different. He had been different, from the very first kiss. And it had been needed. Necessary. A gift and a blessing.

Adam, with nothing between them, not so much as a breath, and certainly not a counter.

And he drove home that point.

Over and over again, until she shattered in his arms, and he broke apart right after, her name on his breath, on a kiss that she took for herself.

When it was over, she lay next to him for a moment. Her body was bare, pressed against his. Lying next to him in bed like this felt as intimate as him being in her, and she couldn't figure out why.

She studied the lines of his face, all the tension gone now. His arms were slung over his head, the blankets barely covering his beautiful body. She wanted more time. But she couldn't stay out all night. Emma and Anna thought that she was out with Mark and…

She really had to go home. She couldn't stay here.

She couldn't sleep in his bed. That was… A faint glimmer caught her eye, and she realized that it was her wedding ring. She was still wearing it. She had worn it on her date. She had worn it to bed with another man. She couldn't sleep in the same bed as another man while she still had this ring on her finger.

Pain crowded her thoughts, her chest, her heart.

Hannah's words roared back to her.

How she'd been here with Adam while Jacob was dying…

Kissing him had been so easy. So easy to let him lean forward and close that distance between them. Like part of her had been waiting to do it for years. Like a secret piece of her had wanted that mouth on hers for far longer than she should have.

"I have to go," she said.

He mumbled something, then his eyes open slowly. "Why?"

"Because I can't be gone all night. People will… You know. People will talk."

She hadn't cared about anyone else this whole time. Only herself.

She didn't care much about them now.

But she was terrified of something and she needed to run. Otherwise it would all spill out of her here and she couldn't handle it.

He nodded slowly, then he reached up and wrapped his hand around the back of her head, pulling her in for a kiss.

Feeling raw, her eyes stinging, she collected all of her clothes and dressed, acutely aware that he was watching her. She dressed quickly.

He got out of bed and heat flooded her as she watched him stride across the room completely naked.

He didn't have a thing to be embarrassed about. She didn't know they made men like him, not in the real world.

"Let me walk you to your car."

He tugged on his jeans with nothing else underneath, then pulled his T-shirt over his head. He followed her down the stairs, barefoot, and she kept her hands clasped in front of her, deliberately not holding his hand. He opened up the front door, and walked her across the street. The street was completely empty, but she was still nervous about being seen.

"I'll see you," he said.

She nodded slowly. She thought about kissing him again. But… No. She shouldn't.

"Good night, Adam," she said softly.

"Good night, Rachel," he said.

She got in her car and started driving back toward the inn, and that was when she started to shake. She had… With *Adam*.

Another truth clicked into place.

He'd been her escape this whole time. Her break from life. From reality. When she'd needed out of her real life, he was there, and when she added this to it, an attraction that had been simmering beneath the surface—even if it had gone unnoticed by her—it made her understand Anna all the more.

There were a thousand rationalizations spinning in her head. That she was more ready for sex than she was for a relationship—true enough—and that it made sense that it was him, because they did have some level of trust in each other.

If she couldn't have Adam's hands on her, she needed to be numb, though.

Better to be numb than to be in pain. And if she couldn't have Adam's hands on her…

Well, numb was the best thing.

She drove all the way home like that, and at some point she started to sing. To drown things out even more. Reality.

Tonight, and everything that had happened before it.

She was singing a hymn, which she thought might be somewhat sacrilegious, but she couldn't think of anything else. She could use a solid rock to stand on, anyway, so it was as good as any other song. If not better.

She pulled into the darkened, private drive that led

up to the Lighthouse Inn, and she parked her car in front
of the Captain's House. And she sat there for a moment,
not quite able to absorb what it was that was wrong with
the place.

The light was on in the kitchen.

It was late.

It was all right for the lights to be on in a guest space,
because people had free run of the house. But they locked
the kitchen at night, and no one was supposed to be in
there.

Which meant, either her mother or Anna was in there,
or the light had been left on.

Without giving it much thought, she parked the car
and got out.

What she was doing was delaying the inevitable. The
moment that she was going to have to be alone with her
thoughts.

This gave her an errand to do. Maybe she would bake
something. Maybe she would stay up, forget trying to go
to bed.

She used the code to let herself into the Captain's
House, and began to head toward the kitchen. And just
as she did, she heard a door open upstairs, and footsteps
on the first landing.

And then, she saw her mother, wrapped in a guest robe.
And there was a man coming down the stairs behind her.

"For God's sake, Mother," Rachel said, before she could
even stop the words from falling out of her mouth.

"Rachel?"

"Yes," Rachel said. "What the hell is happening?"

"What are you doing here?"

"I'm getting home from my date," she said.

And as she said that, she realized that she didn't look

any better. Half in a coat, with her hair looking like Heaven knew what, and it was… Well, it was after midnight.

"Never mind," Rachel said. She turned and started walking toward the door.

"Rachel…"

"I'm not mad," Rachel said. "I'm not mad."

She stumbled out the front door and down the steps, and toward the Lightkeeper's House. The lunacy of it. And she prayed that her mom wouldn't follow her. Because she needed…

Not this. She needed to be by herself now.

She needed to go to sleep. Tonight had been a mistake. A huge mistake.

You really think being with Adam was a mistake?

She didn't know. She didn't know what she felt, except that her insides just felt mixed up. And everything hurt.

Now that she was feeling hurt again, it was a whole new kind.

With shaking hands, she let herself into the house.

And she prayed that Emma wasn't up still. Gave thanks that Anna's house was far enough down the hill that she wouldn't have seen Rachel come home.

She leaned against the door, her eyes closed, and she listened.

The house was silent.

She went up the stairs, and parental paranoia bade that she crack open Emma's door and make sure she was in there, asleep.

She could see her daughter's red hair spread out over the pillow, and then she rolled over once, flinging her arm over her face.

Well, that was one thing she didn't have to worry about.

Then she opened the door to her bedroom.

The king-size bed was still made. Just as she left it this morning. The white bedspread was smooth. Because no one else had touched it. No one else had been in it.

She walked over to it slowly, discarded her coat and kicked off her shoes.

Then she lay down on the edge of it, staring across the space. At all the emptiness.

She let her hand stretch across to his side. And she pressed her palm to the cool blanket.

And she didn't know how she could be so conscious, so bitterly conscious of just how gone he was tonight. When she had let another man inside of her body.

Joyfully. With great *pleasure*.

It was only in the aftermath it felt sharp and wrong.

"My mom hooked up with a guest," she said, a bubble of laughter escaping with a tear. "I would've told you that as soon as I got home."

She looked down at her left hand. And slowly, very slowly, she slid off her rings. "But you're not here."

She set her rings on his pillow.

For a long time, she looked at them, barely visible with the moon shining in through the window. Dark circles against the white linen.

"I still miss you," she said.

But he wasn't her husband anymore. And he wasn't here.

He never would be again.

And when she finally let herself sleep, it was Adam's hands that she dreamed of.

26

I have spent much time hating myself.
I find I've lost the taste for it. Is it so wrong
to try to find forgiveness of ourselves,
and for how we were made?

—FROM A LETTER WRITTEN BY STAFF SERGEANT RICHARD JOHNSON,
JANUARY 1945

ANNA

Anna got out of the car, and walked up to the front door of what had been her home for fourteen years, and found that her heart had frozen in her chest. She felt like she was having an anxiety attack. Like she had returned to that life that she had left. That was clarifying. She didn't want to be going back. This didn't feel like home. She knocked. It didn't even feel weird to have to knock.

She waited. And she honestly didn't even know if he would answer the door for her.

She knew that he would have looked out his office window to see who was there, and that he had a view of the edge of the front porch, just enough to see who was standing there.

This was a splintered piece of her life. And she was ready.

Ready to deal with it, so it could be removed. So she could be remade.

She'd gotten dressed this morning, put on makeup. Put on pants that didn't have an elastic waistband. She'd gone to the Sunset Bay Coffee Company, and she'd been able to feel people looking at her. But she found that she didn't care. And not in that brittle, angry way that she hadn't cared in the weeks after it happened. Not in the way that she'd stared down that cashier.

It just…felt like it didn't matter for some reason she couldn't quite pin down.

No one knew her. They knew a version of her. They knew a version of events. And they knew that she had done some things that were wrong. She knew that, too. And for some reason, when she left the coffeehouse, she found herself driving in a strange, familiar direction. One that had become foreign to her, because she hadn't driven that way in months.

When she pulled up in front of the house that had been her home for fourteen years, she just sat there. It was so familiar. Painfully so. And in its walls, it contained years of relative happiness. And a lot of pain and regret. His car was in the driveway, and she knew that he was home. Working in his office.

She hadn't thought about him very much. She'd been angry with him. She'd been ashamed at her anger.

She waited. And when she heard footsteps, she didn't know if she was relieved or not. He pulled open the door, and her stomach went tight. She hadn't seen him since the night before that Sunday in church, and, of course, none of them had been back since.

It was weird to look at him now.

Detached somehow. Like she was looking at a stranger.

He was a handsome man, her husband. The man who would be her ex-husband soon enough.

He looked at her, and he didn't say anything, and she searched his face. For something. Anger, longing, sadness. She couldn't read any of it there. But, then, she always had difficulty reading him. That calming presence that he had more often than not just felt opaque to her.

"Hi, Thomas," she said.

"What brings you by, Anna?" The question was calm, as he always was, but tight-lipped.

"Believe it or not, I just want to talk to you."

She expected him to say that he was busy. After all, he had been busy for the whole of their marriage. Too busy to talk. Too busy for much of anything.

"Come in," he said, backing away from the door.

She walked in slowly, enveloped by the familiarity like a white-and-cream cocoon. She'd walked through this door every day for years. Arms empty, arms full. With this man and by herself.

Home. For so many years, it had been home.

She didn't know what she expected when she walked in, but it wasn't this.

It was strange, but she didn't miss this house.

Having spent months away, coming back into it, she could recognize all the things in it that weren't hers. So many things. From the carpets to the couches, it was all clean and sterile. Very much Thomas's taste and not hers.

"You can sit," he said.

So she did. She crossed the room and sat down slowly on the couch, trying not to get too caught up in the absurdity of being invited to sit down in the living room that she had called her own for more than a decade.

Except...

It really did feel like someone else's.

This oatmeal-colored carpet and sedate, cream-colored couch.

She couldn't blame him, though, for this room that looked more like him than her.

She had chosen it.

And so she wondered if it wasn't so much that it was his taste, but as if at one time it had been both of theirs, and something had happened along the way that had changed her irrevocably. Something that had taken her from a place where this couch, and this man, seemed like decisions that she wanted to live with for the rest of her life.

Until they didn't.

"I assume you're here because you've been to speak to a lawyer?"

"No," she said, realizing that she *did* need to do that. "I didn't. I—I genuinely wanted to talk to you."

"About?"

"Us."

He crossed his arms, his posture defensive. "Okay."

"Did you care? That I had an affair. Did you care?" Well, that hadn't been what she'd meant to ask, but suddenly it mattered.

A muscle in his jaw worked. "That's an unfair question. Of course I cared. You betrayed me."

"Yeah. I did. You're right. But what did I betray, exactly? Vows? Your pride? Or your heart."

"Why does any of it matter, Anna?"

"Because you were my choice, my life, for fourteen years. And what I do with that life, our life, is going to matter in terms of how I go on. How the two of us continue to live in this town, how you continue to have your ministry. How I continue to have a life. I could leave. But my family's here."

And whether or not things were complicated with her mother, that was true. Her mother was here. Her sister was here. Emma was here, for now. And even if Emma left, this would be her home base.

She was angry at her mother, but did that mean she would leave? She—she didn't know. She didn't know what she wanted or if they could heal their relationship. She didn't know what her future held.

Somehow she felt like her answer was here somewhere. Wrapped up in her past.

"I never cheated on you," he bit out.

"No. You didn't. So what were you doing? When you weren't in my bed, where were you?"

"In my office, writing. Or at the church seeing to issues with the congregation. I was seeing to my work, Anna, not betraying our marriage."

"You know that's not the question I'm asking you, Thomas. I don't need an accounting of what you did with your time. What happened to *us*?"

"I didn't change," he said. "I'm everything that I showed you that I was from the moment we first got together."

She stared at him, and she realized that he believed it. More importantly, she realized it was true. He had always been polite, but not overly impassioned. Had always been a steady presence, rather than an intense one.

And she had imagined in her head that some of those things would change. Because they had been chaste prior to marrying, she had assumed that he'd been holding something back, but now she wondered if he had been.

She took in every detail of his face. So handsome. So... impossible to read. "Are you attracted to me?"

He drew back, and the strangest thing of all was that he looked...embarrassed.

"As much as I am to anyone."

"What does that mean?"

His throat worked. "Desire is not a huge factor in my life."

She frowned. It wasn't like she lived under a rock. She understood that people had different sex drives, and that some people didn't really have them. But it had never occurred to her that...her husband was one of those people.

That he simply didn't want...her. Or sex at all.

"So you're just not that into sex?"

"This entire thing is about sex for you?" He looked flustered. Uncomfortable. Things he so rarely was.

"No. But it's a symptom. A symptom of everything I thought was wrong with me. Of everything I thought was wrong with us. It's why..." She swallowed hard. "Thomas, I've only been with you. Before Michael, I'd only been with you."

"I've only been with you."

"I know." This had to come out, for her own soul more than his. Because she'd tried to show him with actions what she'd felt and she'd asked—in a basic sense—for more. But time had given her a clearer understanding of what she'd been missing and she needed it said.

"And during our marriage I told you that I thought you were an attractive man. I took pleasure in being with you. And I wanted you to do the same with me. But when you quit being interested in touching me at all, I just felt like I was broken. And I felt like it meant you didn't love me, because for me...that's part of being in love. Desiring someone. Being desired. I can't separate those things. And it would never have occurred to me to. So when another man came in and started telling me that I was beautiful, that he did want me, it felt like…more than what we had. And it wasn't fair. It wasn't fair for you to stand up in front of the congregation and make me out to be the one who was weak. It's not a temptation for you, apparently. You don't…miss that. But you were perfectly happy to have me miss it for the rest of my life. To have me…dying up in that bedroom by myself at night wondering what I had done to make you fall out of love with me."

"Anna…" His voice was uncharacteristically rough, and he sank into the chair across from her, looking genuinely upset. "When I was young, I thought…marriage was the path that I would take. Because it seemed to be the path that everyone expected me to take. And the younger I did it, the better. That was especially the opinion of my mentor. Because what you don't want is for a young pastor to be constantly pursued by every woman in the congregation."

He cleared his throat. "I wasn't tempted. But… I thought perhaps that spoke of my spirituality. That I wasn't led into temptation. By the time I realized that perhaps I wasn't all that suited to marriage—"

"We were already married." She tried to smile.

"And had been for a while. I've always cared about you. I loved you. And I was… I was upset by you sleeping with him."

She huffed out a laugh. "Well, I guess there's that."

His eyes met hers and she felt…nothing. Not anger. Just a strange kind of wistfulness that you might feel looking at old yearbook photos. The love she'd felt for him once was a faded memory that couldn't be recaptured.

While the years had knit Rachel and Jacob together, they had left Thomas and Anna isolated.

She'd never made a fuss about the furniture because in her heart, she didn't want this to be her house.

It had never seemed like the right time to have kids because for her, he was the wrong man.

The wrong marriage.

And she hadn't fully realized all that until now. Until she'd become a stranger to her life. Until she had come back to look at it all from the outside.

"I'm sorry," she said. "I'm sorry that I didn't have the courage to end things in a better way."

He looked genuinely shocked with her. "What?"

"I shouldn't have slept with him. I tried to fix what we had. I realize now there was no fixing us. Our versions of love, of marriage, are two different things. I don't think we could ever even bend enough to meet in the middle."

"But you know how the church looks at divorce," he said.

"People in church divorce, Thomas, and life goes on. You made me a villain so that you didn't have to be vulnerable. So you didn't have to admit that you didn't really want to be a husband. That you hid things from me. The way you hid your issues with desire was a betrayal. You let me think I was flawed, instead of just admitting we were different."

"Anna…"

"You could have just said nothing. You could have let people talk, and be above it. Instead, you let them talk about *me*."

"It was true," he insisted.

"Yes. But it was half. I told you I was unhappy. I told you over and over. I didn't want to make waves because

I believed in what you were doing. We're all a mess, and that doesn't mean we don't have things to offer the world. And God knows you've offered more to the broader world than I ever have. But you didn't ever bring it to my life."

She closed her eyes. "And if I've paid attention in church at all, then I've learned that being perfect isn't required to lead. To affect change. Your example is teaching people that perfection is required, and it isn't. I'm not proud of how I ended our marriage. I used him to make myself unforgivable, because I know that if I had done anything less you wouldn't have divorced me. What I did felt like the only way. But I wish we could have found the bravery in ourselves to sit down and talk. To admit that we were wrong for each other. Not that *I* was wrong. I'm sorry that I hurt you. But less sorry than I might have been, because I'm not sure you've ever been sorry you were hurting me. Actively. For years."

He just stared straight ahead. "I didn't do anything."

The truth of it resonated in her. But she knew it didn't echo in him. Knew that he still felt that *nothing* meant *innocent*.

"Exactly," she said. "You didn't do anything. Love isn't passive, and neither is marriage. It isn't stagnant. Someone is always moving, and if you're not moving together… you're moving away from each other. And that's what we did. I just… I wanted to see you. Because I wanted to make sure that you were…damn it, Thomas." Her mild swear word made him jolt. "I was afraid that I'd *hurt* you. Not your reputation. *You*. I didn't. Did I?"

He stared straight ahead for a long time. "Does it help that I wish it could have?"

"No. If we could bring wishes into the equation, then I would have wished us into a different couple. Different people, who could make it work, because I would've spared us this. I would have spared myself this."

She got up and started to walk away.

"I'm sorry," he said. "I used you, Anna, and I didn't mean to. To make a life that looked perfect, and I thought that if it felt perfect to me, then it must to you. That if I took joy in the way things were going…it must be all right to you. And when you would tell me that you wanted something different, I—I lied to myself. I told myself my explanations were sufficient for you, and that they'd handled things. But they weren't."

"No," she said. "They weren't."

He stood and crossed the room, stopping in front of her. She looked up at him and part of her wanted to demand his pain. His anger. And another part of her realized…that wasn't fair. Because if he'd possessed that kind of passion in him for her, then what she'd done was terrible. In the end, it just left her looking at the reality of it all. At a dismantled, broken mess that neither of them felt strongly enough about to try to put back together. Not after this.

And if Thomas had been the kind of man to rail and rant and carry on, if he had been incensed, and wounded by her betrayal, then…it might have been different.

And ultimately, she never would've betrayed him in the first place.

He cupped her chin, his touch familiar in a way that made her hurt. And then he leaned in and pressed his mouth to hers, the kiss dry and soft, and over quickly.

Her body responded, because she'd always been attracted to him.

When they parted, his eyes were cool. It had never been more clear to her that the man she'd loved, the man she'd wanted all this time, had never existed.

The problem was, he wasn't cold, and he wasn't intentionally cruel. He was just a man lost deeply in his perspective, who didn't feel things the same way she did, and who didn't want a marriage that looked like the one she required.

They both thought they could fashion each other into the image of the perfect husband or wife. She'd imagined that her desire for him could fill him, and he would feel the same things she did. While he'd imagined that the fervor he felt for his sermons, for his books, was enough for him, and so it could be for her.

They were two people whose marriage vows had never managed to make them one.

"I guess…we should start doing the legal things now," she said.

"I guess. Do you want…? Just going into things, ahead of it all…should we sell the house, and split the proceeds? I'm not interested in leaving you with nothing, Anna. I'm not. Whatever you might think about me, and what I did after I discovered the affair… I don't actually want to hurt you."

She looked around, and she shook her head. "No. This place is yours. I'm happy for you to have it." There was nothing noble about the gesture on her part. She wanted to be done. That was it.

And she found she wasn't here to place blame. Casting fault on someone else could never—*would* never—heal her.

"What are you going to do?"

"Well, I did all the work of wrecking my life. So now it's up to me to fix it into the thing I want it to be. I hope you're able to do the same."

Then she turned and walked out the front door, and was

surprised to see that the clouds had cleared, and the sky was blue over a much more cheerful-than-usual ocean.

If she'd been waiting for a sign that the conversation with Thomas needed to happen, then this was it.

She didn't necessarily feel fixed, didn't entirely feel whole. But that had confirmed to her that when she was with him she hadn't been, either. That what she'd left behind she needed to leave, even if she could have done it in a different way.

She wished she could've been brave enough to walk away on her own two feet, rather than with the help of Michael, and her affair with him.

"I just have to be that strong from now on," she said, to no one in particular except the blue sky.

And she was determined that she would be. But she needed to start by repairing what was broken with her mother.

Blame wouldn't heal anyone—it would only keep them broken.

And Anna refused to live broken anymore.

27

I hope you get this letter. I'm trying frantically
to reach you. Someone from the college
finally agreed to give me your address.
You should know, I'm pregnant.

—FROM A LETTER WRITTEN BY SUSAN BRIGHT, OCTOBER 1961.
RETURNED TO SENDER UNOPENED. STAMPED: DECEASED.

WENDY

The last person Wendy expected to see at her door was
Anna.

Well, maybe Rachel had moved to the position of last
on the list, after last night. But Anna would have been second to last, and seeing her beautiful, stubborn daughter
standing there with her cheeks and nose flushed from the
cold made Wendy's heart clench tight. Somehow, Wendy
saw straight past all the years and felt like she was looking at her little girl again.

A little girl who might just need a Band-Aid and a kiss
to make the pain of a scraped knee go away.

She missed those days. When you could fix things that
easily.

But they were living in a tangle of betrayal, and lies, largely created by her, and even if she had the power to make all this go away with a Band-Aid, she had taken that right from herself.

"Are you here to yell at me again? Because I'll be honest, I deserve it."

"No," Anna said. "I came to talk. Not...accuse you of anything." She bit her lip, and suddenly, tears filled her eyes. "I don't know why it's so easy for me to realize that things are complicated and have lots of sides to them when it's me. But so difficult for me to see when it's other people. Still. I keep thinking I've learned the lesson, but I haven't. It's also much harder, and more complicated than that. Then just knowing it. And I... Mom, I wanted to blame you for my unhappiness, because I wanted to blame anyone but myself. I went to see Thomas today, to blame him."

"Oh," Wendy said, her heart contracting with sympathy.

"And you know, he does have some of the blame. He married me, and he could never give me what a husband should. Talking with him today confirmed that. But I wasn't brave. I wasn't brave all on my own."

Wendy's heart contracted again as she watched her daughter, pale but determined, saying she wasn't brave while she cut open her soul and let it bleed out.

"I used Michael to escape. I did think I might be falling in love with him, but I don't think I was. I saw a hand being reached down to where I was in the pit, and I just wanted to take it rather than keep trying to climb out on my own."

A tear slipped down her face and Wendy had to put her

hand over her mouth to keep from interrupting. To keep from crying out.

She should have been that hand for Anna. But her fear, her stubbornness and her secrets had driven a wedge between them.

"I knew that Thomas wouldn't be able to forgive me for cheating on him. I knew that it would end it. Because I wasn't brave enough to say the words to him. I wasn't brave enough to ask for a divorce. I made him be the one to do it. And then I was still looking for reasons why. When the reasons were just that we… We're two people who don't see love the same. Who don't see marriage the same. And neither of us love the other enough to set down what we needed, what we wanted."

"Come sit down," Wendy said, making her way over to the stove and turning the heat on for the kettle. Anna followed, and sat down at the tiny table in the kitchen. There were two seats at that table, just the right size for an honest talk, for a breakdown. To heal. To mend.

"I've replayed what you said to me the night I told my secret over and over, Anna. And you're right. I was protecting myself. I was protecting myself from the judgment of everyone else because I couldn't bear any more of it. My mother was always so fearful of who I would become. Any mistake I made she blamed on blood. The weakness from my birth mother, and I began to wonder if she was right. When I got a good look at who I was and what I'd done, at the end of everything… I despised myself."

She swallowed hard and pressed on. "But I did it to you. I was so afraid of the parts of you that looked like me. So afraid of what trouble your wild spirit would find for you. I hurt you more than I helped you. It's a mother's job to help her girls fly, not to clip their wings. I should have been the one to reach out and help you. You should never have had to be that desperate."

"Mom…"

"I'm sorry," Wendy said. "I'm so sorry."

Anna stretched her arms across the table and hugged her, wordlessly, for a long, long time.

"I want forgiveness," she whispered. Then she pulled away, wiping tears off her cheeks. "I want to forgive you and to forgive myself. I want you to forgive you. I keep thinking there has to be a way where you can admit that you did something wrong, but still forgive yourself completely. And I want to find it. That real forgiveness. I don't want to live hating myself. I don't want to live hating you. I want it gone. I don't even want the seeds of it there. I want to dig it out completely."

"I never knew how to do that for me," Wendy said, her heart squeezing tight, because what Anna was saying was so beautiful and compelling, and she wanted it so very much. "Because I was afraid that if I did I would just… stay the same. That I wouldn't change. That I might do something else that later I could see was wrong or repellent. I felt so much guilt for what I did.

"But I look at you, Anna, and I see that you deserve a new life. One where you're happy. And you certainly don't deserve to walk around carrying the weight of your mistakes for the rest of your life. And I don't even mean the affair. I mean your marriage. You and Thomas weren't suited to each other. And you know what? The one thing that I regret isn't the affair that I had that resulted in you and Rachel—I got to the place where I can never regret that, because it gave me the two of you. What I regret is the pain that I caused you. I didn't mean to set up a fake, unrealistic standard for you. And I didn't mean to push you into marriage. But I was afraid. I was afraid of the pain that I knew you could feel in this world. I'm afraid I pushed you into it, anyway."

Anna shook her head. "I loved Thomas. You could never have told me that he was wrong for me. You could never have told me that I shouldn't be with him. Not ever. Because I was sure that I loved him, and that I wanted to be with him. And maybe, knowing what you thought about marriage made it all the easier for me to jump into that kind of commitment... But who knows? I could have found whatever justification I wanted. I was eighteen and thought that I knew the world, and you know how that is."

"Most definitely."

"You don't deserve to be kept in your past," Anna said. "Least of all by me. I think part of moving forward is learning to take my own fault and just deal with it. To accept that what I did was wrong, the method that I went about getting out of my marriage was wrong, and let myself move on, anyway. So what. We made a mistake. We're not perfect."

Wendy looked at Anna, and she felt...proud. Because it had taken her more than thirty years to even begin to move on from who she'd been and what she'd done.

And if she'd known that dragging her secret out into the light would be the beginning of all that ugliness inside her dying, she would have done it ages ago.

"I didn't think..." Wendy shook her head. "I didn't think that it was possible. That exposing all this rot was what would get rid of it. I'm just glad that you figured all this out earlier than I did. That you don't have to sit in a mistake forever."

Last night with John had been a revelation. Not just because it had been wonderful, pleasurable and deeply gratifying to be with a man again in that way, but because she'd allowed herself to have pleasure, and she hadn't been instantly punished. Because she'd let herself feel something wonderful, and she hadn't dissolved.

Because without so many words, that had been part of forgiving herself. And maybe it was a strange thing, that the forgiveness had come when so many other people were angry at her.

But it was like she had taken out her own personal demon into the open and discovered it was old, decrepit and losing its teeth.

In the darkness, hidden away, it had been free to be the snarling, fanged monster that haunted her dreams and made her feel a deep sense of unease with who she was and everything she had in her life.

And seeing Anna like this… It was like all the pieces fit together. Because, of course, she didn't think that Anna should exist in that darkness. Of course, she didn't think she should be punished. Not for the decision she'd made at eighteen to marry Thomas, when she hadn't had the first idea of what she wanted from her life, and who she wanted to be, but also for what she'd done when she'd existed in a state of such despair that the smile from a stranger had been the only hope she'd been able to see.

But that left only one thing.

"The thing I'm the sorriest for is that you couldn't talk to me. And that is because of the lie that I constructed. I might not be responsible for all your choices, but you didn't feel that you could come to me when your marriage was falling apart, and you should have. I should have made it clear that I was here for you. That I supported you no matter what. And that I would love you no matter what happened in the end. But I didn't. I'm sorry. I want you to know, from now on, no matter what you do, no matter who you're with, who you aren't with, I'm proud of you, Anna. Everything you are. You were the light of my life from the time you were born. If I didn't have you, if I didn't have Rachel, I wouldn't have had the strength to carve this new life out for myself. To make this place. You're part of it—you're a part of me. The best part. You were brilliantly and wonderfully loved, no matter what. And I'm saying this too late, but I am always on your side. Even when you're wrong. Especially when you're wrong. Because you have to be wrong in life to get where you can be right. And I will walk with you, through all of that. Because all I want is for you to be happy."

A tear slipped down Anna's cheek, and she leaned across the space, and pulled Wendy in for a hug. Wendy clung to her daughter, a sob lodged in her throat.

"I know, Mom," she whispered. "I know that you love me."

In those words were the absolution that Wendy needed.

And she thought that maybe for the first time in more than thirty years, she might be okay with who she was.

In the end, she hadn't been the one to teach her daughter how to live.

Anna had been the one to teach *her*.

28

Sometimes we're a storm. At night, we are the very waves crashing on the rocks. I wonder what has overtaken me. By day, I don't know how to speak to him. And a smile from him is like the sun is here. Rare. Why do I treasure it so?

—FROM THE DIARY OF JENNY HANSEN, AUGUST 1, 1900

RACHEL

Rachel had intended to go to J's to order a hamburger. Truly. That had been her intent. She hadn't meant to stay chatting until the last customer had conveniently left. And she hadn't counted on Adam locking the door and closing up early. She hadn't meant to start kissing him, and she really, really hadn't meant to end up right back in his bed.

But there she was. Naked, and beautifully, *brilliantly* satisfied, fitted against his hard, muscled body.

And tonight…she just didn't have the energy to run away.

It was done. They'd slept together, and whatever the messy implications this new phase of their relationship added to their previous one, she couldn't turn away from it now.

What she had figured was that eventually, she and Adam would talk about what had happened between them. After all, talking had always been about the easiest thing in the world to do with Adam.

It turned out there was something that was even easier to do with him.

He rolled over on his side and rested his hand on her bare hip. She wanted to purr over how good it felt. The weight of that masculine hand.

"That was amazing," she said. She turned over so that she was facing him. "Really. I don't think that I stayed long enough last time to tell you just how…wow."

"Thank you," he said, his mouth quirking up into a half smile. "I'm flattered."

She turned over on her back. "I know that we didn't ever talk about…things. You know, before."

She didn't know if she wanted to talk about them now. But there were just a couple of things that she felt like he should know, given everything they'd done.

"No," he said. "I didn't get the impression you wanted to."

"I didn't. Because coming and seeing you was… It was an escape. And it was one I needed. I needed it so much. I loved him. I feel like people would never understand how I could be with someone so quickly if they fully knew how much I loved him. But I haven't had this in a long time. A *really* long time. I forgot what it was like to have something for myself. And remembering how good my body can feel… It's…amazing. I'm glad it was with you."

"I'm going to tell you something," he said. "I wasn't just a disinterested listener, you know. I knew you were married, and I respected that. But… I wanted you from the first time you walked in."

She shifted back to her side, away from him, her face heating. "I didn't know."

"I came here because I didn't have anything else. And then there was you. And it didn't matter… Whatever your real life was. Our conversations weren't real life. They were something better than that."

"I felt the same way."

He had been escaping with her, too. It amazed her. Left her in awe. And she wanted to know… She wanted to know why. Even if she shouldn't. Even if she should leave it alone. Because they had this brilliant, beautiful thing. This relationship that she'd never had with anyone else before. Something that transcended reality, like he'd said. And it seemed like adding real things to it would only cause pain.

"What are you escaping from, Adam?" she whispered.

Silence stretched between them and she rested in it. In the heat of his body. The comfort of his touch. Being in an unfamiliar bed and feeling altogether unfamiliar to herself.

Finally, he let out a slow breath, his fingers tracing a pattern on her hip. "I was in finance," he said. "In another life. Made a lot of money. I was busy. Very important. But I had everything you were supposed to have. Big house. Wife. Kids."

Her heart stilled, her breath stopped short.

"You know, I thought I was doing things right. Because you have to support your family. But it was more than that. I cared more about that job than I cared about any-thing. And before I realized it, my best friend had stolen my wife. And my kids right along with her."

"What?"

"I mean, not legally. But you know… They're teenagers, I can't make them see me. There are court agreements, sure. But—but to force kids who don't want anything to do with me to come and stay over? Hell. No. And I would go to work and I would wonder…what the hell it even meant anymore, because I had all that money and no one to spend it on. No life to put it toward. Nothing. My grandpa died, he left me this place. I came."

Rachel didn't know what to say. She was utterly and completely blown away that Adam wasn't this solitary, single man who simply stood behind a counter every night. That they weren't actually so different.

She had assumed all this time that he was single, childless, that he may never have been in a serious relationship. That he was unattached in every way, because that was how he had seemed to her. She had assumed that she was the only person holding back anything of her life, and she'd known full well that he was aware of most of it, whether he spoke about it or not.

Because living in a town this size, there was no way he hadn't heard some details about her, at least whispered when she walked out of the diner.

And she'd thought…

That he was just there for her. Handsome and safe, and then handsome and not so safe when it had become the right moment for her to have those feelings.

But he had been there all along with feelings of his own, and a past that she couldn't have even guessed at.

"How many kids?"

"Two," he said, his voice rough. "My daughter is a year older than Emma. My son is sixteen."

"Neither of them speak to you?"

"No," he said, his voice rough. "I believe that the last time my son saw me he said he never wanted to speak to me again."

"How? How did this happen?"

"I wasn't around," Adam said.

"I can't imagine that. I can't imagine you...were devoted to a job to the point where you weren't with your family."

"But it's true. It's who I was. I thought it was taking care of them, and so it was all that mattered. Yeah, I can see it all now, with a whole lot of clarity that I wish I didn't have, or I wish I'd had sooner. But it doesn't do me a shit lot of good now. I can't fix it. I was commuting into San Francisco every day, and my wife was having an affair in my big house up on the hill. But I left her there to have that affair. I wasn't around. We didn't have a connection anymore. But I was arrogant enough to think that my money was going to keep her with me."

"Did you cheat?"

He shook his head. "No. I probably would have, though. Eventually. My life was split in two pieces. Everything I did at work, everything I did at home. And the work piece just got bigger and bigger. I forgot why I was doing all of it."

He cleared his throat, shifted behind her.

She wanted to look at him but she was afraid of what would happen if he did.

Afraid he would stop.

Afraid he would continue.

Eventually, he did. "When the kids were little, and we were poor, I knew exactly who I was and why I was working like that. To make a better life, for our survival, for their education. But eventually it became all about me. It was like a sickness. Being the best. The most aggressive. The smartest. At every meeting. Always early. My blood pressure was sky-high. I probably would've keeled over before I managed to cheat on my wife, if I'm honest. I was going to have a heart attack before I was forty."

His breath was heavy, jagged. "I can get mad, and I could blame Katie for making the kids hate me, but I made the kids hate me. I was a stranger, so it was easy for her to tell them who I was, and how I felt. They didn't know me well enough to know what was true and what was a lie, and that's my own damn fault. I'm angry. I won't pretend I'm not. But I'm mostly angry at myself. I had the real thing. When it was gone, I realized how little the rest of it mattered. She didn't even take my money, you know. Tad has money of his own. But that's how much she wanted to be rid of me. Everything that I worked for in that marriage... In the end, she didn't even want that. I would have felt better if she would've taken my money from me."

Suddenly it was like she'd switched to the other side of the diner counter, and she saw what they were, what they'd been to each other so differently. She'd thought he was being there for her.

All this time, he'd been lonely. All this time, she'd been there for him.

Just by being.

"Adam, I'm so sorry. But, you know, people heal rifts all the time. They can. They do." She thought of her mother, her sister. They would fix it. They would fix it because they were family. Family always would.

"I hope so," he said. "But the thing is, even if we do fix it... I've only seen Jack a handful of times since he was eleven. And Callie... She goes to her room every time I come over. At first, I took my weekend visitations, but as they got older they started making their own choices. By the time Callie was sixteen she wouldn't come anymore. I tried to keep things going, but I couldn't. Well, I came here three years ago. I haven't been back. Not for more than their birthdays."

Rachel could only give thanks, in that moment, that as difficult as things were with Emma sometimes, they weren't there. And she didn't see them being there anytime soon. No, they wouldn't let it get there.

And she was thankful again for Jacob, and the relationship they'd had. Which would always be a part of who she was. He was part of what had knit her together. An integral thread that made her…her. And he always would be.

She couldn't have banished him even if she'd wanted to. Not without unraveling herself.

She turned over and moved closer to Adam, her eyes on his mouth. "I'm sorry." She kissed him, and somehow that kiss opened up something inside of her. Made her chest expand.

She felt something. More than something.

She felt raw and confused. Wounded. On Adam's behalf, because she considered the man a friend, and knowing he'd been going through so much pain…

"I'm so sorry," she repeated. "I'm sorry I didn't know."

"We never talked about your stuff."

"Yeah, but you knew what I was going through, and I always felt like you didn't talk about it out of respect for me. You gave me a place to go where the fact that my husband was dying wasn't the biggest thing. You were… You were my lighthouse, Adam. You kept me from hitting the rocks. Some nights, knowing that I was going to the diner to talk to you, and to get my cheeseburger, was the only thing that kept me going all day. Knowing that I would have a moment to have a breath. To feel like me.

Just me." Her eyes filled with tears. "It feels awful even to admit that. But I needed it. I needed you look at me the way that you did, not with sympathy, but like a friend. I didn't have anyone else that could do that for me. And I... What was I for you?"

"The most beautiful damn thing in my day, Rachel."

He captured her face, rolled her onto her back, his hard body over the top of hers, his muscled chest pressed against her breasts. "I hadn't been with a woman since my divorce. You were the first one I wanted."

She reached up and touched his face. "Well, I'm glad to have helped with that...anyway." He turned his head and kissed her fingertips.

Their eyes met, and she felt...so much. Too much.

It was impossible.

She moved away from him.

"I should go."

"You can't stay all night?"

"No," she said. "I wasn't even going to do this. In fact, I was going to tell you it was a bad idea. Because it's too soon."

"Right," he said. "I forgot it was too soon for you."

She groaned. "I really need to cancel my date with Mark."

"Damn straight," he said.

"I don't think you get to have an opinion on that."

"No?"

"No. This is...us. Just without the counter between us."

He chuckled, but she didn't hear a lot of humor in it. "Without the clothes, too."

"Sure. Anyway, I'm not ready to date."

"Just ready for this?"

No. She wasn't ready for *this*. Whatever it was. And the way that he looked at her with those blue eyes made her feel like she was coming apart at the seams.

"I'm not going out with him," she said.

"Well, I'm not revising my opinion on that. Good."

"Thank you," she said. "For being there for Emma. I understand now a little bit more about why you're so good with her. I appreciate it. Because you know she doesn't have…"

Her throat got tight, and all of this was a little bit too close to serious. A little bit too close to what she didn't want to be in the middle of.

"Yes," he said quickly. "No problem."

She slipped out of bed and started hunting for her clothes.

"I'll see you tomorrow," he said.

"No, you won't," she said. "I'm not going to be hungry for a hamburger tomorrow."

"Well, I'm going to be hungry for you."

She stopped, her heart fluttering, her whole body warring with just how much that pleased her even while it unnerved her.

"I might make you starve."

"I don't think you will."

"Why don't you think I will?"

"Because you're hungry for me, too."

"I might have a salad."

"You don't like salad."

"Still. Sometimes I have salad, anyway."

"Have me instead."

She got dressed. "I'll think about it."

And as she walked out the door, she knew that this was a challenge she'd already lost.

Because try as she might, she was already planning how they would see each other again.

EMMA

Emma was tossing and turning in bed. She couldn't stop thinking about what her mom had said to her about first love.

She was thinking a lot about Luke, about taking things to the next level with him.

Not just possibly sleeping with him, though she was giving that a lot of thought, but also wanting to share more of her life with him. More of herself.

This, she supposed, was falling in love.

She had been resistant to it. Hadn't wanted to fall in love with him, even while she had wanted to chase the crush between them, because it had made her feel so good.

But it had become so real, so deep, so fast.

She had never envied her mother's life. The way that she had fallen in love so young, and had experienced so much loss as a result. And she had certainly not at all envied Anna recently.

But this felt so new and different and like nothing anyone else in the history of the world had ever experienced.

She was aware of reality enough to know that that was silly, and how everyone must feel.

But it didn't stop her from wanting more.

"What would you do, Lazy Susan?" Emma asked, feeling ridiculous. "Would you sneak out to the lighthouse with a boy? Did you?"

There was no answer. So she picked up her phone.

I'm thinking about you.

There was nothing for a moment, and then three dots appeared at the bottom of the screen indicating that he was typing.

Me, too. Can't sleep.

You should come here.

She sent the text somewhat recklessly.

To your house?

To the inn. No one will think it's weird if a car shows up late.

Are you sure?

Yes. I want to show you something.

Okay. Text when I'm there.

Without thinking, Emma got out of bed and put on a thick woolen sweater, then she got a heavy coat out of her closet. She had a giant, old-fashioned flashlight, metal and substantial, just like the ones in all the guest rooms, with a label that said it was property of the Lighthouse Inn.

She kept it on hand in case she wanted to walk up to the lighthouse, which wasn't an uncommon thing, though she hadn't done it in a long time.

It was an experience, going up there at night, when all eight lights were on and the lens was rotating.

It had been her favorite place to hang out with her dad.

It was hard to believe that she would be graduating in just a couple of weeks.

And he wouldn't be there.

Suddenly, the urge to show Luke the lighthouse felt nearly desperate.

Life didn't wait. That was the thing.

And she'd been playing games. Keeping Luke separate, even if he wasn't a secret. And she wanted him...

Here.

The Light will always lead you home...

She hadn't been able to go there since her dad had died. But it was home, and it always would be. The essence of this place that had shaped who she was.

Life could be scary.

But life was also short, and if she'd learned anything over the last few months it was that. That people could just be gone from your life, and you couldn't have them back. You couldn't say what you hadn't said. You didn't get a chance to do things over.

Her father had always wanted to do great things with his photography, but he hadn't had the chance, because he'd gotten sick.

She didn't have infinite time. She didn't have infinite chances.

No one did.

But Emma had been given a great and terrible gift, in that she knew just how much truth there was in that.

Her father had had such a limited amount of time.

Emma had no idea how much time she had.

It suddenly felt so short and fleeting, and she wanted to make it all count. Wanted to make it all big.

Her phone buzzed.

Here.

She looked out the window, and saw that her mom's car wasn't there.

That was strange.

She'd been out late a bit lately, and Emma didn't have a

clue as to what she was doing. One time, when she hadn't been around, Anna had said something about a girls night, which had irritated Emma, because if it was a group of the old friends that her mom had hung out with before her dad had gotten sick, then they used to be included in that.

And it made her feel angry that her mom would join a group that excluded Anna.

Though, she supposed her mom needed friends no matter what shape they came in.

And, anyway, it was convenient for Emma.

She went down the hall, and paused at her parents' bedroom, her heart in her throat. Then she pushed open the door and went in.

She didn't know what she'd expected to find. A ghost. Pain. But there was nothing but the blandness of an empty bed.

She touched the bracelet on her wrist, and suddenly she understood.

Her dad wasn't here. This wasn't a tomb.

He wasn't contained in the ashes her mom had spread out over the sea.

He was with her.

He was her light. And he would always guide her home.

She didn't have to fear an empty room, an empty bed, a future that stretched out wide before her with no certainty.

Because he and her mom had made her into someone who could endure, find her way, stand strong.

Losing him was sad. There was no other way to see it.

But having him had been an immense gift.

And it was one she had. She couldn't lose sight of that in the middle of her grief. Couldn't lose sight of the gifts because of the loss.

She clattered down the stairs and out the front door,

then turned on the flashlight and watched the beam wave wildly as she jogged across the lawn and toward the little parking lot.

Luke was there, leaning against the truck, and her heart jumped.

"Hi," she said.

"What's going on?"

"I wanted to show you this. The lighthouse."

"In the dark?"

She rolled her eyes, even though he couldn't see. "Silly. That's the best time to go see a lighthouse."

"Okay. Fair enough."

"Follow me," she said.

She aimed the flashlight on a paved path that led across the outside of the picket fence, moving toward a hill. The path turned to dirt then, became narrow and wound up the side of the rocky hilltop.

Trees were dense on either side of the path, though on the left, if you stepped off you were liable to roll right down the hill and plummet into the sea.

But Emma had been navigating this path for most of her life, and in spite of the dark all around her, she didn't feel nervous.

"This way," she said, the trail taking a sharp bend left, and then back right. And then it flattened out, the tower coming into view. There was a small shed, white with a red roof, and the light tower, stark white with a matching red roof, was behind it.

As it turned slowly, the lens up inside the top of the tower glittered like diamonds. The lens looked fractured in the light.

Emma had always been fascinated by it. The way that it transformed in the dark. Each clever cut designed to magnify the brightness of the light in the glass, becoming jewellike in the darkness.

It turned slowly, eight beams rotating along with it, strong and sure. When the light beam would pass over the back, it would illuminate the hillside, catching the trees, the plants, before sweeping back down toward the sea.

"Well," he said.

"I know. This is actually all public land—anyone is allowed to come up. Anytime. We can't go in the lighthouse. My family doesn't own it. It's run by the Coast Guard. The US Forest Service owns the land the house is on. It's…confusing. But, anyway…this is where I grew up."

"A far cry from the trailer park I grew up in," he said.

"I was lucky," she said. "I mean… I really was. It's easy for me to feel sorry for myself now. To feel like I've had it tough. But it only hurts that I lost my dad because he was so great. I wanted more time because…" She swallowed hard. "He used to bring me up here. And we used to just look out at the sea. During the daytime we would watch for whales. He would point out the spouts on the horizon, and I would always sit and stare, hoping that I could see just a little bit of them. There are some natural caves just to the left, around the corner behind the rocks. And the sea lions live there, so we'd always see them swimming around in the waves. I knew from the time I was a little girl that the ocean was my life. That it was what I wanted to spend my life studying."

"But how come you want to go away and study it?"

"Because I want to see more of it. It's so vast. And I'm tied to this piece here, but… I want more. I want to see it. Study it. Experience it. And I know I'm going to end up back here. Because you're right. This is my home, and this is where it started. But…"

"You love it so much you need to see more of it. I can understand that."

"Yeah," she said.

She walked over to the light tower and looked up, watching the beams as they turned. "Come here," she said.

She leaned back against the tower, which made her tilt her slightly, her feet out in front of her, and gave her just the perfect view of the light beams moving slowly over the water, with the perfectly clear sky above them, and the scattering of glittering stars.

Luke leaned against the wall next to her, his hands shoved in his pockets.

"Isn't it amazing?"

"Yeah," he said. "It's amazing. I can't say that I've ever really stopped and looked at anything here. It's just where I was born. I've never really loved it. Not like you do."

"It's not too late. You're looking at it now."

"Yeah," he said. "I am."

Except when she looked at him, his face was turned toward her.

Her heart expanded, and the space between them shrank as he leaned in to kiss her. Softly. Slowly.

And she knew that this place would be changed for her forever. Because it would no longer just be the site of those girlish hopes and dreams, but of these extremely adult feelings that Luke created inside of her.

Love. That's what it was.

Love.

And just like the way she loved the water here, and it created conflict with her desire to go away, he was another thing. Tethering her to this place.

It frightened her.

But she also knew there was nothing she could do but embrace it. Fully and completely.

She was falling in love with him.

And life was short enough that she knew she couldn't put that off.

If she was given love now, she had to embrace it now.

All of it.

All of him.

But she wouldn't tell him, not yet. Not because she was scared, because she wanted this to be about...

Being here. Sharing this.

When the time was right, when it was all about them, when she was ready to... When she was ready to be with him, she would tell him.

For now, she would just let him kiss her here at the lighthouse.

For the first time in a very long time, Emma felt like all the pieces of herself had been crushed together, like she was whole. Fractured and glittering like the lighthouse itself.

29

Is it such a terrible thing to love someone?

—FROM A LETTER WRITTEN BY STAFF SERGEANT RICHARD JOHNSON,
FEBRUARY 15, 1945

ANNA

It was a new day. And Anna was feeling bold. She was going down to town to talk to Adam about how well the pies were doing. And she was excited to find out what she could do to make things work even better.

She was in general feeling…good.

The talk with her mother, and the one with Thomas, had done so much to change the way she felt. It wasn't enough anymore to sit around thinking about the fact that she had changed her life. No, she had taken the first step toward changing her life.

And the rest was all in front of her.

She was figuring out what she wanted. And, depending on what Adam said today, she had another stop in mind.

She pushed open the door to the diner, and the first person she saw was Emma. Waiting tables, her red hair thrown up into a bun.

"Hi," Anna said, crossing the space and pulling her niece in for a hug.

"Hi," Emma said.

"You look tired," Anna said. "Is everything okay?"

"I'm okay. It's… I'm at work."

"If you need something please tell me. Emma, I'm on your team. No matter what."

Emma offered a small smile. "I know. And I'm good."

"Well, if you ever aren't good…tell me."

"Thank you," Emma said softly.

As they separated, Anna noticed her sister. Sitting at the counter, which was not abnormal. But when Adam came out from the kitchen, the color that mounted in Rachel's face was indeed abnormal.

And the way he was looking at her…

Well, Anna would have to be an idiot to miss what was happening there.

She had known that Adam had more than a passing interest in Rachel. He'd made that very clear.

But what she hadn't realized was that Rachel might have an interest in him.

"Hi," she said. "I came to ask about the pie."

"Oh," he said, looking at her as though he was shocked that anyone but Rachel was there at all. "Sure."

"Hi," she said, nudging Rachel, who hadn't said anything to her. She felt like she should say the word one more time just for good measure. It was getting a little ridiculous.

"Yeah," Rachel said, looking edgy.

"I just wanted to know if you were going to want more pie, if you sold the pie, if anyone committed a ritual sacrifice of the pie in my dishonor…"

"No ritual sacrifice," he said. "In fact I have money

for you." He turned away. "Just going to go get the envelope from the back."

When he disappeared into the kitchen, she looked pointedly at Rachel. "And?"

"What?" Rachel asked.

"Adam?"

"What about him?"

"You're staring at him like you want to lick him. Or like you *have* licked him."

Her face went scarlet.

"Oh. *You have.* You've already done it."

"Please keep your voice down. Emma would die. He's her boss. And no one else would understand. Can you even imagine? 'Supposedly grieving widow hops on diner owner mere months after her husband's death.' Her good, sweet, local husband that everyone loved?"

"Does anyone else have to understand? As long as you do."

"You know that they do, or they gossip a lot. And are mean."

"Sure."

"I don't understand, either," Rachel said. "I shouldn't be able to do this yet, right? One dinner date with a guy I thought of only as a friend-ish was one thing, but this is—"

"You having fun?"

A serene smile crossed her face. "Yes."

"Keep having fun. There's a shortage of fun in our lives."

"True." Rachel took a breath. "I just… I feel like you should know. I understand why you needed to escape. And that you did with Michael. What I said to you….about how I would never, it was wrong. I would. I did. With Adam.

We didn't have a physical relationship or anything before this and I wasn't totally conscious that we were flirting. But I took a break from my life and I let myself use him as an escape. Jacob wasn't a burden. But it was hard. It was so hard and I was lonely. Somehow taking a break from the real world and taking about other things made me less lonely."

Adam reappeared with the envelope as soon as Rachel quit talking. "I sold them all. If you want to think of monthly specials, in addition to some of the standbys, that would be great. It was really popular."

"Excellent," Anna said. "That's perfect."

Her mind was still turning over with her sister's apology. With what she'd said.

She supposed she could choose to get mad. Mad that it had taken Rachel this long to acknowledge it, but she didn't have it in her.

Their lives were complicated in ways they never would have chosen. If they could find their way through the mist and to the light, then why be mad over the how, when or why.

They'd connected here. At this point of pain. And suddenly it was like she could see Rachel clearly, and she knew Rachel saw her now, too.

She looked between him and Rachel. "Well, I'm going to leave you. I have another stop to make."

And she marched right down to Fog, money in hand. She talked to Jo about making turnovers. And then, feeling truly brave indeed, she went down to Sunset Bay Coffee Company to make the same offer to Natalie.

It was a strange meeting, and it took a while for Natalie to warm up, but once she did, she was interested in what Anna had to offer.

"Full disclosure," Anna said, "Fog will have some turn-overs, and J's will have pie. But if you want to, I can make you different specials. Things to differentiate between here and there."

"That would be great, Anna," she said. "I'd love to have your baked goods. I miss them at church."

Anna huffed out a laugh. "Right."

"Sorry. I promise I wasn't being snarky. I mean it. I miss seeing you there."

"Thank you."

"You're welcome here. Anytime."

That was entirely unexpected and…nice. It was nice.

She'd felt like a pariah, and had told herself she was comfortable with it. Had told herself she'd blown up her life.

Maybe none of that was true. She'd just rearranged it.

With herself in the center of it. And come to find out… that was okay. More than okay. She didn't have to be colorless.

"Thank you for that, too," Anna said.

She looked over and saw Xavier sitting at a table by the door. He ran a large hand through his dark hair and she paused to watch the motion. He was concentrating on whatever was on his computer screen and he didn't notice her.

She wanted him to notice her.

And she didn't have to just sit back and hope he would.

She walked over to his table and leaned in. "Hey," she said.

He looked up from his computer and smiled. "Anna, hi."

"I'm just headed out. I don't want to interrupt you. Just wanted to say hi."

He smiled at her, and she lit up inside. Before he could say anything else she moved away.

And when she stepped out into the sunlight, it felt like the first step into something. Maybe into that new life that she'd been wanting so very much.

The life that had always been there, waiting for her to make it.

WENDY

When her granddaughter showed up at the Lightkeeper's House unannounced one morning after all the guests had been served breakfast, Wendy was surprised.

Emma had spent a lot of time in the Lightkeeper's House when she was a girl, learning to avoid the times when the guests were most likely to be milling about in the main house, and choosing times instead when she could putter around with her grandmother, or sit in the kitchen with a book.

But, of course, Emma had lost interest in that a long time ago, so seeing her standing on the front porch, reminding Wendy so very much of when she was young, threw Wendy back to a different time.

"Can I come in?"

"You don't have to ask," Wendy said. She looked out at the ocean, at the brilliant blue, the sky clear for the first time in so long. They'd been having beautiful weather for the last few days, and it was a blessed relief.

It was well into May, and it was finally starting to look like spring. It may have been late, but it was welcome all the same.

"Though, if you like, I can bring lemonade out onto the porch. It's pretty out."

"I'd like that," Emma said. "Can I help you with anything?"

"No," Wendy said. "I've got it."

It was a funny thing, she mused as she went into the kitchen and collected lemonade in a cut-crystal pitcher, and a platter with shortbread cookies on it. Of course, Emma was offering to fetch things for her because she was older. But Wendy wanted to bring them to her, like she'd done when Emma was a girl.

But it was strange. How those roles began to shift. It had happened with her daughters a while ago. They tried to take care of her, while she tried to take care of them, and now even Emma was trying to take care of her.

It was just funny how people grew, and things changed. And no matter how much you might like to, you couldn't change them back. You could only move forward and find the beauty in the brand-new shape of things.

She opened the door again, shut it quietly behind her and took a seat in the wooden chair next to Emma's. There was a small round table between the two of them, and she set the tray with glasses, the pitcher and platter there. She let Emma pour lemonade for the two of them.

The roar of the ocean wasn't quite as pronounced today, the water a bit more placid than it sometimes was. But that sound—that sound that had rolled right through her body every day for the past three decades—was there. A steady constant. One that she barely thought about. A presence all the same. Like the hand of God, or a sense of love. Something that she would miss profoundly if it was gone, but often didn't think about.

"I have a question about…the dorms," Emma said. "Have you had any luck chasing down any information about them?"

"No," Wendy said. "The school won't release names. I've posted on an online group for alumnae asking if anyone who was here during the time had letters or stories or memories to share beyond what we have, but I haven't had any responses."

"I'm curious about Lazy Susan. The one who carved on my ceiling. You know, where she was from. If she was far from home when she was here. On an adventure." Emma took a breath. "Grandma... I'm not sure now. I'm not sure about going to Boston."

The words surprised Wendy. Emma had been so certain. It had been a dream of hers for the last two years, and something that she had clung to, even after Jacob had died. She couldn't understand why she was second-guessing herself now.

"We'll be fine," Wendy said. "We'll be fine here. And we'll be here waiting when you get back."

"I know," Emma said. "I mean, I know you'll wait for me, and that you will be here. But... I don't know. What if I leave, and I can't come back. I'm worried about Luke. My boyfriend. And I feel bad about that, too. Because I should be more worried about Mom. But I'm just worried that he could fall in love with someone else. Because I don't know if he loves me the way that I love him. And I..."

Wendy looked at her granddaughter's face, so pale and drawn, and distressed. And Wendy didn't need to know the whole story to understand that Emma was in deeper than Wendy would've hoped she'd be at her age, with so much left to do.

She also knew that...sometimes there was nothing for it.

She'd fallen in love at Emma's age, and she made terrible mistakes with it. Rachel had fallen in love at that age and paid a terrible price.

Anna had fallen in love, and it had been wrong.

But whatever the outcome had been in the end, she knew that nothing could've stopped them from falling.

It was a road you had to walk on your own. A mistake you had to make, or a wonderful, difficult truth you had to take on, like in Rachel's case.

Because her love for Jacob could never be called a mistake, and if they'd fallen in love any later, then they would have had even less than the lifetime cut short that they'd had.

She couldn't tell Emma she wasn't in love. She couldn't tell her not to worry about it.

"You are a strong young woman, Emma," Wendy said softly. "You've had to be. I worry that you had to be too strong. Because everyone around you was doing their very best to hold themselves together, and you saw that, and began to keep your own self all stitched together in one piece, all on your own." Wendy looked out at the ocean. "You have to trust your heart."

"But…hearts lie. And mine is so afraid." She bit her lip. "And it wants different things. It wants everything. You can't… You can't have everything."

"Why not?" Something shifted inside of Wendy. "Why not, Emma? Look at how little we are willing to hold on to in this life. I told myself I couldn't have everything. I thought that I needed to punish myself forever. Because of my sins. The world didn't punish me, God didn't punish me—I did. I came up here with my girls, and I lied about who I was and how I'd gotten myself into my circumstances. I didn't let myself fall in love. I didn't let myself have a companion. Because I had decided that I didn't deserve it.

"I've met someone, too," Wendy said softly. "I never let myself be open to that, not in all the years I've been here. I thought I didn't deserve it. Because of my past. But we don't live in the past. We live now, and we store up for the future. But the past is done. It's over. You can't bring your father back, any more than I can. We can't heal a wound by continuing to make it hurt."

"But what...? What happens if I can't have everything."

"Then maybe it wasn't everything. And as much as it doesn't feel like it, you can fall in love with someone else. Or you can fall in love with another place. Because our hearts are big, and they change. They grow, and they expand. Why don't you demand everything first. See where it gets you."

"But Mom..."

"Your mother is strong. No less strong than you. You don't need to protect her."

"You tried to protect us."

"And look where it got me. It all fell apart, years later. And maybe if it had fallen apart earlier... I wouldn't be learning these lessons now, sitting here with you on my porch. Maybe I would've learned them when I was eighteen."

Emma blinked. "I suppose...that's the greatest gift," Emma said. "That you, and Aunt Anna, and Mom... That I get to learn from you now."

"I hope so," Wendy said. "I hope that I can take all those rocks in my own road and break them down, and give you a smoother path. Because I've made a lot of mistakes. And I can't do anything about the past. But we can all try and have a better future. But what you want, and what you're willing to accept from life, begins with you. I can't tell you what the right thing is. I tried to control your mother, and I tried to control Anna. I wasn't able to keep them from pain. Pain is part of life. It's part of love. I hope you don't have a heartbreak, Emma, but you might. You probably will. But that doesn't mean you shouldn't love. And it doesn't mean you shouldn't have dreams."

"But I'm scared."

"I know. You loved your father. I loved your father. We all did. We knew that we would lose him earlier than we wanted. And we did. But what if we hadn't loved him at all?"

Tears slipped down Emma's cheeks, and Wendy felt moisture building in her own eyes. "I can't think of anything sadder," Emma said.

"Neither can I," Wendy said. "Neither can I. Two things in this world are worth the pain, sweetheart. Love and dreams."

Emma reached across the space between their chairs, and gripped Wendy's hand.

And they sat like that, drinking lemonade and watching the ocean.

She looked at her granddaughter's profile, proud and strong.

She wanted to protect that girl. But she was fierce and strong, and she was a fighter.

And she deserved everything in this world.

And Wendy suspected you couldn't reach for everything without risk.

She couldn't protect Emma.

But she could learn from her. From the bravery of youth.

Wendy suspected that she already had.

30

There is an answer now for my morning queasiness.
Naomi and Rose are thrilled. I don't know
what to feel. I have not told him. Not even
the lavender walls can cheer me.

—FROM THE DIARY OF JENNY HANSEN, AUGUST 15, 1900

RACHEL

It was so strange to do this day without Jacob. Even stranger was wishing that Adam was with her.

She felt like she was caught in the middle of conflicting desires. For the man that she had loved as a girl, and the man who was… She didn't know. He was under her skin. The skin of the woman that she was now, who couldn't quite remember what it was like to be the girl who had fallen in love with her husband.

Life had taken too much from her. Had worn her down.

She felt strong, because she had to be to weather life. But she felt fragile, too. And sometimes the temptation to just lean against Adam was so strong that she wanted to collapse with it.

She'd come to terms with wanting sex. With wanting

to recapture part of who she was as a woman, those pieces that had been lost and worn away by grief.

But she didn't know how to cope with these feelings that were rising up inside of her. With the fact that on the day of her daughter's graduation, the daughter she shared with Jacob, she was thinking of him.

Wishing he was sitting beside her.

Anna was sitting beside her. Her mother was on the other side of her. That should be enough.

Well, not enough. Because not having Jacob left a hole there that wouldn't be filled, she knew that.

But she wanted…

She wasn't going to think about it. She wasn't going to think about him.

She cried, though, when Emma accepted her diploma. And she wished that she could grab hold of Jacob's hand. Congratulate him.

Because he was part of this. Part of her. This beautiful girl that they had raised to womanhood.

Smart and fierce. She loved the sea because of Jacob. And loving Jacob, losing him, hadn't made her afraid to live her life. It had made her follow her dreams.

Rachel was afraid, though.

She had lost purpose in some ways when she had lost Jacob, because caring for him had been such a big part of her life. Loving him had.

And Emma… Getting her through school, seeing her through life, was a change in her role, too.

But she had Adam. And in his arms she wasn't a caretaker or a widow. She was a woman.

When the graduation was over, she hugged Emma. And Emma ran to her friends, because, of course, they had places to be.

"We are going to bake dinner rolls," Anna said, grabbing hold of Rachel's hand. "Unless you want to go to dinner."

"I…"

Anna looked at her meaningfully. "You can also go occupy yourself elsewhere. Since your daughter is leaving for the evening. And I can certainly make excuses for you."

"If you would," Rachel whispered.

She gave her mom a hug, and then she slipped away, giddy like she'd imagined she might have felt if she'd ever sneaked out of the house as a teenager.

Her phone buzzed, and she looked down, saw a text from him.

Dinner?

A smile curved her lips. On my way.

She wanted to keep this a secret, keep it between them.

When she'd been young she hadn't minded talking about sex with her friends at all. She'd proudly told her high-school friends the first time she and Jacob had slept together and had given them details. Physical measurements. It had seemed exciting and fun.

As she'd gotten older, she hadn't done that anymore. She might make general comments with very close friends, before the distance had settled between them.

But this was… Somehow the intimacy of what they shared felt so deep she could hardly stand to think of it in a room with other people, much less speak it out loud, or let anyone know what they did.

What he made her feel.

It was like that corner of the world they'd made for each

other during Jacob's illness had become larger. That space they had created while she was going through grieving the loss of Jacob—and if she was honest, she had been grieving him for years before his death—had grown to encompass not just that diner area, but his apartment, his bed.

What they had was so fierce inside of her. And she wanted so much to keep it just hers.

It wasn't a date.

It was something she couldn't explain.

And if no one knew, then she didn't have to name it or figure it out. Because then she didn't have to deal with the accompanying emotions that were beginning to grow inside of her chest.

It was better that way.

He texted her just before she arrived.

Come to the door in the back. I'll take you straight up.

She hadn't realized that there was a door back there that went directly upstairs, but there was. Adam opened it, and the sight of him, in a worn T-shirt and faded jeans, made it feel like the air had been scooped out of her lungs.

"I can't imagine you in a suit," she said.

"What?"

"You were in finance."

"Yeah. I probably still have the suit somewhere."

"I need to see it."

"Not tonight."

"Why not? Maybe I have a James Bond fantasy."

"Well, when you put it that way. Maybe."

He closed the door behind them and she followed him up the narrow staircase. "What are you doing?"

"We have to eat, right?"

"Sure. But…"

Her words were cut off when they entered the apartment, and she smelled something decidedly undiner like. Pasta. She was certain. And there was a green salad sitting on the table.

A bottle of wine. Two glasses.

"What'd you do?"

"I cooked for you. And I had to make sure that it was different than the way that I normally cook for you."

"Why?" she asked.

He was feeding her. He was giving her…a romantic dinner. And they hadn't done romance. Not at all. Everything they'd done in this apartment had happened in that bed. Well, sometimes the shower. But they'd been naked, and their conversations had been short. Between bouts of hard, fast sex before Rachel ran back to her real life.

"How long has it been since someone took care of you? And I don't mean in that church meal train, feel-sorry-for-you kind of way. When was the last time someone took the time to do something for you?"

"I don't… I don't know."

"You take care of everyone. And the only time you ever let someone else take care of you was when you came into my diner and ordered a hamburger. I like taking care of you, Rachel."

"I—"

"Sit."

She was so shocked that she obeyed. Like she was a golden retriever.

He went over to the stove and took a pan of lasagna out of the oven. She watched him move, his broad shoulders, narrow waist and lean hips. The way that the muscles in his forearm shifted as he worked.

In this context she could imagine him in a suit. He had authority. Wore it with the same ease that he wore those faded T-shirts. Not the kind of authority that was louder, and demanded respect and attention.

It was measured.

Easy.

He poured her a glass of wine, served her, then sat across from her, looking at her with the kind of intent that made her skin heat up.

"Thank you," she said, because it was the polite thing to say, but she wasn't sure she was actually that grateful. Because it was…

She didn't know quite how to do this.

She'd fallen into the role of caretaker for her family. It had been easier. Easier than sitting around and waiting for bad things to happen. Easier than hoping that someone else would do the difficult things.

Easier than sitting around and just having feelings.

And, yes, sometimes she had felt overwhelmed, but then she was able to marinate privately in righteous indignation.

When someone did things for you…

She didn't quite know how to handle it.

He was easy to talk to. Even with her conflicting feelings. He told her more about his house outside of San Francisco. Told her more about Jack and Callie. They talked about good times with them. Not about his estrangement.

And, somehow, that led her into talking about Jacob.

"I knew I was in love with him right away. But, then, I was seventeen. You don't worry about whether or not something is real when you're seventeen. You just feel it, and you know. It was the easiest thing in the world. Our relationship was the easiest thing in the world. It seemed so unfair when he got sick. Because we could've fixed anything. Could have faced anything. In terms of marriage, in terms of those day-to-day problems that you have. But we couldn't…make him well. There was no amount of love that could fix it… People feel sorry for us. For me. But I had a great marriage. I don't feel sorry for me."

She felt sad sometimes, but never sorry.

"What kind of man was he?"

"Nice. Very even-tempered, which is a bonus, since I'm not. He liked to take things slow. He was a photographer, and we would go for long drives, and sometimes… he wouldn't even take a picture. He wanted to look at the scenery, to see it and take it all in first. And then sometimes he would go back for a picture. But he was big on experiencing life. Especially as things went on, and his health deteriorated and it became clear that his life would be short. He was so good at that. At taking in those moments."

"I'm not very even-tempered," Adam said.

No. She could sense that. Even though she'd never really seen his temper, there was a sharpness to his personality, beneath the affability. A firmness about him. That authority that she'd been thinking about earlier.

It was very different than Jacob.

She wondered if that was why they generated so much heat.

A sharp kick hit her chest. She felt guilty having those thoughts. It was just…very different. Things were new between them, but sex wasn't new. You couldn't compare that to two fumbling virgins who had all the excitement and enthusiasm of new lovers, but absolutely no methodology.

Or maybe it was because they'd both lost before. So when they came together they held on a little tighter.

Whatever the reasoning. The sex with Adam was...

Something else.

He'd also made her dessert, which he promised was good, because it was cake and not pie, and therefore not overly complicated.

He was right. It was delicious. And the whole meal, she didn't have to get up.

And for a moment she wondered.

If her life could be like this. A life with a man like this. Who took care of her. Who was passionate, who wanted her.

Panic twisted in her gut, and she kissed him. Because when she kissed him she couldn't think. And when he stripped off her clothes, she couldn't second-guess anything.

Because whatever else was happening between them, this was easy. Or natural. And it didn't require thought.

And when they were through, she curled up against him, exhausted. Sated. He took care of her in bed, too. Made it all about her. About her pleasure. Time after time. He was never satisfied with just once. As if somehow it made his own pleasure less, and she hadn't known men like that existed.

She should leave. But she looked up at him, and his blue eyes, and she didn't want to go.

She wanted to stay in the strange moment. Where she felt like she was someone different.

Where she felt like she could have what she didn't think she really could.

This man who touched her and held her in ways she'd been starving for.

Who created a fire within her that she hadn't known could exist.

She ached for that. For the intensity.

She and Jacob had settled into soft and beautiful, and moments. Just moments. Those moments that he had appreciated so much had been such hard work for her to love. The whole time her mind was just racing ahead to what would happen when that moment was over.

She was glad he hadn't lived that way.

Losing him by inches had altered the fabric of who she was. Her mind had always been on the moments *after*. The time she'd have to live in on her own. Alone.

And who she was in the aftermath…

She had been gentle hands. Soothing voice.

And now she wanted rough, calloused hands and gruff words. A meal cooked for her, and the kind of sex that made heat ignite inside of her whenever she remembered it.

She shut her eyes, and she let exhaustion roll over her. And just for a moment, she let all the guilt drain away.

She let herself admit that she wanted this.

That it was what she needed.

Adam wrapped his arms around her and pulled her close, curling her against him, wrapping his body around hers.

She just wanted to stay. Wanted to lie there and smell his skin, his sweat. Such a strange and primal thing that desire brought out in people. She wanted to enjoy it. Living. Being a human. Being a woman. Stripped back to these basic parts.

The beauty of sleeping against a solid male body.

So she closed her eyes, and she let herself have it. Defiantly.

But when she woke up it was morning.

And she knew that she had made a mistake.

31

I can't come home yet. But I will.
You'll keep my secret, right?

—FROM A LETTER WRITTEN BY SUSAN BRIGHT TO HER SISTER,
FEBRUARY 1962

EMMA

Emma touched her necklace, then let it drop. She was nervous. To the point of shaking, which was silly. It was all silly.

She'd thought about calling Catherine before she'd come. Catherine wasn't a virgin, and her friend could've at least walked her through the basic mechanics. Not that Emma didn't know the basic mechanics. But there was something to be said for hearing a narrative account versus having just read science books, and the odd scene from a romance novel that she'd snuck out of her grandma's room now and again.

She hadn't talked to Luke beforehand, because she felt weird about that, too. Which was maybe not the best sign. If you didn't quite know how to broach the subject of sex with the man you wanted to have it with.

She walked into the garage and looked around. "Luke?"

He came out from the back room, wiping his hands on a rag. He froze when he saw her. She supposed that she was dressed a little bit more…up than normal.

"Hi," she said. "I hope you're…off soon."

"What are you doing here, Em?"

"I came to see you."

"You normally call first."

"I know. I'm a surprise."

Her throat felt impossibly dry. She felt like running away, which was strange, because she was the one who was determined to do this in the first place.

There was no point waiting on anything.

Her father was gone.

He hadn't been here for her graduation. He wouldn't see her off to college. Wouldn't be there for her future wedding, or to ever meet her children.

In many ways, that made her feel like more of an adult than anything ever could. Those milestones that she'd have without him.

"Okay, you look like you're afraid of me," he said. "And I don't like that. So what's up?"

"I'm not afraid of you," she said, the words coming out in a rush.

"Are you breaking up with me?"

She blinked. It had never occurred to her that he would think that. That Luke could possibly have even a moment of insecurity when he…

Well, if anyone should feel insecure about their relationship, it was her. Younger, less experienced and definitely not the kind of thing that he was looking for. He was the object of her long-held fantasy.

Of course, he didn't know that.

Suddenly, she saw all of this from his point of view. That she was standing there looking awkward, and he had no idea what was going to come out of her mouth. That she might be touching her necklace, because she was going to take it off and give it back, not because it was the most treasured thing that she owned, and she wanted to hold on to it now because she wanted to hold on to it forever.

"I've had a crush on you for forever," she said.

"What?"

"Luke, I… I've had a crush on you for forever. I'm going to sound like a crazy stalker girl, but I took a job at the diner partly so that I could be near you. I mean, I didn't go looking for the job. Adam offered it to me, but when he did…"

"You really did that?"

"Yes."

His lips turned up into a lopsided smile. "Hmm."

"You think that makes me sound like a stalker?"

"No. But it makes me feel…good."

"I didn't think you would ever pay attention to me. I was going through one of the hardest things… The hardest thing that I've ever gone through in my life. You were just kind of a hot escape. But then we started talking, and you were more than that. You helped me figure out what to do next. And… I didn't just come to talk."

"Where does your mom think you are?" he asked.

"I told her I was going out with you. I told her I might be late."

"How late?"

"Late enough. Hey…do you have condoms?"

He dropped the rag. "What?"

"My friend Catherine would yell at me and tell me that it was my responsibility to get condoms if I want to have sex because we live in a society that demands we take charge of our own sexuality. But everyone knows my mom, and I couldn't figure out which store to go to that wasn't like…fifty miles away. So, I was just kind of hoping that you had some."

"I—"

"*You're* not a virgin, are you?"

"Hell no," he said. "I mean… I didn't mean it like that. No. I'm not."

"So you have condoms?"

"Yes," he said. "I do."

"Good," she said. "Because I think we might need some."

"Emma, you don't have to."

"I know. Honestly, though, you're making it sound like I just offered to clean the whole garage or something, not have sex with you. You're not exactly selling it. Remember, I've never done it before."

"I know," he said. "And I didn't say it like that because I think it's a chore. I just… I don't want you to think that you have to do this because…you're eighteen, and I'll leave you if you don't, or because you had that feeling that life is short. I felt that way after my dad died. I did stupid stuff. I don't want to be a stupid thing you do."

"That's not why," she said, shaking her head. "I want to."

Because life *was* short, and love helped make you, even if it had pain. She'd watched that play out in her mother, her grandmother and her aunt.

"Emma…" She was pretty sure he was going to argue with her. And, honestly, she didn't want to beg the guy to sleep with her. But if he was just trying to protect her…

"If you don't want to, that's…well, it's not okay. It's

kind of devastating. But if you don't want to, then we won't," she said. "But if you're trying to protect me... please don't, Luke. Don't protect me from you. Don't protect me from life. I'm not a kid. I need to make some of my own choices. I don't need another person trying to protect me when I already know that life doesn't come with a guarantee. I want you. I'm here now, and so are you. Let's make something with that."

She found herself being hauled up against him then, and he kissed her, fiercely, holding nothing back. "It was never a question of wanting you," he said. "But it matters to me. It matters to me to be the first one. It matters to me that you're younger than I am. And I don't want to take advantage of you."

"Well, that's part of why I like you so much, so even if I find that annoying, I can't be mad about it."

"You *could* be," he said.

He picked her up, and she squeaked. "Where we going?"

"To my house," he said.

It turned out they didn't have to go far. His house was a camper, parked out behind the shop.

"Why did you never mention this?" she asked as she stepped inside the small space.

"I live here because I choose to," he said. "I'm saving money. For different things that I want to do with the business. And...since I live by myself, and I'm almost never home. Mostly I just need a place to crash."

There was a tiny kitchen, and a room she assumed was a bathroom stall.

"I shower in the shop," he said.

"Oh," she said.

The thought of him showering was exciting. She was

a little disappointed she wouldn't be able to shower with him, actually. But, clearly he didn't have the facility for that. And it was something that would have to wait.

"What?" he asked.

"Oh, I was just… I was thinking about you showering," she said, smiling slightly.

His brow shot up. "Really?"

"Yeah. I kind of like that."

"I didn't realize you were such a bad girl, Emma."

He said it with humor, and it made her feel a zip of excitement.

"Just for you," she said.

But then he started kissing her again, and she couldn't think of words anymore. It didn't matter. And nothing seemed all that funny, anyway. The lightness that had taken them from the garage to this point, and into the small platform bed in the camper, faded. Was replaced with intensity. Kissing that she knew didn't have to stop. Touching that could keep going on. And anytime she felt nerves threatened to overtake her, she just looked at him. At his face. In his eyes.

It was like a dance she didn't know the steps to, but her partner did, and he knew how to lead. He was slow, methodical. Gentle when he needed to be. And after a while she just got caught up in it. In the motion, in the moment. In her feelings.

But they were so much deeper, so much more than she had anticipated. She had thought she understood the connection between them, but she hadn't. She had thought she'd known what her feelings were, and that she had somehow reached the depth of them, and that was why she was ready to be with him.

But when they were skin to skin, and when he slowly

eased his body in hers, she fought against tears. Not because it hurt, but because she hadn't known.

Pleasure, brighter and hotter than she'd expected, burned away the emotion for a moment, but when it was finished, and he held her, she began to shiver, because she didn't have the ability to contain all of the feelings that rioted through her body. She thought she would break apart with them. How could she leave him?

How could she ever bear to leave him?

That thought had been a quiet echo in her for weeks, but here and now it was like a church bell ringing in her head. One she couldn't ignore or think past.

Tonight, and for school. What would happen if he didn't want her anymore after this? Now that he'd seen her body, seen her naked. Now that he knew her in a way that no one else did.

"I wish you could stay," he breathed. And she didn't know if he meant tonight or forever, and both options scared her, because she couldn't stay all night, anymore than she could stay forever, and it wasn't fair of him to make her feel like she should.

Strange, how close to the surface anger was, along with fear. And an intense vulnerability that made her want to curl into a ball and protect herself. Like a small animal turning out its spikes so that she couldn't be touched or hurt.

But she didn't have any spikes. All she had was soft, naked skin that he was still touching. And with each sweep of his calloused fingers over her, she became more and more aware of how easily he could hurt her.

"You okay?" he asked.

"Yeah," she lied, because what was she going to say?

It had felt good. Wonderful. And she loved him. But

that was the problem. Love was so much more than she'd realized it was an hour ago.

"It'll get better," he said.

She didn't know if she wanted it to get better. She didn't know what she wanted at all.

"I have to go home," she said.

"What? Now?"

"I don't want my mom to get worried. She knew I was going to be out for a while but…you know, probably not this long."

"Okay. I'll walk you to your car."

She watched him get dressed, and she lay there, still naked underneath the covers. His body fascinated her. It was so different from hers, and suddenly she didn't want to go. Not because of his body, but because looking at him reminded her that it was Luke. And suddenly she wanted to cling to him forever. But she'd already said that she needed to go, so she did need to go. She hadn't known that it would make her so insane.

"Let me help," he said.

He dressed her. The guy rehooked her bra for her. Pulled her dress back over her head. Bundled her up in her coat.

"You don't have to go, Emma," he said. "You can stay with me. We don't have to…do anything. We can just sleep."

She wanted to. But she wasn't ready to have that conversation with her mother. Except…she almost felt like she needed to.

"No. I should go. I just… My mom…"

And she wondered if that was really what was happening, or if she was just panicking. Because she was on the edge of something big and it terrified her.

Because she'd been on the edge of love and now she was deep in it.

"Luke... I love you."

It was like he'd turned to stone. "Oh."

"Is that all you can say?"

"I... Emma, I've never..."

"You told me you weren't a virgin," she said, trying to do something about the horrible weight on her chest.

He shook his head. "I've never done the love thing."

"What did you think I was doing?" she asked, her voice hushed.

"Love is a stupid thing, Em. It's just words and it doesn't matter. Why do you need them?"

Emma floundered, trying to breathe past the pain in her chest. "Because I want everything. The school of my dreams, the career of my dreams, love. Am I worth that or not?"

"Emma..."

"Are we worth it, or not?" She knew maybe this was wrong, but she didn't want to wait. Not for this. Not for anything.

He didn't speak. And she couldn't stand there in his silence for another moment.

She scrabbled out of the trailer as fast as she could. She expected him to follow her, because he always did. He always walked her to her car. But this time he didn't. And she fought with herself. Fought to keep from going back and begging him to love her. Saying that she would take whatever he gave.

And maybe she was being unreasonable. Or maybe she was being immature, she didn't know. But she was... It was his reaction. And it hurt.

But her mom was right, her grandma was right. And

watching the way that her aunt's marriage had fallen apart, she knew that she was right.

She had to ask for what she wanted now. She had to make it clear what kind of love she wanted. What it looked like to her.

Because otherwise she would pour years into this relationship, feeling like she did, and he wouldn't be able to give it back.

And she would rather know now than wait until then.

No matter how much it hurt.

32

He was happy. It gives me hope.
Hope hurts so very badly.

—FROM THE DIARY OF JENNY HANSEN, SEPTEMBER 20, 1900

RACHEL

She had so many missed calls. Her poor daughter. Of course, now Emma would know how she felt, but that wasn't fair. At a certain point last night the calls had stopped, and Rachel had a feeling she knew why.

Because while Anna was loyal, and was her sister, there was no way she was going to keep her secret at the expense of Emma's or Wendy's sanity.

Which meant the jig was up for her.

But worse than that...

She had fallen asleep with him. Like they were a couple.

Like they were *married*.

Her husband had died just a few months ago, and she was playing house with another man.

Guilt ate at her. That guilt that she had pushed to the side last night was back now with a vengeance.

She'd spent the night with him. Like a wife. Like a woman in a relationship.

She'd gloried in it. In being alive and happy. In Adam being strong and masculine. Someone who didn't need her care. In the fact that the sex was the best she'd ever had.

She nearly doubled over with the guilt.

She loved Jacob. She loved him. Deeply. Profoundly. And the pain of loss hadn't faded. It never would.

Twenty years of her life had been spent married to that man. He had shaped her. Who and what she was.

How could she…?

How could she?

She stumbled out of bed, and the sound of her feet hitting the floor made Adam stir.

"Rachel?"

"I really have to go," she said.

"Stay," he said.

"I'm not a dog, Adam. Sit. Stay. I don't do tricks. You can't give me a treat and get me to behave."

"You do come when I call, though," he said. The grin on his face was wicked, and she wanted to punch him, because he clearly wasn't reading her panic.

"Stop it."

"Hey," he said. "What's wrong?"

"You're not my boyfriend. That's not what this is. I can't be spending the night with you. Emma's worried about me. And now I'm going to have to explain."

"Is that such a bad thing?"

"Yes. It is a bad thing. Because this was just supposed to be between us. It wasn't supposed to affect my real life."

"I hate to break it to you," he said, pushing himself into

a seated position and crossing his arms over his broad chest. "But this *is* your real life. Everything we've done is part of your real life. All of the conversations that we've had over the past three years are part of your real life. It's not a separate thing that exists in an alternate dimension."

"It was to me. It *is* to me. I have my family, and there's you. You just existed for me. To make me feel better."

"I think you were falling in love with me. For years. I think that's what you've been doing."

"No," she said. "I was not. I was married. I was in love."

She hated this. Didn't want to think of it. Didn't want to believe what Hannah had said about her was true.

"You *are* in love. With him. And that's fine. But that doesn't mean you don't have feelings for me. That doesn't mean there wasn't a reason that you confided in me for all that time."

"You were convenient," she said. "And...that's it."

"You're a liar."

"Don't—don't do this to me," she said, anger rolling over her. "I didn't ask for this. I wanted sex, Adam, not... dinners and heart-to-heart talks."

"If you wanted sex you could have had it with the man that you didn't have a relationship with."

"Well, I'm attracted to you. More than I am...to anyone else. But that doesn't mean that there's anything more, or that I was asking for anything more. Or that I wanted anything more."

He crossed the space between them, over six feet of muscular, irritated, naked man that she found far sexier than she wanted to admit. Even angry. Maybe especially angry.

Because there was a vitality to this. To him. And it felt

so sharp and raw and honest. She wanted... She wanted to have a fight. She wanted to yell at him.

"You say that you want to give to me, but you don't. If you did, then you would just...stop it. You would quit pushing me. Quit challenging me. I've had enough, Adam. I wanted some orgasms, that's it."

"You want me," he said, his voice rough. "You could have had an orgasm with Mark."

She laughed. A short, huffed-out sound. "That's up for debate. And, in fact, I didn't sleep with him because that is *so* up for debate."

"You want me. Admit it. Not anyone else."

The words hooked onto something in her chest and tugged hard. Made her feel wounded and fragile.

"I had a marriage. I had a whole twenty years of beautiful, wonderful, hard commitment. I don't want it again. I don't have it in me to care for another man, not like that. That is the last thing that I want. On this earth. Don't tell me that I have feelings for you. You don't know me. You don't know what's in my heart. I loved *him*. And that's it."

He hauled her into his arms, and she wanted him. Immediately. Even while she was angry. So damned angry.

"You need me," he growled.

"No," she whispered.

The word was fractured, weak and fragile, because what he'd said was the most terrifying thing anyone had ever said to her.

Need.

She couldn't afford to need anyone.

She knew what happened with people. They left. They died.

She had grown up never needing a father because she didn't have one. She hadn't needed Jacob because she'd had to learn not to. She thought that she did. Oh, at first in their relationship she thought that she did. But as the years progressed and it became clear she was going to lose him, she had to learn how to make it so that he needed her, but she didn't need him to survive. Because when she lost him it was bad enough, but if he'd been a requirement for her survival where would that have left her? All the days when he couldn't be with her. All the days when she had to be strong for him… If she needed him, everything would've collapsed.

She couldn't need. It was simply impossible.

Love was too heavy. It was too heavy, and the kind of need that he was talking about, the kind of feelings he brought out in her… They only led to one place.

You were in love with me then.

No. She rejected that.

"No," she said again, finding her strength. "I don't need you. I don't *need*. Least of all you. You don't matter to me. You know what matters? My family. And you're not part of my family. You couldn't even handle your own, why would I trust you to handle me and mine?"

He drew back like she'd struck him, and she might have felt guilty if she wasn't so terrified. Of him. Of herself.

"Low blow, Rachel. Really low."

"You're the one that went and changed the rules on me, Adam. You had a woman offering you no-strings sex, and what do you do?"

"I was in love with you before this started," he said. "What hope did I have once we were together like this? Once I'd kissed you and touched you…"

Her stomach cramped up. "Don't. We're not teenagers. We don't… We don't need to do this, ridiculous, intense, *love* thing just because we had sex. We are adults. We've both been in love."

"Yeah. We have. So we know how to recognize it when it comes up, don't we?"

And that was the thing that scared her the most. That she did understand what love looks like. That she understood what it looked like at two weeks, two years, twenty years. That she knew what a lifetime looked like, because she'd had a lifetime with a man. His whole damned life. Her whole life. She already knew what it meant.

And she was tired.

Tired and scared. And the guilt. So much guilt…

"I have to go home. I'm not going to see you again."

"Rachel…"

"I have to grieve! I have to… My daughter graduated from high school and she's going away to college. My husband is dead. I am *a mess*. I can't begin to figure out how to clean it up, and God knows I can't do it with you."

"Why not?"

The question was so simple. Asked so flatly. As if it was the easiest thing in the world to just bring him into her life while she was dealing with all of that. As if he didn't have to compartmentalize and do things in a certain order. And wait a certain amount of time *and*…

"I can't talk to you if you even have to ask that question. There's no answer that I can even give you. It's just ridiculous. You have to know that."

"But I'm ridiculous. A damn fool for you, that's for sure. You're right, I have been in love before. And you're right, I did fail my family. I regret it. With every fiber of my being, and I know how to be better now. But it's too late for me to fix that. I know how I want to love *now*. I want to love you that way. It's all right if you're scared. I'm brave enough for the both of us. It's all right with me that you love him, too. I can handle that. We're not starting from square one. We had lives, you and me. Separate from each other. I don't want to erase all that. I just want to give you—us—something new."

"I don't."

On a choked sob, she collected her things and ran out of the apartment. And she cried. She cried the whole way home, like she had lost something. Someone. Which only made her angrier, because she had lost someone. Lost them to death. The man that she loved, the man that she had her daughter with. The man that she'd spent twenty years of her life loving and caring about and caring for.

How could she cry over this? Over him?

It wasn't right. It wasn't fair.

All this time, all these months, these years, and Rachel hadn't despaired.

But she did now. And she didn't know how she was going to climb out of it.

EMMA

At around 8:30 a.m., her mom's car finally pulled into the driveway. She saw her mom look up at the house for a moment, then turn and walk down toward the beach.

Emma grabbed a sweater and a pair of shoes, and headed out the front door, running down the path that took her down to the rocky beach.

"Mom?"

Her mom turned, and her face was streaked with tears. "I'm sorry," she said. "I'm sorry that you were looking for me, and you couldn't find me. Just one of the many stupid things I've done lately."

"Are you okay?"

She shook her head. "No."

"Adam didn't hurt you, did he?"

She didn't want to acknowledge what her mom had been doing with Adam, but she wasn't stupid. It was even weird to have to admit it to herself now that she wasn't a virgin, and knew just what sex was like.

Her aunt Anna's words—about how Emma hadn't known—flashed back to her mind, and she had to admit to herself, her aunt was right.

She knew now, and that made certain mysteries in the world close and intimate, rather than gauzy and faraway.

She didn't like realizing how complicated all of the women in her life were. She preferred to put them in neat boxes. Her grandma, her mom, her aunt. They'd existed only in those roles to her. But they'd seen too many messy, terrible things happen in the world, to each other, recently, and it was impossible to pretend that they were anything but women. Who made mistakes, who tried to fix them.

And like her grandma had said, they were women who deserved to have all the good things that life could offer.

Her mom deserved to be happy. Whatever that meant.

"No. He didn't… He didn't do anything. I mean, he *did*. I don't want to have feelings for anyone. No one but your dad. I've already been there and done that. I've already loved a man, and I can't love another one. Not more. Not more than him."

"You wouldn't be crying if you didn't have feelings, though."

She had to wonder if her mother was feeling the vast, terrifying things that Emma had felt when she'd slept with Luke. Which…horrified her on every level, but also made her feel a deep amount of sympathy. It was strange. This full realization of the humanity of the women in her life.

That they could be uncertain. That sex could feel as big and terrifying to them, too.

"Why don't you want to love him?"

"Because," her mom said. "It's not… It's so different. It's so different, what I have with him. And it makes me feel like I'm betraying what I had. The timing is awful. If I was going to meet him it should have been in ten years, you know? Not a minute before then. I don't want this now."

"I understand that." Emma nodded. "Every time I start feeling happy I think it's not time yet. I feel that way whenever I don't think about Dad being dead for more than a few minutes. And I felt that way about going to school. I just wish it could all happen later and I could sit around being sad now."

"I don't want that for you."

"I know. I don't know if… I don't know if it'll ever quit hurting. But…can we have things that don't hurt around it?"

"It's different, though," her mom said. "I loved your dad. I *love* him."

It was hard, so hard to not let her heart close up and want to save all the feelings—hers and her mom's—for her dad.

But he wasn't here.

And she…she knew what it felt like to be touched by a man. What it felt like to be held and kissed. And what it felt like to worry that man she loved would never hold or touch her again.

Her mom had lost the man she'd loved like that. There was no getting him back.

She could never, ever wish her mom a lifetime of knowing she couldn't have it ever again.

"Is there a rule that says you can't love Adam, too?"

"I don't think that's how it works."

"I want to stay here. And I want to go to school. And I want to make you happy, and I want to be with my boyfriend. And I don't know how to have all those things," Emma said. "I don't... I don't know how to ask for all of that. And it means that I have to believe that everything somehow is going to work out. Even though it's messy."

"I'm afraid that he wants more from me than...than I want to give him. Than I can give him."

"You gave more than Dad could give you for a long time. What's wrong with taking more than you can give?"

That seemed to stop her mother completely. "That isn't true, though," she said. "He loved me. And that made it... Not a burden to take care of him. He gave everything he had."

"Well, maybe that's all Adam wants from you."

"Oh. Just everything I can give? Like that's nothing?" If it wasn't all so painful it would be funny to watch her mom contort her face like she was the bratty teenager, waving her arms in broad, dramatic strokes.

"I don't know," Emma said. "I don't know. Grandma said... Grandma said that we shouldn't be afraid to want everything. She said that she didn't. That she didn't want everything for herself for a long time. And that...she wished that she had."

"I don't want everything," her mom said, wrapping her arms around herself. "Because it hurts too much when you lose it." She took a jagged breath. "Besides, he's nothing like your father. Why would I want to be with a man who's completely different?"

"That makes more sense to me, anyway," she said. "If you had someone who was like him...it would be replac-

ing him. Or trying to. Trying to make that person like
Dad. I don't know—doesn't it say something that the person that you're with isn't like him? Something about how
real it is?"

"I'm not taking love advice from you. As much as I
admire you."

Emma sniffed. "I *am* in love."

"Don't give everything up for him," her mom said. "I
did love your dad. So much. And it makes me feel guilty
to even…think the thing that I'm going to say to you next.
I went into marriage not knowing what I was going to
sacrifice. Not realizing just how much the sickness part
of the vows would be part of who we were. Don't walk in
knowing that you're sacrificing. Don't start sacrificing
from the outset. Because when you marry someone, it's a
series of sacrifices. You choose, every day in ways small
and large, to set aside your way of doing things. Your vision of life to make your shared vision of life. And sometimes you have to set everything aside and give that person
all that you are. Because they needed it. Marriage is not
fifty-fifty, Em. It's two people giving everything they've
got, and sometimes that's not equal. It can't be. But you
do it, anyway. You carry the portion of the burden you
can shoulder. That's how you have a marriage that's real."

A tear escaped and slide down her mom's cheek. "People want a happy marriage," she continued, "but that is…
It's not that simple. You want a marriage that's deep. One
that's fulfilling. But it means that you give. And give and
give."

She looked squarely at Emma. "Go have your life for
a while. Do what you want. He'll love you enough to be
here when you come back. Just like we do. Don't sacrifice
anything for me, either. Because I love you. And I'm going

to be here when you get back. Love is patient, Emma. Let it be patient for you."

She reached her hand out and squeezed Emma's.

"Thanks, Mom," Emma said. "I… I'm going to do that. I'm going to go to Boston, and I'm going to come home during break. I'm going to end up back here."

"You might not," Rachel said. "You might stay there. You might meet the man of your dreams there. You might meet the whale of your dreams there. The aquarium might be the place you want to stay. You might fall in love with a building, or the air. You don't know. But it's okay. Because…" She closed her eyes. "I was selfish. I'm sorry. I did want you to stay. I felt like I was losing you. And it all felt like loss in the face of losing your dad. And I couldn't cope with that. But it's not the same. It isn't. My whole job loving you was to love you into a strong woman who made her own decisions, and could follow all of her dreams. It wasn't to keep you here as part of mine. So you go off, and you live. Don't worry about living the way that I did, or making me proud. Because you already have, Emma. In every way."

Emma flung her arms around her mom's neck. "I love you," she whispered.

"I love you, too. And I'm always here for you."

"I'm always here for you, too, Mom. And I know…it isn't the same. But I want you to be happy. It sounds stupid. But I am so proud of you. Because I don't know very many people who could've loved Dad the way that you did. And he had that. All the bad things, but he had you. You deserve to have whatever life you want."

"Emma," Rachel said. "You're so sweet. I had a marriage. I had love. It's okay if I can't have it again."

"Well, I'll love you either way."

"I know you will."

They hugged and the only sound was their breath and the waves. Emma closed her eyes. "Sometimes I think I can hear them," Emma said. "All the people who were here before us. Soldiers and sailors and lightkeepers. Students."

Her mom moved away and wiped her eyes. "I've always liked thinking about them. Life moves on. The older generation passes, but life keeps moving forward. And at the same time I can feel everyone, every year contained in this house."

"Jenny Hansen had to start over, too," Emma pointed out. "With nothing but a letter and the hope of a place she hadn't even seen."

She smiled, small and sad. "I'm not sure I'm as brave as Jenny."

While Emma was resolute in her decision, and what she was going to do next, she didn't feel satisfied.

Because she knew that her mom was heartbroken. And there was nothing that she could do to fix it.

33

*As the baby grows, so do my feelings for him.
I couldn't recognize them at first because
they weren't what I knew before.
But, oh, how deep they have become.*

—FROM THE DIARY OF JENNY HANSEN, JANUARY 5, 1901

RACHEL

Rachel stayed out at the beach until it was dark. Until the beams of the lighthouse split the night. She was sitting in the cold sand, her wedding bouquet clutched tightly in her fists. Like it might bring him closer to her.

She didn't have any clarity.

Everything she'd said to Emma was true. Except she just felt...guilty. Because it wasn't that she couldn't find it in her to have feelings for Adam.

It was that she did have feelings for him. And she didn't understand how. It confused her.

It made her question herself. Everything she knew about who she was.

But who are you, anyway?

She knew exactly who she had been when she had married Jacob. A young woman who had been largely shielded from the pain of life.

Yes, her mom had been single, and she had never known her dad, but for the most part, the sense of community, the joy that she'd gotten out of growing up here at the lighthouse, overlooking the sea, had compensated for any of that pain.

It had always been secure and warm.

They'd always had food.

She hadn't learned how truly cruel life could be until she'd watched illness steel Jacob's vitality, take his dreams and move them out of his reach.

Take their plans and twist them, bend them so that they had to take on an entirely different shape.

They had refused to be broken.

They had refused to allow his sickness to drive them apart.

She had stayed with him. Through seizures and surgeries, the side effects of those surgeries, medical event after medical event.

Cancer. Chemotherapy.

Everything.

And she had gotten hard. Because she'd had to. She learned to stand strong, because she had no other choice.

You need me.

Those were the most terrifying words he could have said to her. Most especially because she was afraid they could be true.

She'd had that moment, that fantasy in his apartment about sinking into that life.

And on top of it all she felt disloyal. Because so much of her craved this thing that Jacob hadn't been able to give her. That he never would've denied her if he had a choice.

It didn't feel fair to want it so very much. To glory in the physical aspect of her relationship with Adam, and to crave having someone in her life who would take care of things. Who would be able to carry some of the weight.

She could carry it all on her own. She knew she could. As long as she was loved. Because she had done it.

But she didn't want to anymore. And Adam created such a tempting vision of life.

But she didn't know how she could let herself have it. Didn't know how she could let herself have him.

Jacob.

She whispered his name beneath the roar of the waves.

But there was no response.

The lighthouse illuminated the ocean, guiding in the ships.

She remembered the history of the place. When three lightkeepers had been needed to keep it lit.

No one kept it lit now—it was automated.

And suddenly, something clicked inside of her.

She was still acting like a lighthouse keeper, tirelessly keeping the flame lit. And it just didn't matter anymore. It wasn't needed.

Emma was ready to go off on her own.

And Jacob's ship was home.

He was no longer in danger of being dashed on the rocks. It was finished.

It was like the fog had lifted away.

And she could...love.

She could simply love Jacob.

The work, the sacrifice... It was done.

She didn't have to *quit* loving him. But there was nothing left to do. The love wouldn't shrink, wouldn't go away, but it would need to shift. Otherwise, she was just lighting a flame that wasn't in danger of going out. Doing work that no one had asked her to.

And it wasn't selfless. It was selfish. It had made Emma feel like she was beholden to her, like she might need to stay here instead of going to the school of her dreams.

Jacob was gone. Emma was grown.

There were no dreams left to follow but her own.

That was the terrifying thing. The one that scared her down to her bones. Beneath everything else, she told herself. Grief, guilt and responsibility.

What scared her most was the idea that she could reach out and take something she wanted. That there would be nothing holding her back.

Something just for her.

Giving had been her life. Because she'd been sure giving would keep her from being selfish. From being the kind of woman her mother had warned her not to be. It had also preserved her. Given her tasks to perform so she didn't have to sit with the weight of her emotions.

Now she was free to be whatever she chose. Free to have the life she wanted.

She could think of nothing more frightening. She stood, and the breeze caught her hair. Then she ripped the petals off of the flowers, those flowers she'd thought before were so much like her. Tired and worn from the years. And she let the wind carry the petals out of her hand, into the air and over the sea. She couldn't keep flowers in a vase and pretend they still lived. She couldn't hold a memory like it was a person. But that didn't mean that love went away. Love remained. And when she turned away and began to walk back to the house, it wasn't grief that burned brightest in her chest. It was love.

ANNA

Anna hummed while she finished doing the dishes in the kitchen, and surveyed her morning's baking as it cooled on the counter.

It was two weeks into her expanded baking initiative, and Anna was feeling good. She'd been out and about town since she'd started making deliveries to the different coffee shops and J's every day.

She'd also had coffee with Laura earlier in the week.

Laura was interesting. Genuinely happy with her husband of five years, with a two-year-old, but not as overly sunny as Anna had first taken her for.

She had a dry wit and her jokes slipped in under the radar sometimes. Anna liked it.

Laura, for her part, wanted to understand Anna, not so she could judge her, or chide her for the decisions that she made.

She no longer felt like the town was full of enemies. Yes, there were people who avoided her. Somebody literally crossed the street to avoid running into her, and Anna had to pretend that she didn't notice, because she wouldn't give the woman the satisfaction.

The older lady in the grocery store whose name Anna still didn't know always looked sour-faced when she rang up Anna's groceries.

But it was fading. And it would fade even more, she knew that.

She had ripped off the Band-Aid with the interaction with Thomas. She had sought it out.

But it was funny the way that interactions with people that weren't Thomas remained more uncomfortable most of the time than any potential interaction with him.

But they were finished. And it was mutual.

Anna walked into the sitting room, where her mother was clutching a stack of letters in her hand. "I was wondering if you wanted to read these and put them into a book. Something for the guests."

Wendy's eyes were bright and damp-looking, and Anna wondered why. "Mom, are you okay?"

"Fine," she said. "I think that you'll find something in here. Something that might... I know how much you always loved the history of the soldiers. I think you'll appreciate this more than anyone else."

She handed the stack of letters to Anna, and then walked quietly out of the room. Anna unfolded the first one and sat down slowly on the couch, and began to read.

By the time she was finished her cheeks were wet, her shoulders shaking.

She went into the bathroom and splashed water on her face, and looked at her reflection.

I have spent much time hating myself. I find I've lost the taste for it. Is it so wrong to try to find forgiveness of ourselves...

Those words, and others echoed in her mind. Wisdom from the past. A gift from the past.

From her mother, who had known what it would mean to her.

Her heart felt swollen, sore but happy.

Things felt...bright. Like it was the first real sunny day in a long time. Or maybe it was just how it felt to be remade. That pastor's-wife coat had been shed and she could feel light and warmth on her skin. All those protective layers gone.

She was...visible. All her flaws known. To her town, her family, herself. But there was a freedom in that. Not the same as that jaded lack of caring she'd felt a few weeks back.

Like she'd found a way to love all that was flawed in her. To accept that others might never understand, but that she could be at peace with herself, anyway.

So Anna found herself walking in bravery and vulnerability out in the sun. And it was glorious.

During her Monday delivery, she didn't think of Thomas at all. She didn't think about people staring at her. She didn't worry about her interactions with anyone.

Xavier was at Sunset Bay Coffee Company again, at the same table. This time, he was the one who came to Anna.

"Hi, again," he said.

"Yeah," she said. "Hi."

"We keep running in to each other. And I've missed my chance all these other times. I wanted to give you my number." He handed her a piece of paper that already had his number on it. "You can put it in your phone if you want. Or lose it. Up to you."

"I… I'm not going to lose it," she said.

And she didn't feel the need to warn him about the rumors, or ask him about them, or try to talk him out of making a connection with her. Because she wanted one with him. And whatever it became, whatever reaction he had when he found out—if he didn't know already—she'd deal with it then.

"Good," he said, grinning. "I hope you call it soon, too."

"I think I will," she said. "I have to run, I'm doing deliveries. But I will call it."

She was feeling downright buoyant as she headed out of the coffeehouse, which was why it was doubly shocking when she ran in to a wide-eyed Laura, and was nearly physically accosted by her on the street.

"Anna," she said. "I can't believe I ran in to you."

"I make deliveries here are a few days a week."

"Did you hear about what happened in church yesterday?"

"No," Anna said, frowning.

What happened now? Had Thomas burned her in effigy? Was there a scarlet *A* set up somewhere that she should know about?

"He apologized. For what he said about you. He said that it was wrong. He said that it wasn't fair. That it was only one side of the story, and it was an easy side. He said that he hadn't been a good husband to you, and that being faithful was only part of the equation when it came to marriage. He absolved you."

Those last three words settled strangely in Anna's brain, and everything kind of went fuzzy. "He...*absolved me*?"

"Yes. In front of everybody."

"Oh."

"He said that everyone was supposed to quit being awful to you. That—that Jacob dying had broken something that was already fractured. That he sees it a lot when he does counseling in church and...well, that it wasn't surprising your marriage didn't withstand it because it was stressed."

"Wow," she said.

And, oddly enough, that almost made her angrier than when he had dragged her name through the mud. Because mostly she just wanted it all to go away now.

And he was still putting the power in his own hands. Except...what other choice did he have? If he believed that he'd made a mistake, and she had been certain that when they'd spoken there had been a change in him. An agreement, and the sense that his own part in the failure of their marriage was real…

She had to assume, she supposed, that he was doing the best he could. That he felt genuine remorse over the way that he'd handled it.

She'd made a mistake. However their relationship had been in the end, her husband had seen her coming out of a bedroom with another man, directly after she'd had sex with him. She had hurt him. Even if it wasn't in the way part of her petty heart might have hoped.

And then he'd hurt her with the way that he'd spoken about what had happened to the church congregation.

But all they could do now was their best to fix it. All they could do now was their best to move forward.

And this was his effort at…at healing. She had to believe it.

Because that was part of letting it go.

"Right. Well… I don't even know what to say. I didn't expect that."

"Neither did anyone else. Least of all me. I still think we're leaving the church."

"You don't have to. Not on my account. If it serves your spiritual needs, that's why you should be there."

"I'm not comfortable," Laura said. "I can't…go there again."

The solidarity felt real, and it felt good.

"Thank you."

"I'll let you get on with your day. But let's have coffee again?"

"Yes," Anna said. "Let's."

With numb fingers, she found herself dialing Thomas's

phone number while she started her car. He picked up on the second ring.

"Why did you do that?"

"I had to try to fix what I did to you."

It was sincere, the note of pain in his voice, and it made it hard for her to yell at him, even though she wanted to. What was the point, anyway?

"Thank you," she said, instead of everything else she thought.

She felt her heart break open. There was a lot to be said, but not between them. Not anymore. Again, he thought he'd done the right thing, and maybe he had. She didn't know.

But it wasn't their problem to solve, not now.

That made her feel free. Much more than sad.

"I want you to know," he said. "I think I loved you the very most that I can love someone like this. But I also realize that isn't going to be enough."

"I loved you, too," she said. "So much. But I wanted to love you into a different person. And neither of us can do that for each other, or to each other."

"Be happy, Anna."

It took her a moment. But she finally figured out a way to mean the next words she spoke. "You, too."

She got off the phone, her palms slick. And she realized that neither of them had offered each other forgiveness. And she was glad of that, because she didn't want his.

She didn't need his.

No, she needed her own. That was why the idea of him absolving her sat wrong.

They weren't together. She didn't require absolution from him. It needed to come inside herself. A spiritual reconciliation. With God, with her own heart. With those that she wanted to continue to have in her life.

That was where her love was—it was where her life was.

The lessons from those letters, from finding forgiveness and acceptance in her own family.

And it was all she needed.

She drove home, her thoughts spinning. And when she pulled up to the inn, she froze. Because Michael was standing there at the front door.

34

We are coming home. These years away have been hard, but through these trials I have been given a gift. I know what life I want to lead. I know what manner of man I am, and I will stand firm in that. I will not allow those who would seek to destroy us decide how we are to live.

I have seen what hate brings to the world. I would choose love.

Dearest Robert, I cannot wait to see you again. Finally.

—FROM A LETTER WRITTEN BY STAFF SERGEANT RICHARD JOHNSON, SEPTEMBER 1945

ANNA

"What are you doing here?"

She stared at this man in the bright sunlight and had… the strangest response. There was memory in her body, of what it had felt like when he'd touched her, and that was real. Very real.

But she didn't look at him and feel like he was the most interesting, exciting man on earth.

She was much more excited by Xavier's phone number than by Michael's presence now.

She felt like she was staring her own desperation full in the face. The desperation she'd felt at that point in her life. In her marriage.

"I miss you," he said.

"It's been months," she responded.

"I know. I didn't know how to handle that whole thing with your husband. I can't say that I've ever had that happen before."

"Yeah," she said. "Me, either."

"I'm sorry," he said. "I didn't handle it right. But I thought maybe we could start over."

Anna realized with sudden clarity that she didn't need him. To make her feel good about herself. To feel like a woman.

Just like she didn't need Thomas to absolve her in front of the church.

She was so much stronger now. She wouldn't have needed to use Michael to escape now. Her life stretched before her, full of endless possibilities.

She didn't have to fall from one life to another, from one relationship to another. She didn't have to shroud herself in shame and pain. She could have whatever life she chose.

She could call Xavier. She could find more places to sell her pastries to. She could open a bakery. Or she could stay working at the inn, living there with her mom and sister.

"I don't want to," she said. "I already started over. Here. By myself. I like where I'm headed."

"Anna... I really cared about you."

"I needed you to care. At that time I needed you more

than I can express," she said. "But I've been...dealing with myself. And I've changed. I need different things now. But...thank you. Thank you for caring for me when I was lonely."

He looked at her for a long moment, then closed the distance between them, touching her face briefly. She felt warm, but not fluttery. Affection, but not love.

"If you change your mind..."

She smiled. "I don't know what I'll do. I have...so many choices and I don't know where any of them will take me yet."

He walked toward his car, got in and drove away. Toward what, she didn't know. It suddenly seemed clear she hadn't known him at all.

It hadn't mattered who *he* was, since she hadn't fully understood who *she* was.

Now she had some work to do. Work on her own. To figure out exactly what she wanted. What mattered to her.

And if she ever did get married again, when she did have another relationship, exactly what she wanted from it.

But today had brought home some very important facts.

She forgave herself. And she wasn't bound to those two men anymore.

She was free.

And more than ready to stand on her own.

35

It's a girl, El. She was so pretty. With red hair. I wish I could have kept her. I barely got to see her. I thought the most important thing was making sure Mom and Dad weren't disappointed in me. But it's not the most important thing. All I want is her happiness.
I wasn't supposed to see, but I did. The family who adopted her is named McDonald.

—FROM A LETTER WRITTEN BY SUSAN BRIGHT TO HER SISTER, MAY 1962

WENDY

The mood in the kitchen that morning was subdued. Everyone was on hand to help. Well, Emma wasn't helping so much as she was sitting in the corner, her chin in her hands. Anna had a straight posture, her chin held high, her movements bright and aggressive as she whipped about the kitchen, going in and out and serving guests, taking the helm like she was powered by caffeine and the Holy Spirit.

"What exactly is going on?" She directed that question at Rachel, who could not have looked more down-trodden if she tried.

"What do you mean?"

"Anna has a literal spring in her step, you look awful and Emma…" She looked over at her granddaughter.

"I think Luke is going to break up with me," Emma said glumly.

"Why?" Rachel and Wendy asked at the same time.

"I told him I loved him and he got weird. He couldn't tell me he loved me, too, and I told him I needed to hear it."

"Oh," Rachel said.

"I didn't think it seemed unreasonable. We're talking about being long-distance for years. And I…"

"You don't have to justify yourself," Rachel said. "You asked for what you wanted."

"But I'm sad. Because I don't want him to break up with me."

"Why are you afraid he's going to break up with you?"

"Because I told him if he couldn't give me what I wanted, then he was the one that had to do it. I'm not giving him an easy out."

Wendy laughed. "Well, I'm proud of you for that," she said.

"Why didn't anyone warn me how terrible this was?" Emma asked plaintively.

"I think we are all literally walking examples of how terrible this is," Rachel said. "If you couldn't make that observation, that's on you."

"I'm only *eighteen*," Emma said.

"I thought you were wizened," Rachel commented.

"Against my will," Emma responded.

Anna came back in looking chipper. "What did I miss?"

"What did *we* miss?" Wendy asked.

"Thomas told the whole church that he was wrong about the way that he handled me. Then Michael came back, and I told him to go away. I feel...like I'm finally living my life. And it's amazing."

"Wow." Wendy looked at Anna, pride coursing through her. "I'm proud of you. You did what I couldn't manage for years. You're strong, Anna. And I'm so glad you're here, on the other side. I'm so glad you got yourself out, and didn't let yourself stay so unhappy."

Anna's eyes went misty. She cleared her throat. "And someday...well, I'm open to finding someone. I hope I do. But it won't be good unless I know who I am first. Unless I love me."

"Well, you know we love you," Wendy said.

"We love you, Mom," Rachel said quietly. "I'm sorry about what I said. When you told us the truth. I'm sorry about everything. I'm sorry that it was so easy for me to judge both of you," she said, looking between Wendy and Anna. "Because I knew hardship, a very particular kind, and I thought because I did that I understood everything. But I had someone that I loved, and I had a lot of security in that. I hadn't... Hadn't dealt with how things can get so...messy."

She stopped. "Even Emma has more experience with it than I do. And is probably handling it better."

"Adam?" Anna had mentioned that Rachel was with Adam the other night, and Wendy knew enough to put the pieces together. The diner owner was a good man, and a handsome one. It didn't surprise her that Rachel had feelings for him.

"Yes. I miss him. I miss him, and I miss him right over

the top of missing Jacob, and I don't know what any of that means. I don't know…"

Wendy grabbed hold of Rachel's hand. "You're not going to stop missing Jacob. You don't have to. I spent some time with a man recently who talked to me a bit about the death of his wife. And one of the things he said stuck with me. It doesn't go away. I don't think it ever does. It doesn't shrink or grow smaller. But your life can grow around it. All of this love—your family, Adam— can expand. And that pain will be there, always. Something that you carry with you. A remnant of that love that you had. But everything you have now can grow brighter. Bigger. And eventually you don't think of the pain every day. Eventually, it's not the biggest thing."

She nodded slowly. "I realized the other night that there was nothing more I could do for him. And part of me is still…trying. Because I know how to do things. I know how to show love that way. I know how to hold pain at bay that way. Adam wants to take care of me. And I—I have no idea how to let myself have that."

"You just have to get out of your own way," Wendy said. "It's as simple and as hard as that. But if there's one thing we've learned over these last months, it's that life moves on whether you wanted to or not. Things happen to us, and we do things that have consequences. But in the end, we get to choose what to do with the changes. Nobody gets to tell us what we are. Nobody but us." She turned and pulled an egg soufflé out of the oven just in time. "And you don't have to know right now. None of you do. We don't need any epiphanies here. Not right at this moment. Because I'll be here no matter what. Always. Because I love you right where you're at."

And then they all crowded in around each other in

that tiny kitchen, and Wendy took all of her girls into her arms. And the real beauty of it was, she didn't have to regret any of the years past. She might have found something new, something special, the revelation that she could have things she hadn't previously believed she could. But she'd had the most important things all along, and she had them still.

She had her family. And they had her. No matter what. And they would grow and change even more over the years, but that fact would remain. Always.

36

*Love takes as many shapes as the ocean here.
Sometimes it roars, sometimes it sneaks to the
shore, a massive wave that consumes with no
warning. I have come to love the place. I have come
to love the people. I have come to love the man.
It is not what thought I wanted. But it is what I need.*

—FROM THE DIARY OF JENNY HANSEN, MARCH 11, 1904

RACHEL

Rachel jerked open her front door and nearly ran into a young man standing there. His short, dark hair was sticking out at odd angles, and he had grease spots on his shirt, and his forearms.

Even without the grease, Rachel would've been pretty sure who she was looking at.

"Can I help you, Luke?"

He looked slightly surprised when she used his name, but didn't express it. "Is Emma here?"

"Well, that depends. Are you going to upset her again? In which case, no, she isn't here."

He looked uncomfortable. "Did she tell you...? What happened?"

"She told me enough." She desperately didn't want further details on what was going on between Emma and her possibly-ex-boyfriend. It wasn't her business. She didn't need to know anything beyond what her daughter had offered up freely.

"I don't want to hurt her again," he said. "It just took me a few days to get my head on straight."

"Is this going to be a pattern?" Rachel crossed her arms and regarded him. He looked tired. Much more so than someone his age should. She hoped that he was emotionally tortured by the whole situation. Because poor Emma was heartbroken, and if the boy wasn't also heartbroken, then he didn't deserve to breathe the same air that Emma did, much less speak to her.

"No," he said, certainty in his tone. "I'm a hard worker. I know how to do that. I know how to fix things when they're under a hood. I don't know anything about...loving somebody. But I'm trying to learn. Because I do love her. I just... I need to... I need another chance."

There was something about what he said that made her heart turn over. Maybe because she related to him a little bit too much. Not because she didn't know how to love—she did. But because she didn't quite know how to love Adam. Or how to accept that she might be in love. And she had handled it badly.

Whether his age, or thirty-nine, she supposed that second chances would always be necessary. She didn't know if he would find that comforting. But she did.

She nodded slowly. "Well, if Emma loves you as much as I think she does, then I think she'll be more than willing to give you that second chance. But don't ask for too many of them. And when she needs one…give it to her. That's all I ask."

She couldn't say they were too young, because she had fallen in love at eighteen, and it had been real. A love that would stay with her always, even if the man hadn't been able to stay with her as many years as she might have wanted.

Whether they were destined for forever or not, he mattered. He would be part of Emma's story.

Every person you loved was part of the story.

The story of the world, the story of the Lighthouse Inn.

Jenny Hansen had come here for a second chance.

Rachel had read the letters from Richard Johnson. He'd found himself while defending this place that she loved with all of her heart.

The college students that had stayed here… They had found adventure, the beginning of their lives, she assumed.

Rachel, Anna, Emma and Wendy were all part of the story of Cape Hope Lighthouse. Part of the history.

A continuous thread in a brilliant tapestry that made a picture of life, of love, loss and hope.

And it was up to them now to decide what picture their thread would make.

It was up to them now to choose love.

"She's at the lighthouse."

EMMA

"I thought I would find you here."

Emma turned and saw Luke walking up the hill toward the lighthouse.

"Did my mom rat me out?"

"Yeah. She did. I would like to pretend that I just found you because I knew you. But…she told me. She also said that if you threw me off the cliff and into the ocean she would deny all knowledge of my ever having been here."

"That sounds like my mom." She hesitated for a moment. "Did you come to break up with me?"

"No. I didn't. I came to tell you that I love you, actually."

Emma stomach tightened. "Really?"

"I'm sorry that I didn't tell you sooner. I'm in awe of you, Emma. The way that you hope for good things. I had that beaten out of me pretty early. And learning to trust in the world again is… It's weird. I'm not sure that I actually ever trust in love. No one ever gave me a reason to. Until you. I'll come visit you. And I'll be here when you need me. I'll be here when you come back. I'll wait for you. There's no one else I want. No one else I want to be with. Now, you may be able to do better than a mechanic in a small town, but I'm never going to be able to do better than you."

Emma closed the distance between them, and kissed him, her heart thundering wildly. "You're an idiot."

"Yeah, that's my point."

"Nobody can do better than love. It's the best. It's what holds us all together. Trust me on that one."

"I do. I do trust you. And I'm going to need you to be patient with me while I figure all this out."

"I promise. Because I love you, and it's worth it."

"I'm proud of you. I'm going to tell everybody that my girlfriend is on the East Coast going to school. That she's following her dreams."

"It'll be tough. Because one of my dreams will be back here waiting for me."

"I'm one of your dreams?"

"You're my favorite one. But I want to do everything."

"You can."

"Thank you for making me believe that."

She kissed him again as the sun sank into the water. And they stayed there until the lighthouse lit up the sky.

RACHEL

She didn't want to meet in the diner. She didn't want to meet at his apartment. She asked him to meet her on the beach, because she couldn't continue pretending that what they had together was separate.

No, she knew it wasn't. Because she carried the pain of letting it go into her real life, and she carried her regret over the way that things had happened in her real life. And it was time to face up to that.

To deal with the realizations that she'd been having over the past few days. Over the past few months.

She didn't know if he would come. She crossed her arms, staring out at the water, resolutely not looking back at the parking lot by the beach. The wind whipped past her ears, and she tightened her jacket more firmly around her body.

And then she saw movement out of the corner of her eye. Adam. He was wearing a coat, his hands stuffed in the pockets.

"You came," she said.

"Of course I did."

"There is no 'of course' about it. After all the things I said to you… Especially about your family."

"Believe it or not, I have pretty ample experience dealing with wounded creatures. I know that they attack when they feel backed into a corner."

"I'm a wounded creature?"

"Sure."

She would love to be mad about it, but he wasn't wrong. Not entirely.

"I've done a lot of thinking," she said. "And I've done a lot of talking with my family. And I realized something. All I ever wanted was to be safe. I thought that getting married young, keeping my life, myself, my dreams here, would keep me safe."

"But it didn't," he said.

"No. It didn't." She sighed. "I'm not the same woman that I was when I married Jacob. I'm not the same woman that I was all those years during our marriage. When we had to face worrying diagnoses becoming awful prognoses. When our roles shifted and I had to begin to care for him. I'm not the same woman I was at the beginning of that. I'm not even the same woman that I was when I had to face the fact that he was dying. 'Safe' was out of the question at that point. But I was going to lose him so much sooner than I thought. And I thought that I had a realistic worldview, a pretty clear-eyed vision of the truth that he and I wouldn't grow old together. But it still hit so much sooner. So much faster. And I realize now that I would never have been ready. I'm not the same woman I was the day of the funeral. I've changed. When you go through something like that you don't worry about little things. And then you quit worrying about bigger things. Like what you want, because all you focus on is what needs to be done. It's been scary for me to deal with what I want. Because it's so different than I imagined it might be. Because on some level it has felt like a betrayal of him. To admit that there is joy in having those pieces of myself back again. To admit that another man has captured my heart, and in a way that I didn't expect.

"But my heart is scarred, battle-scarred. And that requires a specific kind of love. And I think…as difficult as it is to think this, or try and work it out, I think that in some ways meeting you was me being prepared for what would come next. I saw what kind of man you were during that time. You did take care of me. Even then. And it was easy for me to think that I didn't know you because we never talked about our lives. But I did. I knew you based on how you treated me. Every interaction we had, you made it about me. About making me feel good, without making me feel pitied, and no one else ever managed that, Adam."

She blinked, her heart swollen. "I think I'm falling in love with you. And I didn't want to. I never wanted to fall in love again. It scares me, to want more. Because what I've done is keep my head down and grimly accept that certain kind of pain I was living in. Wanting something new, wanting something more… I've always been afraid to want too much, Adam, and I'm afraid this is too much. That you're the right man, but it is the…wrong time."

"You don't have to do anything but be with me," he said. "Because I do love you, Rachel. I'm already in love. And I'll wait. As slow as you want to take it. Until the time is right. Because if I'm right for you, knowing that… I can wait."

"I don't want to take it slow. It sounds crazy, but honestly… I loved Jacob so much. I loved that marriage that we had so much, and for a while, I loved the idea of being free. But…love was never prison. I know it isn't. Sharing your life with someone might be work sometimes, but it's the best work. And that is the future that I want for myself. But not just with anyone. With you."

"I'm a big enough man that I can take you on, and your past. If you can take on mine."

"Yes," she said. "Absolutely."

"I'm coming to you pretty scarred. This has been a rough few years, and I've got things left to work through myself. Because I can't stop until I fix the relationship with Callie and Jack."

"Good. I think if we add our shattered dreams into one pile, we can work on fixing them. Together."

"Only if we can do it while we watch sports."

She huffed out a laugh, and she closed the space between them, wrapping her arms around him, and just holding him.

They hadn't made vows, not yet, but she was pretty confident that they would. And she knew that when they did, it would be different. Different than it had been when she'd been eighteen, standing there bright and new with the man she loved, not understanding what it would ask of them in the end.

No, this was a man who had loved already. Who'd made mistakes with that love, and who wanted to be different. And she was a woman who knew that sometimes love would ask everything of you. And you would have to give it.

And they were still choosing to love each other.

And that was the bravest, brightest miracle she could think of.

Rachel Henderson had known that she would be a widow for quite some time.

But she had never guessed that she might be a wife again.

And she had never guessed that she would find a sense of wholeness inside of herself. Not like this.

But she had. And it was all because of love.

The love that she had for Jacob. That she still had for

him, and that she always would. The love that she shared with her family, a brilliant thread that had been there from the very beginning of her life, strong and unbreakable, no matter what happened to test and stretch those bonds.

In the love she had never expected to find with Adam.

The secret was love.

It was that simple, and that hard.

Love of every kind that made you weak, made you strong, made you brave and made you scared. Love that you chose, anyway, every day.

Love that shone like a lighthouse on a hill, always there to guide you safely home.

37

I'm a single mother, and I don't have experience
in the hospitality industry, though baking has always
been a talent of mine. What I lack in experience,
I will make up with hard work. I'm willing to devote
my life to this inn. I don't know why, but I just
know this place is meant to be my home.
That feeling I had is something I want to give
to everyone who comes to stay.

Maybe that doesn't mean anything to you.
I don't know why it should. Feelings won't run a
business. But I believe in my heart that love will.
The love I have for my girls most of all.
They need this new life even more than I do.

All I want is their happiness.

—FROM A LETTER WRITTEN BY WENDY MCDONALD
TO THE UNITED STATES FOREST SERVICE, IN RESPONSE
TO AN AD OFFERING THE CHANCE FOR ONE ENTRANT TO WIN
THE CHANCE TO BE THE INNKEEPER AT THE NEWLY PROPOSED
CAPE HOPE LIGHTHOUSE INN, JUNE 1987

WENDY

Summer was over far too soon. It meant that Emma was
going off to Boston, and the cold weather would be with
them again shortly.

But Wendy wasn't sad. She couldn't be. Not now.

They were having a big going-away dinner in Emma's honor, and they'd had to get more chairs for the table, because there were no longer empty seats—it was over-flowing.

Adam was there, of course, and Rachel, with the brand-new ring that she had accepted from him only a week or so earlier. Emma's friends Catherine and Prathika had come, and so had her boyfriend, Luke, who'd come bearing flowers.

Luke was learning what it meant to be part of a family. Because whether he'd wanted it or not, he'd been pulled into theirs.

Anna had made all the sweets for the going-away dinner—including a spread of Jenny Hansen's breads, which made the past feel like it was right there with them. Anna was also working on getting a storefront set up in town. It would mean doing a little less work with her here at the inn, but it was all worth it as far as Wendy was concerned.

She was so proud of the way her daughter was standing on her own feet. Of the life that she was building for herself.

She had also seemed downright giddy the past few weeks. Wendy wondered why. And she wondered all the more when Anna paid much more attention to her phone that evening than usual.

And as for Wendy...the house was full. And she couldn't ask for anything more.

There was a knock on the door, and she looked around the room, taking inventory of everyone in residence. They were all here. There was no one who should be looking for them, unless a guest had wandered over from the Captain's House.

She opened it.

It was John.

Her breath left her body in a rush. "What are you doing here?"

"I went for a drive," he said. "The road brought me here."

"All the way from California?"

"It seems to lead here no matter where I start."

"I… Why don't you come in," she said.

"Really?"

"Yes. Why don't you join us for dinner?"

He smiled, and he came inside.

"I'll get another chair," she said.

She came back in, and made introductions, putting him next to her. He held her hand underneath the table.

Wendy McDonald looked around the room, feeling a sense of satisfaction.

Life hadn't been without its troubles, not for them.

But in the end, they were together.

And that was all that mattered.

Across time, and geography, through sickness and health, death and new life, secrets and ugly truths, love was what mattered.

Love rolled on, through the ages, through each one of them.

And when they were another piece of history in this brilliant, wonderful place, and their story was pieced together through letters and journal entries, through photos and the memories of the next generation, their legacy would sing out like a golden thread in that great tapestry.

Family. Forgiveness. Hope. Love.

Through all of history, those things endured.

And they always would.

EPILOGUE

Dear Wendy,

Recently I stumbled across your post requesting tokens from the Lighthouse Inn at Cape Hope, from the era when the building was used as a dorm for the community college.

I was a student there in the '60s, and it holds a great many memories for me. Both painful and wonderful.

These posts from you led to my reading about all that you've done with it, about how you raised your girls there. How you won your position as innkeeper with a letter.

I was moved to tears by your story. And by the fact the lighthouse found you. And I believe in my heart that it did.

There is so much to say, but I fear I could never write a letter quite so complete or stirring as yours.

I have made a reservation to come and stay at the inn for a week at the end of this month, and I hope we get a chance to sit and talk.

I have so much to tell you.

With warmest regards,

Susan Bright-Carlson

—FROM AN EMAIL WRITTEN TO WENDY MCDONALD, SEPTEMBER 2020

* * * * *

ACKNOWLEDGMENTS

I owe many thanks to the staff at the Heceta Head Lighthouse Bed & Breakfast in Yachats, Oregon, for letting me pester them with questions, and poke around the B and B so that I could satisfy my curiosity. To Nicole Helm for reading this book chapter by chapter as I wrote it, and giving her honest feedback as always. To Megan Crane, who read it when it was done and yelled at me because she loved a character so much, and felt she wasn't getting a fair shake. That feedback changed some major elements, and the book is better for it. To my agent, Helen Breitwieser, for pushing my career in any direction I ask for her to, and for helping make this particular book a reality. The team at Harlequin, who is so supportive of me, and for that I'm truly grateful. And finally, I have to acknowledge my editor, Flo Nicoll, who edited this book with so much insight, and spent hours discussing such deep, meaningful things with me, helping me find the deepest parts of the emotion, and offering me her own wisdom on such tough subjects. Flo is a writer's dream.

FROM THE AUTHOR

Sometimes it takes a special place to bring an idea together. I knew the characters in *Secrets from a Happy Marriage* from the beginning, but didn't know quite where I wanted to put them. Then I remembered visiting a beach on the Oregon coast and seeing a lighthouse up on the hill. A quick internet search revealed not only what the lighthouse was, but that it was also a bed-and-breakfast. I immediately made a reservation to stay there.

It was late January, the weather was a misery and I had serious concerns about getting to the lighthouse—it's Oregon, we're not equipped to drive in snow!—but I made the trip, and I'm so glad I did. The rich history of the location provided the backbone for this story.

Built in 1894, the house has lived many lives. From the original lightkeepers' residences, to barracks, to dorms and finally to a bed-and-breakfast. Lives have started, and ended there. Children have taken their first steps in the parlor, and old men have breathed their last in the upstairs bedrooms. The stories of ghosts, mail-order brides and soldiers give a sense of the generations of people whose history is wrapped up in this place.

I wasn't sure how I wanted Wendy to have come by running the fictional Lighthouse Inn, until I heard the very real story about how the innkeepers of the Heceta Head Lighthouse came into that job. It was, in fact, a contest run on the radio by the United States Forest Service in the '90s. And they really did write a letter and win their position there.

I love that story. A chance letter that changes the course of your whole life, and I knew it belonged in the book.

Sometimes the real history of a place is more interesting than any fiction that could be created, and the history of this house is definitely one of those cases. It is, to me, as important a character as any others in this story. Because it's the anchor that holds Wendy, Rachel, Anna and Emma to each other, and to the town.

Which was a lesson to me, I think, as much as to the characters in the book. That we're one thread in a much bigger story, and it's the full perspective of time and history that creates the beautiful picture we enjoy around us. Which is inspiration to make our own thread a brilliant one.

Turn the page for a sneak peak of
Confessions from the Quilting Circle,
the enthralling new book by Maisey Yates...

**The Ashwood women don't have much in common...
except their ability to keep secrets.**

When Lark Ashwood's beloved grandmother dies, she
and her sisters discover an unfinished quilt. Finishing
it could be the reason Lark's been looking for to stop
running from the past, but is she ever going to be brave
enough to share her biggest secret with the people she
ought to be closest to?

Hannah can't believe she's back in Bear Creek, the
tiny town she sacrificed everything to escape from. The
plan? Help her sisters renovate her grandmother's house
and leave as fast as humanly possible. Until she comes
face-to-face with a man from her past. But getting close
to him again might mean confessing what really drove
her away...

Stay-at-home mom Avery has built a perfect life, but at
a cost. She'll need all her family around her, and all her
strength, to decide if the price of perfection is one she can
afford to keep paying.

This summer, the Ashwood women must lean on each
other like never before, if they are to stitch their family
back together, one truth at a time...

CHAPTER ONE

March 4th, 1944

The dress is perfect. Candlelight satin and antique lace. I can't wait for you to see it. I can't wait to walk down the aisle toward you. If only we could set a date. If only we had some idea of when the war will be over.

Love, Dot

Present day—
Lark
Unfinished.

The word whispered through the room like a ghost. Over the faded, floral wallpaper, down to the scarred wooden floor. And to the precariously stacked boxes and bins of fabrics, yarn skeins, canvases and other artistic miscellany.

Lark Ashwood had to wonder if her grandmother had left them this way on purpose. Unfinished business here on earth, in the form of quilts, sweaters and paintings, to keep her spirit hanging around after she was gone.

It would be like her. Adeline Dowell did everything with just a little extra.

From her glossy red hair—which stayed that color till the day she died—to her matching cherry glasses and lipstick. She always had an armful of bangles, a beer in her hand and an ashtray full of cigarettes. She never smelled like smoke. She smelled like spearmint gum, Aqua Net and Avon perfume.

She had taught Lark that it was okay to be a little bit of extra.

A smile curved her lips as she looked around the attic space again. "Oh, Gram…this is really a mess."

She had the sense that was intentional too. In death, as in life, her grandmother wouldn't simply fade away.

Neat attics, well-ordered affairs and pre-death estate sales designed to decrease the clutter a family would have to go through later were for other women. Quieter women who didn't want to be a bother.

Adeline Dowell lived to be a bother. To expand to fill a space, not shrinking down to accommodate anyone.

Lark might not consistently achieve the level of excess Gram had, but she considered it a goal.

"Lark? Are you up there?"

She heard her mom's voice carrying up the staircase. "Yes!" She shouted back down. "I'm…trying to make sense of this."

She heard footsteps behind her and saw her mom standing there, gray hair neat, arms folded in. "You don't have to. We can get someone to come in and sort it out."

"And what? Take it all to a thrift store?" Lark asked.

Her mom's expression shifted slightly, just enough to convey about six emotions with no wasted effort. Emotional economy was Mary Ashwood's forte. As contained and practical as Addie had been excessive. "Honey, I think most of this would be bound for the dump."

"Mom, this is great stuff."

"I don't have room in my house for sentiment."

"It's not about sentiment. It's usable stuff."

"I'm not artsy, you know that. I don't really…get all this." The unspoken words in the air settled over Lark like a cloud.

Mary wasn't artsy because her mother hadn't been around to teach her to sew. To knit. To paint. To quilt.

Addie had taught her granddaughters. Not her own daughter.

She'd breezed on back into town in a candy apple Corvette when Lark's oldest sister Avery was born, after spending Mary's entire childhood off on some adventure or another, while Lark's grandfather had done the raising of the kids.

Grandkids had settled her. And Mary had never withheld her children from her. Whatever Mary thought about her mom was difficult to say. But then, Lark could never really read her mom's emotions. When she'd been a kid, she hadn't noticed that. Lark had gone around feeling whatever she did and assuming everyone was tracking right along with her because she'd been an innately self focused kid. Or maybe that was just kids.

Either way, back then badgering her mom into tea parties and talking her ear off without noticing Mary didn't do much of her own talking had been easy.

It was only when she'd had big things to share with her mom that she'd realized…she couldn't.

"It's easy, Mom," Lark said. "I'll teach you. No one is asking you to make a living with art, art can be about enjoying the process."

"I don't *enjoy* doing things I'm bad at."

"Well I don't want Gram's stuff going to a thrift store, okay?"

Another shift in Mary's expression. A single crease on one side of her mouth conveying irritation, reluctance and exhaustion. But when she spoke she was measured. "If that's what you want. This is as much yours as mine."

It was a four-way split. The Dowell House and all its contents, and The Miner's House, formerly her grandmother's candy shop, to Mary Ashwood, and her three daughters. They'd discovered that at the will reading two months earlier.

It hadn't caused any issues in the family. They just weren't like that.

Lark's Uncle Bill had just shaken his head. "She feels guilty."

And that had been the end of any discussion, before any had really started. They were all like their father that way. Quiet. Reserved. Opinionated and expert at conveying it without saying much.

Big loud shouting matches didn't have a place in the Dowell family.

But Addie *had* been there for her boys. They were quite a bit older than Lark's mother. She'd left when the oldest had been eighteen. The youngest boy sixteen.

Mary had been four.

Lark knew her mom felt more at home in the middle of a group of men than she did with women. She'd been raised in a house of men. With burned dinners and repressed emotions.

Lark had always felt like her mother had never really known what to make of the overwhelmingly female household she'd ended up with.

"It's what I want. When is Hannah getting in tonight?"

Hannah, the middle child, had moved to Boston right after college, getting a position in the Boston Symphony Orchestra. She had the summer off of concerts and had decided to come to Bear Creek to finalize the plans for their inherited properties before going back home.

Once Hannah had found out when she could get time away from the symphony, Lark had set her own plans for moving into motion. She wanted to be here the whole time Hannah was here, since for Hannah, this wouldn't be permanent.

But Lark wasn't going back home. If her family agreed to her plan, she was staying here.

Which was not something she'd ever imagined she'd do.

Lark gone to college across the country, in New York, at eighteen and had spent years living everywhere but here. Finding new versions of herself in new towns, new cities, whenever the urge took her.

Unfinished.

"Sometimes around five-ish? She said she'd get a car out here from the airport. I reminded her that isn't the easiest thing to do in this part of the world. She said something about it being in apps now. I didn't laugh at her."

Lark laughed, though. "She can rent a car."

Lark hadn't lived in Bear Creek since she was eighteen, but she hadn't been under the impression there was a surplus of ride services around the small, rural community. If you were flying to get to Bear Creek, you had to fly into Medford, which was about eighteen miles from the smaller town. Even if you could find a car, she doubted the driver would want to haul anyone out of town.

But her sister wouldn't be told anything. Hannah made her own way, something Lark could relate to. But while she imagined herself drifting along like a tumbleweed, she imagined Hannah slicing through the water like a shark. With intent, purpose, and no small amount of sharpness.

"Maybe I should arrange something."

"Mom. She's a professional symphony musician who's been living on her own for fourteen years. I'm pretty sure she can cope."

"Isn't the point of coming home not having to cope for a while? Shouldn't your mom handle things?" Mary was a doer. She had never been the one to sit and chat. She'd loved for Lark to come out to the garden with her and work alongside her in the flower beds, or bake together. "You're not in New Mexico anymore. I can make you cookies without worrying they'll get eaten by rats in the mail."

Lark snorted. "I don't think there are rats in the mail."

"It doesn't have to be real for me to worry about it."

And there was something Lark had inherited directly from her mother. "That's true."

That and her love of chocolate chip cookies, which her mom made the very best. She could remember long afternoons at home with her mom when she'd been little, and her sisters had been in school. They'd made cookies and had iced tea, just the two of them.

Cooking had been a self-taught skill her mother had always been proud of. Her recipes were hers. And after growing up eating "chicken with blood" and beanie weenies cooked by her dad, she'd been pretty determined her kids would eat better than that.

Something Lark had been grateful for.

And Mom hadn't minded if she'd turned the music up loud and danced in some "dress up clothes"—an over-sized prom dress from the '80s and a pair of high heels that were far too big, purchased from a thrift store. Which

Hannah and Avery both declared "annoying" when they were home.

Her mom hadn't understood her, Lark knew that. But Lark had felt close to her back then in spite of it.

The sound of the door opening and closing came from downstairs. "Homework is done, dinner is in the Crock-Pot. I think even David can manage that."

The sound of her oldest sister Avery's voice was clear, even from a distance. Lark owed that to Avery's years of motherhood, coupled with the fact that she—by choice—fulfilled the role of parent liaison at her kids' exclusive private school, and often wrangled children in large groups. Again, by choice.

Lark looked around the room one last time and walked over to the stack of crafts. There was an old journal on the top of several boxes that look like they might be overflowing with fabric, along with some old Christmas tree ornaments, and a sewing kit. She grabbed hold of them all before walking to the stairs, turning the ornaments over and letting the silver stars catch the light that filtered in through the stained glass window.

Her mother was already ahead of her, halfway down the stairs by the time Lark got to the top of them. She hadn't seen Avery yet since she'd arrived. She loved her older sister. She loved her niece and nephew. She liked her brother-in-law, who did his best not to be dismissive of the fact that she made a living drawing pictures. Okay, he kind of annoyed her. But still, he was fine. Just… A doctor. A surgeon, in fact, and bearing all of the arrogance that stereotypically implied.

One of the saddest things about living away for as long as she had was that she'd missed her niece and nephew's childhoods. She saw them at least once a year, but it never felt like enough. And now they were teenagers, and a lot less cute.

And then there was Avery, who had always been somewhat untouchable. Four years older than Lark, Avery was a classic oldest child. A people pleasing perfectionist. She was organized and she was always neat and orderly.

And even though the gap between thirty-four and thirty-eight was a lot narrower than twelve and sixteen, sometimes Lark still felt like the gawky adolescent to Avery's sweet sixteen.

But maybe if they shared in a little bit of each other's day-to-day it would close some of that gap she felt between them.

Lark reached the bottom of the attic steps, and walked across the landing, pausing in front of the white door that led out to the widow's walk. She had always liked that when she was a kid. Widow's walk. It had sounded moody and tragic, and it had appealed to Lark's sense of drama. It still did.

She walked across the landing, to the curved staircase that carried her down to the first floor. The sun shone in the windows that surrounded the front door. Bright green and purple, reflecting colored rectangles onto the wall across from it. The Dowell house, so named for her mother's family, had been built in 1866, and had stood as a proud historic home in the town of Bear Creek ever since.

The grand landscape, yellow brick that had mottled and taken on tones of red and rust over the years, was iconic, and had appeared on many a postcard and calendar. It had been part of her Gram's family, but to Lark it had always been Grandpa's house. When he'd died ten years earlier, it had surprised everyone that the ownership of the place passed to Gram, considering the two of them had been divorced for over forty years at the time. But it had been clear that however deep her grandfather's bitterness had been, it hadn't extended to making sure his former wife didn't get the home that had been passed through her family for generations.

But even after Lark's grandfather had passed, Addie had never lived in it. A couple of times Lark's uncles had stayed there when they'd come to town for visits, but for the past two years it had been largely closed up. And the attic had clearly been used as her grandmother's preferred storage unit.

It was The Miner's House that her grandmother had called home. She had made a little candy shop in the front, and had kept a bedroom in the back. The yard had a small dining set and the porch had rocking chairs. That, she'd said, was all she needed.

But as a result, The Dowell House was in a bit of disrepair, and in bad need of a good dusting.

Lark walked through the sitting room, and into the kitchen. The two rooms were divided by a red brick wall with another stained glass window set into it, and a large arched doorway. At one time, it had been an external wall and door, the change just part of one of the many expansions and remodels that had taken place over the years.

Another thing Lark had never given a whole lot of thought to. Because it was simply how Grandpa's house had looked. Now, she saw it for the slight architectural oddity that it was.

She could see her sister through the window, the pane cutting across her face, the top of her head green, and the bottom half purple. Lark walked into the kitchen, where her mother was already seated at the table, and her sister was in the process of wiping it off. She had brought...

They looked like insulated bags, which Lark could only assume had food in them.

"I figured you guys would be pretty hungry by now."

"I'm always hungry," Lark said. "And hi." She closed the space between herself and her sister and drew her in for a hug.

"Good to see you." Avery dropped a kiss on to her head.

Lark took a step back. Avery looked tired, her blond hair piled on top of her head, an oversized sweater covering her always thin frame. She had on a pair of black leggings and a pair of black athletic shoes. She looked every inch the classic image of the supermom that she was.

Avery had all the self possession and poise of their mother and the effortless femininity of their grandmother. She'd been popular and stylish with ease and Lark had envied her. When Lark had reacted to things it had always been big, and often messy. Until she'd learned to get a grip on herself. Until she'd finally learned her lesson about what could happen when you acted, and didn't think it through.

"But what food did you bring?" Lark asked.

"I had a potpie in the freezer. I also brought salad and rolls. I figured Hannah would probably be hungry too, after flying cross country."

Her sister had also brought wine, and sparkling water. Lark helped herself to the water. Without asking for assistance, Avery finished cleaning off the table, then produced paper plates. "I didn't know what kind of a state the dishes would be in. And I didn't know which appliances in the house were functional. I don't hand wash."

"No. Why would anyone? It's why God gave us dishwashers."

"Agree. Mom?" Avery asked. "How much potpie do you want?"

"I can serve myself."

"No," Avery said. "You don't have to. Just sit. I'll get you some wine." Avery was a flurry of movement, and even when Lark and Mary had their food, Avery didn't sit. She opened up the cupboards and looked in each of them, frowning. Lark could almost see an inventory building in her sister's head.

"What exactly are you doing?"

"I've been thinking," Avery said. "Didn't you talk to Hannah at all about what her idea was for this place?"

"No." Lark felt vaguely wounded by that. There was a plan, and Hannah hadn't said anything to her?

That made her feel more like the baby sister than anything had for a while.

"Finally!" Laden with suitcases, Hannah pushed the door open with her shoulder, her bright red hair, a shade or two down the aisle from the color their grandmother had used, covering her face. "I couldn't seem to get a car. I had to rent one."

Her suitcases were flung out in front of her, her violin in a black case slung over her shoulder. Lark didn't see a purse. She was sure her sister had one, but the violin was obviously her most important possession.

"Yeah, I don't think ridesharing has really caught on around here," Lark said.

"Do you mean those apps? Aren't all the drivers serial killers or something?" Avery asked. Everyone looked at her. "One of my friends shared a post about it online."

Hannah and Lark exchanged a glance.

"Well, I've managed to use it for about five years now and not get serial killed. But I'm keeping my fingers crossed," Hannah said. "It will be good to have a car, but I don't really want to pay for a rental for the next three months."

"Dad said you could borrow the car," Mary said.

"Thanks," Hannah responded.

"I drove," Lark said, only then registering that her sister had not in fact asked if she needed the car. "So I have my car," she finished lamely.

Dad and Hannah had always had their own special thing. Not that Lark thought he loved Hannah more. She just wasn't shocked that he'd set the car aside for *her*.

"That smells good," Hannah said. She grabbed a paper plate and served herself a large portion of salad, and a small wedge of pie, passing on the wine and taking a sparkling water the same as Lark.

Soon they were all sitting around the table, except Avery, who was standing, leaning against the kitchen counter, holding a glass of wine.

"Do you want to sit?"

Avery blinked. "Oh," she said. "I just get so used to not having a chance to sit."

But she didn't move from her position.

"Avery says you have an idea?" Lark pointed that statement at Hannah.

"Oh," Hannah said. "Yes. I do. Well, we're doing a scaled back concert series this summer, and I wasn't needed for the next three months." Lark couldn't read her sister's emotions. She was laying it out matter-of-factly, but Lark had the sense she wasn't all that happy to have three months off. "I'm clear until end of August."

"You can just…leave for a few months?" Avery asked.

"I don't even have a houseplant," Hannah said. "Easily mobile by design, thanks." Lark knew that sometimes the orchestra sent people to other orchestras on loan. Her sister had spent seasons in New York, London and Moscow.

On paper, she and Hannah were pretty similar. Creative professions, the chance to move around. But there was a tenacity and intensity to Hannah that had skipped Lark. Avery had it too. She just channeled it into school events.

But Hannah was an island. An island of isolated, locked down emotion. Whatever her sister really felt about things was tough to get a handle on. She might be outspoken, but that wasn't the same as sharing feelings.

Hannah was allergic to feelings.

"I have the summer, free and clear. And I thought I could spend that time helping revamp everything here and... When it's over we can turn this into a vacation rental."

"It's a great idea," Avery said, using her school meeting voice. "Because none of us want to live here, right?"

"No," Mary said. "I'm not antsy to move back into my childhood home."

"David hates this house," Avery said. "The last thing he wants to do is fuss with potentially faulty plumbing on a day-to-day basis. Old houses are charming and wonderful, but they can also be a pain in the butt. Hannah isn't staying. Lark, I assume you're going back to New Mexico."

"I think it's a good idea," Lark said, bypassing the question she'd been asked. She was happy to linger over their plans for a moment, which would give her more space to address her own next. "A vacation rental. The house is famous. I think people will really enjoy staying here." She took a deep breath. "I want to stay here. In town. Permanently."

Avery and Hannah looked shocked. Her mother's expression was smooth, except one divot on the right side of her mouth, which suggested pleasure.

"Have you ever been to a Craft Café?"

That earned her a couple more blank stares.

"They're these cafés where you can come in and work on crafts. I think that's pretty self-explanatory."

"Does anyone *do* that?" Avery asked.

"Yes. They're getting more popular in places, and I think it could work here. We get all the tourism in the summer, and the kinds of people who move here are... Well, they have a lot of leisure time on their hands. They're either retired, or they have family money of some kind."

"What about your illustrations?"

Her heart squeezed uncomfortably. "I... I'm taking a break from it. But I have the money to put into the place. I don't need to use Gram's. But we all own The Miner's House and I am proposing that I use it for business. So, I need all of you to be on board with it."

"I don't have plans for it but..."

"Do you have a business plan?"

Her mom and Hannah spoke at the same time.

"I do have a business plan," Lark said.

And she was thankful for her friend Rusty who had told her in no uncertain terms that "starting a crowdfunding campaign is not a business plan."

Then had helped her make an actual business plan.

"And I know it's going to take some time and money to rehab the place, but, if we're working on the house here, I can easily get the same crew to go down the street and do some work there too. Two houses, one stone. Or one phone call."

She took a breath. "I sold everything. I mean, all my

furniture. And my lease was up. I… I want a fresh start here."

The deep irony of looking for a fresh start here. This place that had made her, then unmade her. Tearing out each and every stitch that had held her together so she'd been forced to go off in pieces and find a way to repair what was.

It wasn't holding. That was the problem.

All these years later. Nothing was healed, just hidden.

She felt like she'd left pieces splintered of herself all over the country. On rivers and lakes in the Midwest, in the Atlantic Ocean. In different towns and different cities, different jobs and groups of friends.

She'd been searching for things there, but it had only left her more fragmented. And none of it had brought her healing.

She'd been everywhere else looking for it. But she hadn't been back home, not really. Visits with her parents, the will reading, the funeral, that wasn't the same as really being here. When she came back she didn't spend time on Main Street in town, didn't visit old friends. She usually holed up in her parents' house and went between there and The Miner's House to spend time with Gram.

"If you can open this shop, you'll stay?" Her mother's expression was neutral, and Lark couldn't really tell what her feelings were on the subject.

"Yes," she said.

"Then try it," Mary said. "Why not?"

"A ringing endorsement," Lark said. "What about you two?"

"I figured I'd just line up the renovations for The Dowell House," Hannah said, in her typical, straightforward fashion. "Avery and I have already gone back and forth on furniture, and I ordered some."

"You didn't ask me?" Lark asked.

Avery and Hannah both had the decency to look slightly guilty. "I didn't think you'd care," Avery said.

But they hadn't asked.

Their skepticism about her ability to run a business combined with this felt...

Like something you've earned?

She ignored that. Even if it was true.

She felt nearly divided sometimes, into before and after. Before she'd left home, and after. When she'd been young she'd been...well, young. And probably a little bit spoiled because she was the youngest. She'd always wanted to have fun, to have good feelings because bad ones had been unbearable and she didn't know how to keep them in, and when they came out it was always a whole meltdown.

And then after...

She'd just stopped letting herself show those feelings. She'd stopped...letting herself want so much. And if her family thought she was sort of a shiftless drifter then fine. It suited her. It kept her a little mysterious, which also suited her.

Except now you're mad about it. And hey, you've moved home. So much for your distance.

"Do whatever you want with The Miner's House," Hannah said. "I can't run a shop and I don't need a little house."

"Same," Avery said.

It was, maybe, the most tepid unanimous yes of all time, but Lark would take it.

She put her hand on top of the swatch book, and held

the silver Christmas ornaments to it, looking at the silver glinting against the worn leather. Her grandmother would approve of the idea, she knew she would.

Gram had loved art. And she had fostered the love of it in Lark. In all of them, really. The Miner's House had been the only place the three of them had ever gotten along.

"I'll keep a bowl of candy on the counter," she said.

Because her Gram would want the kids to be able to come in for candy still.

She just knew it.

"What's that?" Mary pointed to the book that was on the table next to Lark.

"It's not your business plan, is it?" Hannah asked.

Lark rolled her eyes. "No. Even I'm not a big enough hipster to put my business plan in a leather bound book."

"I don't know about that," Avery said.

"I don't know what it is. I grabbed it off the top of the craft boxes before I came down. I wanted to see what was in it."

It was worn, the edges looking chewed and tattered. The leather cover was pale in the places where someone's hands might have rested while holding it. She opened it up, and saw small, neat handwriting on the first page.

Memory quilt.

On the next page was a graph. A design for a quilt, with each piece laid out on the grid.

"Grandma was making a quilt," she said. "This is…"

She turned the page. There was a scrap of lace affixed to it, and underneath it in that same handwriting it said: *wedding dress.*

"It's like a swatch book. With fabric for the quilt."

"That's interesting," Hannah said. She got up from her

seat and move down to the end of the table, peering over Lark's shoulder. "What else?"

She flipped the page where there was a very colored fabric in silk and velvet. "'Parlor curtains.'" She went to the next page, which had a fine, beaded silk. "'Party dress.'"

"There's all kinds of stuff like this up in the attic," she said. "Remember when Gram used to let us go through her collection and choose things to craft with? Broken earrings and old yarn and fabric. And always tons of unfinished projects lying around. Obviously she intended to make this quilt. Maybe she even started it. And it's somewhere up there with all of the…the unfinished things."

Unfinished.

That was the word that kept echoing inside of her.

Because it was why she was here. She was one of the unfinished things.

Being here, opening the café, it would give her a chance to finish some of what her grandmother had started.

Maybe along the way she'd manage to join up some of the unfinished pieces inside her own soul.

***

Don't miss
Confessions from the Quilting Circle
available May 2021 wherever
Harlequin Books and ebooks are sold.
www.Harlequin.com

Copyright © 2021 by Maisey Yates

Get 4 FREE REWARDS!

We'll send you 2 FREE Books plus 2 FREE Mystery Gifts.

FREE
Value Over
$20

Both the **Romance** and **Suspense** collections feature compelling novels written by many of today's bestselling authors.

YES! Please send me 2 FREE novels from the Essential Romance or Essential Suspense Collection and my 2 FREE gifts (gifts are worth about $10 retail). After receiving them, if I don't wish to receive any more books, I can return the shipping statement marked "cancel." If I don't cancel, I will receive 4 brand-new novels every month and be billed just $7.24 each in the U.S. or $7.49 each in Canada. That's a savings of up to 28% off the cover price. It's quite a bargain! Shipping and handling is just 50¢ per book in the U.S. and $1.25 per book in Canada.* I understand that accepting the 2 free books and gifts places me under no obligation to buy anything. I can always return a shipment and cancel at any time. The free books and gifts are mine to keep no matter what I decide.

Choose one: ☐ **Essential Romance**
(194/394 MDN GQ6M)

☐ **Essential Suspense**
(191/391 MDN GQ6M)

Name (please print)

Address   Apt. #

City   State/Province   Zip/Postal Code

Email: Please check this box ☐ if you would like to receive newsletters and promotional emails from Harlequin Enterprises ULC and its affiliates. You can unsubscribe anytime.

> Mail to the **Harlequin Reader Service:**
> **IN U.S.A.:** P.O. Box 1341, Buffalo, NY 14240-8531
> **IN CANADA:** P.O. Box 603, Fort Erie, Ontario L2A 5X3

Want to try 2 free books from another series? Call 1-800-873-8635 or visit www.ReaderService.com.

---

*Terms and prices subject to change without notice. Prices do not include sales taxes, which will be charged (if applicable) based on your state or country of residence. Canadian residents will be charged applicable taxes. Offer not valid in Quebec. This offer is limited to one order per household. Books received may not be as shown. Not valid for current subscribers to the Essential Romance or Essential Suspense Collection. All orders subject to approval. Credit or debit balances in a customer's account(s) may be offset by any other outstanding balance owed by or to the customer. Please allow 4 to 6 weeks for delivery. Offer available while quantities last.

Your Privacy—Your information is being collected by Harlequin Enterprises ULC, operating as Harlequin Reader Service. For a complete summary of the information we collect, how we use this information and to whom it is disclosed, please visit our privacy notice located at corporate.harlequin.com/privacy-notice. From time to time we may also exchange your personal information with reputable third parties. If you wish to opt out of this sharing of your personal information, please visit readerservice.com/consumerschoice or call 1-800-873-8635. **Notice to California Residents**—Under California law, you have specific rights to control and access your data. For more information on these rights and how to exercise them, visit corporate.harlequin.com/california-privacy.

STRS21MAXR